Sovereign Chance

Also by CJ Murphy

frame by frame

The Bucket List

Five Point Series

Gold Star Chance
Forever Chance
Redemption's Road

Sovereign Chance

CJ Murphy

Desert Palm Press

Sovereign Chance
(Five Points – Book 4)

By CJ Murphy

©2020 CJ Murphy

ISBN (trade) 9781954213005
ISBN (epub) 9781954213012
SBN (pdf) 9781954213029

Desert Palm Press
1961 Main Street, Suite 220
Watsonville, California 95076
www.desertpalmpress.com

Editor: CK King, Raven's Eye Editing
Cover Design: Murphy's Law Ink

Printed in the United States of America
First Edition December 2020

Acknowledgment/Author's Note

In book four of the Five Point series, I attempt to tackle the plight of a young boy with severe hearing loss brought into the lives of my main character through tragedy. If you have read the other books, you might remember Hunter, a small boy who overdosed on drugs left lying around. It also led to an unexpected overdose of my main character, Jax, as she performed duties as a paramedic. Hunter was born into poverty and hasn't had the advantages available to many born with hearing. I realize there are great difficulties faced by real individuals in their ability to communicate with those around them. Their educational opportunities are different, and without intervention they could be left at a disadvantage.

In my first draft of Sovereign Chance, I unknowingly glossed over many of those issues until I consulted with those who have lived with the struggle and those who have educated children with hearing loss. I will admit that romanticizing the character and his abilities at six might make for a good book, but it would feel like I was diminishing the achievements of those in the deaf community. I've tried to explain some of those struggles and admittedly have taken some liberties in finding solutions to make the book enjoyable for the reader. What I don't want to do is offend those individuals who walk through life with this reality. As Hunter grows, I hope to accurately bring attention to the difficulties and be an advocate for realistic solutions. There are those among us who are differently abled than others. They are part of the fabric of humanity and deserve their rightful portrayal in the pages of a book. Everyone needs to recognize themselves in the characters and dialogue authors write. I just hope I've done them justice.

Don't worry, there is still plenty of action and adventure between these pages, but I pride myself in being able to blend those scenes with romance, love, and family. Enjoy.

Dedication

As always, this book is dedicated to the woman who has made all good things in my life possible, my wife, Darla. Thank you from the bottom of my heart for putting up with my crazy musings, the necessity of my backside being in the recliner to write, and the madness that editing brings.

Tha goal agam ort.

Chapter One

SHERIFF CHANCE FITZSIMMONS SAT at her desk opening her mail. One piece of correspondence caught her eye, and she read through it with concern. She looked up to see her chief deputy, Taylor Lewis, leaning in the doorway with her K9, Midas, at her side. "Are you headed home?"

Taylor yawned, stepped in, and sat down. "I am. I'm going to run Jace to your mom, so I can get a little sleep."

"His omas will be happy to see him." Chance smiled at the thought of her godson. They'd settled on calling him Jace. The little boy had been named after both Chance and her wife, Jax. He was born on their wedding day.

"Take a look at this." She passed over an informational sheet sent out by the local ATF office out of Clarksburg. "It seems a few of our new county residents have made claims of sovereign citizenship. The information states that a Division of Natural Resources officer had a run-in with one of them. They refused to produce a valid fishing license."

Taylor perused the pages. "If I remember right, these folks don't think they need a license for anything, not even to drive a car. Most of them are wrapped up in conspiracy theories about the US Government, but aren't most pretty harmless? I know they tie up the courts with frivolous lawsuits and try to scam the IRS."

"They do have many conspiracy leanings, but they are definitely not all harmless. If you recall, Timothy McVeigh was convicted and executed for the Oklahoma City bombing. He and his accomplice, Terry Nichols, had declared that they were sovereign citizens. According to my research, as of two years ago, forty-two law enforcement officers have lost their lives to domestic extremists. Sovereign citizens are among those extremists and have been involved in several horrific incidents that I don't want our people unprepared for. I'm going to bring in a friend of mine from the FBI to do a seminar for all of us, including the communications center. They have to be able to recognize the signs if one of our officers calls in with confusing information."

Taylor nodded her agreement. "It certainly can't hurt. If we can get a class outline beforehand, I can check with the Sheriffs' Association to make sure we can get law enforcement continuing education credits. Knowledge is always critical in our job. It's what we don't know that can really hurt us, and there's too much of that already. I'm going to head home." Taylor stood and turned. "Well, hello there."

Jax Fitzsimmons walked in with a smile on her face. "Good to see you, Taylor. I just snuggled my godson. He's getting so big."

"He certainly is. I'm actually taking him to Maggie and Dee, who have graciously offered to keep him for the day so I can sleep."

Chance stood and came around the desk to Jax's side. "Taylor, take the night off to be with your family. I've got your midnight shift."

Taylor stood and rubbed her face. "Thanks. I could use it. See you two later."

Chance wrapped Jax in a hug. "To what do I owe the pleasure?"

Jax kissed her. "I had to stop in at our attorney and sign some papers to make sure your name is on all the right documents. After the hell we went through last year, I don't want anything up in the air with our property or the clinic. I'm headed to work to interview my new vet candidate. By the way, I have some things I need help with at some point."

"No problem, I can try and schedule a completely off-duty day soon."

Jax rolled her eyes. "Honey, if there is one thing I've learned since coming back here it's that you're never off duty."

Chance kissed her again. "I can't argue with that."

***

Chance walked down the steps of the courthouse after retrieving some paperwork from the county clerk's office. Sergeant Harley Kincaid was jogging across the street headed for her cruiser.

"Hey, Chance."

"Something up, Harley? Catch a call?"

"I did. I'm headed to an abandoned pickup in a cattle fence, up on Dry Fork Road. There's no one around it, but it's got a few radical stickers that match things on that bulletin we got today."

"Want some backup?"

"Might not be a bad idea. I'm the only trooper in the county, with one off sick and one out of state at training."

"I'll follow you. From what I've been reading, it's a bad idea to deal with them alone." Chance loaded Zeus, her K9 partner, back into her cruiser.

After a forty-minute drive, they approached the older model Chevy straddling a ditch line. The pickup was partially blocking the road. The property owner was in the field, attempting to put up temporary fencing to keep the cows from escaping. Cattle chewing their cud dotted the lush green pastureland.

Chance and Harley reported on scene and exited their vehicles to inspect the scene. The blown tire likely caused the accident that tangled the pickup in barbed wire and jammed a piece of fence post up under the skid plate. Zeus watched the cattle but didn't bark or disturb them. Danny Cooper dropped his tools and walked over to meet them.

Harley shook his hand. "Damn, looks like we've got a bit of a mess here. Dispatch said you didn't have a tow truck on the way, so I called for one. Granger's coming with their flatbed."

"Hell, I didn't even know what happened until the neighbor called and said my cows were out in the road. His wife about hit one of them before she even got to the wreck. Took me over an hour to get them all rounded up and back inside the fence. Sheriff, good to see you." Danny put out his hand to Chance, who accepted the greeting.

"I wish it was under better circumstances," she said.

Danny pushed his ball cap up. "Got any idea who this damn thing belongs to?"

Harley shook her head. "I'm going to see if I can find a VIN to run. Hopefully, we can find an owner."

"That sticker on the tailgate is from a group that doesn't believe in paying taxes or in anything they think supports an illegal government," Chance cautioned Danny. "So that paper license is bogus."

"Horse shit. Taxes are just part of life. No one likes them, but only two things in this world are for certain, death and taxes. What's the chance they believe in insurance?"

"Slim to none." Chance jumped the ditch line and peered in the window of the beat-up truck.

Danny took a deep breath and walked back over to continue his work. "Once they pull that truck out of my fence, I can do a permanent repair job. If those damn cows get loose and someone hits them, I'm responsible."

Harley tried to open the truck door. "They've pulled the vehicle identification plate off the windshield. Should be one on the inside of the door but those are locked. If you can pop the driver's side, we can see if that one's there. If not, when we get it to the impound lot, I'll see if I can find it on the engine block."

Chance looked around the area. With no one in sight, it was hard to even tell when the accident had happened. They'd need to question some of the locals about their travels, narrowing down when they went in or out to try and pinpoint the time it took place. "Harley, is the engine cool?"

"Yes." Harley nodded. "Best guess, this happened sometime last night."

"Danny, ever seen the truck before?" Chance called out.

"I can't say that I have, but I don't live on this road either. I rent the land for grazing. You might check with Leon Stanley. He and his folks have lived on this road their whole lives." He continued to pound plastic fence posts into the ground.

Chance turned at the sound of a vehicle and saw the tow truck arrive. Two men jumped out and approached just as Harley came from the front of the pickup. She went to speak with the driver as Chance began to look through the truck's windows. *Maybe I can see a piece of mail or something.* Zeus followed on her heels as she looked inside with her hand against the window. She came up empty. Zeus stared off into the tree line, eyes scanning, ears twitching. "What do you see boy?" She put a hand up in front of her eyes to shade the sunlight. Nothing caught her eye, but Zeus stared intently. "Someone watching us?"

Harley stepped to her side "Zeus catch wind of someone?"

"I can't say for sure, but he's zeroed in on something across that field. Are they towing this to the impound lot?"

"Yes. There'll be a property damage claim against it and a leaving the scene charge for the driver, if we figure out who that was."

"Let's see if we can identify an owner once we have that vehicle run through NCIC. It might even be stolen. No way to tell until those checks are run. I think Granger is getting ready to pull that thing out of the ditch."

***

They followed the wrecker, and Chance pulled in behind Harley at the impound lot. Granger had been advised to put the truck inside the security fence. She hoped he'd find enough room. She'd walked Zeus around the vehicle, but they'd found nothing in the way of narcotics.

The sticker on the back still concerned her and finding the truck's owner was the priority.

Harley stepped to the front of the truck. "Pop that door and let's see if we can find one of the VIN plates that's a little harder to remove."

Chance brought out the lockout kit and had the door open within seconds. The hinges creaked and groaned in displeasure as she turned her head to check out the spot below the latch. "The plate is off the door as well."

"Let's see if we can find the one on the engine block."

Chance pulled the latch, and Harley lifted the hood. "This is an older model. Unless I'm wrong, there should be a stamp right near the oil filter. Want me to check?"

"I got it." Harley climbed on the bumper and stuck her head in the engine compartment.

Chance leaned over and pointed. "I think that's it right there."

Harley rubbed at the grease and oil with little success. "Can you find something for me to wipe this off with?"

Chance went back to her vehicle, found a rag, and took it to Harley. "Can you get a cellphone in there to take a picture?"

"I think so."

Chance handed her the phone. After a few flashes, Harley hopped down from the bumper. They examined the photo. "Gotcha." Chance called the vehicle identification number into the communication center, and they soon had a name and an out-of-state address. "Well, that helps some but not enough to pinpoint someone here. I'm going to have them run the name and see if there are any ties to this area."

Moe Granger approached them with a clipboard, his boots crunching on the gravel. "We'll keep this behind the gates with a hold on it. I'll call you if anyone comes to claim it."

Chance shook his hand. "Thanks, Moe. If you can eventually get it inside, we'd appreciate it. The fact that they had a fake license plate and missing VIN plates tells me they don't want us to find out who it belongs to. I want to look around the cab a bit more before we go. Sometimes there are hidden clues under or behind the seats or in the glove box. Even when you think you've cleared everything out, a receipt or an old insurance card falls down in a crack you can't see."

Moe nodded. "You wouldn't believe what I've found in vehicles that have been abandoned because someone didn't want to pay the tow bill or impound fee. It's like a treasure hunt. Sometimes that's not so fun either. One time I found someone's pet snake. The guy said the snake got out of his glass cage, and he never could find him. After the guy wrecked it, I was parting it out and found the snake living inside the firewall. I called the guy, and he came and got him out. I'm not ashamed to say, I damn near shit myself."

The group laughed at the admission as Chance pulled on her Kevlar gloves and covered them with nitrile pair. She began to rummage around the pickup. Harley opened the opposite door and did the same as Moe went back to his office. Old coffee cups, fast food wrappers, and the odd bits and pieces of trash littered the interior of the truck. It smelled of body odor and cigarettes. Chance switched on her flashlight and leaned the bench seat forward.

"Got a set of jumper cables and a tire iron over here." Harley continued her exploration.

Chance pulled out a zippered sweatshirt, turned the pockets inside out, and examined a slip of paper. "This is a credit card receipt from an Exxon station in Kentucky, from six months ago. Might give us a timeline of where the truck's been. The jacket has a business logo on it." She laid the hoodie on the seat and continued to look for anything useful.

"Done on this side." Harley moved to check the glove box.

With nothing more found, Chance returned the seat to the upright position. She leaned down on the floorboard, shining her flashlight up under the seat. "Well, what do we have here?" She pulled a Smith & Wesson snub-nose .38 Special from a holster attached to the springs. She was careful to avoid areas that they might be able to obtain prints from.

Harley came around the vehicle and whistled when she saw the revolver. "I'm doubting they meant to leave that."

"I agree. Maybe whoever wrecked the truck didn't realize it was there or was in a big hurry. I've borrowed Mom's Jeep before and never looked up under the seat. She could have a case of dynamite stashed there and I wouldn't know it."

"But the owner will realize it's missing. Can you see a serial number?"

Chance looked at the flat area where the numbers should have been. "It looks like someone tried to scratch them off. When I get it back to the office, we'll take pictures and see if we can decipher it. We should dust it for prints too. I'm not leaving it with the truck. With the hold order, Moe will call us first if the owner makes a claim."

"I didn't find anything in the glove compartment. I was hoping for something with a name."

Chance unloaded the revolver and placed it and the bullets in an evidence bag she pulled from
her pocket. "That would make it too easy. Let me take a picture of the logo on that sweatshirt. I think we've done all the damage we can for now. I've got to get back to the office. After the bluegrass festival, I'll turn Taylor loose to decipher the information we do have."

Harley nodded. "Sounds like a plan. I'll work up the accident report, and we'll work together on the rest."

***

In her office, Jax looked over William Tolliver's resume. He'd graduated five years ago from Virginia Tech's veterinary program. "Your internship was with a large practice in Blacksburg. Any reason you didn't stay there instead of seeking a position here?"

William nodded. "My wife, Amber, is originally from Elkins. Her father has Alzheimer's, and we're moving in with her parents to help take care of him and help out with the family business. They own Cloverfield Cattle Farm. Amber has one brother still at home, but with the care Tom is going to require, it's going to take all of us to keep that farm going. It's been in the family for over a hundred years, and we'd like to keep it that way, in case Andrew wants to continue the business after college. I'd like my kids to grow up the way my wife did, with plenty of green grass and clean air. That's becoming harder to find than a job these days."

Jax nodded. "I imagine you checked out my practice before applying?"

"I did. I'm interested in working with you because of your large animal practice. That's important to me because those skills are so easily lost when you spend years examining cats and dogs. I grew up on a farm in the Midwest, so I'm no stranger to barn calls."

She closed his file on her desk and sat back in her chair. "The reason I'm hiring someone is multifaceted. First, I got married last December and want to spend a bit more time with my wife." Jax let the statement sink in for a few seconds. She wanted to judge his reaction to her being married to another woman.

William nodded. "Amber's mom said they know your in-laws and that the Sheriff's bought beef from the farm before. I can relate to wanting to spend more time together. I remember the days right after I was married. I had my boards coming up and a job interview. It was hectic and there was little time to enjoy being married for the first few years. That's the other reason we wanted to move. We've been trying to start a family and working seventy hours a week isn't t helping much."

Jax chuckled and rocked in her chair. "That first year after graduation is a bitch. It was nonstop from morning until night. Secondly, the practice has been steadily growing beyond what I can handle by myself. My workload has increased three-fold with one of the vet offices over in Oakland, Maryland shutting down. I've been trying to keep up with the barn calls for a three-county area, and I'm worn out. Lindsey, the vet tech you met, just started vet school. I have plans for her to join the practice after she finishes out. My sister-in-law's girlfriend will be graduating in two years and has expressed a desire to work here as well. I'm not ready to retire anytime soon, but if there's enough business, we could expand with a second clinic at a later date to make use of all three of you."

"I can definitely tell it's a busy practice." He pointed to the numerous photos on the walls of Jax with her patients.

"It is, and there's no sign of it slowing. I've already called your references, and they were all very positive. Your current employer is sad to lose you but said he'd hire you back in a second if you decided the West Virginia mountains weren't for a flatlander like you."

"That sounds like Dr. Kelly."

"With that, I'd like to offer you a job, William."

"I'd like to accept your offer, pending discussions about salary and benefits. Please call me Bill. William is what they call me when I'm in trouble."

Jax smiled and nodded at the sentiment. "My original plan was for part time, but with a candidate like you, I'd be kicking myself later." She handed him a few sheets of paper. Here's the offer I can make. If it's acceptable, we'll sign some employment paperwork and talk about when you can start."

Bill looked over the papers and stuck out his hand toward Jax. "Deal. Thank you for this opportunity."

Jax shook hands with her new employee. "Welcome aboard, Bill. You're now part of the Three Rivers family."

***

Jax stood at the counter with Lindsey Kincaid, her vet tech, discussing the day's events. "Bill's a good hire. I hope it lightens our load a bit. You've got some major classes coming up."

"I'm glad. He seemed like a great candidate on paper."

"Oh, I got to hold Jace this morning before Taylor took him to spend the day with Maggie and Dee." Jax looked over the appointment schedule.

Lindsey propped up her chin on her hand. "He's adorable."

Chance walked in with two bags dangling from one hand and a drinks carrier in the other. Zeus padded close behind. "He certainly is. He's got his omas wrapped around his little finger. Thank God for friends with babies who can ease that need for grandchildren."

Jax unconsciously put her hand on her stomach, feeling a slight pang of envy that she'd never fill that need for Maggie and Dee. That ache didn't even begin to block out the larger one that she felt at never having a child with Chance. In her heart, she knew she was beyond the age it was practical to be pregnant. It made her think about all the years she'd wasted with Lacey in a loveless marriage. *Water under the bridge.* She felt strong arms wrap around her from behind.

"I know exactly where your mind went. The past is gone. All we can do is look forward. I will tell you that I would have loved to watch you go through pregnancy. We'll just have to spoil Jace as if he were ours."

Jax reached a hand up and cupped the back of Chance's neck, pulling her closer. "You always could read my mind." Jax's stomach growled.

"Right now, I'm reading your body. Let's go eat. I love you."

Jax turned in Chance's arms and looked into the eyes that were so unique to her wife. "And I love you."

CJ Murphy

Chapter Two

CHANCE DROVE THROUGH THE bank parking lot in Thomas. Several days ago, a bulletin had been distributed about a group that was casing banks located in small, rural areas. Chance picked up her mic.

"SD-1 to Comm Center."

"Go ahead, Sheriff."

"Miners & Merchants premises check. All clear."

"We'll put the check in the shift notes."

"SD-1 clear."

All of her officers, and those of the state police, were being vigilant in their patrols. Any vehicle on the premises after hours was checked for occupancy and ownership. If there were any doubts, the communication center called the contact person to determine if the vehicle had permission to be on the property. If the vehicle was questionable, it was towed to an impound lot.

"Let's go check Grant County Bank in Davis, Zeus."

Her K9 partner barked his approval as she pulled out onto Seneca Trail. It was a little after two in the morning and she yawned. *I need some coffee.* She planned to stop in at the twenty-four-hour convenience store beside the bank after she did her check. Less than three miles separated the two small communities. Fifteen minutes later, she'd made a quick trip around the building and reported her findings. At the BFS, she went inside to refill her travel mug. She waved to the woman at the register.

"Hey, Betty. How's your evening?"

"Longer and longer every year. I'm not sure I have too many more midnight shifts in me. I'm too damn old for this."

Chance grinned at the silver-haired woman. She'd been working the graveyard shift for as long as Chance could remember. "The older I get, the more toll staying up all night takes on me."

Betty shook her head and clicked her tongue. "You're still a young pup. Try doing it when you're seventy. Hell, even if I am home, I don't sleep. I guess they'll find me in here one day, colder than the stock in the beer cave."

Chance paid for her coffee. "Let's hope that's many years from now." Her radio beeped, alerting her that dispatch was getting ready to broadcast.

"All units, we have a 911 call with an open line. Address is…"

Chance didn't bother saying goodbye as she ran from the store to her Suburban. The address the comm center gave was one she knew well.

"SD-1 to Comm Center. I'm in Davis and responding to that call on Fairfax Ave."

The year before at the annual Run For It, a little boy had overdosed on drugs his mother's live-in boyfriend left out. The child had been hospitalized for an extended period but was fortunate enough not to suffer any long-term effects. Chance knew there were special circumstances, as little Hunter had a profound hearing loss. "Lord help me remember how to sign."

Hunter was the reason she'd brought in someone from the high school to teach them how to communicate with those who were unable to hear or speak. Hunter had just turned six. She'd kept a close eye on him and his mother since last year's incident.

Chance jumped from the vehicle and released Zeus and he immediately took a working position at her side. She grabbed a small trauma bag from the back and pulled her service weapon out of its holster before she cautiously approached the house and used a Dutch K9 command to bring Zeus to working mode. "*Bewaken.*" The living room lights were on and she stepped to the side of the door, peering quickly into the living room. She could see Hunter on the floor shaking his mother. She wasn't responding. Hunter likely wouldn't hear her knock, so she entered and flicked the lights on and off to draw his attention, remembering what the instructor had taught her.

Hunter turned quickly, fear on his tear-stained face. When he saw Chance, his eyes grew wide and his hands rapidly began to sign as he spoke with broken language. Chance halted him and signed for him to slow down as she slid on a pair of nitrile gloves. She reached down and held her fingers over the carotid pulse. *Barely detectable.* She signed to Hunter.

"Are you here alone?"

Hunter shook his head and signed that it was just him and his mom.

Chance looked around the room, noticing the tourniquet on Crissy's arm and a used needle beside her. Chance grabbed her radio. "Comm Center, I need an ambulance to this location, possible overdose.

Adult female found unconscious." She walked quickly through the other rooms. "Scene is secure."

She was advised that the ambulance was en route as she knelt by Crissy Kenton. She opened her kit and pulled the ever-present Narcan from her bag, administering the first dose without any response from Hunter's mother. She had Hunter sit on the couch and instructed Zeus to stay with the boy as she continued her resuscitation efforts. "Come on Crissy, come on." She rubbed a knuckle on Crissy's chest and prepared to administer a second dose when Sarah and her crew came through the door laden down with a plethora of equipment from their ambulance.

"Twenty-five-year-old female, unconscious on my arrival. Weak, thready pulse, shallow respirations. Signs of drug use." Chance pointed to her arm and the tourniquet and needle. "I've given her one dose of Narcan with no response. I was just getting ready to hit her again."

Sarah nodded and began to pull out an intravenous line set up, while her partner administered another dose of naloxone before attempting to establish a set of vitals. "We've got it. Take care of the boy. He doesn't need to see this."

"No, he doesn't." Chance rose and went to kneel before Hunter and began to sign.

Hunter sat with big tears rolling down his face as he buried a hand in Zeus' coat.

"Come into the kitchen." She softened the command with a smile.

He sniffed and nodded.

Chance gritted her teeth as she thought about what this small boy had already been through and what he was likely to go through as a result of the catastrophic choices his mother had made. The judge had gone easy on her because of Hunter's special needs. She'd been ordered to do community service and attend parenting classes. *He's going to end up in the system, because I don't think a judge is going to let her keep custody while she's using.*

She pulled her phone from her uniform pants and dialed Jax's cell number. She stood up and had Hunter take her hand and led him into the filthy kitchen. She still had work that needed to be done documenting and investigating the case. She sat down and pulled Hunter into her lap. There was little choice in who she could call, though a notification to Child Protective Services would be necessary. Jax picked up on the second ring.

"Chance?"

13

"I need your help. Hunter's mom has overdosed, and there's no one I can call to be with him while I clear up this mess. I know it's a lot to ask, bu—"

Jax cut her off. "Let me throw on some clothes and I'll be right there. He must be scared to death."

Chance nodded to herself. "He is. Thank you, honey."

"No thanks necessary. I'm on my way. I'll be there in fifteen minutes. I love you."

"I love you, too."

When she hung up, she hugged Hunter then adjusted so she could sign to him.

"Your friend Jax is coming."

Hunter wiped tears from his cheeks and sniffed before he signed okay. Chance knew he was in a bit of psychological shock. Sitting in a cold hospital waiting room was the last place he needed to be right now. She held him close again and rocked him gently. *I might even need Rhebekka and Naomi by the time this is all over. Heaven help us all.*

***

The ambulance was pulling away as Jax exited her vehicle and ran to the house. She pulled open the door to the place where she'd suffered an accidental overdose the previous year while treating Hunter. She shivered as the memory of the small boy who'd nearly died washed over her along with the smell of rotting garbage. She moved into the room and called out. "Chance?"

"In here."

Jax stepped into the kitchen that didn't look any better than the last time she'd been there. Sitting on Chance's lap was one of the sweetest little boys she'd ever met. Fat tears rolled down his cheeks. She stooped and wiped them away before she signed a greeting to him.

"Hi, Hunter. Would you like to go to my house for some cookies?" Jax watched as he wiped his nose on his pajamas and nodded. *"Please, show me where your clothes are."*

Chance lifted him from her lap and put him on the floor. "I'll be amazed if he has anything clean, given the way this place looks again. I'll make a call to CPS and let them know he'll be at our place."

Jax let Hunter lead her and shook her head in acknowledgment of what Chance had said. Her heart was breaking for Hunter. He was small for his age, likely the result of poor nutrition now and while his mother was pregnant with him. When they got to what she assumed was a bedroom, she choked up. A bare mattress lay on the floor with a thin blanket and a rumpled pillow on top of it. Hunter looked up at Jax and the sight nearly broke her. She forced a smile and asked him if this was his room.

"Mommy and me sleep here."

Jax nodded and knelt near a black garbage bag with clothes hanging out of it. *His things are likely in here as well.* She gently probed through the bag, concerned that there might be dirty hypodermic needles hidden among the clothes. The stench in the room was nearly overwhelming as she located a pair of jeans and a sweatshirt that were far from clean.

"Show me your shoes and coat, please."

Hunter ran back out of the room toward the living room. Jax quickly followed and ran into Harley, who had apparently arrived after they went to look for clothes. The six-year-old pulled his coat from the door handle of a small coat closet and pointed to his well-worn tennis shoes by the door.

"Good. Please put them on."

Hunter nodded and pulled on his coat as Jax helped him with his buttons.

Chance stepped to her side and kissed her temple. "He trusts you. You're doing exactly what he needs, making him feel safe and cared for." Zeus sat beside him and licked his face. Hunter put his arms around the dog and squeezed.

Jax could only nod as she bent to help Hunter tie his shoes. He stood and spontaneously hugged her legs, nearly bringing her to a full-blown ugly cry before he put his hand in hers. She ran her other hand through his greasy hair and somehow managed to keep the tears at bay.

Chance held open the door for them and handed Jax a booster seat that was sitting by the coffee table. "I'll call you as soon as I can."

Jax led Hunter to her vehicle. "You know where we'll be. Be careful and I love you."

"I love you, too. Thank you for doing this."

"This is criminal, Chance. He shouldn't have to live like this. No child should." Jax opened the car door and put the seat in place before she buckled Hunter in.

And if it's the last thing I do, I'm going to find a way to make sure he never has to go through this again.

***

Chance watched them pull away and turned to Harley. "So unfair."

Harley sighed and nodded as if in agreement. "He's seen far too much for six years old. Have you called CPS?"

"No, but I will. After he overdosed last year, Crissy was required to do a few things to get him back. CPS is familiar with him, but what they told me the last time was they have a hell of a time finding any suitable placement because he can't hear. I feel so bad for him. How would you like to be six years old and unable to tell someone something that there is no picture for?"

Chance slapped her Stetson on her leg before slamming it back on her head. She pulled out a notebook and started documenting the scene for her report. "Did you bring a camera in?"

Harley held up her scene bag and pulled out a small digital camera. She began taking pictures. "How do you let your kid live like this?"

"It's not even something I can begin to relate to. I know the easiest cop-out is to blame it all on the addiction, but that's only part of it. I don't know if you noticed, but there isn't a stove or a refrigerator in that kitchen. I saw a cooler with a few cans of soda in it. From the looks of it, I'll bet my life savings the only thing he's eaten in a long time is dry cereal or microwaved macaroni and cheese. I won't be surprised if he fixes it himself. Hunter's mom doesn't seem capable of taking care of herself."

"And yet the court will want to give him back. Sometimes, the powers that be need to recognize that there are people that aren't capable of raising a child safely."

Chance used the toe of her boot to open a soft-sided lunch box revealing more drug paraphernalia. "Guess we need some evidence bags. I need to call and get a warrant for the blood tests they'll do at the hospital. Garrett Memorial is pretty strict about releasing that info without one. I'll make a call to the hotline later this morning. I should call Jax and tell her to take pictures of Hunter's condition before she cleans him up."

"Why don't you let me process the scene. You go do what you need to do about Hunter. I'm not stepping on your toes, but that little guy has bonded with you two since his hospitalization last year. You took the time to learn sign language for him along with your moms. Hell, you made your whole department learn. That will mean something to him. Any rookie can do what we're doing here. I'll make sure to document and collect everything. We'll do a joint investigation and make sure we get Hunter into a safe environment. Right now, that's with you and Jax."

Chance looked around the room, disgusted with the conditions that hadn't improved much from her previous visits. She typed out a message to Jax about pictures. If it was within her power, Hunter had spent his last night in this pigsty with a woman who cared so little for his well-being. "Thanks, you know how to reach me. Let's go, Zeus."

***

Chance wasn't the least bit surprised to see the small dark-haired boy curled up in Jax's arms, both of them fast asleep with a blanket over them. For the first time since the call came in, Chance sighed with relief. She was so thankful that her partner in life was willing to walk this road with her, no matter how many potholes the blacktop delivered. Hunter's hair was damp, and a hot chocolate mustache dotted his upper lip. She heard a car door shut and turned to look out the window as her mother climbed out.

Maggie walked in with an armload of clothes and kissed Chance on the cheek as she passed. "Jax called me. I kept some of the clothes Eddie outgrew. I can't tell you how many times I thought about sending these to charity. Something always made me stop. I guess now I know why."

Chance touched a blue and green item on the top of the stack. "I bought him this dinosaur shirt. I'm sure Hunter will love it just as much."

"How is he?"

"Clean, fed, and asleep, which is a thousand percent better than when Jax picked him up." Chance crossed her arms over her chest and clenched her teeth so tightly she could feel her jaw starting to spasm.

Maggie reached up and cupped Chance's face. "Don't crack a molar over this. You did the right thing. He's safe now. The rest we can figure out in the morning." She touched the clothes. "They might be a little big on him, but they're clean. I couldn't find any shoes, but I'll take care of that in the morning. Have you heard anything about his mother's condition?"

"No, I called but they would only say she was being seen. They won't tell us anything that would violate HIPAA. Privacy laws are a double-edged sword. I'm more worried about Hunter."

"Dee and I'll come back by around nine and make breakfast. She can make her famous Mickey Mouse pancakes for Hunter. That should make him smile."

Chance took a deep breath and said a small prayer of thanks for the blessing of her family and the love that surrounded them all.

***

Over the next few hours, Chance made calls to obtain warrants. She'd urged Jax to lay down on the couch. Hunter was curled contentedly at her side and the two of them slept soundly. *She was born to be a mother. If only we hadn't been torn apart. We'd have our own kids by now.*

At eight, Chance called CPS and relayed everything she knew. The woman on the other end of the line was someone she was familiar with. April Reeve had been with the Department of Health and Human Resources for many years. She was damn good at her job, and Chance had witnessed the toll the job had taken on the woman now in her sixties.

"This one is going to be tough, Chance. Very few people know any sign language, and Hunter doesn't read or write well enough yet to express his needs in that way. The place he was at while Crissy was in rehab had a picture board and they used for him to point to. They aren't available because they already have two new children in their care. His limited communication skills really cause an issue. We could try to put him at the West Virginia School for the Deaf and Blind over in Romney. I can start working on that, though that could take a while."

Chance looked in to see that Jax and Hunter were awake and playing on the floor with some toy fire trucks and police cars from a keepsake collection she kept on the mantle. Jax's smile lit up the room as Hunter used her bent knees as a tunnel. Jax had canceled her morning appointments so that she could stay with him while Chance followed up on the case. "April, hypothetically, what would Jax and I need to do to foster Hunter? We both know some sign language, and he's familiar with us."

Chance turned and looked out the window as the phone line went silent for a few minutes. She could hear the tapping on a keyboard in the background.

"I'd need to get back to you on this. As I've said, he's a hard placement."

"My sign language is par at best after the classes I've taken, but he always seems to understand Jax."

"That's another point in your favor. We'd have to do a home evaluation. There are forms and background checks you'd both need to have, not that I'm worried about them. It's standard procedure."

"Let me talk with Jax, though I'm sure I know her answer. Go ahead and get the ball rolling on an emergency placement with us if that's possible. If not, maybe with my moms?"

"Hunter's mother is the only blood relative we've ever identified. His father is unknown. No one was listed on his birth certificate. For the time being, he's a ward of the state. I'll get everything ready and make the calls to see if this is acceptable. Talk with Jax and let me know. We've placed different kids over the years with Maggie and Dee, so I'm sure we can make that happen. For the time being, as long as it's acceptable with you, I'll leave Hunter there. If Jax declines, I'll start checking with the School for the Deaf."

Chance blew out a long, slow breath. "This kid has been through hell. I know the school is an option, but he needs some personalized attention right now. Last year he almost died and now his mother might. He's been living in squalid conditions. If we can keep him with us, I think it will be beneficial to him."

"I don't disagree, Sheriff. Let me know."

"Thanks, April."

Chance disconnected the call and swiveled in her chair to see Jax leaning against the door frame. "Hey. How much did you hear?"

"Enough. My answer is yes." Jax came around the desk and sat on Chance's lap. "He fell asleep with one of your trucks in his hand a few minutes ago. I covered him up. You were so engrossed in that call. You didn't hear me come in. If they can do an emergency placement with us, we'll gladly take him, for however long he needs us. He's been through enough."

Chance pulled her close and rested her head on Jax's shoulder. "I'll make the call and let April know."

***

Maggie and Dee came through the door, hands laden with bags. Chance and Jax followed them into the kitchen before helping to pull food out.

"Moms squared to the rescue." Jax came in and helped unpack the items.

Maggie sorted out the basic necessities for a six-year-old boy including toys, shoes, and a variety of clothes. Jax hugged her while Chance pulled down the skillet Dee requested from the rack above the stove.

Chance squeezed Dee's shoulder, then walked over to Maggie. "Thanks, Mom, both of you. You didn't have to do all this, but we appreciate it. We need some advice, along with breakfast."

Jax came to Chance's side and snuggled under her arm. "We're going to try and foster Hunter."

Maggie clapped her hands and pointed to Dee. "We called it. I assume you'd like some pointers on how to go about the process?"

Chance nodded at her parents. "April's checking on an emergency placement. You two have done this numerous times, and if you can help us get a jump on what we need to do for the home evaluation, we'd be that much farther ahead when the time comes."

Maggie drew both women into her arms. "That's a given. For now, let's feed everyone and we'll see what we can do. I still have a little pull, and if they won't put him here on the emergency placement, we're still certified. Hunter is welcome to come to our place."

Jax clutched her arm. "You'd do that for us?"

Maggie cupped her cheek. "Of course, we would and for Hunter too. His mother, Crissy, wandered into this town pregnant. We used to deliver provisions to her from the food bank. After Hunter was born, I watched her go down the wrong track with Austin and the likes of Leland Kurst. I even offered her a cleaning job at our rental houses, but she couldn't stay off the drugs. I had to let her go after she failed to make it to work one too many times. After last year's overdose, I tried again once she got out of rehab. I'll always hold out hope that she'll turn her life around."

Chance's phone rang, and she pulled it from her cargo pants. "This is Sheriff Fitzsimmons." She listened as the hospital notified her that Crissy Kenton had passed away after a cardiac arrest. "I see."

The caller went on to ask if she was aware of any next of kin. It was sad not to be able to provide them with any name other than the six-year-old boy who'd just wandered into the kitchen rubbing his eyes and motioning for Jax to pick him up. She watched Jax step over to the window with Hunter.

"No relatives that we know of, and her son is too young to make any decisions. If we locate anyone, I'll call you back."

After listening to a few more pieces of information, Chance thanked the caller and hung up. She looked at the adults in the room who stared eagerly at her. She shook her head.

Jax held Hunter and rocked him softly as Chance came to her side and rubbed his back.

Dee slid plates off a shelf above the stove. "Let's try to eat and keep things as normal as possible until we have more information. This family will do what we always do, take care of those in need."

Maggie kissed Chance on the cheek and joined Dee preparing breakfast. "She's right, it's what the Fitzsimmons clan does."

Chance wrapped her arms around Hunter and Jax, forever grateful she'd been born into a family of givers.

***

The horses were content to stand and graze in a shady spot under a huge maple in the field. Chance looked out the window in her home office, digesting all the research she'd done on the computer. Since breakfast, she'd buried herself in research on how to help Hunter communicate. She'd called April earlier with the news about Crissy and was now waiting on a call back from her. She'd also contacted their sign-language teacher and asked several questions. Her phone rang, "Sheriff Fitzsimmons, how can I help you?"

April Reeves spoke. "We were able to get the emergency placement."

"Thank you, we'll take good care of him." She sighed in relief. Fifteen minutes later, Chance released the tight grip she had on her phone, her head swimming with information but her heart pounding with excitement. She hit Taylor's icon and waited for the call to connect.

"Hey, Sheriff. Aren't you supposed to be sleeping?"

Chance explained the night's events and how Hunter came to be with them. "As you well know, a little boy in the house leaves very little time for sleeping. Hunter wants to explore everything, and he's in love with the horses. Zeus might as well be surgically attached to him because he spends most of his time under Hunter's arm."

"What does CPS have planned for him?"

Chance looked into the kitchen and watched Jax fix Hunter a peanut butter sandwich. She'd stop frequently to sign a question to him about what kind of jelly he liked or to ask about his favorite cookie. Chance was so grateful for the class she'd arranged for her department after her first encounter with the young boy. "We're trying to get long-term placement with us due to his special circumstances. I just got off a call with April and they're leaving him with us for now. There are so few foster homes available in general and finding someone equipped to handle what he needs is apparently quite difficult."

"As far as I'm concerned, he landed exactly where he's supposed to be. I've tried everything I can to find a relative for Crissy. I've been completely unsuccessful. I found her birth certificate, and it seems she was left at a fire station in Pennsylvania as an infant. A little more digging revealed that she grew up in an orphanage until she aged out at eighteen."

"Seems like a vicious cycle that her son is now an orphan too. There's a lot of logistical things to work out, though Maggie and Dee have offered all the babysitting services in the world. Looking back now, that sign-language class everyone took seems a bit fortuitous."

"As Pastors Rhebekka and Naomi would say, 'God works in mysterious ways.'"

Chance looked at the shift schedule she pulled up on her computer. "True. I need to rearrange the department schedule a bit in a way that I think will be beneficial to both of us. I'm going to take midnights for a while until Daniel gets back from his K9 training next week. From the reports I'm reading, he and Athena are exceeding all expectations. I had little doubt. It'll be good to have him on shift."

Chance heard papers shuffling and imagined Taylor at her desk finding the paper copy of the shift schedule.

"Okay, I've got the lineup. Let me work on this a bit and I'll send you an updated electronic version to approve. Oh, by the way, I'm happy to report that Jace slept an entire six hours last night. I don't know what Maggie and Dee do when he's with them, but I'm writing it down and taping it to my forehead."

"Moms squared has some kind of magic touch when it comes to babies. You'll get there. Jace knows he has you two wrapped around his tiny hand. He'll settle soon. Now, work that schedule for me, please?"

"Will do. Deep breath, Sheriff. You've got this."

Chance did just that as she wiped a hand through her hair. "I'd better. Hunter is depending on us." She rose and went to give the good news to Jax, who looked at her with expectant eyes.

"Well?"

Chance nodded with a smile then went to Hunter's side and watched his smile, as she slowly slid one of his tiny fish-shaped crackers off his plate and pretended like it was swimming into her mouth. She poured more out of the container for him, to his delight.

Jax exhaled as if she'd been holding her breath. "Thank God."

Chance pointed up. "Thank God indeed."

The house phone rang, and Chance watched as Jax answered then put her head back in frustration. *I'm apparently not the only one who's never off duty.*

***

Chance handed over the small bag Jax carried back and forth to work.

"I don't want to go." Jax sighed as she slipped on her shoes.

"I know you don't. If it wasn't an emergency, I'd tell you to send it to one of the vets in Randolph County. This is a sick horse, honey, they can't just put it in a cat carrier and go. I promise you, Hunter and I will be fine for a few hours." Chance leaned in and rested her forehead against her wife's as Jax's arms came around her neck.

"I know you will be, that's not the issue. I want to be here. Hunter needs to know he can depend on us."

"He'll learn that over time." Chance nodded. "We have to go to work, honey. He'll get used to it and eventually believe that, no matter what, we'll be back. You need to get going."

"If it's colic, I could be there for a while."

Chance chuckled as she handed Jax her keys. "I don't expect us to be alone very long. I'll bet you that one or both of the moms squared will show up later this afternoon. There is no way the two women who raised me are missing out on time with their first grandchild. Call me when you can and let me know how it's going. I'll do the same."

Jax nodded and pecked Chance on the lips. "I love you."

"Right back at you."

Chance watched her head out to her work truck and drive away. When she was out of sight, Chance turned to watch Hunter. He sat on the floor putting together a puzzle Dee had given him. His little hands manipulated the pieces shaped like cars and trucks into the right spots, then patted them in place as if they'd drive off if he didn't. She chuckled softly. Once he'd finished, he held the puzzle in front of Zeus for his inspection. Chance brought a hand to her mouth. *So sweet.*

She made her way beside him and tapped the coffee table under his hands to get his attention. *"Want to go outside?"* she signed.

He enthusiastically nodded. *"Can we see horse?"*

"Yes."

Chance laughed as Hunter scrambled up from the floor and raced toward the door where he'd left his shoes. Zeus followed and dutifully sat at his side. Hunter struggled to tie his shoes and it took all Chance had to not bend down and do it for him. Carefully, he made a large loop, his tongue sticking through his lips. His small hands pulled the other string around the loop until he could pull the loop through the knot he'd made. He pulled the shoelace tight and smiled up to Chance with pride. The look of accomplishment on his face was worth the extra few minutes of patience. *Dad, if there was a time in my life that I needed you to guide me, this would be it.*

***

Jax walked the sorrel mare around the paddock, patting her neck to soothe her. The anxious owners paced back and forth near the barn door. After twenty minutes of watching her paw at the ground, stretch, then eventually roll back and forth in the dirt, they'd made the call to Jax's office.

"The mineral oil should start working it's magic soon."

Martin Jenkins pushed his hat back on his head. "I can't thank you enough for coming out."

Jax reversed course, holding the halter and guiding Sadie around the fence line. "This is what I do. I did want to tell you that I've taken on a new vet. He will be full time with my practice. I think you'll like him. He comes highly recommended and has great credentials."

Linda, Martin's wife, started to walk beside Jax. "Is he cute?"

Martin shook his head. "Stop trying to find Missy a husband."

Jax chuckled. "Sorry, Linda. Dr. Toliver is already happily married. I have no doubt Missy will find her special someone all on her own."

After a few more laps, Sadie finally ridded herself of the gas that had built up in her intestines. It wasn't a pleasant procedure the horse had to endure. Jax had inserted a tube through her nose down into her stomach, then pumped in a gallon of mineral oil to help lubricate the intestinal tract. The administration of the anti-inflammatory, Banamine, had helped ease the pain until the gas could pass. Jax rubbed the velvety nose and spoke softly to the horse. "Good girl, Sadie. You should feel better now."

Linda grabbed Jax's hand. "I don't know what we'd do without you. Missy had to go to work this morning, or she'd be here. Sadie is the most important thing in her world. I need to send her a text." Linda pulled her phone from her back pocket, fingers flying across the screen.

Jax handed Sadie's halter to Martin. "Keep walking her for as long as she'll tolerate it. She's likely not done passing the gas, but I think a large pocket is gone. I can already tell she feels better."

Jax's phone pinged, and she pulled it out of her coveralls. The photo in the notification made her put a hand on her heart. Hunter stood on a crate, brushing Glenny. She wanted more than anything to be there. It would take her close to an hour to pack up her gear and drive home.

"I think we've got this if you need to go, Doc. Get us an invoice and we'll pay it," Martin said.

"Thank you. If you need anything else, don't be afraid to call. I'll have Lindsey send it out sometime this week."

"Much appreciated. Be careful on your drive home."

Jax waved and headed to her truck. She pulled the boot covers off and put them in a biohazard bag, along with her gloves and the tube she'd used to administer the mineral oil. She made a mental note to replace the items in her truck later. Once she'd shucked her boots and coveralls, she slid her feet into her Ropers. With everything loaded on the truck, she drove toward home. Her phone rang with a call from her office. It was Lindsey.

"I hate to bother you, but we have an emergency that just came in. Bill is back in the exam room with Booney. They were out doing some training and he fell into a hole. Looks like he might have broken a leg, and Bill's worried about internal injuries."

Jax slightly altered her route to drive to her office. "I'm on my way."

"It's not that Bill can't handle it, but you've worked with Pete on several calls, and I'm betting he'll feel better with you here. He's ready to come out of his skin."

"Tell Pete to relax, I'm on my way." She hung up with Lindsey and called Chance.

"Are you on your way home?"

Jax could hear laughter in the background and wished more than anything she could tell Chance she was. "Unfortunately, not. Sadie's going to be fine, but my new vet is treating Booney at the clinic. I'm not sure of all the details, but I know I'd feel better being there."

"Damn, Pete's probably all tore up. You go, we've got things handled here. Moms squared are here spoiling Hunter and he's soaking it up."

Jax could hear a bit of trepidation in Chance's voice. "What's wrong? Before you say nothing, remember I know you."

Chance sighed audibly over the phone. "I'm trying to figure out how we are going to tell that sweet boy his mom is dead."

"Has he asked about her yet?"

"No, that's the strange thing. He has to be wondering where she is."

"We'll talk about it when I get home. Maybe we can sit down with him and explain before he asks. There's no way we can avoid it."

"I don't want to hurt him."

"Neither do I, but we have to tell him sometime. He needs to know that we will be right there and that he's not alone."

Jax and Chance spoke for a few more minutes before she disconnected and concentrated on driving. A million things were running through her head. Losing a parent was difficult, no matter what your age. Chance had experienced that. Jax's estrangement from her mother was different, though no less painful. *We'll make it through, together. We'll be there for him.*

***

It was late in the evening when Chance heard Jax drive up. *She's got to be exhausted.* Chance met her at the door and enveloped her in her arms. "Hey you, welcome home."

Jax melted against her. "The minute I turned onto our road, I felt like I'd been run over by a bus."

"How about a glass of wine and some of Mom's cheeseburger casserole?"

"That sounds better than a five-star restaurant. Did Hunter like it?"

"Three helpings later and he was finally full, until the chocolate cake came out. He's in watching *Tom and Jerry* cartoons with Zeus."

Chance took Jax's coat and hung it up as Jax pulled off her boots. "How's Booney?"

"He's going to be okay. We had to put a plate and some pins in. It's going to take some recovery time. We aren't sure if it's going to affect him long term or not."

"Damn, I hate to hear that."

"I know." Jax grabbed her foot. "My feet are killing me."

Chance kissed her on the forehead. "After you eat, I'll rub them for you. Go sit on the couch and be with Hunter."

Jax sighed with relief. "Sounds good. Can I have a beer with that instead of wine?"

"Your wish is my command."

Jax kissed her passionately. "I have a lot of wishes I'd like to command, but dinner and a foot rub first."

Chance saluted. "At your service. Go on, go see the dynamic duo."

Jax made her way into the living room as Chance went to the kitchen. Her phone rang and she put it on speakerphone to answer so she could retrieve Jax's plate.

"Hey, Taylor, what's up?"

"I just sent you a new copy of the schedule with the changes you requested. Sorry it took so long. I'm sure you've heard the calls we've got going on."

"I have, sounds like you're handling it fine."

"Just another day in paradise. Anyway, look over that schedule. I left you off tonight. Khodi and Echo are going to pull overtime tonight. He's trying to remodel some of the rooms of his parents' farmhouse and is glad for the extra money. Get some rest and enjoy being together."

"Thanks, Taylor. I owe you."

"Far from it. I'm happy for you. Now put work out of your mind. That's an order." She paused then continued. "From Penny, since I don't rank."

Chance was able to picture Penny pointing her finger with one hand, the other firmly planted on her hip. "Tell the boss, I said, yes ma'am."

Chance retrieved a fork and a few slices of homemade bread, which she slathered with Amish butter. She pulled a growler of Savior's Red. The craft beer from Redemption's Road Brewing had become one of their favorites. Knowing that a portion of the proceeds from their purchase went to Rhebekka and Naomi's kids' program was a bonus.

She carried the plate and pint glass into the living room and was warmed seeing Hunter sitting on Jax's lap, showing her a picture book.

Hunter looked up and smiled at Chance as he scrambled off to sit beside her. *She looks so content.*

Hunter signed how much he'd liked all the cheese then explained that Oma Maggie promised to leave the chocolate cake she'd made for them.

Jax smiled and leaned in to bump Hunter's shoulder, making a show of taking a big bite.

Watching the beginnings of what Chance hoped would be many more evenings together stirred her emotions. She hated to get her hopes up too high if CPS didn't allow them to keep Hunter on a more permanent basis. *Cross that bridge when you come to it.*

***

Later that night, as they tucked Hunter into bed, the question they'd been dreading came. Jax had just placed a stuffed horse under his arm and kissed his forehead.

Hunter rubbed his eyes, then signed to them. *"Where's mommy?"*

Jax drew in a deep breath and looked to Chance who nodded. While Hunter had played in the bathtub, they'd talked about how to tell him and formulated a plan.

Jax did her best to explain. *"Remember she was sick? The ambulance took her to the hospital."*

Hunter nodded.

"I'm sorry. She didn't wake up. She died."

"Will I see my mommy again?"

"Not for a long time, but you can stay with us. You will be safe."

Hunter didn't communicate anything for a long time as tears ran down his face. Jax drew him into her lap and Chance surrounded them both with her arms. She could feel her shirt growing damp as he cried. Her cheeks grew wet with tears, as she wept for the stolen childhood Hunter had experienced so far. She vowed that if it were within her power, he wouldn't suffer one more loss. Jax kissed his head, sifting her fingers through his soft, dark hair. Without looking at Chance, she made a declaration.

"Whatever it takes, Chance."

Chance echoed the sentiment. "Whatever it takes."

Chapter Three

CHANCE SAT AT HER desk, staring off into space as she absentmindedly petted Zeus, who had his head on her thigh. Taylor and Midas walked in to start the day shift.

"You look like you're a million miles away."

Chance straightened. "I guess I am. I'm waiting for a call from April. They're supposed to make a final decision about letting us become Hunter's foster family."

"You said the house inspection and background checks went well. What's left to worry about?"

"April says there are a few people that have concerns about placing Hunter with us because we are a lesbian couple. If you remember, the federal government has recently proposed gutting an Obama administration provision that prohibited foster agencies from discriminating against LGBTQ couples. The other day, a West Virginia legislator proposed the same thing. Several states around us have already proposed or passed legislation giving adoption agencies the right to deny couples based on orientation."

Taylor sat down hard in the chair in front of Chance's desk. "Are you shitting me? With all the kids looking for homes in the foster system, someone is worried about you and Jax?"

"Seems so. April doesn't think it will hold things up, but she wanted to make me aware of the issue."

"That's just fucked up. Hunter is doing great with you guys. How many families are they going to find where both adults know some sign language? No one is better for that little guy. How idiotic."

Chance rubbed her tired eyes from her midnight shift. "I know it and you know it. Moms squared is making some calls. You can bet someone is getting an ass chewing. They haven't tried to foster since the jackass who stirred this all up was elected president. It's amazing how far we've come and with a single election, how far we've been set back."

"Christians my ass. I've never been very religious, and if hating people who live differently than you do is what's required, I never will be."

"That's one of the reasons I've become so comfortable with Rhebekka and Naomi. They offer a completely different view. Anyway, forward we go." Chance pulled a file folder off her desk and handed it to Taylor. "A few days ago, Harley and I handled a truck wreck in Dry Fork with a vehicle that had some symbols on it like that sovereign citizen information sheet from the other day. I have some investigative work for you to do. I found this." She opened an evidence box with the mystery .38 in it and went on to explain what she wanted Taylor to do. "J.D. Hamilton from the FBI will be coming this weekend to give us that in-service on the group in general. I talked to Ms. Newlander over at Valley Institute, and they've offered us the use of their multimedia auditorium. I want to get this out of the way before the bluegrass festival."

"Anyone else joining us?"

She pointed to a printout on her desk. "Harley is sending her available troopers, and I've invited several of the local agencies to come. I'm expecting about twenty or twenty-five. Let's see if we can round up someone who will donate some sandwich platter fixings, chips, and sodas. That would help keep the costs for the agencies at a bare minimum. If not, we'll take it out of our training budget. JD is coming over for free, so there won't be any speaker-related costs."

Taylor turned her hat in her hand. "I ran into our local Department of Natural Resources officer, who filled me in on that fishing license incident. Did you know that the guy threatened him with a gun?"

Chance nodded. "I read the report. We live in dangerous times to be wearing a badge. Somehow, we've become the bad guy. Don't get me wrong. You know as well as I do, we have some rotten apples among our ranks. Sadly, those few seem to be overshadowing the thousands of officers that strive every day to uphold the laws that keep the general public safe. We need to do better all the way around. Without good police officers, the bad guys hurt good people. We just have to make sure good police officers don't end up being the bad guys."

"Preaching to the choir, boss."

Chance leaned back and put a booted foot on her desk edge to rock the chair. "True. Sometimes it just feels good to say it out loud."

Penny poked her head in the office door. "Sheriff, you have some visitors."

Chance put her foot down. "Show them back."

April Reeve walked in the door with Jax following. Chance knew that Hunter was spending the day with Dee in her office while baby Jace spent the day with Maggie. Chance rose and shook the CPS worker's hand. "April, I wasn't expecting to see you. I thought you'd call when they had a decision."

Jax joined Chance behind the desk and stood at her side.

"Normally I would have, Sheriff. I thought this was too important to say over the phone, and I wanted to be able to share the news with both of you personally. I ran into Jax at the gas station and asked her to join me here."

Chance could feel her stomach knotting so tightly it hurt. *Please.*

"We'll take off if you need privacy." Taylor wrapped an arm around Penny's shoulder.

April smiled at them. "I don't think it's necessary, unless Chance and Jax are uncomfortable."

Jax shook her head. "No, they can stay. They're close friends. There's nothing we won't tell them anyway."

"Then I won't keep you in suspense. You've been approved as Hunter's foster parents. This is the fastest I've ever seen this process happen. The fact that you both can communicate in sign language weighed heavily in your favor. I will tell you there were a few strong objections, but in the end, both of you couldn't have been more suitable for this. It didn't hurt that Maggie made a few calls. I don't need to tell you how much weight she still pulls."

Chance relaxed and smiled for the first time that morning. "No, you don't."

Jax put a hand on Chance's chest. "What does this mean for him long term?"

April came around the desk and opened a folder for Chance and Jax to see. "There's some training that you both need to take. Everything at the house checked out. You live in the same school district as his former home, so he can go to school as normal when it starts up again unless you make other arrangements. You've taken him to the doctor for a checkup and his health is relatively good, all things considered."

Jax pointed to some numbers on the patient report in the document. "He's slightly malnourished. We're taking care of that by feeding him regularly with plenty of snacks that should help him get where he should be."

April nodded. "Basically, you've already done many of the things that we would have required you to do. Now it's a matter of getting him comfortable living within your home and dealing with the trauma of his mother's death. I highly recommend you find him a therapist that specializes in childhood trauma. Preferably someone familiar with deafness. I can help with that."

Chance spoke up quickly. "Anything he needs, he'll have, regardless of what it is. We'll do all we can to provide him with the safety and security he's never known in his young life."

Jax asked the question on Chance's mind. "How long would we need to foster him before we can put in to formally adopt him?"

Chance looked at her wife and her heart swelled. They truly did think on the same wavelength. They were already deeply attached to Hunter and had no desire to see him go anywhere else.

April looked at both of them. "It's a big decision. He'll be permanently tied to you until he is at least eighteen. Make sure you both discuss it before we start looking at the process."

"April, I can speak for both of us on this right now. We want to be there for a lifetime for Hunter, not just a few weeks or the next twelve years. He's been through enough and deserves a full-time family. We don't need to think about this at all, do we, Jax?"

Jax put her hand in Chance's. "No, she's right. I'd adopt him today if you'd let us. Start the process, we can give you our attorney's number."

Penny and Taylor stood in the door with broad smiles. Even the dogs knew something was happening because both turned in circles and barked.

April nodded. "It looks like everyone agrees, so I'll start the paperwork. As Maggie will tell you, initially, it seems like an easy thing to do. Saying yes is the easiest part. Now the hard work begins. I'll be back in touch. The process can take anywhere from twelve to eighteen months."

"However long it takes, we're not backing out. Hunter deserves it." Chance pulled Jax close. *And so does she.*

***

The days passed quickly. Jax was busy integrating Bill into her practice. The timing of his employment seemed like a godsend after Hunter's placement with them. Chance and Jax both made it a habit to be home to have dinner with Hunter and to put him to bed. They were truly settling in as a family. Jax discarded the scraps into the trash, then handed the plates to Chance to put in the dishwasher. Hunter's job was to help carry the plates to the sink before he fed Zeus two cups of food.

The boy had taken on both chores with great enthusiasm. They noticed that he thrived on routines.

Chance turned to Jax and handed her a large pot. "I'm glad he's finally stopped wolfing down his food. Do you think he's figured out that there will always be another meal coming?"

"I think he went without for so long it's instinctual. I found Goldfish crackers under his pillow when I changed his sheets."

"It breaks my heart what he's been through."

"I know but look at him now." Jax nodded toward Hunter as he was making the sign for Zeus to sit. "He's settling in and has Zeus wrapped around his paws."

Chance pushed the dishwasher door in place and started the cycle as she watched the boy. "Not just Zeus. That little guy has this whole family wrapped. I haven't seen my parents this happy since they brought Kendra home."

"I thank God for them every day. I'm not sure what we'd do without them. On days I can't take Hunter to work with me, he's content to help Oma sell houses. Maggie says he charms the signatures right out of the buyers."

"Momma D says he is exceptional at helping her pick colors for her advertising."

"I wonder what kind of in-depth hearing tests or examinations he's had. In everything I've read, it said from birth, he's never been able to truly hear anything except extremely loud noises. I wonder if they ever tried hearing aids?" Jax poured herself a cup of coffee as she watched Hunter put the ketchup in the door of the fridge.

"No clue." Chance picked him up and tickled him as he tried to run by her. At six, he was about the size of most four-year-old boys. She sat him down. *"Time for your bath,"* she signed. *"Please get your PJs and slippers."*

Hunter hugged her, then sprinted off in the direction of his room. Jax followed behind Chance as they made their way to the large bathroom. She smiled as she went down the hall, noticing the pictures they'd recently taken and framed. *I want him to know this is his home.* She hoped the pictures made him feel like he fit in as an integral part of their family.

Chance poured bubble bath in the water, then threw in a Spiderman scrunchy and a toy fireboat. Hunter came running in with his PJs in his arms. He sat on the closed toilet as Jax helped pull his sweatshirt off and Chance untied his shoes. He stood and fumbled with the button on his jeans until he was stripped down to his Batman boxer briefs. Once those and the rest of his clothes had been placed in the hamper, Chance held his hand as he climbed into the bathtub.

"*I can make you old,*" Chance signed.

Hunter questioned her, "*How?*"

Chance piled soap bubbles all over his head then formed a beard with even more. Jax handed her a mirror and she showed Hunter his reflection. The giggles from both of her two loves filled the room. It was music to Jax's ears, but she knew the sound was silent to Hunter. *I think Chance is right, we need to have a thorough hearing check done. I wonder if there's anything we can do to enhance what hearing he might have.*

With bath time complete, they helped him into bed. Jax slid his covers up and tucked his stuffed tiger and horse in with him. She pushed the dark hair off his forehead and kissed it lightly as Zeus settled on the end of the bed. She whispered to herself. "I love you, little man."

Chance kissed him, then turned on his night light before flipping the overhead one off.

They stepped into the hallway as Chance closed his door.

"I understand why it's safer, but I hate to think of him waking up that separated from us."

Chance kissed her. "I know you do, but if there is a fire, it will keep the smoke and heat away from him. It's important. Plus, Zeus is in there with him. These are lever door handles Zeus has been trained to open. I have no doubt he'd come and get us if there was a problem."

Jax wrapped her arm around Chance's waist as they made their way to the library. "Yes, Mrs. Firefighter." They'd installed a special smoke alarm in his room that vibrated his bed and flashed a bright light in his room to awaken him in the event of a fire. They'd spent a few evenings practicing his escape plan. These were just a few of the small but vital changes they'd made to their house to keep him safe. She paused for a moment and took Chance's hand. "I was thinking."

Chance led them down the hall. "About what?"

"We need to move quickly with a hearing specialist. It won't be long before he starts school."

"I'll call around and see about some recommendations."

They sat on the couch, and Jax curled up against Chance's chest. "Maybe his pediatrician would know."

"Good idea. Don't forget, I have that symposium tomorrow."

Jax turned her head to look at Chance. "The one on the right-wing extremists?"

Chance nodded.

"Are they becoming a big problem?" Jax pulled back to look Chance in the eyes.

"In this current political climate, yes. Suddenly, everyone is a constitutional expert who no longer must follow the actual laws of the land. Instead, they follow their interpretation of them. Sadly, most of the time, they get it completely wrong."

Jax snuggled in. "It seems like as soon as we rid ourselves of one problem, another pops up. Just be careful."

"Always."

"You have a family now, Chance. It's not just me depending on you, there's Hunter too." *And we both need you.*

***

Saturday morning, a group of law enforcement officers sat listening intently to Special Agent in Charge, J. D. Hamilton. Chance sat on an outside row, watching intently as the man in his early sixties paced back and forth highlighting a large projection screen with a laser pointer.

"Watch for visual clues that the individual you've pulled over is a sovereign citizen. They may have a homemade license plate that has no validity. Wording like Kingdom of Heaven, private traveler, and DOT exempt will often be accompanied by the words right to travel or not for commerce."

He flipped through several slides with examples of confiscated bogus license plates.

Chance watched as Taylor and her other officers took notes. She was pleased to see they were taking in the information that she hoped might help keep them safe.

"They may also display a flag similar to the one shown here." He zoomed in on a bumper sticker on an older model van. "Notice that it's a variation of the American flag, except the stars are now blue on a white square and the stripes are vertical instead of horizontal. It's vitally important that you recognize, as soon as possible, what you're dealing with. Some groups recognize only the sheriff as an elected official, while others recognize no government authority. That means they don't feel the need for a license for anything they do. No fishing license, no hunting license, and especially no driver's or vehicle license. They will do anything and everything to avoid paying taxes or fines. We are the enemy, in their mind. According to them, law enforcement has zero authority over them."

Chance raised her hand and asked a question when acknowledged. "We've heard rumors that there have been some run-ins over in Randolph County, near the Tucker County line. Do you have any intelligence on those we have living here?"

JD nodded. "We have our eye on more than one, specifically in the more remote areas of Dry Fork and down in Laneville. The Joint Terrorism Task Force and the Fusion Center have collected several pieces of information. My colleague is passing around information packets on the two I've just mentioned. One is the paper terrorist type. You pull him over and he'll try to bury you in legal mumbo jumbo that means absolutely nothing. He might even try to sue you or charge you a fee for signing the citation you try to issue. A few of these encounters have turned violent over the years."

He pointed to his temple. "Remember, the individual likely doesn't have a valid driver's license. His vehicle probably hasn't been inspected and is lacking a valid registration. By law, you can tow the vehicle and cite the driver. This is when they tend to get belligerent and start threatening a great deal of legal action through a system they don't recognize."

Taylor spoke up. "And the other one?"

"The other is a hard-core militant type. He has ties to both sovereign citizens and a white supremacist group called Posse Comitatus. Moved to this area about ten years ago from Missouri."

Neither were names Chance recognized from anything other than the flyers the ATF sent, but she committed the faces and particulars to memory.

Taylor nudged her shoulder and pointed to the hard-core sovereign, Ted Eichland.

"I saw this guy at Kinder's Feed Supply a few weeks ago when I picked up our horse feed."

Chance tapped the papers. "Let's make sure we keep copies of this in the cruisers. I'm glad the communication center folks are here as well. If they get a call involving either of these locations, no one responds alone."

***

The group took a lunch break before JD and his team went over procedures they'd developed in handling encounters with domestic extremists. The officers practiced different approaches, with the FBI agents playing the part of the sovereign citizen.

Chance carefully approached the vehicle and spoke to Zeus. "*Bewaken.*" She stood to the side of the car window, talking through the glass to the agent pretending to be the sovereign citizen. He hadn't rolled down the window.

"Sir, turn off your vehicle and roll down your window."

The agent inside the car rolled it down an inch and handed her a slip of paper. "I want you to be aware that you are being recorded. I'd like you to put your name and badge number on that form."

Chance ignored the paper and glanced at Zeus before addressing the driver again. "Sir, I've pulled you over for driving with an invalid plate. May I see your driver's license, registration, and insurance card?"

"I'm not driving, I'm traveling."

Chance knew that these phrases were distinctive sovereign citizen lingo meant to confuse and distract. She kept her hand on her gun. "Please step out of the car, sir."

"As a free person, I do not recognize your jurisdictional authority. As a free person, your license plate taxes do not apply to me."

Chance reached for her radio and simulated calling for backup assistance with a traffic stop. "Sir, as you are operating on a state-maintained roadway, you are subject to the fees associated with its usage. As a duly sworn officer of the law, I am requesting your driver's license, registration, and insurance information. If you fail to provide them, you will be cited."

The agent inside the car became belligerent. "Are you detaining me? What crime have I committed? Who is the injured party?"

The mock traffic stop went all the way through removing the subject from the vehicle by simulated force directed by JD and his agents. Each move carefully orchestrated to achieve taking the person into custody, without harm if possible, using the means legally available to them. As each officer went through the simulation, they made adjustments to reduce the danger.

Chance was grateful they'd started using body cameras since her election. All interactions were recorded and served as evidence when cases came to court. It also made her a better officer, knowing that her actions could be subject to legal requests. *It gets more complicated to do our job with so much against us.* The last thing any officer wanted was to lose a critical case because they failed to do something required or did something inappropriate. It was as much a protection for them as it was the public.

***

The hands-on portion of the training ended, and all the officers went back inside for a debrief. JD and the rest of his agents talked about the good officer responses and the ones that needed changes for the best outcome. Chance took notes and mentally planned a department training day to address some of the concerns.

JD finished his remarks to a round of applause. Chance walked to the front of the room with Zeus at her side and shook his hand. "I'd like to thank you and the members of your team for sharing your knowledge and skill with us." She turned to the officers sitting before her. "We face new challenges every day from criminals that grow more violent, even as the public trusts us less and less to protect them. Our actions are always under scrutiny, and it's our job to continue to uphold the oath each one of us takes to protect and serve. Thank you for coming. Keep your head on a swivel and have each other's backs."

The officers rose and chatted with the agents. Taylor approached them. "I can't thank you enough for that hands-on training. I certainly feel more confident."

The agent put out his hand to shake hers. "This group is no joke, and they are all over the board as to their beliefs and actions. Knowing their game is the only way we can keep ahead of it."

Taylor shook with him. "I worked as a US Marshal and had to take them into custody. I can remember the planning was pretty thorough, and it required a good bit of backup."

JD nodded. "If you think about the Ruby Ridge incident, you know how quickly things can go south. Fatalities aren't uncommon, but it certainly leaves a black eye on the agency in the public's opinion. To an outsider, who doesn't understand how radical these people can be, it appears that we used deadly force first. The reality is that's our last option when we are given no other choice."

Chance brushed a hand over Zeus' head. "I hope we can avoid an encounter with either of the individuals we now know live here. I feel better knowing my officers always have K9 backup with them. I'd appreciate some standard operating procedure recommendations. With this training and a policy in place, our officers will have a playbook to follow."

JD slid his hands into his pants pockets. "Not a problem. I've gathered several of them traveling around doing this training. You can look over them and adapt to your needs. I'll be happy to review your SOP to make sure it covers all the bases."

They talked a bit more as they closed out the session. When everyone had departed, Chance and Taylor had a few minutes to talk.

"How're you doing with the visiting in-laws?"

Taylor adjusted her Stetson. "Given the fact that we've barely seen them since we got married, it's going better than I could have expected. Having a grandson apparently softened her stance on our marriage. Brenda has been extremely helpful at night when he fusses. Nana has the same magical power as Maggie does at getting him back asleep. In the morning, Warren takes over and plays with him, or they sit and watch fishing shows together. It's been nice having them there to let us get a few things done while they keep him entertained. They shooed us out of the house the other night and told us to go have a date night."

Chance stared at her. "You're kidding?"

Taylor raised her hand. "Swear to God."

"Well, my friend, the old saying is 'miracles can happen.' Looks like you're getting some firsthand knowledge."

The pair watched Midas and Zeus chase each other.

Chance saw Taylor open her mouth as if to say something, but she didn't. "What?"

"How's Hunter doing?"

Chance took a deep breath. "He has good days and bad. He wakes up screaming some nights. We're looking for a therapist for him, but with his hearing issue, it's a tall order. Jax is making calls for recommendations. It breaks my heart."

"He's been through a lot in his short life."

"Jax and I are going to do everything we can to make it better."

"He doesn't know it yet, but he hit the jackpot for parents."

"I guess that's still to be seen. The state could reject our adoption request, and it's still possible an unknown relative could pop up and decide they want to raise him."

Taylor shook her head. "I don't see that happening. If his mother had anywhere to turn, I can't imagine she wouldn't have done it while she was alive. Hunter will have questions when he's older, and you'll be there to help answer them. Don't doubt yourself, Chance. He's where he needs to be."

"Let's talk about the bluegrass festival for a few minutes. Is the schedule done?"

Taylor pulled out her smartphone and pulled up a document. "Daniel and Athena are now on the schedule as well. That makes us fully staffed. Carl has asked to move over as court bailiff full time, but he's agreed to work overtime in the evening if needed." She continued to lay out the schedule for the rest of the deputies. Most would work the festival, except for Khodi and Echo who would remain on road patrol to handle any calls. The state police would also have officers there.

"The good thing is that this festival is relatively calm. I can't remember anything beyond a few public-intoxication calls in the last fifteen years. Last year's numbers were close to 2000, with no serious arrests." Chance pointed to a specific spot on the schedule. "Friday and Saturday night draw the biggest crowd."

Taylor nodded. "I'm going down to talk to the organizers at the campground and see if we have a firmer estimate on the attendees. Most of the headliners bring their own personal security staff, and the last I heard was that the organizers were hiring some off-duty officers from Randolph County as stage security. We've never had any issues there, but the bigger the acts get, the more likely someone is going to get a little too close."

Chance pulled out her phone and checked a text message. "Let's make some calls over to Randolph and get familiar with the names. I'm going to go pick up Hunter. Jax is still out with the Saddlebacks working on the route for the endurance race."

"Duty calls."

Chance couldn't help the grin she felt creep up. "Best duty ever."

Chapter Four

JAX PULLED UP ON Mac's reins and patted his neck. Matt Carson rode up beside her. In front of them was an embankment leading out of a stream. Jax checked her trail map. "I don't think there will be a problem here unless someone goes too far to the right." She pointed to a rocky outcrop at the top.

Matt nodded. "We can mark that as a hazard and put it on everyone's course map to stay to the left. I've had a ton of inquiries from all over the place. The main trails are well known, it's how we've tied them together to avoid some of the more dangerous spots that are in question. If they live close, some will certainly practice beforehand."

"Letting them out in groups of four or less should help stagger it. To compete in the limited distance race of twenty-five miles, they have to run the course four times."

"And eight times for the fifty-mile endurance race. Did you ever run the Ironhorse?"

Jax folded the map and put it back in her shirt pocket. "I have. I rode in the Tevis Cup in 1992 and finished tenth. One hundred miles in one day, and I've got the silver buckle to prove it. I had a great horse. It was one of the hardest things I ever did, and I've never done one like that since."

They moved on, riding through some dense brush headed back to the trailhead where the horse trailer was. As they rounded a bend, Jax noticed Raider flinching slightly. "Hold up, Matt. Something's not right with your horse. I need to check him."

They dismounted and Jax noticed where a piece of laurel had broken off and gotten stuck under the girth strap. When she touched it, Raider snorted at her and moved sideways. "I think this rubbed a sore spot. We need to pad the girth strap to try to alleviate it."

Matt adjusted the strap that held the saddle in place and mounted the tall Arabian. He pointed to the sky. "That will have to do for now. We might want to double-time it to get back. Those look like storm clouds to me."

Jax's ponytail blew around her face, and she checked the horizon while she got back on Mac. From her vantage point, she could see dark clouds rapidly approaching. "I agree, let's go."

Both riders picked up the pace until the horses were in a trot. On open ground, they let the horses break into a gallop until they were forced to slow for laurel or trees. The sky had moved from pale gray into threatening swirls of charcoal as the winds continued to pick up. As they crossed over a stream and started up a small embankment, Jax saw Matt's saddle slip. She prepared to stop again when she watched the girth strap move back until it was more of a bucking strap. Raider let out a trumpeting whinny before he reared and threw Matt off into the creek bed.

"Matt!" Jax had only a second to call out before Raider careened into her and Mac.

Her horse stumbled and pitched Jax sideways, forcing her to grab onto the saddle horn. Cold fear ripped through her as Mac took off at a frantic gallop with Raider right beside him. Jax struggled to find the reins she'd dropped when she was nearly thrown off. The horses were running full out as the trees got closer and closer. *Oh shit.* She braced herself as Mac slammed into one, launching her out of the saddle. She landed among the rocks and forest litter; the breath knocked out of her. A bolt of lightning split the darkening sky as she tried to clear the cobwebs out from the fall.

Seconds later, a clap of thunder boomed. The skies opened up and began pelting the ground with huge raindrops. Jax pushed herself into a sitting position and attempted to take inventory of any injuries. She was thankful for the helmet that she knew had saved her from a serious head injury. She could taste copper as she ran her tongue across her teeth only to stop from the pain where she'd likely bitten through the skin on the inside of her lip. "Ouch, dammit." Jax slowly got to her knees and stood with a wobble. Neither horse was in sight as she tried to peer through the heavy downpour. "Matt! Matt, can you hear me?" With weak legs, she started back to the creek where she'd last seen him. The horses had run a considerable distance from where Raider bucked Matt off. It took her ten minutes in the blinding rain to get back to the water. "Matt?" She shaded her eyes from the rain, looking for the fluorescent vest he'd been wearing. She nearly missed the streak of safety yellow at the creekbank but not the scream he emitted as he tried to pull himself up farther. Jax ran down and dropped beside Matt who was half in, half out of the rapidly swelling creek. She leaned close to him and wiped the streak of rain-diluted blood from his face. "Are you hurt?"

"Pretty sure I broke my femur. Do you have the horses?"

"No, they took off after Mac ran into a tree. We need to get you out of the stream. Let me go see if I can find something to splint that leg." Jax ran over to a small group of saplings and broke two off. She stripped off the small branches and brought them back to where Matt lay on his stomach holding on to the roots of a large maple. The leaf cover helped protect them somewhat from the pounding rain, but Jax worried about the lightning that continued to break through the darkness. She pulled off the backpack she wore, found the headlamp, and slid the light into place on her helmet as she turned it on. She grabbed the webbing and used her knife to cut two three-foot pieces off.

"Just do it, Jax." Matt looked at her. "I know it's going to hurt like hell."

She pulled off her leather glove and jammed it in his mouth. "Bite on this so you don't break a tooth." She climbed down in the stream and measured the saplings against his leg. She broke them into the right length and tied them on with the webbing. She could hear him screaming around the glove as she tightened the last strap. Jax looked at his pale face. "Okay, I'm going to wrap the other part of my webbing under your arms. There's no easy way to do this, Matt. I'm just going to have to drag you up. All I can hope for is you pass out and then it will be over. I'll figure out what to do after we get you out of the water. Help with your good leg if you can."

"It's okay. Let's just get it done."

Jax threaded the webbing under his arms and around his chest forming a type of girth hitch. She sat a few feet back from the bank and dug the heels of her boots in the wet ground. "One...two...three!" Jax pulled with all her might as Matt's blood-curdling scream drowned out the thunder. She choked down on the webbing and pulled a second, then a third time. Matt came farther and farther up the bank and out of the stream. As she'd hoped, sometime during one of the pulls, Matt had passed out. She used the webbing and dragged him closer to the trunk under the shelter of the tree. *Not the best place to be in a lightning storm, but we can't stay out in the open either.*

Her chest heaved from the exertion as she pulled a sheet of plastic out of her bag and draped it over Matt. She had an emergency blanket but thought better about covering him with something that resembled tin foil. She pulled her phone out of her coat pocket and cursed as she looked at the cracked screen. "Fuck!" *Now what, Jax?* She put her head back against the trunk of the tree, trying to clear her head. *Matt has to have a phone on him.* Matt lay unconscious as she patted his pockets, trying to find his phone. She located it in his inside jacket pocket and stood. *Thank God for waterproof cases.* She looked at the display. Her heart sunk. *No fucking service.*

The rain finally let up. She watched something large and dark moving through the woods. Raider, Matt's horse, cleared the trees and trotted up to her. She strained to look past him hoping to see Mac. When he didn't appear, she turned back to Matt who had started to come around.

"Hey there. I'm not going to ask you how you are. We did manage to gain some company. Raider is back."

Raider leaned over and snuffled Matt's face. A shaky hand reached up and patted the horse's snout. "Jax, you need to ride him out of here and get help. There's no way I can ride."

"I can't leave you here alone."

"Yes, you can. Get in my saddlebag and grab the GPS."

"Dammit, Matt."

"Do it, Jax. It's what you'd have me do. Get the coordinates and send help back. There's a first aid kit in there, too. Should be some over the counter pain meds."

Jax busied herself trying to make Matt as comfortable as possible. She dressed the large cut on his chin and pulled the Advil from another pouch in the kit. He drank water from a bottle in his pocket and swallowed as many pills as was safe. Once she covered him with the plastic sheeting as well as she could, she stood and took Raider's reins in her hand. With the coordinates locked in, she took a deep breath. "I'll be back as soon as I can."

Matt nodded then closed his eyes. "Go."

She adjusted the girth strap and made sure it was in the correct position before putting her foot in the stirrup and climbing onto the black horse's back. "Let's go, Raider. We need to get your dad some help." With a slight nudge of her heels, Raider took off down the trail. The entire ride, she watched for Mac along the way without success. Like an oasis in the desert, she located the truck and trailer.

The minute she secured Raider in the trailer, she jumped in the truck and headed off the Sods, back down to the Red Creek Ranger's Station. A quick look at the dash told her she had less than half an hour to get there before they closed, forcing her to travel farther to a phone or to find cell service. The gravel was rutted with the heavy rain, the ditch lines overflowing. Her anxiety was through the roof as she concentrated on seeing the narrow road and the windshield wipers struggled to clear the heavy rain. She stifled a cry as the ranger station came into view. The transmission made an unpleasant grinding sound when she threw it into park before the truck was completely stopped. She jumped out and ran up the rain-slicked stairs causing her to slide to a knee before she righted herself and rushed through the door.

"I need help! I've got a man up Little Stone Creek trail with a fractured femur. Our horses spooked, and he was bucked off into the creek!"

A tall man in a tan ranger's shirt and green pants came around the counter. "Slow down. Where's he at again?"

Jax relayed the coordinates where she'd left Matt and waited until the ranger contacted the Tucker County 911 center. Jax got on the phone and gave the particulars of Matt's current condition and location. The radio tones in the background told her that units were being dispatched. Jax recognized that she was talking with one of the senior telecommunicators. "Pam, I need to talk to Chance. My phone broke. Can you call for me?"

"I won't have to, Jax. I've got the Sheriff right here. Hold on."

There were clicks on the line before the one voice Jax needed to hear more than anything came through.

"Jax, are you okay?"

She tried to hold back a sob but couldn't. It was a few seconds before she could get herself back under control. "I'm banged up but not as bad as Matt. I'm pretty sure he broke his femur. It was pouring down rain when I left him near the creek under a big tree."

"My parents were visiting Hunter. They'll watch him for us. I've got Kelly trailered and headed your way. The rescue truck responded from Canaan and I put the helicopter on standby. Sarah is headed to you in the ambulance. It's okay, we're on our way, baby. Promise me you'll stay there until I get there."

"I can't do that. I'm making my way back to Matt. Macallan is missing too." Jax finished telling the story of how she'd ended up at the ranger station.

"Jax, wait there, please."

"I love you, Chance, but I'm going. Matt wouldn't leave me out there alone. I'll see you when you get to us." She hung up and spoke to the ranger. "It appears the cavalry is coming. They have the coordinates. I'm headed back out there."

"Ma'am, are you sure you should get back on a horse? You look like one of them dragged you a country mile."

Jax grimaced as she limped back out the door. "That's closer to the truth than you know."

***

A hard ride up Stone Creek Trail brought Jax back to Matt's side. She checked his pulse and took what vitals she could without a blood pressure cuff. His pulse was steady, though his respirations seemed a bit shallow.

"I think it's because I cracked a rib or two on a rock in the creek." Matt tried to adjust his position and cried out in pain.

"Try to stay still. We don't have any idea about internal bleeding." Jax cut the laces of his boot. "Can you feel your foot?"

"I'm not sure. Everything hurts. I think I'm moving my toes."

Jax watched his foot. "That looked like movement. I don't want to try and cut this boot off until they get a Sager splint on that leg to relieve the pressure."

"When that saddle slid back, it had to hurt Raider. Did you check him?"

"When I put him in the trailer, I ran my hand down his flanks and around his belly. I think it pinched him."

"Where's Mac?"

Jax grew quiet and began a more detailed trauma evaluation of Matt's injuries. "I know you said your ribs hurt, how about your hips or back?"

"Jax, where's Mac?"

Her voice trembled as she told him the truth. "I don't know, Matt. After he hit that tree and dumped me, he took off. I'll find him once we get you taken care of. I can't think about that right now."

"I'm sorry, Jax."

"It's not your fault. Oh, I almost forgot." Jax held up a handful of chemical hand warmers before she opened them and put them under his armpits, around his neck, and let him hold one in his hands. "If we'd had my truck, I'd have had my go pack with my IV set up and some good pain meds. They'll try to get as close as they can with the vehicles, then it's going to be a hike or a ride in. If Chance gets here at the same time as Sarah, she'll ride her into us. For now, let's try and keep you calm. I know you're probably chilled, and if I could, we'd get those wet clothes off you. With that makeshift splint on your leg, we'll do our best to keep you comfortable. I've got a few more of those warmers."

"Let's hold on to them in case these go cold. They're making a big difference."

Jax watched him close his eyes for a minute. She looked for the rise and fall of his chest to make sure he was still breathing. When she shifted her position to get off her sore hip, a small groan slipped out. Matt opened his eyes.

"Jax, how bad are you?"

"Stiff and stoved up. Mac took the brunt of the hit. I can tell you I'm grateful we ride with helmets." She knocked her knuckles against the side of it.

Matt nodded weakly. "I'd hate to know what would have happened to me if I hadn't had it on. My chin feels bad enough. Pretty sure my season is over."

"Good bet. Looks like the only thing you'll be riding is the stats table for a while."

They chatted about inconsequential things until Jax heard twigs snap somewhere behind her. Her eyes flooded as Chance broke out of the trees with Sarah tucked in tight behind her.

"Jax!"

Jax stood up and waved her arms. "Over here!"

"Hang on!"

Jax watched Chance cover the distance between them as if she were riding in the Kentucky Derby. She brought Kelly to a halt and helped Sarah slide off. When Chance dismounted, Jax threw herself into her wife's arms and let the tension go. Tears poured down her face as Chance held her tightly.

"Baby, are you okay?"

Jax tried to pull herself together as she buried her head in Chance's chest. "I am now. Nothing that will kill me. Let's take care of Matt. I can't deal with anything else right now."

***

Chance knew Jax had to be worried sick about Mac wandering around in the woods with the predators that came out at night to hunt. All that was on top of her concern about Matt. They positioned the

Sager to stabilize the broken femur. Matt screamed initially, then passed out from the pain as they finished the application.

Sarah pushed the earpieces of her stethoscope back in her ears and pumped up the blood pressure cuff. "Jax take his pulse, please?"

The two conferred and agreed he was as stable as he could be at this point.

Chance set about putting out flashing beacons to draw the responders in before she grabbed her radio. "SD-1 to Comm Center."

"Go ahead."

"Can you make contact with the team and see how far they are from the coordinates given?"

"Stand by."

Jax walked up beside her and slid under her arm. Chance pulled her in close and felt Jax relax into the comfort offered.

"Comm Center to SD-1. They think they are about fifteen minutes from you. They tried you on the radio but were unable to make contact. I've advised them to switch to Tac-2 direct."

"I'll try to reach them there. Let them know I've marked the scene."

"Received."

As the darkness continued to surround them, Chance turned up the intensity of her helmet light and helped Sarah do the same. She broke several glow sticks and stuck them in the ground around the area where they were tending to Matt.

Matt smacked his lips. "Can I have a drink of water, please?"

Chance was hesitant. "Just a little. You're likely headed straight for surgery when we get you out of here. They're going to want that stomach as empty as possible." She held the bottle to his lips, allowing him a small sip.

"Rescue-1 to SD-1."

Chance held her radio to her mouth. "SD-1. Go ahead."

"We have a visual on your flashers. We should be with you in about another five minutes."

"We'll be waiting."

They readied Matt by slipping on a cervical collar and gathering their supplies. It wasn't long before they heard voices behind them. A crew carrying the stretcher and the transport wheel arrived along with several horseback riders carrying other supplies.

Jax pointed. "Those are other members of the Saddlebacks."

Matt clasped her hand. "A welcome sight."

Over the next several minutes, Sarah gave Matt another dose of morphine right before they moved him onto a backboard and placed him inside the basket. The crew maneuvered the travel wheel under the basket and attached it. With that in place, the litter bearers took positions at the rails with Sarah directing the extraction process.

Chance looked at Jax and made a decision. "I want you to ride with me. One of the crew can bring Raider down." She swore she could see relief blanket Jax's face when she nodded her agreement. "You're exhausted, both physically and emotionally. Truth be told, I need you close to me."

Jax leaned against her. "I need you too."

As they rode down the mountain, Jax continually called out for Mac. Chance did the same and hoped he'd follow the sound of her voice. The crew maneuvered the stretcher down the trail, switching out crew members as needed. Logically, one would think that the trip down would be quicker, but the reality was the process was slow and methodical in the dark. Walking down a rain-soaked gravel and dirt path made the crew members susceptible to slips and falls. Sarah stayed alongside Matt the entire way down.

When they were near the halfway point. Chance yelled for everyone to take a break before exhaustion truly set in. Sarah updated Matt's vitals and administered meds as necessary.

With everyone rested and rehydrated, they started down the trail again using their headlamps to illuminate the uneven terrain. It took them another hour to make it to the waiting ambulance at the trailhead. Sarah jumped in the ambulance with Matt, who was taken from the scene and moved to a landing zone in a large field down on Laneville Road. He would be transported to Ruby Memorial Hospital by helicopter.

Chance led Kelly and Raider over to the trailers. "Let's get them loaded up. We can board Raider at our house tonight. I promise, at first light, we'll come back and look for Mac with Glenny and Zeus to help find him."

"I can't imagine him being out here all night alone."

"He's a big horse and fast as hell." Chance heard a horse nicker and turned toward the sound. She smiled. "Well, I'll be."

***

Jax broke into a run, slipping on the mud. Coming down the road was Mac. He skidded to a stop in front of her as she fell against him, wrapping her arms as far around his neck as she could. "Oh, Mac, you scared me to death." She cried into his neck for several minutes as he nuzzled her. "Let me check you."

Jax led him closer to the command post where large lights had been set up to illuminate the area. Chance finished loading the other horses and came to hold him while Jax performed her examination.

Mac threw his head up and down as Jax ran her hands all over his flanks and down each leg. There was an area around his right front hoof that was scraped and some abrasions on his shoulder where he hit the tree. He drew it away when she tried to probe it and pawed at the ground.

"It's okay, boy. We'll fix it. Let's get you home where I can really check you over." She felt tears pour down her face when she looked at Chance. "I've got Matt's truck and trailer. Since you've got the other two loaded, let's load Mac and go home. I have no idea how bad his shoulder is, and he's got some serious cuts around his fetlocks. Poor guy must have had to go through some serious brambles."

Chance came around and drew Jax into her arms. "Whatever it is, we'll take care of it."

Jax melted and once again cried in the familiar strong arms she depended on. "There is very little of my old life I brought back here with me. I wouldn't have survived all those years of misery without Mac and Glenny."

"Everyone knows what they mean to you. It's going to be okay. Let's get him loaded."

For the next several minutes, they worked on securing the three horses and making sure they couldn't injure themselves during transport. Jax was wet and cold and didn't object in the least when Chance asked one of the members of her rescue squad to drive her truck with the horses to their place. Jax had no idea when she'd fallen asleep and jumped when Chance woke her.

"We're home."

Jax opened her eyes to see they were in front of the barn at their house. She let out a groan of pain as she straightened.

"Are you all right?"

"Just stiff from the fall. I'm fine. Let's get them in the barn so I can check Raider and Mac properly and dress those wounds."

With Andy, the other driver's help, they unloaded and brushed down the horses. Chance and Andy took care of the tack while Jax carefully examined all the horses and treated any wounds she found. Raider had a variety of scratches that she cleaned and applied salve to. Mac had some major swelling in his shoulder as well as some deep gashes around his legs that she treated and dressed appropriately. When she was done, she leaned into Mac's neck and hugged him tightly. "I'm so glad you're okay. Glenny and I would be lost without you."

Mac nuzzled and nipped at her hair, snuffling contentedly, and accepting the molasses treat from her pocket. "Get some rest and I'll be back in the morning to change those bandages." She stepped out of the stall and gave Raider, Kelly, and Glenny the last of her treats.

Chance and Andy came out of the tack room. Jax squeezed his arm. "Thank you so much, Andy. I wasn't in any shape to drive."

"It was a pleasure, Jax. I'm going to head to the station and see if they need any help. If Matt's wife needs me to take Raider home, I'll be glad to do that for him."

Chance's phone pinged with a text. "It's Sarah. She says Matt's headed to surgery but is in good spirits. He said to tell Jax thank you and get some sleep."

Jax wiped tears from her eyes and felt the salt sting her cheeks. She had no words and instead responded with a nod of her head.

Andy went out to catch a ride with another squad member who pulled in.

Chance wrapped an arm around Jax's shoulder. "Let's get inside. Everyone out here is good, and I'm pretty sure some little guy is going to be happy to see you. Mom texted me that he refused to go to bed until we got home."

They walked arm in arm back to the house. Jax stumbled up the steps, exhausted. Chance caught her and held her tight.

"You okay?"

"Tired, so tired."

"Then let's show Hunter you're okay and head to bed."

"I think that's the best idea I've heard all day." Jax was right where she longed to be, home with her family.

***

Chance pushed open the kitchen door and led Jax inside. A few steps down the hall and she found everyone curled up on the couch watching another *Tom and Jerry* cartoon. Chance chuckled at the choice. Rarely were there any spoken words in the cartoon, the actions of a cat chasing a mouse needed little explanation. Hunter was tucked under Dee's arm watching the screen, oblivious to their presence, until Zeus looked at them and wagged his tail. Kendra and Brandi were curled up together in one corner of the couch. Hunter's eyes followed where Zeus was looking. "*Jax is home.*" Chance signed and pointed to Jax.

Hunter climbed off the couch and ran to Jax, wrapping his arms around her legs. When she dropped to her knees to hug him, Chance nearly lost it and barely managed to hold back the tears.

Hunter moved back and looked at Jax before running off.

Jax quickly stood and started to go after him before Chance stopped her. "Let's see what he does."

"I'm afraid he's upset," Jax said, pulling off her coat.

"Then we'll deal with it. We have to let him work through things on his own and help when we can."

Hunter came running back into the room with his toy doctor's kit in one hand and the other dragging Brandi off the couch. Jax knelt in front of him. "*What's this?*" Jax signed.

Hunter pointed to her cheek then to Brandi and himself. His little fingers formed the signs for "*We fix you.*"

Chance wiped a tear away as Hunter pulled Jax to the couch and made her sit. Watching him use the toy stethoscope and thermometer to check her out under Brandi's supervision was one of the most endearing things she'd ever witnessed. She joined them on the couch, then Hunter ran out of the room again. He brought back a wet washcloth to clean a small scratch on Jax's face, then asked Brandi to open the Band-Aid to put on it.

Jax hugged him and thanked him for taking care of her.

Chance ran her hand across the crown of the small child's head. "*Thank you, Hunter,*" she signed to him. "*Please go to bed. We'll be there soon.*"

He nodded, then wrapped his arms around them before rubbing his tired-looking eyes. He yawned and took Dee's hand.

Dee smiled at Hunter and turned to her daughter-in-law. "We'll handle this. I'm glad you're okay, Jax. This family could use a break."

Chance took a deep breath. "Amen."

Jax hugged Maggie. "Thanks, Mom."'

"You're both welcome."

Kendra stepped up and hugged Jax as well. "We'll be here to help take care of the horses tomorrow. You need some rest, and it's the least we can do."

Chance smiled at her sister and pulled her into an embrace. "Thanks. Hunter seems to be smitten with Brandi."

"Those two are thick as thieves. I can't tell you how happy I am that Hunter is with you guys. He's going to have some awesome parents. You've had some pretty good role models for the job."

"Thanks, Kendra, for everything."

Kendra turned to Jax. "You okay? The whole thing was making us nuts not being out there to help."

Jax hugged her. "I'm okay now. I'm grateful you kept Hunter occupied."

"That's one of the best jobs ever. If you need someone to watch him, Brandi and I are up for it anytime."

"We'll remember that." Chance took Jax by the hand as they made their way to the bedroom where she methodically undressed Jax who was nearly as limp as a rag doll. Chance ran the bath water and poured in citrus soap. Jax sank into the steam and groaned with pleasure as Chance soaped up a loofa and gently began to clean off the day's grime.

"That feels so good. I wish you could climb in here with me, though I'd likely fall asleep against you."

"You're bruised from head to toe."

"I can feel it."

"Lean back, let me wash your hair."

Jax did as instructed and leaned back into Chance's hands.

"My heart stopped when I heard that call drop. I knew you and Matt were up there scouting the trail. Something told me it was you guys. I just didn't know which one it was until they gave the full size-up. The relief at hearing your voice was overwhelming. I didn't know what to say to Hunter. He's had enough trauma in his life." Chance poured water to clear away the soap from Jax's long, dark hair.

Jax yawned. "It's not just the two of us anymore. Everything we do from now on affects him."

"Trust me, that isn't lost on me." Chance helped Jax stand after which she wrapped her in a bath towel. "Let's find you some PJs and check on the doctor in training."

"We're quite the family, aren't we?"

Chance nodded. "Indeed we are."

***

Sunday, Jax and Chance decided the family needed a day to do nothing but play games and heal up. Kendra and Brandi headed back to Morgantown after taking the horses out. Jax sat beside Hunter, helping him communicate with Grampa Mike. Jax's dad didn't know sign language yet, but he'd already solicited a class with a local instructor.

Jax signed for Hunter's benefit as she spoke to her dad. *"Grandpa wants to know if you have any sevens."*

Hunter grinned then signed, *"Go fish."*

Mike giggled and picked a card off the pile.

"Do you have any queens, Grandpa?" Hunter signed and Jax continued to interpret. Chance set a cup of hot tea and two Advil in front of her. She tipped her head and kissed Chance. "Thank you."

"I've got a hot pack heating in the microwave for your back."

"I'm so stiff." Jax helped Hunter put the queen her dad passed with the others Hunter had. The grinning boy pulled them out and laid them on the table with a triumphant smile.

"Later tonight, we'll soak in the hot tub. I'm glad we went ahead and added one of those after our Valentine's Day trip."

Jax leaned back and stretched. "Me too."

After several more rounds of card and board games, Chance grilled hamburgers for everyone. Jax poured Hunter a glass of milk. The small boy helped bring the ketchup and mustard to the table before running back outside to be with Chance.

"He seems like he's settling in." Mike put plates and silverware down at each place setting.

"That little guy has had a rough existence for his first six years. Our goal is to make his next thirty the best they can be."

Mike hugged his daughter. "With you guys as his parents, he's got it made."

Jax leaned into her father. "Thank you for being so supportive. It means the world to me to have you in my life and now in his."

Mike sighed. "I let far too many years go by, and I'm committed to not missing one more."

Hunter ran back in with a package of napkins. "Why don't you help him with this. It won't take much in the way of communication for that. Don't worry, you'll get it. Eventually, Hunter will be able to help you as you learn."

"No matter what it takes, I'm going to learn this. It's too important not to. Hunter needs to know he matters in this family. Not just to you, but to me and everyone else as well. I'm hopeful that someday he'll be your son permanently. If there's anything I can do to help make that happen, you make sure you let me know."

Jax squeezed his hand as Chance came back in carrying a plateful of grilled burgers. "Don't worry, Dad, we will. For now, let's eat."

***

Later that afternoon, Jax wandered out of the barn to rest her arms on the top of the fence. She'd checked on Mac's wounds and redressed them. She stood watching her family enjoy a ride. Chance sat Hunter on her lap as they rode around the paddock on Kelly. The look on Hunter's face was pure joy and Chance's was of pure love. She waved at them and clapped as they rode by her. *I don't know what I did to be this blessed, but whatever it was, please let me keep doing it.*

Chance brought Kelly to a stop where Jax was standing.

Hunter's helmet slipped down in his eyes. His hands were flying. *"Did you see me?"*

Jax clapped and signed to him. *"I did. Good job."*

He nodded excitedly. *"Do again."*

"Go ride."

Chanced nudged Kelly forward, and they took several more laps before she stopped by Jax and let her help Hunter down. She dismounted, and together, they led Kelly into the stall. Chance took off the bridle and handed it to Hunter before she signed. *"Come help me."*

Over the next hour, Hunter was involved in all aspects of the care that each horse required. They'd just finished when they heard a vehicle pull up. Matt's wife got out and Jax walked over to hug her.

"How's Matt doing? I want to come and see him as soon as I can."

Holly Carson pulled herself together. "He came through the surgery fine. It will be harder for us to get through airport security from here on out, but they said he shouldn't have any long-term issues. There's also plenty of therapy in his future. I'm trying to figure out how to keep him off a horse long enough for him to recover."

Jax smiled. "You don't have to explain that to me. If you remember right, I got married on horseback with my foot in a walking boot."

"That's true. I can't thank you enough for what you did, Jax. Matt feels the same way. He wanted me to tell you how grateful he is that you were out there with him."

"It could so easily have been reversed. I did exactly what Matt would have done for me."

"Still, our whole family is grateful. How's Raider, anything I need to be concerned about?"

Jax looped her arm in Holly's and walked her toward the barn. "I couldn't find anything other than a few scratches, one across his nose. I cleaned it and applied some antibiotic salve."

They watched Raider stick his head out of the stall and nicker at Holly.

"I think he knows his mom is here."

Holly rubbed his jaw. "Hey there, big boy. Are you ready to go home? The rest of the family misses you." She turned to Jax. "You know how they are when one of their herd is missing."

Jax nodded. "I certainly do. Let me get Chance and we'll help you load him up."

"I appreciate it. Misty is with me to drive the car home. She can help. He's not usually too difficult to put in the trailer with a treat or two." Holly pulled a few carrots from her pocket and fed one to Raider.

"They have us right where they want us."

The two women laughed and started the process of loading Raider for transport. Chance put the ramp up and fastened everything in place while Hunter sat off to the side with Zeus beside him.

With the goodbyes said and promises of a visit soon, Jax held out her hand for Hunter to take. Chance made the sign for them to go inside and the family made their way in. A simple dinner followed, and by bath time everyone was ready to settle in for the night. Jax sat on the couch with Hunter's head in her lap. It didn't take long before he dropped off. She sifted her fingers through his hair.

"Life is so much better now."

Chance pulled her a little closer. "I agree."

"What's on your agenda tomorrow?"

"Preparation for Pickin' in Parsons. The campground has been filling up for the last few days. Taylor is ready to go with the schedule. I want to spend some time with Daniel and Athena now that they are back from training. He has some shifts at the festival, and that will be a good time to watch the two of them interact with the public."

"Do you have many calls during the event?"

"Actually, no. It's much tamer than the 4WD races. It brings in a different crowd that comes to enjoy the music. Most evenings, a dozen or more small groups are sitting around a campfire playing together. On rare occasions, someone has too much to drink and has an issue with someone. They do a lot of self-policing and the event hires some security."

"Let's hope this is an uneventful festival. We've had plenty of excitement for a while."

Chance chuckled and kissed her. "From your lips to God's ears. How about we put this little guy to bed, and we do the same?"

"I love the way you think, Sheriff. Lead the way."

CJ Murphy

Chapter Five

CHANCE AND ZEUS MOVED through the festival on Friday afternoon, the sound of bluegrass music resonating all around them. A large crowd gathered around the main stage, sitting in their camping chairs and listening to a local group. Her department's preparation over the last few days was paying off as the music festival being as uneventful as she'd hoped. She pulled a portable water bowl from her cargo pocket and filled it for Zeus.

"Get a drink, boy."

It was important to stay hydrated. Between the bulletproof vests and the heat of the day, she knew it was easy to become overheated. Chance looked up at the sky that was once bright and sunny, now dotted with dark gray clouds moving in on a sticky breeze. The weather forecast was calling for thundershowers later. The hope was the rain would break the heat that seemingly arrived with the campers.

"Comm Center to SD-1."

Chance depressed the button on her shoulder mic. "SD-1. Go ahead."

"We've just received an alert from the National Weather Service that a strong front is pushing in. There is a possibility of damaging winds and hail along with a heavy downpour. We're getting ready to announce a weather watch over all channels. Do you have contact with the festival organizers?"

"Comm Center, affirmative. How much time do we have?"

"National Weather Service says twenty minutes maximum. Our neighbors to the west are already experiencing downed trees and electric lines. They will be sending out a weather alert to all the cellphones as well."

"I'm on it."

As she released her mic, the alert came across her radio. She made her way to the administration booth. Harry Filler stood staring at his phone.

"Harry, I assume you're watching the weather?"

He nodded and showed her a large red line of storms headed their way. "Jeremy just stepped on the stage to announce it. There isn't enough cover for everyone under the pavilion."

A high-pitched tone sounded as she watched as those in attendance grab for their phones. She grabbed her own and listened.

"The National Weather Service is issuing a severe thunderstorm warning for the following counties, Upshur, Randolph, Tucker, and Preston County, West Virginia until 4:30 pm today, Friday, August 7th. A strong line of thunderstorms has been reported near Montrose, moving northeast at thirty-five miles an hour. Damaging winds, quarter size hail, and heavy rainfall have been reported. Seek shelter."

People were already gathering their things as Jeremy took the mic. "You heard it from the horse's mouth. It sounds like we're in for a rough patch. If it's safe to do so, we'll resume the schedule as soon as we can."

A rumble of thunder sounded off in the distance as Chance went to help an elderly couple gather their items.

"Thank you, Sheriff. We're not as spry as we used to be. That's our camper over there." The gentleman pointed to a twenty-five-foot RV sitting near a Silverado pickup truck.

"We'll get you there. I've got these chairs and your cooler, go ahead and help your wife." Chance picked up the small Igloo cooler and walked behind the couple, trying to protect them as much as possible from the dispersing crowd.

The woman struggled to get her key in the door but managed to do so by the time her husband took the chairs and placed them in a compartment outside the camper. Chance handed him the cooler as he stepped inside.

"I appreciate your help, Sheriff. Do you need a place to get into? You're welcome to stay with us."

Chance smiled and shook his hand. "Thanks for the offer, but there's still a lot of work to be done to make sure everyone's heard the warning. You two be careful now."

The man waved and closed the door. Chance felt a noticeably cooler wind blow across her neck as she watched small bits of detritus blow around. "Let's go for one final walk around, Zeus, make sure everyone got in." She walked near the pavilion again. The grounds crew had secured the sound equipment in cases and stored them in a truck. She ran into Harry.

"Sheriff, we've got things buttoned up for now. I called into the 911 center and let them know we have a good bit of day-trip folks planning to ride this out in their cars on the grounds in hopes this will pass quickly. It seems like everyone else took the warning and are hunkering down in their campers. I'm headed into mine. I'll see you when this blows over. Stay safe."

She shook his hand. "I'll do that. I need to check in with my officers." On her way to her Suburban, she contacted each officer and was assured they were all headed for the underground garage at the courthouse to protect the vehicles from the hail. She and Zeus climbed in and headed that same direction. "I think it's time to go, Zeus."

The first raindrops began to fall as she passed through the streets of Parsons, their abundance forcing her to turn her windshield wipers on high. The sky was angry, a roiling cauldron of black and gray clouds intent on swallowing up the daylight. Two blocks away from the garage, the wind picked up. Street signs were flipping back and forth, and the overhead power lines began to swing. The trees' limbs whipped around violently as their great trunks swayed, and lightning streaked the blackened sky. Zeus barked from the passenger seat when a large tree limb fell into the street blocking a lane of traffic. Chance put the Suburban in park and reached for the door handle. She threw her Stetson on the dash, afraid to lose it to the storm.

The wind pushed the vehicle's door back at Chance as she tried to open it and caused it to slam shut once she'd exited. Hail the size of marbles pelted her and littered the ground like a bag of spilled mothballs. She grabbed the massive oak limb to drag it out of the street. Lightning hit a tree fifty yards from her, breaking off the top and hurling it onto a nearby car. She abandoned the limb and ran back to the safety of her vehicle. Climbing in, she wiped the rain from her face and slicked her hair out of her eyes. "We gotta get out of here, hang on."

She put the vehicle in reverse and made a three-point turnaround. *I need to get us to cover.* She used a side alley to get access to the parking area under the courthouse. She was glad to see the rest of her officers had taken shelter in there as well. Several civilian vehicles had squeezed in, preventing Chance from getting her entire vehicle inside. The hail increased in size until the ground was covered in pieces of ice the size of golf balls.

Vicious winds howled through the garage as blinding rain deluged the area outside of the protection. Chance startled and ducked as the sound of breaking glass filled the Suburban. Rain poured in the rear window that had taken a direct strike from a large hailstone that now bounced around on the ground. The fire whistle on top of the station went off and wailed like an air raid siren, and her phone alerted with another weather announcement. Simultaneously her police radio blared a warning.

"All units, all stations. Possible tornado on the ground, Moore area. Seek shelter immediately!"

While the announcement repeated, Chance's breath stopped in her chest even as her heart pounded out of control. *All those campers.*

If the tornado continued into town, there could be a huge loss of life in the flimsy shelters that weren't connected by a foundation. There was absolutely nothing she could do until the storm died down enough for her to get out of the garage. A thought even more terrifying than the danger to the public sent panic through her system. *Jax and Hunter.* The last time she'd spoken with her wife, they were on their way back to Tucker County after a trip to Tractor Supply in Oakland. She turned and saw Zeus, unharmed, looking toward the rear of the vehicle. She grabbed her cellphone only to drop it on the floorboard with trembling hands. She found it and tried desperately to hit Jax on the speed dial. The call dropped over and over. *Text her. Text messages should go through.* Her hands shook so badly she was unable to type anything. She hit the voice to text button. "Jax, tornado on the ground near Parsons. Find shelter!" She watched her words appear on the screen and hit send as soon as she could. She prayed her message went through. Chance knew that if Jax was in the area, she too would have gotten the weather announcements and followed the warning to seek shelter. This was her family, hers to care for and worry about, and at the moment, she could do nothing for them.

The wind was relentless, lashing at everything in its path. Chance watched out the other opening of the garage as unidentifiable debris flew past, followed by a sidewalk sign from the business next to the garage. The metal scraped along the ground like fingernails on a chalkboard.

Please, God, let this be over soon. As if her prayers had been answered, the wind soon died down and the rain calmed to a light shower. Chance looked at her phone for an answer to her urgent text. *OMG, stay safe! We're home and fine. No severe weather here.* The relief that washed through Chance was like finding the surface when you'd been deep underwater and running out of air. Now she could concentrate on helping those who were affected by this disaster. She got out of her vehicle and moved Zeus up into the front passenger seat as she called her staff over to her.

"Taylor, we've got to get down to the campground. That wind could have easily done some major damage. Carl, you and Daniel come with us." She depressed the mic on her shoulder. "SD-1 to SD-6."

"SD-6. Go ahead, Sheriff."

"Status check?"

"I'm trying to make my way down Backbone Mountain. It's slow going with all the trees down."

Chance stopped for a moment and heard calls for the fire department and the ambulance being dispatched to various locations throughout the county along the Cheat River. Dispatch advised that they had multiple reports of injury and entrapment at the campground where the bluegrass festival was being held. "If you can't get here, handle calls as they come in from your area."

"SD-6, received."

Chance turned to her deputies. "Let's go. I can't imagine what we're going to find when we get there." She climbed back in her damaged Suburban. "SD-1 to Comm Center. Have you heard from the state police units?"

"We've had contact with 207. She's making her way into Parsons from Route 72 in St. George. She has one trooper on the mountain."

"See if she can have her mountain unit handle calls up there. My guess is we're about to be knee deep in it here. Contact Fish and Wildlife, see if any of their folks are out and can give us a hand handling calls as well."

"Comm Center received."

"SD-1, 2, 3, and 4 are responding to the campground. I'll give a size up as soon as possible." She backed out of the garage and began to dodge the debris in the street. Bricks from a collapsed corner of the bank building, tree limbs, and a runaway trampoline littered the paved surface. The storm had torn off part of a house roof, and the owner stood in the street looking at the gaping hole it left. She rolled down the window. "You all right?"

The man pushed his ballcap back. "I'm good, Sheriff. We're all safe."

She waved and continued her difficult path toward the campground. Once, she had to back up and reroute. A fire department pickup was blocking access where a downed powerline dangled in the street across two cars. Chance finally pulled into the campground, horrified to see more than one camper crushed by the large butternut and maple trees that earlier had provided shade from the hot sun. A few overturned campers lay on their sides, and a strong smell of propane saturated the air. "SD-1 is on scene at the campground and establishing command. Comm Center, advise incoming fire units we have a propane leak somewhere, likely from a broken RV line. Stay upwind or those diesel engines will run away." She looked at the disaster in front of her as people began to crawl out, bleeding and broken. "Get me every ambulance you can. We've got a mass casualty incident on our hands. Check with EMS about protocols for mutual aid. Advise the county emergency manager that I'm going to need temporary shelter arrangements. This place looks like a war zone. I count four campers lying on their sides and at least three that may have entrapment from trees on them. Alert search and rescue and get me some help down here off the mountain."

"Comm Center copy. SD-1 assuming command. I'm sending everyone to TAC-2. We're making calls and dispatching additional units. Leading Creek Fire Department is coming in from 219, and Phillipi Fire Department is approaching from Rt. 38."

Taylor pulled up beside Chance and she jumped out and moved Zeus into her chief deputy's vehicle to protect him from the broken rear window and the unknown hazards on the ground. She went to the back to grab her rescue helmet, gloves, and a small crash ax. "Zeus, *blijf*. Let's go, Taylor."

Thumbing the knob on her radio to the assigned channel, she saw the first ambulance and fire truck approach the scene. Sarah jumped out and began directing her team of three to start triage. She reached Chance's side.

"This is going to be bad, Chance. Chip was down at the firehouse. I imagine one of the two of you are going to have to run point as Incident Command. I'll let you two fight that out. I'm going to get triage set up."

Daniel and Carl ran up to her. She pointed to the pavilion. "Let's start directing the walking wounded over there. Carl, help Sarah get a triage area set up. The pavilion is missing a few pieces of metal roofing but stands mostly intact. It has a concrete surface. Taylor, you and Daniel come with me."

On their way to the first camper, they ran into Chip.

"Chance, I heard you establish command? Do you want to keep it or handle operations?"

She ran a hand through her hair. "Take command. I'm going to be needed for the technical side of getting folks out, and the incoming units will need direction and staging. There's only one way in and out of here, and somewhere, we've got a flammable gas leak. Sarah and I thought the stage would give the incident commander the best overview." She grabbed her radio. "Comm Center, this is SD-1 formally transferring command to Chief 10. SD-1 will be rescue operations chief." She turned to Chip. "Find that leak."

Chip nodded as he raised his mic. "Chief 10 assuming command. Command post will be at the music stage."

"Comm Center received."

She grasped his shoulder. "I'm taking Daniel with me. We're going to start a camper-by-camper search. Send me your manpower when you can."

He nodded and turned to his firefighters as she ran to a twenty-five-foot camper that was tipped on its side. Randy showed up, and she directed him and Taylor to check a small fifteen-footer on its top. Daniel helped her scramble up the side of their target. She lay on her stomach near one of the broken windows and cupped her hands around her mouth. "Is anyone in here!" She listened for anyone to answer.

Finally, a frail female voice called out. "My husband and I are. He's trapped in the bathroom. Our fridge came loose and is up against the door."

Chance stood and slipped on the Kevlar gloves she used to pat suspects down as she shouted to the occupant. "Stay back from the window area. I'm going to pry on the frame and make my way in." She did just that with her crash ax, Daniel by her side.

"The dogs aren't happy to be in the vehicles." He pulled at one of the aluminum-clad windows.

"Too much glass down. They're safer where they are. If you can pull that out of the way, I think I can get in."

"You got it. Be careful."

Chance lay down on her stomach and flipped herself in the window, gripping the opening until she could see where she would land. Her boots crunched broken glass inside when she jumped down.

"Thank God, you're here."

Chance made eye contact with the woman, who looked to be in her seventies. "Are you all right?"

"A little banged up but nothing serious. Tom is in here, and I can't move this to get him out."

Chance made her way over to the full-size refrigerator that was face down, covering a doorway. "Daniel, make your way in here. The area's tight, and I'm going to need your help."

He dropped through the opening and helped her push and pull the appliance until it was no longer blocking the doorway. Chance pried it open to find Tom sitting tucked between the sink and the toilet, holding a hand towel to his head. "Tom, are you hurt?"

He tried to get up and grimaced. "Mostly my pride. I've got a gash on the head, but other than that, I'm okay. Ressie, are you all right?"

Chance offered him her hands to help him to his feet. He wobbled a bit, then grabbed onto the door frame. His wife came to him and kissed his cheek.

"I'm okay now that I can see you. Thank you, Sheriff."

"You're welcome. If you two are okay, we're going to go help a few others in trouble. We'll come back and get you out as soon as I get someone with some equipment to make a new exit for you. Okay?"

Tom waved her on. "You two go, thank you. We'll be fine for a bit."

Chance and Daniel climbed on a kitchen island and made their way back outside. She spotted two of Chip's firefighters. "There's an elderly couple in here that appear medically stable but won't be able to make it out the way we got into them. If you have something that can peel this tin can open, they'd appreciate it. We're headed to that big one over there with the tree on it."

The firefighters nodded and went to work opening the camper as Chance and Daniel ran. The propane smell was dissipating, making Chance hopeful they'd found the source and secured it. A hefty butternut tree had crushed the center of the large Jayco camper in front of them, its branches impaling other sections. A broken picture window in the slide-out made access easier than the last trailer.

"Watch yourself, Daniel." Chance cleared some of the glass with her ax then grabbed the sides and pulled herself in. "Sheriff's department. Is anyone in here?" She flipped on the flashlight attached to her helmet and made her way through the camper to the area crushed by the tree. Water streamed in where the metal and fiberglass had been compromised. She slipped on the wet floor and went down on one knee, and something slashed through her right forearm. Aiming the flashlight to pinpoint what caused the injury, she saw a screw sticking through a piece of particleboard. "Dammit. Good thing it's not been that long since my last tetanus shot."

Daniel was behind her. "You're bleeding pretty good. Hang on."

She stopped momentarily, long enough for him to tie a bandanna around her arm. "Thanks. I haven't heard anything yet, have you?"

"No."

"Let's move forward." She pushed through fallen items that had spilled from cabinets and drawers as she tried to make her way around a large piece of the tree that blocked her way to the rest of the camper. "I'm going to have to go over this. Everything below it is crushed."

She pulled herself up onto what used to be the countertop and wrapped her arms around the massive limb until she could scramble over it. On the other side, a hand stuck out from beneath a jumble of tree and camper. "This is Sheriff Fitzsimmons. Can anyone hear me?" She bent down and pulled off her glove to check for movement in the hand or a pulse. Neither were present. Chance tried to find a way to get better access but was at a standstill without using a chainsaw to cut pieces of the fallen tree away.

She grabbed her mic. "SD-1 to Chief 10."

"This is Chief 10. Go ahead with your traffic."

"I'm inside the Jayco camper with the tree on it. My access is blocked. I have at least one entrapment."

"I'm sending a crew with extrication equipment to you."

Chance stared at the hand, willing it to move before she turned to Daniel. "I've got a patient here that I can't confirm is dead or alive. There may be someone else in here. See if you can get back out and make access from the other direction. Here's my ax."

"Will you be okay in here by yourself?"

"I will. Go on."

She watched him climb back over the fallen items and disappear out the window. There were pieces of a broken cabinet door near the hand. A large blood pool appeared when she moved one. *Damn.* There would be nothing she could do for whoever the blood belonged to. There were moments when she felt so helpless. She'd seen others lose their lives, and she'd taken lives in the process of doing her duty. Each was difficult. It was highly likely that she had no personal connection with the person. This affected her on a different level than friends and family, though the tragic loss of life was still painful, regardless of its familiarity. The sound of her name brought her out of the reflective moment.

"Chance?"

"Yes, Daniel, I'm here."

"I think I have a viable patient over here. She appears to be unconscious, but I can't find any wound on her."

"I'm going to head your way." With a last look at the hand, she turned toward the window. "There's nothing I can do here."

***

The next few hours were hell. Three campers were impacted by trees, while several others were toppled. Most injuries were minor because of the age of the victims, all needed care and transport. Chance was inside the camper of the elderly couple she'd helped inside before the storm hit. She held Betty's hand as they waited for firefighters to come and open the camper. The extraction crew had been diverted to more urgent calls. Bob sat holding Betty's other hand. The couple appeared bruised and slightly battered, but Chance hadn't been able to find any serious injuries from being tossed around.

"Betty, you've got a pretty serious skin tear. I need to cover that up before we start moving you around. Okay?"

Betty nodded. "Trust me, Sheriff, I bump myself against a dishrag and my skin rolls back. It's about as durable as tissue paper." She turned to her husband. "Bob, are you okay?"

Bob leaned over and kissed his wife. "I am honey. I came back to you after the Korean War, this little bump on the head is nothing."

Chance smiled at the couple. Bob had a large goose egg, and she had concerns about his knee. She took Betty's hand and placed a bandage and dressing over the paper-thin skin, avulsed back in a long strip. The wound would need to be cleaned at the hospital. For now, she wanted to make sure it didn't get caught on anything and tear away, leaving a larger injury. She noticed Betty was rather pale.

"Betty, are you still feeling okay?" She pulled the blood pressure cuff from the trauma kit she'd pulled inside with her.

Betty put a hand to her cheek. "I do feel a bit poorly. Probably just all this excitement."

Chance knew that trauma patients could often appear fine for a long time as their body compensated for a hidden injury. She'd done the best she could at assessing possible injuries. Betty's blood pressure was on the low side, but that wasn't unusual for someone of her size. Chance grabbed her mic.

"SD-1 to EMS command."

Sarah answered her. "Go ahead."

"I think my patient's condition is changing. Requesting a medic in here."

"I'm on my way, I just cleared the triage area."

It felt like hours before Sarah climbed down in.

"What do you have?"

Chance relayed the vitals as Sarah hooked Betty up to a monitor. She handed the strip to Chance. "She's throwing PACs. We need to get them out now."

Chance looked at the paper strip and saw the premature atrial contraction indicators that could be caused by the increased adrenaline from the incident or something more serious. "SD-1 to Command."

"This is Command. Go ahead."

"We need an expedited extrication at my location. My patient's condition requires a rapid extraction." She held Betty's hand and tried with everything she had to display cool confidence.

"Received, the crew just finished at a location beside you. I'm short on manpower, Chance. I've got calls all up and down the Shavers Fork and the Cheat."

"I copy, Command."

"Sheriff, am I going to be okay?"

Chance put on her most reassuring face. "Betty, you have the best medic in the county working on you now. I trust her with my family because she's a part of that family. We're going to speed this up because we don't like a few of those beats. It's likely because of the excitement. I just don't want to take any chances, okay? Bob, don't worry, we're going to get you two out of here. You can't see what's going on, but those winds toppled several campers the way it did yours."

Bob's eyes pleaded with her for reassurance. "I'd certainly like to get out of here and anything you can do to make that happen, I'm all for."

They heard the power tools begin their assault on the metal and fiberglass keeping them from the outside world.

Sarah pulled an IV setup from her bag. "Betty, are you having any chest discomfort? Even a little?"

Betty looked a bit sheepish as she nodded. "I didn't want to bother anyone. Everyone is so busy."

Sarah patted her hand. "It's no bother. I'm going to give you something to help with that."

Chance helped her assemble the IV and watched Sarah deftly start the line before hooking up the fluids. With the line established, Sarah injected medication to help soothe the irritated heart.

"You should start feeling some relief. Your blood pressure is pretty low, so I don't feel comfortable giving you any nitroglycerine. Let's get this oxygen on you."

The crew outside finally started to make some headway and peeled back a large section of the roof a few feet from them. Chance could finally see some outside light coming through. It was late in the afternoon, and thankfully, the sun had come back out after the storm. A large hole opened up, and two firefighters came inside and helped Bob out.

Sarah called for a stokes basket. "Betty, with that chest pain, I don't want you walking out of here."

Chance grabbed the basket that held a backboard already in place. "Let us do all the work, and we'll carry you out of here."

"You won't hear any complaint from me. I'm about as weak as a day-old kitten about now."

Chance and Sarah shared a look of concern and urgency. As they were moving Betty into the basket, the heart monitor let out an alarm. Sarah turned her head. "She's crashing. Let's get her out of here. I need to shock."

Chance grabbed the basket and began moving out of the camper, holding the rails, and directing the maneuvers. "Let's go!"

Outside the camper, they put the stokes basket down and removed Betty from the metal basket with the backboard and lowered her to the ground.

Sarah waved an arm. "Everyone clear! I'm shocking."

Bob had already been moved to the waiting ambulance. Chance glanced there, debating whether to go tell him or wait until she had more information.

"Chance, start CPR while I push drugs." She pointed to the two firefighters. "Get that cot out of the ambulance. We need to get her to the hospital now."

Chance followed the bottom of the woman's ribcage up with her finger until she felt the sternal notch. She placed the heel of her hand down and interlocked her fingers over the top. She said a silent prayer as she pushed down and felt a rib pop. This wasn't unusual in older people, but Chance hated it. The crew lifted Betty and the backboard onto the cot as Sarah pushed oxygen into her system and Chance compressed her chest to keep blood flowing. Once they were inside, Sarah could shock Betty again and hopefully put her heart back into rhythm. Only time would tell.

Inside the ambulance, Sarah took the airway seat and looked at the heart monitor. "Shockable rhythm. Stop compressions."

Chance lifted her hands and stood back from the metal railing as Sarah pushed the shock button to start the heart beating on its own again. Chance held her breath as she stood there with her hands in the air, fingers spread. She watched the monitor screen until a set of beats skittered across the display, then settled in.

"Sinus rhythm. Let's go!"

Taylor stuck her head in the ambulance. "Zeus can stay with me, don't worry. We'll pick you up at Davis Memorial."

"Call Jax for me, please. Thank you."

Taylor waved as Chance shut the back door. The driver pulled away with Chance settled on the bench seat assessing Betty's color. It was still pale, and the frail woman lay unconscious.

Sarah stood and dug through one of the built-in compartments. "I'm going to intubate her, then we'll switch seats so you can bag her while I call this in and deliver meds."

Chance nodded and watched as Sarah chose an endotracheal tube, opened the lighted laryngoscope, and slid the tube past Betty's lips. *She's so damn good.*

Sarah attached the bag valve mask and squeezed. "Listen for breath sounds and let me know if I'm in."

Chance grabbed the stethoscope and listened, moving the bell around to hear the air rush in and out. "You're in." Chance stood and grabbed the bag from Sarah as they exchanged positions in the back of the ambulance. She squeezed the bag at a measured rate and listened to Sarah give her report to the ER while she continued with her cardiac arrest protocol. Sarah was a sight to see when she was in her element. Every patient was a member of her family, whether she knew them or not. Inside the body of this ambulance, the patient's life was in her hands, and Chance knew she intended to turn every patient over to the ER in better condition than when she'd found them. "Don't ever let anyone tell you this isn't where you're meant to be, Sarah, ever."

Sarah's lip curled in a slight smile as she injected another medication into the IV tubing. "Coming from you, I believe it. The feeling is very mutual. Betty's doing okay, Chance. She's holding her own. I'm surprised we didn't have more heart attacks with the way that storm blew in."

"I can't argue with you about that. Couldn't have happened at a worse time. It had to feel like being inside a pinball machine the way they were tossed and thrown about. Thank God it didn't last any longer. It sounds like this was localized to the lowlands."

Sarah's eyes suddenly grew wide. "Jax and Hunter?"

"Safe. I heard from her before I took command in the campground. They were on the mountain and at home."

Sarah pulled an automatic blood pressure cuff from the pocket of the heart monitor. "I'm not the only one that was pretty outstanding on that scene. I watched you take charge and get that organized before you started going into rescue mode. You have such natural leadership abilities, Chance. The county's residents and visitors have no idea how lucky they are. Your dad would be so proud."

"I hope so. I try to live up to what he taught me."

"How's the fostering going? I swear, every time I see Hunter, he has a smile on his face."

"We wait. We have temporary custody for now. It's no wonder there are so many kids waiting on foster homes or to be adopted. The hoops they make you jump through are never ending. We'd adopt him tomorrow, but Child Protective Services has to do an exhaustive search for relatives. Since his mother was abandoned and grew up in a group home, they're basically looking for an unknown dad in an unknown city."

They pulled up to the ER doors. "Well, all I know is that he's where he needs to be. Let's get Betty inside. Bob's ambulance is just behind us. Kristi and I are thrilled for you. By the way, we're grateful you're watching over our son. He couldn't have a better mentor."

Chance stepped out of the ambulance and helped unload the frail woman. "Thank you, Sarah. That means a great deal to me. Thanks for this too." She nodded to indicate Betty. "We lost too many today. Thanks to you, Betty isn't one of them."

Chapter Six

CHANCE WAVED TO SARAH and the crew that had given her a ride back to her cruiser. Daniel had met her and dropped off Zeus. She grabbed her mic. "SD-1 to SD-2."

"Go ahead, Sheriff."

"Call me on your cell."

Chance was going to have to tell Taylor something that would be another devastating blow, something she didn't want to say over the radio. When Taylor called, Chance gave her the news.

"We've got another fatality."

"Damn. A local or a visitor?"

"Local. We've confirmed identity. It's Travis Parker. We're going to need to make a death notification down at Leadmine. He was working at the festival as a stagehand. We found him under a block wall that was knocked down by one of those big trees."

"Doesn't he live with his grandparents?"

"Yeah. If you remember, his dad was killed in Afghanistan and his mom passed from cancer a few years ago."

"That family has been through hell already. Wasn't he one of Rhebekka's after-school kids before he graduated?"

Chance nodded to herself. "He was. I'll call her. Maybe it would be best if she went with us. Let me see if she's available. They're going to take this incredibly hard. They already lost their son and daughter-in-law. Now it's their grandson. No family should have that much tragedy. Mr. Parker has a bad heart, and Mrs. Parker isn't in much better shape."

"I know. See if Rhebekka can meet up with us at the church near the intersection of Horseshoe Run and Leadmine Mountain Road."

"Thanks, Taylor."

"All part of the job. One of my least favorites but an unavoidable one. We barely have radio contact down there. I'm betting they don't have power or phone service after this storm."

"Not likely. I talked with the emergency manager. There's no estimate of when we'll get power back. There are widespread outages in several counties. They have the shelter, with a generator, opened for anyone who needs it. We have a ton of folks on oxygen, and eventually, they'll run out of their reserve bottles. The fire department is trying to go out and do welfare checks on the ones we know and see if they need transport. Our folks know how to deal with a power outage when it's winter. The heat of summer is another thing."

"What a mess. Okay, call Rhebekka. I'll catch up with you at the intersection."

"You got it. Be careful."

"Always, Sheriff."

***

An hour later, Chance and Taylor stood on the porch with Naomi as Rhebekka continued to talk with the Parkers inside the house. Notifying them had been gut-wrenching. Chance wasn't sure she'd ever get the sound of Mrs. Parker's wail out of her head. The woman had collapsed on the floor. Mr. Parker was stoic, but he spoke with glassy eyes and a cracked voice.

Chance leaned against the porch railing, squinting in the dim light coming from the house. They'd been able to help the family get a generator running. "This never gets any easier."

Naomi stepped up beside her and squeezed her arm. "You two handled that with great respect. I admire you. I know it wasn't easy."

Taylor stepped beside Chance. "I knew Travis' mother. She worked at the medical clinic in Parsons. Rhonda patched me up more times than I can count."

Chance sighed. "She did the same for me. This is one of the worst parts of the job."

Taylor pulled her Stetson off and ran a hand through her hair. "I know you and Rhebekka believe in God's love, but days like today, I have a hard time seeing it."

Naomi nodded. "Rhebekka can sympathize. It took her many years to see the comfort God brings in times like this, to witness His grace and not the wrathful God so many others perpetrate. I hope, someday, we might be able to share the God we know."

"Thanks, Naomi. We'd better get going; I get the feeling this is going to be a long night."

Chance stepped down off the porch and headed to her car. "I hope you're wrong about that, but you rarely are."

"Peace be with you both. Be safe."

Chance waved. "From your lips to God's ears."

***

Chance started back toward Parsons with Taylor right behind her. They'd settled on a route that would take them by a small clinic that had recently been burglarized. With the electricity out, it would make an easy target for those seeking to raid the pharmacy of narcotics. It was almost midnight, and it was eerie driving by homes that she knew were always well lit. There were no dusk-to-dawn lights illuminating the yards she passed. On the outskirts of St. George, her eyes keyed in on an unusual glow in the sky. Black smoke rose into the inky darkness. She drove her Suburban around a bend to find flames licking up the outside of a two-story home.

"SD-1 to Comm Center, in the blind. Urgent traffic! Structure fire, Holly Meadows Road past the clinic, Roger Thomas' house. I'll update when I can."

She threw the vehicle into park, releasing Zeus from the back as she went. She hoped the dispatcher had heard her. Her boots crunched on the gravel as she pulled on her gloves before pounding on the front door with the flashlight she'd pulled from her belt. She could hear a generator running in the background as Taylor and Midas came to her side.

"Go check the back door." She pounded on the door in front of her. "There's a fire! Roger, wake up!"

She continued to pound on the door, then ran around to a side window and rapped on the glass. When she got no answer, she circled to the back door, Zeus on her heels and barking an alarm.

Taylor was there with her long, black Maglite in hand. "It's locked too. I'm going to break the glass.

Back up, Midas!" When the K9 had cleared the area, she used the butt end to bust the window in the door then reached in.

Chance laid out the plan. "We'll do the search together. The fire is on the outside for now. His mom might be in here as well." Both dogs stood looking at them. "*Blijven!*" Chance couldn't have Zeus or Midas following them in and ordered them to stay. In a crouch, she trained her flashlight on the room already hazy with smoke and spoke to Taylor. "Stay with me."

The two officers began a right-handed search. Chance kept her knee touching the wall to stay oriented. When she came to a door, she banged on it and pushed it open. Crouching, she made her way around what appeared to be a bathroom. *Bedrooms are normally upstairs in these old houses.* She pulled her T-shirt up and covered her mouth and nose, coughing from the smoke.

They searched until Chance found the stairs and made her way up them. At the top she found Roger collapsed a few feet away. "Taylor, get him out of here. I'll look for his mom." She coughed and dropped completely to her knees. She helped her chief deputy roll him over, then watched Taylor bunch up his T-shirt at the shoulders before dragging him down the steps.

Chance continued her search alone and found no one in the other bedroom. She crawled down the stairs and came upon Taylor being pulled toward the door by Zeus and Midas. Roger was nowhere in sight. *Damn the living room just lit off.* Flames were licking inside a broken window and pushing into the space. The room filled with thick acrid smoke and heat.

"Good, dogs. Go out, I've got her." She slid her arms under Taylor's, grabbed her hands, and began to pull backwards until they were outside. "Taylor! It's Chance. Look at me! Come on, take a breath."

Taylor's eyes were unfocused, and Chance could see she was barely breathing. Midas whined beside her and licked Taylor's face as Zeus pawed at Chance's leg. A siren wailed in the background.

"It's okay, guys. Come on, Taylor. Take a breath. That's it. The ambulance is coming. Just keep breathing."

Taylor tried to roll on her side, so Chance grabbed her vest and helped her seconds before she retched and gulped in big breaths of clean air.

Chance continued to hold her. "Cough it up, Taylor. Sarah's here." She put a hand on her injured officer's shoulder. "Taylor, it's okay. Don't sit up. Lay still and let Sarah help you."

Taylor tried to get up anyway. "Midas, check Midas."

"Taylor, listen to me. I've got him. Let Sarah help you."

Taylor lay back down but watched Chance put a pet oxygen mask over her K9's snout.

Sarah shook her head. "We've got to get her to the hospital. Her oxygen level is shitty. You both likely took in way too much smoke. Taylor, the cot's right here."

Taylor nodded and looked at Chance. "Penny, call Penny."

Chance leaned over her and slid her arms under her shoulders. "I've got that covered, and I'll call Jax for the dogs, don't worry. Let's get her on the cot. On three. One, two, three."

When Taylor was seated on the litter, Sarah elevated her head.

"I'll meet you at the ER after I drop the dogs at the clinic for examination." She stumbled a bit.

Sarah frowned. "I don't think so. Hannah has Taylor and the other crew has Roger. My chase vehicle is right there. Sit your ass down and I'll help you drop the dogs off, then we'll go to the hospital. No arguments or I'll call Jax and Maggie myself. How much shit do you want to be in? Even Dee won't be able to save your ass."

Chance sighed and coughed. "I know you're right. Let me get one of the firefighters to stay with the vehicles until someone from my staff can come to get them. There's far too much equipment in there to leave it unsecured with that broken window."

Sarah nodded. "Five minutes."

"That's all I'll need." The only other thing she needed was for Taylor to be all right. *If you can help me out, Lord. I'd appreciate it. Her family needs her and so do I.*

***

Chance stood at the foot of Taylor's bed watching as Penny sat beside her and held a straw to her chief deputy's lips. "Small drinks. Your throat will be sore from the smoke you inhaled," Penny coaxed.

Taylor looked around wide-eyed. "Where's Jace?"

"My mom and dad are with him, and before you ask, Midas is with Jax."

Chance stepped to the side of the bed and held up her phone with a short video of Midas and Zeus lying in Jax's office. "She knew you'd want to know. Our boys are fine. Jax did a thorough examination of them. And the next question you'll have will be about Roger. He's alive and has been moved on to Pittsburgh to the hyperbaric chamber. He's got severe smoke inhalation and burns to his respiratory system. The exhaust of the generator he had running was up against the house. Eventually, the exhaust from the muffler heated the wood siding and started the fire. The good thing is his mother was out of town."

Taylor nodded to her boss. "Was I dreaming or did the dogs pull me out?"

Chance leaned on the bed rail. "They did. Our K9 partners got you to the kitchen as I was crawling back out after looking for Roger's mother. Apparently, you have a bit of undiagnosed asthma. The smoke irritated your lungs and shut you down."

Taylor held up a shaky hand. "I had no idea. I've never had any issues. I crawled back in to help you. I guess it's a good thing I became a cop and not a firefighter."

Chance waved it away. "Maybe so."

Taylor swallowed hard and turned to Penny. "I'm sorry, honey." A coughing fit came over her as she spoke.

Penny stood up and helped her take a drink before kissing her. "Don't be. All I ask is you be careful. You were determined to be a law enforcement officer when I met you. I knew you'd be in danger and it was a risk I was willing to take. I love you, Taylor, and so does Jace. Someday, he'll know how incredibly brave his momma is."

Taylor used a palm to wipe the tears she felt running down her cheek. She cleared her throat. "Let's get down to brass tacks. Tell me the damage I've done to myself and how soon I can get out of here."

Chance stood with her hands resting on her hips as Penny went on to tell her about the superficial burns and the smoke inhalation that the doctors wanted to make sure didn't develop into respiratory failure.

"They were concerned about burns to your respiratory tract. Your nose and mouth were full of soot." Chance pointed to her own face. "Yes, they checked me too, but I must have been lower to the ground than you or at least less susceptible. There's a big worry that you could develop pneumonia later. The burns are minor, and your gloves likely saved your hands from being too bad. That would have gotten you a flight to a burn center. Speaking as someone who's lived through burn treatment, be grateful it isn't worse."

Penny kissed her forehead. "They're going to keep you overnight and monitor your oxygen levels for any signs of trouble. They haven't told me when they'll release you, but don't push it. Let them make sure you're all right before we go home. We need you, but we need you healthy."

Chance winked at Penny. "She's right. You're officially off duty until you're cleared to return. When you do, that means light duty. Desk work and no more for a while. Sheriff's orders. We're going to take Midas home with us until they release you. Penny will have two children for the next few days, and Hunter will enjoy having another playmate." Chance winked. "When you're ready, we'll bring him to you. I know he'll be worried."

Taylor held her hand out and took Chance's in her own. "Thank you, Chance."

"No thanks necessary. Midas and Zeus did all the hard work by the time I got to you. Now you know why I insist on them. We're a unique department with as many as we have, and they aren't cheap. However, they are an invaluable part of our staff. Which reminds me, when you go on light duty, you can start getting everyone's training scheduled for recertification and start working on that gun I found."

Taylor groaned. "You're going to enjoy having a paper pusher, aren't you?"

Chance smiled. "Indeed I am. Now rest. I'm going to go home. Jax was taking the dogs to our place. Grandpa Mike is hanging out with Hunter and moms squared. Mike is taking a beginner's sign-language course and is doing pretty well. He's trying so damn hard."

"You guys are turning into great parents. He's one lucky little boy, having so many people love him." Penny sat back down in her chair and linked her fingers through the railing with Taylor's.

"Given what he's gone through in his young life, it's so much less than he deserves. Okay, I'm out of here. Rest, that's an order." She pointed to Penny. "Don't piss the warden off. She has my full permission to ground you." She waved and headed out the door, feeling secure that Taylor would be all right and back to full health soon.

Chapter Seven

CHANCE PULLED INTO THE house. It was close to two in the morning and she was exhausted, mentally and physically. When she stepped on the porch, Jax met her and wrapped her in a hug.

"Your neck muscles are tighter than a bowstring. I can also tell you have a headache, probably from that same tension."

Chance sighed. "It's been one of the worst days I can remember. We had citizens die in that storm, and I nearly lost one of my closest friends in that fire. I'm not afraid to say how terrified I was when I saw them dragging Taylor toward the door." Chance's words faded off.

"That's why you put a dog with every deputy. Decisions like that are why you're the sheriff. Taylor's still with her family because of a decision you made to fix the backup your dad didn't have." Jax paused. "Think of it this way. She's alive because of your dad."

After a shuddering breath, Chance nodded. "That's a unique way of looking at it. I just wanted to come home and hold you and Hunter. It's been an incredibly shitty day."

The drive had given Chance time to compartmentalize the events and tuck them into the files in her head. She'd process everything later.

"Looks like the gang's all here." She felt Jax take her hand.

"How about we go in with smiles? Your moms are going to freak out because you smell like smoke. You have soot smudges all over you. A shower is first up on your to-do list. I gave both dogs a bath and they're curled up in bed with Hunter." Jax started walking, pulling Chance along with her.

"Good plan."

Once inside, Chance looked to both her mothers and mustered a smile. "Before you two get too excited, I'm okay and Taylor will be too. I'm going to go shower." She hugged them both on the way by. She lingered in Maggie's arms a minute and spoke softly. "Hunter in bed?"

Maggie wiped a stray tear away. "Yes, it took all we had to get him down. He was determined to wait for you both. I sometimes think he's afraid you aren't coming home."

Jax ran a hand across Chance's shoulders. "Give me your vest. I'll set it aside and let it breathe for a bit. We're going to have to wash the cover, honey."

Chance nodded and pulled at the Velcro closures before handing it over. She looked at her uniform covered in dirt and blood. Whether it was hers or a stranger's, she didn't know. She unbuttoned the shirt and pulled it off. "I think this thing is trashed." Bone deep exhaustion was starting to take over. "You two are welcome to stay the night. You know we have the room."

Dee nodded. "We plan to. We were just waiting on you to get home. We needed to see you for ourselves. Now we have."

Chance hugged Dee tightly again and made her way to the master bath. She turned on the hot water and stripped down. Her scar tissue seemed particularly tight tonight. *Just my mind playing tricks on me.* Inside the shower, she let the hot water run over her head as she planted her right hand on the cool tile, being careful to keep the stitches dry.

Flashes of Midas and Zeus pulling Taylor through the kitchen merged into sheltering a young boy and his dog in her emergency fire shelter many years ago. The memory flicked through her mind like changing channels on a TV. She scrubbed her body before stretching her left arm and side, turning into the hot water where the healed burns still marked her skin. *Steel is tempered by fire, and gold is refined by it.* Maggie's mantra helped ease the discomfort she felt from the close call. She hadn't been completely truthful about how close their encounter was. The entire ceiling had been on fire when she'd reached Taylor, with flames licking over the surface like ocean waves rolling into the shore. It was a miracle that the dogs had suffered no burns. According to Jax, both K9's had a clean bill of health.

"Stay low and go." Chance repeated one of the school fire-safety presentation points she often mentioned to small children when telling them how to exit in the event of a fire.

Warm arms wrapped around her from the back. "I can go very low if you'd like." Jax's hands snaked down her flank and stopped on Chance's hip bone as gentle kisses peppered her back.

A deep moan escaped her tired body as Chance leaned into Jax's warmth. "Safety first, you know."

Jax kissed her shoulder. "I love you, Chance. Today was scary. When I heard that emergency alert come in, you were my first thought."

She stood enjoying the feeling of Jax's gentle hands caressing her. "You and Hunter were mine. The thought of the two of you being caught out in that storm terrified me."

"We were home safe and sound."

"Once I knew that, I could keep my mind on what had to be done. I know I can't protect either of you from everything, but I'd give my life trying."

Chance felt Jax lay her head on her back as the arms surrounding her waist tightened.

"I'd rather you stay with us. I'm not ready to be a single mom. Hunter's been through losing a parent once, I'd rather him not have to experience that again until we're old and gray."

Chance turned and pulled Jax into her embrace, reveling in the softness of her skin against her own. "I wish I could promise you that. There are too many factors I can't control to do so. I can say, I'll promise to do everything possible to always come home to you both."

"I'll take that."

"And I'll take you." Chance cupped Jax's chin and slanted her lips across her lover's. "I need you." She slid a hand between their bodies and cupped Jax's center. Chance swallowed the groan that escaped her wife. She turned her soulmate until Jax was pinned against the tile with a leg wrapped around Chance's hip. "You are so sexy when you do that. I love touching you."

"Chance, I need you inside of me, now. Don't play with me tonight. Fast and hard. Show me you're still here, make this fear go away."

Chance's heart nearly broke at the words as she slipped two fingers into Jax's depth and began to thrust. "I'm right here." She delved her tongue into Jax's mouth, feeding on her kiss as she pistoned her fingers in and out. She leaned in, pushing Jax hard into the tile while the hot water rushed over them. "I'm right here, baby, let it all go."

Jax whispered into her skin. "Oh, God, Chance. Stay with me, please stay with me."

"Look at me, Jax, I'm right here, I'm not going anywhere. Let it all go." Chance pushed deeper and deeper while Jax's eyes bored into her and fingernails raked down her back. "I've got you. Hold on to me."

Jax shifted and threaded her hands in Chance's hair, leaning in and nestling her face close. "So good with you."

Chance shivered as Jax's mouth slid along her jaw until she gasped at the feeling of teeth at the juncture of her neck and shoulder. Fueled by the pleasurable pain, she thrust into Jax, steadily pushing her closer and closer to climax. Jax's whole body began to tremble as Chance curled her fingers before the telltale clenching started. With a deep moan, Jax came and shuddered in her arms.

"Jesus, Chance!"

She held Jax tightly and gently stroked her through her orgasm before she withdrew. Her heart was beating out of her chest as she leaned into the woman who was deeply embedded in her heart.

Jax sighed and kissed her. "So good with you. So damn good."

"With us, Jax. It's so good with us. Love at its very best."

***

Jax woke to the smell of bread baking. She took a deep breath and rolled over into a cool space that should have contained a warm body. She smiled when she heard Hunter's laughter and a deeper one she recognized as Chance's. She climbed out of bed and slipped into a pair of yoga pants and an oversized sweatshirt. Barefoot, she strode down the stairs, wrapping her long hair into a messy bun.

She stood in the doorway watching for a moment. Chance was letting Hunter use the biscuit cutter to portion out the dough into perfect circles. He had flour on his cheeks and a dot on his nose. *This is what life should have been all along.*

Jax moved into the kitchen and tapped her foot on the cabinet to get Hunter's attention. She signed to him as she spoke aloud. *"What are you two doing?"*

Hunter made the sign for eat.

Jax kissed the top of his head before moving to kiss Chance good morning. "Why didn't you wake me?"

Chance pointed to Hunter. "He wanted to surprise everyone. The omas were ordered back to bed."

Jax accepted the cup of coffee Chance held out to her. "When's the last time those two slept in past six?"

Chance laughed and slid the pan of biscuits Hunter finished into the oven. "Never. It has to be killing them."

"It is." Maggie walked in and picked up a dishtowel, wiping flour off Hunter's cheek. After putting it over her shoulder, she signed to Hunter. *"Good morning."*

Hunter's face rivaled the sun for brightness. Jax slipped in under Chance's arm and rested her head on the muscled chest wrapped in a soft WVU T-shirt.

Chance murmured in Jax's ear. "They're enjoying being grandmothers. I've never seen either of them like this."

Jax nodded as she watched Maggie and Hunter chat in sign. "I know. My dad is almost goofy. I remember him being like this when the twins were born. He always was so good with them."

"Hunter loves him. I caught him trying to walk like your dad the other day. It was comical."

Jax took a drink then covered her mouth. She wiped off the small drop that had escaped and rolled down her chin. "Don't say things like that unless you want to wear what's in my cup."

They stood there watching Maggie teach Hunter to crack eggs into a bowl. Dee wandered in and stopped to ruffle Hunter's hair, then kissed Maggie on the way to the coffee pot.

Dee leaned against the counter beside them and watched the show. "Like a bee to honey. Years ago, if I couldn't find her and there was a kid around, I'd head in that direction. She's always been such a natural."

Chance leaned over. "Hey pot, meet kettle. You're both that way. That's why you're a great coach and a great mom."

Jax snickered at the banter. She was so grateful for all the women that surrounded her. Life had finally given her all she'd ever wanted in the family that filled her kitchen. She looked forward to adding Kendra and Brandi, who would be with them next weekend. "You can't say much, Chance. All of you are drawn to making the lives of children better. I've been lucky to fall right in the middle of the most kid friendly family I've ever known. What I wouldn't have done to have grown up among you." She felt Chance's arms tighten around her.

"We can't change what you grew up with, but we can certainly make sure the family you live with now makes up for the past."

Jax knew nothing could make her forget the vitriol her mother had filled her entire childhood with. What those experiences did was inspire her promise to make sure Hunter's childhood would never resemble her own in any way. "How long before breakfast?"

Maggie looked at the biscuits in the oven. "I'd say another ten minutes. Hunter and I are about to start the scrambled eggs."

Jax nodded. "I'll set the table."

Chance moved toward the door. "I'll feed Zeus and Midas. I put them out back to explore for a while."

Dee sipped from her cup. "I think I'll stand here and watch."

The crew continued to cook breakfast until everything was done. Each person took their place at the table and dug in when their plates were full. Chance buttered a biscuit and enjoyed her family around the table.

When Dee went for a third piece of bacon, Maggie glared at her.

"What? I'm hungry." Dee grumbled but withdrew her hand. "You're going to kill me trying to keep me healthy."

Maggie rolled her eyes and turned to Hunter, signing to him. *"You'll start school soon."*

Hunter pushed his eggs around, causing Chance to grow concerned. She questioned him.

"What's wrong?"

He shrugged. Hunter didn't seem to be forthcoming with an explanation for his issue with school, and Chance wasn't sure what to do about it.

"Maybe we should contact his kindergarten teacher and see if she can enlighten us. This might even be something Hunter doesn't know how to explain. I'll make some calls tomorrow and see what I can find out. The bottom line is, we'll find a solution."

Maggie nodded. "That we will. It's what we do in this family, fix the problem and make it better for others."

Chance sat back and enjoyed the time with her family. She loved knowing there was nothing they couldn't overcome together.

***

Jax stood at the edge of the stall watching the pinto mare with her baby. Bill stood beside her. They'd been called out by a concerned owner. There was nothing like the smell of an active barn. The combined scents of sweet feed and hay mixed with horse were some of her absolute favorites. She thought about how Hunter starting a new school year compared to the tentative steps of the wobbly foal in front of her. Its red ears twitched as it stood to nurse. "Nothing much better than watching new life find its footing."

Bill nodded. "I can't argue with that."

"I've been meaning to ask you, is your wife enjoying being back home?"

Bill smiled with a wide grin. "She loves the time she's getting to spend with her dad. He drifts a little more each day. This time is so precious, while he can still recognize her."

Jax nodded. "I know how she feels. My dad moved here less than six months ago, but I've seen him more lately than I have in thirty years."

"That wouldn't have anything to do with that little guy who came in with your dad and Uncle Marty earlier would it?"

"Oh, I've come to believe the men in my family are all cut from the same cloth, biologically related or not. Hunter is bound to be a fisherman even if it kills the other two."

"I saw a photo the other day with all three of them and a fish about this long." Bill held his fingers about five inches apart.

Jax pushed off the fence. "Dad wouldn't have been prouder if that trout had been a monster, and Hunter acted like he'd caught a whale."

"Life is all about little moments."

Jax's phone rang with an unfamiliar number. She answered with trepidation. "This is Dr. Fitzsimmons. How can I help you?"

"Hello, this is Mrs. Macguire, the principal at Davis-Thomas Elementary School. I have a message to call and talk with you about your son, Hunter?"

Jax swallowed hard at the word *son*. She moved away from the fence and walked out of the barn. "Yes. Thank you for calling back so soon, Mrs. Maguire. Currently, we foster Hunter, but we hope it will be long term and eventually turn into an adoption."

"Mrs. Fitzsimmons, I was informed by Child Protective Services that Hunter is now in your care. Will his mother be involved in this discussion as well?"

"I'm sorry, no. She passed away, which is how we ended up with Hunter in our care."

"Oh my, I'm so sorry to hear that. I only dealt with her when she registered Hunter. How can I help you?"

"He'll start first grade this year, and we want to give him every opportunity possible to succeed at an education. When we try to talk with him about school, he shuts down on us. As I'm sure you're aware, he has limited communication skills."

"Mrs. Fitzsimmons, do you have time to come over to the school to discuss this? As you know, we have limited resources when it comes to children with issues like Hunter has. My schedule is always full, but I'll do my best to be flexible with your schedule."

Jax moved over near her truck. "Let me go home and check with Chance. We'd both want to be there."

"I'd actually prefer it that way. I've worked with Chance on many occasions. Is this a cell number I'm talking with you on?"

"It is."

"I'll text you a phone number and send my basic schedule to you at the email you provided on the contact form. That way, you can look and see what time would be best for you."

"Thank you, Mrs. Maguire. I look forward to meeting you."

When the call ended, Jax stared at the phone and felt a smile cross her face. At least the school was willing to discuss options. Hunter was so much more to her than just a foster child. Every day, he wound his way tighter around her heart.

Bill was loading equipment into the truck. "Everything all right?"

She held her phone up. "More than all right. That was the school. We're trying to head off any problem before it has an opportunity to take root. I might have to take a few hours here and there to deal with getting his school issues settled."

Bill looked at her over the hood of the truck and chuckled. "Jax, I think we can handle it. Remember, you're the boss. This is family, and family matters more than an appointment every single time."

"Did you finish everything back there, or do we have more to do before we head back to the office?"

Bill patted the hood. "All good. I told them we'd be back in two weeks unless there's an issue."

Jax nodded. "Good man, let's head out."

The two of them climbed in and headed to Bill's truck at the clinic. She was grateful Bill had been available to come along. She needed to get the farms she worked with used to a different vet coming out when she was otherwise occupied. As she drove, Bill filled out electronic forms on a tablet that would be uploaded into the system when they got back to the office. *Thank God for Bill.* Hiring him had added a great deal of flexibility to her schedule. It was one of the smartest business decisions she'd made since coming to Tucker County.

The thought of Hunter being at school made her anxious. *I'm sure every parent feels this way. No doubt someday Taylor and Penny will feel exactly like this when Jace starts school.* She turned onto the main road that would take her to the office, and eventually, home to her family.

Chapter Eight

CHANCE SMILED AT PENNY as the door swung wide for her. "Is she awake?"

Penny waved her in. "She's resting on the couch with your godson. Come on in."

Chance entered her previous home and smiled at the way it had been transformed from a bachelor pad into a family home. Zeus sniffed the area then went to greet Midas lying by the hearth. Chance waved Taylor back down as she started to sit up. "Relax, I'm just checking up on you."

Taylor smiled and moved Jace on her chest so she could talk with Chance more comfortably. "He's been a little clingy since we got home." She laughed a bit and pointed to Midas. "Both of them."

Penny gestured to the chair. "Please sit down, Chance."

Chance acquiesced. "I can't stay long. I just wanted to stop by and check on the reluctant patient. How are you feeling?"

Taylor sighed. "I'm just glad to be home."

"I have no doubt the whole family feels the same. I'm ordering you to stay home until Tuesday." She pointed to Taylor. "Desk duty only when you're back. No arguments."

Taylor held her hand up in surrender. "My keeper there will make sure I behave. Do you have a final count on our fatalities from the storm?"

Chance ran her hand through her hair. "As of now, the official total is three. Two from the campground and an electrocution from a resident trying to wire up some temporary power out at Moore Station where the tornado touched down."

"Anyone we knew?" Penny questioned.

"You know about the Parker boy. We ran into that fire after being down in Leadmine delivering notification to his grandparents. I had to call family for the Moore Station guy. He had just moved here from Steubenville, Ohio a few months ago. The other was someone from out of town, here for the festival."

Penny's mother, Brenda, came out of the kitchen with a tray full of coffee cups and a pot. "I'm sure, at this point, you need a cup of strong coffee, if your night was as late as I imagine."

Chance accepted the cup. "You are a godsend, Mrs. Clancy."

"Please, call me Brenda."

Penny took a cup as well. "Thanks, Mom. She's right, Taylor and I were so grateful you were here to watch Jace."

Brenda looked at her sleeping grandson and set a cup of coffee on the table for Taylor. "I missed the first few months of his life out of stupidity. I won't miss an opportunity again. If I'd have listened to your father and not been so stubborn, we wouldn't have missed anything. He's as at home here as he is at our place. Currently, he's outside mowing the grass with that tractor. I swear, he'll try and buy one for our half-acre of ground if I let him."

Taylor chuckled and Jace stretched, opening his sleepy eyes before settling back down. "I haven't had to do any outdoor work since you two got here."

Chance sipped her coffee, then pointed at Brenda. "I hear Warren likes to fish."

Penny's mother nodded. "He does."

"Then I'll have to hook him up with my father-in-law. He's been taking Hunter fishing a good bit lately. I'm sure they'd be happy for him to join them."

Brenda beamed. "If it gets him out from under my feet for a few hours, I'm all for it. Have your father-in-law call Warren the next time they go. We'll be here for another week before I need to get back. Warren's retired, but I babysit for a family in our neighborhood. They went on vacation and will be back for the kids to start school."

"I'll do that. Brenda, thanks for the coffee. Sorry, I wish I could stay longer, but I've got an appointment I need to get to. I just wanted to check on my right hand. Taylor, I'll call you tomorrow. When you get to work, Tuesday, I want you to work on tracing that firearm and those prints from that abandoned vehicle." She and Zeus stood.

"I'll be there. Thanks, Chance." Taylor held Jace close and kissed the top of his soft head. "For everything."

Chance came over and pointed at Taylor. "No thanks needed. I'm pretty sure you'd have done the same thing. Rest up. I'll see you back at work." Chance pointed to Penny. "Call me if you need her put in line, or for anything. I'm off to see about getting that rear window fixed. I'm tired of hearing the plastic flapping."

"I'll see you out. I assure you, she won't be any trouble." Penny rose and walked Chance to the door and hugged her. "I can't thank you enough for making that scene in there still possible. When I got the call, I almost passed out. I can't imagine life without her, Chance."

"I know. Jax has had those same feelings. It's a difficult job, and we rely on our families to remind us why we do it. You're also the reason we take every precaution. Loving you makes us safer and gives us a reason to come home."

"She had close calls when she was at the Marshals, but none that were this bad. I know tomorrow isn't a given, but Jace and I need her the way Jax and Hunter need you. Don't ever forget that."

"I can promise you we never do. Now, try and keep her quiet for a few days, and I promise to give her plenty of work to keep her ass in the chair at her desk when she gets back."

"Thanks. I've worked for more than one person, but none that I ever considered family. That's what you are to both of us."

"I've always felt the same. Now, go enjoy your family. The jobs will still be there when you both get back. I've got a press conference I'm not looking forward to."

"Try not to let Maya get under your skin. I keep wondering when she'll get the call to go to another station."

"Not soon enough, if you ask me. See you tomorrow."

***

God it's been a long day. Chance loved coming home to her whole family gathered in the kitchen. Kendra's truck sat in the driveway with their mother's Jeep Cherokee. She needed some laughter and levity, some true family time. The press conference had been brutal. The names of the victims were released along with some brief information detailing the circumstances around their deaths. Maya had questioned if enough notice had been given and if there was anything that could have been done to prevent the deaths. *Typical Maya, always looking for someone to blame.*

There were at least a dozen counties that had suffered a similar fate and were without power. The storm had ravished the area, knocking down large electrical towers, and causing severe havoc all along the electrical grid. Chance was beyond grateful the mountain still had power, so only half of the county was affected.

So tired. She had a massive headache that was probably from her lack of food since breakfast. A feeling of relief came over her as the worries of the day faded like the daylight. Hunter was likely in the bathtub, and she didn't want to miss time with him. Putting him to bed had become one of her favorite parts of the evening. "Let's go see the family, Zeus."

From the porch, she could hear the welcome sound of laughter. Pushing through the door, Zeus immediately made his way to the damp haired Hunter. "Did I miss bath time?"

Jax came to her and wrapped warm arms around her neck before kissing her. "Hunter took his bath early so he would have more time with you when you got home. He was adamant about not going to bed before you got back. Thanks for coming home. I know you had more to do."

"Nothing more important than this." Chance held her close.

Maggie walked over to her. "Go take that stuff off and sit down. I've got dinner for you and a handful of Advil. I'd be able to see your headache from Davis. What do you want to drink?"

"I could really use a Coke for the caffeine."

Maggie kissed her cheek. "Coming right up."

Chance went to remove her vest and store her gun before she found her way to the kitchen, taking in a deep sniff of the roasted chicken, potatoes, and carrots. "Mom, this smells amazing. Thank you."

"You're welcome. Go eat."

Chance made her way to the table where Hunter hugged her before he went to do his evening chore of feeding Zeus. She pointed to boy and dog. "He never forgets."

Jax grabbed Chance's fork and picked up a piece of chicken and slid it into Chance's mouth. "Eat. Let me guess, you didn't bother with anything for lunch?"

Chance chewed and watched Hunter pull the plastic tub out of the cabinet. He used the cup to gently measure food into Zeus' bowl, then gave him the signal to eat. "It was a madhouse. I did stop by to see Taylor. She's doing fine, and for once, following orders from Penny. The rest of the day was mayhem."

"Eat. You can tell me about it after we put Hunter to bed." Jax rose and handed her the fork. "I'll get you some dessert."

Chance nodded and focused on the delicious dinner her mother had prepared. Hunter ran back in and climbed onto her lap. Chance stopped eating long enough to greet him. *"I missed you."*

Hunter straddled her legs then hugged her.

"We worked on his archery skills." Kendra pulled her arm back as if she were shooting a bow.

Hunter smiled at Kendra, apparently recognizing the movement.

"Was that fun?" Chance signed to him raising her eyebrows and widening her eyes to indicate a question.

He nodded again and mimicked Kendra.

Chance chuckled as Hunter jumped down and ran over to Maggie, obviously on a mission to tell her something.

Dee was taking a call when Brandi came in. Kendra dropped into a chair beside Chance. "The horses have had a ride, been groomed, and fed. Damn, Chance, you look beat."

Chance rolled her neck and swallowed. "Thank you for spending time with him and teaching Hunter to shoot."

"He's going to be awesome at archery."

"Hey, Brandi." Chance waved at her sister's girlfriend. "Good to see you."

Brandi walked through the kitchen. "Always good to see you, too. I need to tell Jax something about Mac. I'll be back."

Chance watched her sister's eyes follow the woman she was obviously head over heels for. "What classes do you have this year?"

Kendra listed off what she was taking in the accelerated schedule that would have her graduating early. She pulled up a website to show Chance a few of the professors. "I think you know some of them. They're former law enforcement officers and federal agents."

Chance scrolled through the headshots and accompanying bios. "Yes, I do." Chance pointed at one of the pictures. "Damn. This woman is a former Washington DC federal prosecutor. Samantha Lynn has put away some big names in organized crime from all over the world. She even had a bounty on her head for several years from a Russian mobster."

Kendra's eyes were as big as saucers. "No shit?"

Chance held a hand up then took a drink of her Coke. "I swear. She is a badass. Believe it or not, she has a house up in Canaan." She set her plate down and used the last bite of a homemade roll to wipe up the leftovers as a small boy crawled into her lap again. Chance signed to him. *"Are you tired?"* She felt him lean in and nod against her chest. She stood with him in her arms and walked toward the stairs. "Someone is ready for bed, dessert can wait."

Jax crossed the room and took Chance's hand as they said goodnight to their visitors. The three of them ascended the stairs to what had become Hunter's room. It was filled with cars, trucks, and dinosaurs. Chance set him on his bed and grabbed a flashlight. Hunter sat curled in Jax's lap with Chance in front of them. She made shadow puppets on the wall until Jax pointed to Hunter. Chance saw he'd fallen asleep. Zeus was curled protectively at his feet. She tucked him in with the bedraggled tiger they'd salvaged from his previous home. Jax had washed and repaired the tiger, then placed it on his bed to find. The two women stood looking at Hunter. Jax wrapped her arms around Chance.

"So innocent. It scares me sometimes, being responsible for him. What if I miss something or don't do something I'm supposed to?"

Chance nestled her in closer and tightened her hold. "I'm sure all parents feel that way. If you ask moms squared, I'll bet they'll tell you the same thing. Kendra was about his age when she came to live with them. I was older and more capable of fending for myself. Right now, our family is his whole world."

Jax looked up to Chance. "I just don't want to screw up."

Chance kissed her nose. "We're both going to screw up, but you're a great mom. Don't spend another moment thinking about that. Let's go see if anything else needs doing and go to bed. I'm beat."

"That sounds like one of the best ideas I've heard all day."

Jax pulled from her arms and tucked the covers over Hunter's shoulder, stopping to kiss his head before stepping back. Chance kissed him as well and slipped out of the room, turning off the light and shutting the door. They'd put a baby monitor in his room the week before, so they'd hear if he had another nightmare. Those incidents were fewer and farther between but still present.

Chance stood with her hand on Hunter's door and felt slightly choked up. She knew she and Jax were doing the right thing by trying to adopt Hunter. There were things to talk about, schedules to coordinate, and information to obtain. *Tomorrow.* All of it could be done tomorrow. Tonight, she needed to hold Jax and let the day fade away.

***

Jax lay in Chance's arms, content. "Oh, I forgot to tell you. The principal from the elementary school called. I didn't expect it, since it's Sunday. She wants to fill us in on last year and talk about solutions."

"There isn't anything that's insurmountable. We'll adjust our schedules if necessary."

Jax nodded against Chance's chest. "Bill told me that same thing."

"You like your new hire, don't you?"

"I do. They moved here not only because they needed to but because they wanted to. I can't help but think there was a little divine intervention, as Rhebekka would say. He needed a job close to his wife's family farm, and I needed a vet willing to do more than just cats and dogs. The timing was perfect with Hunter coming into our life. He's already told me not to worry about the office, to focus on our family."

"I knew I liked that guy."

Jax rolled until Chance was spooned up tight to her back, a protective arm around her middle, and cradled between her breasts. This was home. The security and love Jax had spent a lifetime waiting to have. She fell asleep thinking about how Hunter coming into their family had allowed her to fill one more role she never thought she would. *Mother.*

***

Monday morning, Jax dropped Hunter off at Maggie's office. She had a few different missions for the day, and some even involved the animals from her practice. After enjoying a lazy Sunday, it was the beginning of another busy work week. *I can't forget to schedule that appointment with Mrs. Macguire.* Her day's agenda included a trip to Blackwater Bikes with her dad to pick out a bicycle for Hunter to start riding. They'd asked him if he'd ever ridden one. The small boy had kicked at the dirt, embarrassed. She thought about the pained expression on Hunter's face as he shrugged it off.

It was likely that Crissy hadn't been able to afford one. *Don't be angry at her, Jax.* She and Chance had talked about it and decided that they wouldn't wait for Christmas. They didn't want to spoil him, even as easy as that would be to do. As new parents, they did feel it was important to provide him with more than a roof over his head and food on the table. Life needed to be joyful, and they wanted him to experience the exhilaration of peddling on his own for the first time. Her dad insisted that it was a grandparent's right to buy him his first bike. *Sometimes I think he's more of a kid than Hunter is.*

Her phone rang, and she answered it with the onboard system. "This is Dr. Fitzsimmons."

"Well, Dr. Fitzsimmons, this is Matt. How are you?"

"Matt, I'm fine. It's so good to hear from you. How're you feeling?"

"Physical therapy is a bitch, but much better. I called to talk about the endurance race. Any way you can come to my house later?"

Jax thought about her schedule. "How about I stop on my way home? I've got a pretty full plate until about three. Will that be okay?"

"Sounds perfect. Tell Chance hi for me."

"Will do, Matt. See you later."

She disconnected the call and turned into the parking lot of her office. *Let's get this day started.*

***

Jax walked through the clinic door. Trooper Meg Kincaid stood with a list in her hand, talking with Lindsey. "Good morning you two. Meg, it's been a long time since I've seen you."

Meg grinned. "Midnight shift. I hate it. At least I get to see my wife for dinner. We were just going over her class list."

Jax turned to Lindsey. "Are you excited?"

Lindsey beamed. "I am. When does Angie start?"

"Day after tomorrow. Thanks for that recommendation."

Lindsey handed her some mail. "My cousin was tired of driving to Oakland every day. This made more sense. Even though she isn't making as much on the hour, she didn't have insurance there, and her travel alone cost her a quarter of a day's wages getting back and forth. None of that even touches the fact she didn't care for her employer's disposition."

Jax nodded. "Let's hope she doesn't find me as disagreeable. Angie's smart and has the training to do the job. With two vets on duty and you in school, she'll fit in nicely. I'll hate not having you around as much, but I know Bill will appreciate a competent assistant on the weekends. Megan, it was good to see you. I'd better go answer the ninety-nine emails in my inbox and get ready to see the shelter's new intakes."

Meg waved. "Good to see you too, Doc. Thanks again for the scholarship. She always wanted to be a vet. Because of you, she will be."

"Remember, I'm planning to retire someday. Someone has to take over. I'm hoping between Lindsey, Brandi, and Bill, I've covered all my bases. Be safe out there."

Meg saluted. "Always."

Jax walked back to her office, sorting through the envelopes. She sat behind her desk and opened a letter on business quality stationery from an attorney's office in Vallejo, California. She read through the paperwork and laughed sardonically. Lacey was being sued for sexual harassment, and Jax had been named a co-defendant. She read farther down in the document to see who was suing. She had a guess and wasn't surprised to see the name listed. Tonya Harris had worked for them for over five years. She was the woman Jax caught Lacey with that finally led to the divorce. "This is rich."

Jax pulled out her cellphone and started to dial the number of the attorney she'd used in California, then realized the time. It was only five in the morning there. She set an alarm on her phone to remind her to call Alex. "Just fucking great." Her hands clutched the arms of her desk chair as she let her head rest against the back.

"Problems?" Bill's deep baritone filled her office.

"Ex-wives tend to be that."

"Oh, that can't be good."

Jax shook her head. "No, it isn't. A vet tech from the California clinic I co-owned with my ex-wife is suing us." She held up the papers. "I left the clinic and my then wife because I found out this same vet tech was sleeping with her at the time."

"What a shit storm." Bill came in and sat down in the chair across from her.

She appreciated his frank assessment of the situation. "I'm not sure what she thinks she'll get from me. The minute I found out, I left Lacey and our business. My guess is my ex dumped her shortly after. For all I know, she fired her. I sure as hell didn't condone the affair or Lacey's actions. I'll be damned if I'm getting dragged into her mess. Sleep with dogs, expect to get fleas."

"Or mange, which is what I came in here to talk about. Do you have an attorney?"

"I do. The one that handled my divorce, but his office handles all types of legal matters. He'll flip his lid over this. He's good and I'm not worried. It's just a pain in the ass, just like she was. Good riddance to bad rubbish, as Aunt Mary used to say. Now, about this mange."

"Maddie from Doggy Sods called. She picked up a rescue that has one of the worst cases she's ever seen. I told her to bring him in and we'd set up a room to treat him in."

Jax threw the paperwork from the attorney on the desk. "This day gets better and better, and it's only just begun. Lead on, Doctor. There's work to be done."

* * *

Chance opened the door for Zeus and greeted Penny. "Good morning, boss. What's on my desk today?"

Penny handed her a cup of coffee and several small, pink slips. "You have three messages from a certain reporter. She would like you to personally call her. She said she knows you still have her number."

"Wishful thinking. I don't keep phone numbers I do not need, and after yesterday's grilling, I don't have anything else to say. What else?"

"A few background checks for county employment applications. Oh, and Quade called. Wanted to know what your schedule looked like for lunch."

Chance looked confused.

Penny rolled her eyes. "I know more about your schedule than you do and he knows it. I told him that unless you had plans that weren't on my calendar, you were free. He said he'd come to you. He has some business at the courthouse anyway. Give him a call."

"I'll do that. How's Taylor?"

Penny huffed, then handed her a printout. "That is from your chief deputy. She's as bad as you are about being out of the loop. She sent me this damn list of things she was working on at home that she thought you might want to see. There's a schedule for firearms qualifying, K9 recertifications, and who knows what else in there. She's doing fine physically. The burns aren't too bad. She'll be in tomorrow, whether you want her or not. I put my foot down on the road patrol. No calls that can't be handled by phone. If those burns get infected, I'll bust her ass and she knows it."

The phone rang. Chance waved at Penny before she headed back to her office to answer. Chance picked up her desk phone and called Quade.

"It's about time you called. It's after eight. Are you slacking these days since you aren't worried about reelection yet?"

Chance laughed at the banter from her old friend. "Good to hear from you too. So, lunch?"

"I have fairly accurate information that you're free unless that wonderful wife of yours has dibs on you."

"It just so happens, she has some things she needs to do during lunch, so I am indeed free. What's going on?"

"Not much. I wanted to pass on some information to you. We haven't caught up in a while, and we have to eat. We might as well do that together."

Chance moved some papers on her desk and searched for the background checks Penny mentioned. "We might as well. The diner at noon?"

"Works for me. See you then."

"Head on a swivel until then."

"Always."

Chance hung up and noticed an application she wasn't expecting. Kristi Ryker was applying for a job at the Tucker County Board of Education for a vacant nurse's position at the high school. Chance dialed Sarah.

"Hey, Chance. Seems like I haven't seen you in about three days. You doing okay? How're your stitches?"

"Itchy as usual. Overall, I'm doing fine. How are you handling the campground incident, mentally, I mean?"

Sarah sighed. "If we'd have lost Betty, I'd be having a harder time. We got a save there, and that makes the others hurt a little less. That doesn't mean the deaths weren't significant, it just doesn't feel like we failed them all."

Chance heard the disappointment in her friend's voice. Sarah was the most skilled medic she'd ever worked with. The losses added up over time. Guilt for those Sarah couldn't save weighed heavily, and Chance knew it. They'd drank far too many beers together, and she'd heard Sarah's numerous thoughts at her perceived failures. Sarah carried each death in her subconscious. "You didn't fail any of them. They were dead before we got to them, Sarah. I was there, I feel those losses as well." Chance vowed to spend some time with Sarah soon.

"Hey, enough about that. How's Hunter?"

"It's unreal, Sarah. I know we haven't had him with us very long and that we didn't give birth to him—"

Sarah interrupted her. "Chance, that doesn't matter one bit. I didn't give birth to Daniel, but he's my son."

"That's the weird thing. It feels like he's the child we should have had. It's like he's always belonged. I couldn't love him more if I'd watched him come into this world. To see Jax with him is one of the greatest joys of my life."

"You and Jax were meant to be together and Hunter completed it. Any word on his formal adoption?"

Chance closed her eyes, thinking about the mountain they were climbing in the attempt to adopt. "Lots of paperwork. We start parenting classes later this week. We're making an appointment with the school to see what he needs."

"You've been busy."

"Hey, that's not what I called about though. I see Kristi applied for a school nurse position. Did something happen with her job at the Harman clinic?"

"No, I think she wants to feel like she's doing something. The clinic is busy with the locals who need their blood pressure medicines or some blood tests. At the end of the day, she wants to feel like she's influenced someone's life. I think she's also missing Daniel as a teenager. He's a grown man now, a police officer. He's looking at building his own place on that far left field where they used to pasture the lambs. I think he's going to ask Dezi to marry him. She has one more year of school to finish her engineering degree."

"That might mean grandbabies for Kristi to snuggle."

"Maybe, but I hope not for a while. I don't want them to struggle the way Kristi and I did."

Chance put her hand on the top of Zeus' head and scratched near his ear. She looked at a picture of Daniel and Kendra when they were young. She and Sarah had taken them fishing up in Bowden. "He seems to have turned out pretty well, regardless of how difficult it was."

There was silence on the line for a few seconds. Chance waited her out.

"Yeah, he did. I think that was more Kristi than me."

"I beg to differ. It took both of you, and you didn't even have to attend parenting classes."

Sarah's laughter made her feel better. The emotional well-being of her best friend since childhood was important to her. After she'd come home from the burn center, Sarah had helped Chance get through some of the worst days of her life.

"No, we were left to figure it out by ourselves. You're going to do fine. You and Jax were meant to be parents. A little later than most people start, but Kristi will be glad to tell Jax to be grateful she missed the stretch marks part."

"I'll let Jax know that. I miss you, Sarah. We need to do a family barbeque. How about we get together soon for a cookout? I'll fire up the grill, and we'll tip a few beers."

"I'd like that. I know Kristi would like to meet Hunter."

"You look at your calendar and let us know."

"Will do. Chance?"

Chance held her breath. "Yeah?"

"Thanks."

"That's what best friends do."

***

Jax took a break when her alarm went off. She wanted to call Alex and find out what the hell was going on. She'd need legal representation in California, and Alex Laquinta could handle it. The first thing she decided to do was call Mrs. Maguire and schedule their meeting. She dialed the number and told the receptionist who she was. The line clicked and the principal came on.

"Mrs. Fitzsimmons, it's good to hear from you. Did you find some dates for me?"

"Please, call me Jax. We did. We've cleared our schedule in the afternoon each day for the rest of the week."

"Great. How about tomorrow? Unfortunately, Hunter's new teacher can't be with us."

Jax started writing on her desk calendar. "What time?"

"Can you be here by two?"

Jax wrote down the time as she answered. "We'll be there. Thanks for seeing us so soon. With the school year about to start, we already feel like we're behind."

"I assure you. We're willing to work with you as much as possible."

"That makes me feel much better. See you tomorrow at two." Jax hung up and called Chance.

"To what do I owe the pleasure of a phone call from you this early in the day?"

No matter how many times Jax heard Chance's voice, it still sent a thrill through her. She ran a finger over a wedding photo on her desk. "Maybe I just wanted to hear your voice."

"I'd buy that if I didn't know how jam-packed your schedule is today. What's up?"

"We have an appointment at the school tomorrow at two. I wanted to make sure you know about it, so you don't commit to something else. I know Penny cleared your schedule in anticipation of the parenting classes."

"She did, so no issues. Taylor will be back tomorrow, on desk duty, which will free me up from the office as well. Oh, I invited Sarah and Kristi over for a barbeque soon. I think Sarah is having a hard time dealing with the recent string of fatalities we've had."

Jax doodled on a scratchpad. "I think that's a great idea."

Jax sighed looking at the legal papers on her desk. "I need to tell you something else too. Apparently, according to the paperwork that came in the mail today, I'm being sued as a co-defendant with Lacey by a former employee."

"For what?"

Jax put her head back and stared at the ceiling. "Don't choke when I tell you. Sexual harassment. The kicker is the suit is from the woman I caught Lacey with at the office when I finally left her. I need to contact my attorney in California and see if he can figure out what the angle is. I never condoned her actions and even left the business after that. How I'm involved, I'll never understand. I never touched her nor encouraged anything inappropriate. Once again, Lacey is dragging me into her mess, and I won't tolerate it."

"My guess is she knows about Lacey's other affairs. Probably thinks that in not divorcing her, you had no issue with it."

Jax sat up and pinched the bridge of her nose. "Like hell, I didn't. I confronted Lacey numerous times. It may have taken catching her in the act for me to say I'd had enough, but I certainly was not okay with her infidelity. Knowing Lacey, someone in the family will pay the complainant off. This isn't something I want to deal with. I left her and California behind. I won't be dragged into her muck."

"Call the attorney. Let me know what he says."

She took a deep breath and doodled on a note pad. "I'm sorry, Chance."

"Stop. You have nothing to be sorry for. Call."

Jax took a deep breath and looked at the initials she'd traced doodled on the notepad. Her initials ending with an embellished capital F. "I love you."

"And I love you back. I'm meeting Quade for lunch, so I need to finish a few things up before then. I'll pick up Hunter on my way home. Don't let this worry you."

"I'll try. Give him a hug from me. I'll see you at home tonight."

Jax hung up before she leaned her elbows on the desk and straightened up the papers from the attorney. "Tonya, get ready. You've got a fight coming, and I don't plan on losing." She picked up her desk phone and dialed. *Time to start swinging.*

***

Chance slid into the booth on the other side of Quade. The diner was one of the few businesses in town with a generator. "Good to see you. It's been way too long. You need to stop by the house soon."

Quade nodded. "It always seems like the only time we see each other is on a call. The days of the giant riverbank parties seem so long ago."

"Boy, you're reaching into the way-back machine. The last one had to be what, ten or twelve years ago?" Chance picked up the menu.

Quade signaled the waiter. "Probably longer. Ready to order?"

The waitress took their orders and left.

Chance pushed her straw into her Coke. "So, to what do I owe this unexpected lunch date?"

Quade blushed and wadded up the paper from the straw. "Jenna's pregnant."

Chance let the smile on her face grow wide. Quade's first marriage hadn't worked out. Finding Jenna had been the best medicine for a broken heart. "That's great news. How's she doing?"

Quade ran his hand across his shorn hair. "Other than making me worry myself to death, fine. We made it through that first trimester, so she said it was okay to start telling people. I'm forty years old, I didn't think I'd ever be a father. To tell you the truth, I'm petrified."

"Try being in your fifties, though Jax doesn't have to go through the pregnancy part."

"I heard you're trying to adopt Hunter. You'll be great at this."

Chance nodded. "There's a lot of hoops to jump through, but we hope it all works out in our favor. So, when's she due?"

For the next several minutes, Chance and Quade talked about the changes in their lives. When she'd left the US Fish and Wildlife Agency, she and Quade had made a promise to keep in touch. On occasion, his agency worked with the US Forest Service, another one of Chance's former occupations. Now they mostly worked together on the law enforcement issues within the county and his jurisdiction of the Nature Preserve.

"That class that JD put on was really good. I've seen those symbols around the Canaan Valley area."

Chance nodded. "We've got a vehicle at the impound lot with a sticker related to the movement. Someone removed most of the VIN tags. I'm putting Taylor on desk investigation tomorrow. Since it was in the area where we know some of them live, I'm betting it's related."

Quade pointed a fry at her. "Let me know if you need any assistance. I'm always here for you. How's Taylor doing, by the way?"

"She's chomping at the bit. I promise to always let you know if I need something. I appreciate the agency cooperation more than you know, Quade."

The two finished their lunch discussing colleagues from her time with the agency, paid their bill, and left. Chance stood at the door to her Suburban. "You tell Jenna how happy I am for you both. Let me know if you need anything. Be safe out there."

Quade patted her shoulder. "Will do. Watch your six, my friend."

"Always." Chance wanted to check down at the campground on the cleanup efforts. Work to clear the downed trees and damaged campers was ongoing.

As she pulled in, the sound of chainsaws filtrated into her vehicle. Large wreckers were on the grounds attempting to pull out the mangled wrecks of twisted sheet metal. The stage had suffered significant damage that hadn't been visible during the incident. She pulled up and let Zeus out to join her. She spotted Harry. The look on his face told her he was having a hard time taking it all in. He sat in a chair, watching his son heft blocks up into a front-end loader. Chance sat down beside him.

"I'm sorry, Harry. I know you thought a lot of Travis."

He nodded slowly. "Hard worker and such a good kid. I still can't believe it."

"That storm came up so fast. We just couldn't get everyone to safety in time. You know as well as I do, that we certainly tried."

Harry wiped a grimy hand down his face. "I don't know that I can ever recover from this. We can clean everything up and repair the stage but losing Travis and one of our guests took the wind out of me. I don't know that I have the heart."

Chance put a hand on his shoulder. "Give it some time, Harry. Rely on your family. Is there anything I can do?"

He shook his head. "No, not unless you have a time machine."

She was silent for a few minutes, thinking about the man they couldn't get to in the camper. His wife had survived but was severely injured. There was still a question as to whether she would make it or not. The helpless feeling hadn't gone away. Every time the stitches in her arm pulled, she thought about him. *Comes with the territory.*

"If you need anything, let me know. I'm over at the office or a phone call away."

Harry shook her hand. "Thanks, Sheriff, for everything."

She and Zeus got back in her Suburban and made their way back to the office. An emergency glass technician was waiting to install a new rear window. She passed several power company boom trucks headed into town. They were a welcome sight. The sweltering heat had Sarah and her crew running their asses off, dealing with those in respiratory distress. Without air conditioning, many of the elderly were suffering. *Thank God for the generator at our office.*

***

Jax sighed with relief at the activity in her kitchen. Her visit with Matt had lifted her spirits. They'd worked on more of the planning for the endurance race and had commitments from a few more volunteers. At times, she felt completely overwhelmed with everything she had to do. *Balance, I need balance.*

She and her dad had taken an hour to stop in at Blackwater Bikes and talked to them about what Hunter would need. In the end, they decided to wait and have Hunter come with them so that he would feel like he was part of the decision. What she wanted more than anything right then was to be surrounded by her family. The wonderful smells of garlic bread and red sauce drifted out and made her stomach rumble.

Chance stood at the stove stirring a pot of spaghetti sauce as Hunter laid silverware at each place setting on the table. When he saw Jax, he came running over and wrapped his small arms around her with a smile as wide as the Blackwater Canyon. *"Good to see you."*

Hunter pointed to Chance before signing back to her. *"Eat."*

Jax knelt and pulled him in for a hug that melted the day away. Chance stood watching them, and Jax caught her wiping a tear away.

"Thank you."

Hunter nodded and went back to making sure things would be ready. Jax walked over to kiss Chance. "Hi."

"Hi. You look tired. Go shower. We've got a while yet on the sauce. I haven't put the pasta in."

"It smells heavenly."

"It's Mom's famous recipe. Are you hungry?"

"Starving, like always."

Chance took a piece of bread and dipped it in the sauce. She cooled it before she fed it to Jax. "Let everything go for now. We'll talk about it later. Right now, we've got a six-year-old boy to make us laugh and smile. That's all we need."

Jax nodded and headed to the shower. Once inside, she let the hot water wash away the call she'd made to her attorney. *Chance will flip out.* She worked shampoo through her long hair. The smell of oranges and ginger filled the steamy shower. They'd found this shampoo on a recent shopping trip. It was supposed to help relieve stress. *If it doesn't do that, at least it smells good.* A few more minutes enjoying the steamy heat and she'd get out. It was amazing how a simple hot shower could completely rejuvenate a soul.

She stepped out, dried off, and changed into comfy clothes. This was family game night. The simple pleasure in a game of Candyland or Uno had become one of their favorite pastimes. A few strokes of a wide-toothed comb through her hair and she made her way back to the kitchen. *Time to feed my stomach and my heart.*

***

Hunter slurped the last piece of spaghetti into his mouth, and Jax hid her laughter as the sauce ran down his chin. With her napkin, she wiped away the drip before it found his shirt. Zeus sat dutifully at his side. Once Chance went off duty, Zeus became Hunter's dog. It was a sight to watch Zeus interact with the small boy. Hunter's verbal language skills were greatly lacking, but Zeus always seemed to know what Hunter was saying. She hoped hearing aids and a qualified tutor would open new possibilities. She'd started the process of emailing people from a list she was given of recent Gallaudet University graduates.

Jax turned to Chance. "How was your lunch with Quade?"

"He had news. They're expecting a baby."

Jax clapped her hands. "How exciting!"

"Quade said Jenna's doing well. He's tickled pink and hoping for a girl."

"That's unusual. Most men want a son."

"He said that all the good things in his life have involved amazing women. His childhood, his job, and now his family. I like that thought process." Chance turned to look at Hunter. "Though boys are pretty awesome too."

Jax leaned her head on Chance's shoulder, watching Hunter show Zeus a toy car. To Zeus' credit, he showed intense interest by nosing at the Hot Wheels. "Yeah, they are. Let's get this cleaned up and play a game with him."

"Let's go climb Gumdrop Mountain together."

The nightly routine of washing the dishes, feeding Zeus, and settling into the library was comfortable and grounding. The low coffee table they sat around was the perfect height for the boy. Hunter pulled the Uno cards out and handed them to Chance to shuffle. Once they were well mixed, Hunter carefully dealt each player seven cards. Jax was fascinated to watch her son smile and laugh as they skipped Chance on one turn, then made her pick up four additional cards. The simple game of colors also brought a look of pure joy to Chance's face.

Hunter slapped down a red two, then held up his index finger. He clapped.

Jax signed to him. *"Good."* Hunter beamed back that hundred-watt smile at them.

On his next turn, Hunter went out and jumped up to take a victory lap, landing in both their laps on his way by. He hugged them both fiercely, then leaned back and used his thumb, pinky, and index fingers to form a sign he'd never directed to them before. He formed the sign for *"I love you"* and hugged them again.

Jax held the small boy close as the tears trickled down her cheek. Chance held them both. When Jax finally composed herself, she leaned back and looked at Hunter. She used the same sign he'd given them. *"I love you too."* He handed the cards to her to shuffle. *More than you'll ever know, little man.*

***

Hunter's bath was always a joy-filled time as he played with toy boats, frogs, and ducks in the bubbles. Chance stayed close, allowing him to drain the water and dry himself off before handing him a pair of Spiderman underwear and the Paw Patrol pajamas that he'd picked out himself from his drawers. She caught his attention. *"Please brush your teeth."*

Hunter nodded and climbed on the stool that she had used. Her dad had made it for her when she couldn't reach the sink. Maggie and Dee had used it for the kids they'd fostered, including Kendra. Now the stool had come full circle.

Hunter spat the toothpaste into the sink, then rinsed his mouth. He put his Star Wars toothbrush in the cup and climbed down from the sink. He was tiny for his age. *I wonder if he'll grow out of it now that he's eating regular healthy meals.*

Zeus climbed into Hunter's bed and settled at his feet. Chance shared a picture book with Hunter, until the book slowly slipped from his hands.

Jax pointed. "He's out like a light."

Chance covered him, then put her arm around Jax. "How about a beer and we talk about our day?" At her nod, they made their way back downstairs. Jax turned on the small monitor that showed a video feed of Hunter sleeping. They had these small cellphone-sized devices around the house to watch him.

Chance grabbed two bottles as Jax walked into the library. They sat on the comfortable leather couch, and Chance handed her a beer.

"I'll need to go into the office and get Taylor started on a few things in the morning."

"I'm taking the whole day off. Bill looked over the schedule and felt he could handle everything. Uncle Marty told me he'd be on standby if there was an issue."

"Good. Hopefully, we'll get some good information and have a solid plan when we leave the school." She put an arm around Jax's shoulders. "Now, let's talk about the elephant in the room. What did your attorney say about the lawsuit?"

Jax took a long drink, inhaled a deep breath before she let her head lean back against Chance's shoulder. "Alex has to look over the paperwork and do a little digging for some more information. From what I could understand, Tonya Smith is suing the clinic as well as Lacey and me individually. The basis of her claim is sexual harassment and wrongful termination. I'm not sure how I have anything to do with either, since I didn't have the affair with her, nor did I fire her."

"I'm sure Alex can fight that, given the fact you divorced Lacey and left the practice. Do you think Lacey forced herself on the woman?"

Jax shook her head. "That's not Lacey's style, or wasn't when I was with her. She never needed anything other than her charm to attract women. Tonya latched onto her as soon as she was hired. I was opposed to bringing her on after I called some of her references. Lacey made the sole decision to hire her. We had a huge fight over it, and I informed her I didn't want her working on my service."

"Was there something in her file that gave you a bad feeling?"

"When I called one of her former employers, I asked if they'd hire her again. Some laws limit what they can say about it, but they told me they would not. That was enough for me. It was a well-respected clinic, and I personally knew several of the vets on staff. I think I knew right away Lacey would go after her."

"This isn't your fault, honey."

Jax picked at the label on the beer bottle. "I don't know, maybe I could have stopped it. I guess, in the end, I didn't care anymore. My heart was already closed off to her, and I had one foot out the door of our business. Finding them together in one of the exam rooms in a, let's say, more than compromising position told me all I needed to know."

"How much is she suing for?"

Jax held up three fingers. "Three million."

"Does the clinic have insurance?"

"It did when I was there. It's not unusual to have disgruntled employees. Unless Lacey dropped it, there is a substantial policy, though she's suing us personally as well. I'm more irritated than worried. I had nothing to do with it, and I'll be damned if my family will pay a penalty for someone else's indiscretions."

"I agree."

Jax drew a finger down Chance's cheek. "Can we make out here on the couch and take my mind off all that?"

Chance took the half-empty beer bottle out of Jax's hand and set it on the coffee table beside the pack of Uno cards. "Absolutely." She drew Jax into her lap and planted a languid kiss on her lips. The kiss was soft at first before Jax requested more, her tongue sweeping across Chance's lips, demanding entrance. The feel of Jax in her arms was like a fire that had been banked down and was now getting fresh air to renew the inferno.

Jax cradled her face. "I need you."

Chance moved Jax aside and rose, stretching out her hand. "I need you too." Arm in arm, they climbed the stairs. They stopped by Hunter's room and peeked in on him. Zeus' head raised, and they watched

Hunter pull his tiger and horse closer. Chance closed the door and led them to their bedroom.

Inside, she pulled Jax close and smothered her mouth with a deep, probing kiss. She let her tongue wrap around Jax's and tasted a slight bitterness from the beer. She felt Jax run her hands deep into her hair and the slight sting as she tugged. That slight bit of aggression fueled her, and she pulled at the hem of Jax's T-shirt, lifting it over her wife's head and revealing the navy silk bra.

"You are so beautiful."

"I love you. Please, Chance."

Chance didn't need any more encouragement. She slid down the loose lounge pants, taking everything beneath with them. She kissed Jax hard again as she wrapped her arms around the soft skin and released the clasp on her bra, letting it fall to the floor to join the rest of the clothes. Jax tugged at her T-shirt, and Chance helped her by jerking it off over her head. With trembling hands, Jax shoved up the athletic bra. While Chance fumbled with the button on her jeans, Jax's mouth found a nipple.

They ended up in a heap at the foot of the bed, laughing. Chance cursed trying to get her pants off. Jax cupped Chance's jaw. "Have we gotten too damn old for hot monkey sex?"

"Not on your life." Chance stood and slipped a hand under Jax's knees. The other went around her lover's back. She lifted her and tossed her onto the bed. Jax scurried up to the top and lay with her head on the pillows. Chance looked over the naked body of the woman she'd spent a lifetime dreaming about. The fact that she was here and would be for the rest of their lives, thrilled Chance. "When I'm eighty, I'll still want you just as much as I do right now. If my body will let me make love to you as I take my last breath, you can bet that's exactly what I'll be doing."

"That's kind of gross but really hot."

Chance stalked up the bed like a great predator, playful and yet determined. "I'll show you hot." She climbed up Jax's body and hovered above her before wrapping her lips around a rock-hard nipple and swirling her tongue against the taut flesh. Jax's moans encouraged her to continue as she kneaded Jax's other breast in her hand and rolled the hard peak in her fingers. Jax arched into Chance until they were touching along the entire length of soft flesh and sculpted muscle. These sensations pushed Chance's desire even higher. She lay down on the warm skin beneath her, reveling in the smell of oranges and ginger when she kissed a spot behind Jax's ear. She lifted her head and caught Jax's lips, delving her tongue deep into Jax's mouth and feeling her lover shiver in pleasure. Her body tingled with the anticipation of touching Jax's center as she rolled slightly to the side.

Chance watched Jax's chest heave with every pant. She broke the kiss and glided her hand over Jax's side, across her hip, and down to the damp curls that lay bare the evidence of her lover's desire. Her own center pulsed, and her belly clenched as her fingers slid through liquid silk. A moan of desperate pleasure left her lips. Nothing in her life had ever felt like this. *So soft.* Chance smiled as Jax gasped and spread her thighs in invitation and allowed Chance to settle between them. She kissed and nibbled at Jax's lip and her jawline, finally settling at the pulse point of her neck as she slid two fingers deep inside.

"Oh God, Chance."

"Hold onto me. I've got you," she whispered. Once again, they were joined together, anchored in place for all time like the mountains that surrounded them. Chance moved in and out of Jax, her fingers dripping from the liquid need that surrounded them. She moved her face until her lips were poised at Jax's ear. "You are incredibly wet for me. I love that you need my touch this much." She could feel Jax responding to her words with hips that bucked with each thrust. She moved her thumb over Jax's clit and grazed it slightly. The response was a near keen and a tensing of Jax's body.

"Don't stop, baby. Please don't stop."

"I'll never stop wanting you. I'll never stop loving you. I'll never stop, Jax."

Chance bit down on Jax's earlobe and felt her lover tighten around her fingers with the force of an impending climax. She increased the speed and force of her thrusts, moving down to take Jax's nipple in her mouth again. Touching Jax was like nothing she'd ever done in her life. Nothing ever made her feel this complete. Jax threaded her fingers in Chance's hair and directed her head down.

"Please, Chance."

Those two simple words were all the encouragement Chance needed to move down the bed. On the way, she began kissing the swell of breast, the ripple of ribs, and the hollow just inside the hip before she settled her shoulders between Jax's legs. Being with the woman she loved in this way rejuvenated something deep inside Chance. Jax's desire fed an elemental need, something just as vital as the blood that ran through her veins or the oxygen she breathed. *So good.*

She lowered her mouth, inhaling the unique musk of the one woman she'd loved her whole life. Her lips touched Jax's center as her tongue swept through a river of desire. Jax's hips bucked and she was forced to wrap her arms around Jax's legs to stay in place. She licked and sucked, drinking in Jax's very essence, the sweet tang coating her lips and igniting her own need. Hands gripped her head, holding her in place. She set a rhythm she had no doubt would drive Jax over the edge. She flittered her tongue and hummed against Jax's center. She wrapped her lips around Jax's swollen clit and sucked until Jax exploded in her mouth, filling it with the sweet taste of completion. Chance softened her stroke but kept a steady rhythm, drawing out the climax. She could feel Jax's legs tremble as her body came back down onto the bed.

A gravelly voice filled the silence of the room. "Oh my God. What did you just do to me?"

Chance kissed up Jax's body until she lay face to face with her. "I loved it away." Glassy eyes stared back at her. "I will always be by your side, Jax. Together, there is nothing we can't deal with."

"I love you, Chance."

"And I love you, now and forever."

Chapter Nine

CHANCE'S PHONE RANG ON the bedside table. She tried to reach it without disturbing the sleeping woman beside her. She wiped at her face and focused on the clock. *A little after three in the morning.* "This is Sheriff Fitzsimmons."

"Sheriff, this is the Comm Center. Deputy Ryker is out at Granger's impound yard with a silent alarm. I've got a domestic going on at the other end of the county that the state police are handling. I'd call Chief Deputy Lewis, but we don't have any notification that she's back on road duty."

The short night of sleep made her eyes feel as if they were full of sand as she rose from the bed. "No, she's not. Let Daniel know I'm on my way. I'll be there in twenty or less."

"We'll advise him."

Chance hung up and stepped into her jeans. She pulled on one of her long-sleeve T-shirts and searched for a pair of socks in her drawer.

"What's wrong?" Jax rolled over and sat up, brushing the hair back off her face.

"Daniel's out on a call with no available backup. I'll be home as soon as I can." Chance pulled on her socks and stepped into a pair of tactical boots, zipping up the side. She leaned over and kissed Jax. "Go back to sleep. I'll be back."

"Be careful. I love you."

Chance strode to their bedroom door, sliding her cellphone into her back pocket. "Love you, too."

She made her way down the hall and opened Hunter's room, calling for Zeus. She stared at the sleeping boy for a few seconds, closed the door, and made her way down to her gear closet. She slipped Zeus' vest on before putting on her own, along with her gun belt. Unlocking her gun safe, she pulled her Glock from inside and loaded a few extra magazines into her tactical vest's pouches before jamming a sheriff's department ball cap over her bed head.

"Let's go, partner."

Outside the house, she opened the door to the Suburban and spoke to Zeus, letting him know they were in work mode with his load up order. "Laden."

She drove as quickly as possible to Granger's Wrecker Service, just inside the county line in Red Creek. She spotted Daniel's Tahoe and pulled close. "*Bewaken.*"

Zeus was all business as they exited, reacting to the alert command. Chance pulled her Glock as Daniel came from around her right side with Athena at his heel.

He pointed and spoke in a quiet voice. "I've done a basic perimeter check. The fence has been cut on the back side, near the creek."

"Okay, I've got the code to the small door on the fence over there."

The two officers, with their K9 partners, made their way inside the enclosed area. Three areas would need to be investigated. The building, the tow yard, and the area containing the impounds. Chance pointed to the building and indicated she'd go to the right. Daniel skirted off with Athena to the left as Chance checked to see if the entrance door was locked. Finding it secure, she continued to move around the building, checking all the windows and the locks on the roll-up door. Everything was still locked up. She met Daniel back where they started.

Chance spoke to him in a hushed tone. "We'll let the dogs search the cars in the open lot, then move to the back."

Daniel nodded. "Athena, *reveiren.*"

Chance followed suit, giving the same command for Zeus to search as she moved behind him. Within a few minutes, the dogs had swept the area and looked to their handlers for further instructions.

"Good girl, Athena. Now what, Sheriff?"

Chance smiled at Daniel's use of her formal title. The young man was destined to accomplish a great deal. "Let's move to the outside of the fence where you saw the breech. The fence and gate should hold them as long as we have their exit behind us."

They moved back outside the main gate and worked their way around to the cut in the chain link, both dogs moving quietly with them. Chance gave Daniel the hand signal to indicate she and Zeus would enter first. Zeus moved four feet inside and sniffed the ground. He stood at readied attention as Daniel and Athena made their way in as well. Chance whispered to Zeus the command to seek. If he showed any type of intense interest, she'd decide how to proceed.

She motioned Daniel to her side and whispered her plan to him, pointing him off to the left as she broke right with Zeus. Daniel signaled

Athena and the pair moved off. Chance listened for any out of place sound, metal creaking, glass breaking, or voices that might carry on the warm night air. Zeus stopped and stared into the dark. Chance came to his side and narrowed her eyes. Thirty feet from her was the pickup truck from the accident at Dry Fork. The door was open and the overhead light on. She raised her gun and spoke with authority.

"This is the Sheriff's Department, put your hands where I can see them, or I'll send the dog."

Chance listened carefully but heard no movement. She crept closer with Zeus right beside her. She again announced her presence and her intentions if the suspect didn't come out. Finally, she was close enough to see the entire truck and that there was no one inside.

"Daniel, do you have anything over there?"

"Not a thing. Couldn't have been gone long, Athena is still sniffing the ground." He came to her side, his weapon still in his hand.

"Let's check the rest of the lot, but I think I know what they were after. She grabbed the mic attached to her shoulder. "SD-1 to Comm Center."

"Go ahead, SD-1."

"We've checked the area and need you to make a call to Moe Granger to meet us at his office."

"Received. We'll make the notification."

Chance turned to Daniel. "Whoever it was must have been gone before we got back here. They might have had a lookout who warned them. The truck was in a wreck the other day, and the VIN plates were missing. I found a pistol jammed up under the seat that someone forgot to grab when they fled the scene. Taylor is supposed to start the investigation when she comes back today."

Daniel walked around the rear of the truck. "It's got one of those sovereign citizen stickers on it."

"Exactly. The wreck was close to one of those residents we have the information on. We have no proof it belongs to them, so we need more information. I'm hoping when Moe gets here, he can check his surveillance cameras and get us a better idea of who we're looking for."

"He doesn't live far from here, so it shouldn't take long. I'm going to get some photos of the cut in the fence."

"Good idea. I want to get this truck fingerprinted and get them run through the system. Maybe we'll get a hit."

"I'm up for it if you're willing to trust me."

Chance walked up to Daniel and put her hand on his shoulder. It was time for her to show him she was much more than his godmother. "Daniel, if I didn't believe in you, you wouldn't be working for me. I want this done right. We're going to pull this inside, lock it up, and come here in the daylight to dust it. I'd like you to take the lead on completing that."

Daniel beamed. "I won't let you down."

"Not even a concern of mine." The headlights from a vehicle illuminated part of the yard. "That must be Moe. I'll go fill him in. Take some pictures with your department cellphone and meet me at the building in a few minutes."

Daniel nodded and set about completing his assigned task as Chance and Zeus walked away. She stood on the other side of the gate as it slowly moved out of place after Moe hit a remote to unlock it from his truck. Once he was inside the lot, he stepped out.

"You had a feeling something like this would happen, didn't you? I should have taken the time to put it inside, but I've been so busy, I just didn't get to it."

Chance pushed her hat back. "Not your fault, Moe. I'd like to see if we can get it in now. They ransacked the truck. I'm pretty sure they didn't find what they were looking for. Once we secure it, we'll show you where they made entry."

For the next hour, Chance helped Moe move vehicles to be able to accommodate the Silverado and shore up the fence where the perpetrator had cut an opening. When they'd accomplished that, they checked the surveillance tape. The camera caught a tall individual with his face obscured by a mask. The individual continually looked back toward the cut in the fence, leading her to believe there had been an accomplice. Chance would need time to study the footage for any subtleties or identifying characteristics. With a copy of the footage in hand, Daniel and Chance went back into service. It was almost six in the morning. She had enough time to go home, shower, and spend some time in her office. It was more important than ever to get Taylor started on chasing down the truck's current owner and the weapon found inside, likely the item that prompted the break-in. Soft yellow light poured from the kitchen window when she pulled into her driveway. "Home sweet home, Zeus. Let's go see who's up."

***

Jax stood at the door as Chance and Zeus made their way up the steps. She held a cup of coffee for Chance in one hand and her own in the other. Chance stepped in and pulled at the Velcro of her vest.

Jax moved close, took off Chance's hat, and kissed her. "Morning. Everything okay?"

Chance pulled the ballistic protection over her head and set it against the door. She took the steaming cup. "No one got hurt, that's all that matters. I've got footage, but it will need more analysis. I'll give that to Taylor when I go in. Hunter still asleep?"

Jax nodded. "I checked on him when I got up. I'll let him sleep as long as he can. Do you want anything for breakfast?"

"No, just the coffee. I'm going to grab a shower and head to the office." Chance placed her weapon in the safe, then leaned over and kissed Jax. "Want to join me?"

Jax raised an eyebrow and smirked. "If you're on a tight schedule, I don't think my showering with you will help you get to the office."

"True, but it would be worth it."

"Go." Jax pointed in the direction of the bathroom.

Chance sipped her coffee and saluted. She pointed to the monitor on her way up the stairs. "Check that out."

What Jax saw warmed her heart. The Belgian Malinois was once again curled up beside Hunter. She went to the pantry and grabbed a box of Pop-tarts. Chance was partial to the frosted strawberry variety. Jax was determined to send her off with something to eat. Her wife was always going a hundred miles an hour, running on coffee and adrenaline. The only thing that slowed her down was family. For that, Jax was grateful. It was heartwarming to watch her take a horse ride with Hunter or to see them throw a baseball during a simple game of catch.

She'd never dared to imagine these small moments she was privileged to witness, and it wasn't something she'd ever take for granted. The day would be long and busy with the school visit and the parenting classes required by Child Protective Services. *It will all be worth it.* Jax pulled the Pop-tarts out of the toaster and fixed Chance's travel mug of coffee. Fifteen minutes later, Hunter came into the room holding onto Zeus' back and rubbing his eyes. Chance was right behind him. She signed as she spoke to Jax. *"Look who I found."* She ruffled Hunter's hair, and the small boy went over and pulled the measuring cup from Zeus' food container and dropped food into the bowl. Zeus looked at him expectantly.

Hunter patted Zeus' head and made the sign for him to eat. Zeus obediently did so, and Hunter climbed onto his stool at the breakfast bar.

Jax set a cup of juice in front of him. *"Good sleep?"*

He nodded, then took a sip before licking his lips with a smile. She pulled two more Pop-tarts out of the toaster for Hunter, before wrapping the other two in a paper towel. She handed them and the travel mug to Chance, as she came out of her gear closet dressed and armed for her day. "Breakfast on the go."

Chance kissed her and took the offered meal in one hand. She tickled Hunter on the way by, giving him the *"I love you"* sign. "Be good, you two. I'll call when I'm on my way home."

Jax watched her out the window as she strode to her vehicle with Zeus. *And another day has begun.*

***

Chance drove to the office, her thoughts on her family. "We're pretty lucky, Zeus." He barked in agreement. She'd told Daniel that she'd go with him to fingerprint the truck, but there were other things more important in her life. The time with her family was of greater importance when she had qualified people to turn to. He'd understand. She'd make a call to Randy and ask if he'd go to the garage and assist so that she could return home sooner.

Once at the office, Penny greeted her with a smile. "Good morning, Sheriff. Nice to see you. Can I get you anything?"

"Good morning, boss. Can you call Randy and put him through to me in about twenty minutes? I need to give your half unit her assignment for the day."

Penny nodded. "As concerned as I am for her, I'm thankful she's back to work. I swear the two of you are cut from the same cloth. Downtime for you doesn't exist. On the plus side, your godson has started sleeping through the night."

Chance beamed. "I miss that little guy. The other day, Hunter asked if Jace liked Legos. I get the feeling those two will be best friends like Daniel and Kendra."

Penny handed Chance a stack of messages. "I hope so. Now go, you've got a tight schedule and your wife has given me strict orders to get you out of here before noon."

"Don't worry, I'm planning on it." Chance saluted. She checked through her messages as she and Zeus made their way down the hall to Taylor's office. Zeus immediately went to greet Midas.

Taylor looked up. "Morning, Sheriff. I heard you had a late night, or should I say early morning."

Chance rubbed a hand down her face. "I think someone finally remembered they'd left that gun in that wreck. I'm going to have Daniel and Randy fingerprint that truck from the accident the other day. Whoever broke into Granger's only seemed to be interested in that one vehicle. I need you to start hunting down the owners of both the truck and the gun from under the seat." Chance pointed to the opened box on Taylor's desk that had the .38 zip-tied to it. "The serial numbers were scratched off but see what you can do. You should have pictures of the vehicle identification number from Harley. The plates and identifying stamps were missing from the easily accessible places, but no one bothered to get rid of the one on the engine block. Here is the DVD of the security footage at Granger's yard. Maybe you can find some enhancement that will give us a better view. The guy's got a mask on, but you never know."

"I've been running down that logo and receipt from the jacket you found. Hopefully, we can identify some players on this before it escalates any more. I'm going to be making calls about the information from the truck. You didn't need to make a trip to the office this morning. You've got important business at home, and you know, we have these things called phones." Taylor held her cellphone up.

Chance laughed. "I know. I'd just like to watch you work it out for a bit."

Taylor pointedly looked at her. "That's fine, but once you leave here, I want you to concentrate on nothing but your family. Your life is changing. Enjoy every step of it instead of worrying about this place. You have good people. Let them do their job. None of us will let you down; you can count on that."

Chance nodded and stared at her friend and most trusted coworker. Taylor and Penny had waited a long time to add Jace to their family. Now she stood at the precipice of having her own. Taylor's advice wasn't lost on her. The few things she needed to handle couldn't wait, but the rest of it could. She was looking at the printout Taylor handed her when Penny came in.

Taylor had done a bit more research into the name they'd gotten off the vehicle identification number. "Paul Leonard, of Springfield,

Missouri, purchased the vehicle in 2017. Unfortunately, after 2018, there are no indications that he still lived at the location listed. The vehicle showed nothing in the system for current registration tags. I'm going to focus on finding the name of the property owner of the address where it was last registered." She shifted in her seat. "If I can locate that individual, he might have a forwarding address for the former tenant. It's a long shot, but at least it's something. Frustrating."

"Okay, I need to talk with Randy. I'll call you later. Thanks for taking this on." Chance left, confident she'd placed the investigation in the right hands. "Time to do what I need to and head home."

***

Hours later, Taylor pushed back from her computer and rubbed a hand across her face. "Damn frustrating."

Penny walked in and put a sandwich down in front of Taylor. "What's frustrating? Why don't you take a break and eat? You've been at it nonstop since you got here. Are you making any headway?"

"There was a reason I didn't go into cybercrimes. My investigative skills on the computer are underwhelming."

"Somehow I doubt that. How can I help?"

Taylor's stomach growled like a hungry animal at the smell of the BLT. She took a bite and chewed as Penny pulled a chair up beside her.

"Seriously, let me help run things down. I'm pretty good at tracing ownership, tax parcels, and the like. It's part of what I do for Chance when it comes to tax liens or property disputes."

Taylor handed Penny a printout. "I'm trying to run down that guy, Paul Leonard. He's the last person listed as the owner of that wrecked truck."

Penny smiled and slid a brownie across to Taylor.

Taylor finished the sandwich quickly and grabbed the brownie. "Why didn't you tell me you had brownies?"

Penny glared at her. "Because you are worse than a kid. You'd have eaten it first and left half the sandwich on the plate. What about the receipt?"

Taylor took a drink of the cold coffee she'd been sipping on for the last hour. "Those are a bit harder to run down. I need to get a subpoena to get information on the card owner. It's going to be tricky. It will be easier if I can determine the vehicle or this gun has been used in the commission of a crime. Everything I'm reading says Taurus released this particular gun in January of this year, so the records are easier to narrow down."

"What if we worked it backward?"

"What do you mean?"

"If the gun is newly released on the market, then maybe there is a way to drill down in sales or registration information to see if any were sold in the city or county of the address on the truck. I'm assuming you've already run Paul's name for guns that might be registered to him?"

Taylor nodded. "No weapons registered to Paul, though I'm not surprised. From what I can find, he was convicted of selling illegal substances in 2002. That alone would have prevented him from ever being able to legally purchase a firearm or have it registered in his name." Taylor pushed back in her chair and ran a line of connective thought. "I still think the key is to figure out where he went if he left Springfield and somehow see if this gun ties to him." She pointed to the cardboard box.

Penny picked up Taylor's phone and handed the receiver to her. "How about we call up to the 911 center and talk with Pam? There's nobody better at the teletype. Give her the parameters and let her run with it." Penny stood and grabbed the plate she'd brought the sandwich in on.

"She's been running the info I've given her already. I'll explain what I need and tell her to explore every avenue. Thanks for the advice and lunch. It's nice to bounce things off you."

Penny placed a kiss on her cheek. "That's the benefit of being married to someone who understands."

Taylor clasped her hands. "It absolutely is. Is Jace with his omas?"

"Yes, I think he likes being with them as much as he does us. I enjoy knowing he's safe."

"So do I. I don't think your dad wanted to leave his little buddy."

Penny sat down in her lap. "No, he didn't, and neither did Mom. It's amazing how far she's come. They say grandkids will do that to you."

Taylor rubbed Penny's back. "I wouldn't have believed it until I saw it. I hope things go smoothly for Hunter's adoption. It will kill Chance and Jax if they can't keep him."

"It'll be devastating for Hunter. He's so attached to them both. Fingers crossed that the school visit goes well for them. I know it's weighing on Jax's mind. She called me twice about making sure Chance's schedule is clear."

"Okay, let's get back to work finding this gun's owner before something else happens. I got a few prints, and Daniel just texted me that he and Randy are finished up at Granger's. Let's hope we get something off the truck that will tie everything together."

Penny stood and stretched her back. "Okay. Email me that name and address information. I'll do some digging on my end."

Taylor winked at her wife. "You got it, partner."

***

Taylor concentrated on getting the fingerprints ready to go off for identification. Once everything had been properly labeled and packaged for the state crime lab, she set it to the side. "Now it'll be up to the lab folks." The courier service would pick up the package and deliver it to Charleston for examination. If prints off the gun or truck came back with a person of interest or were linked to a crime, there might be the need for testing through the National Integrated Ballistics Information Network. NIBIN would identify if the gun had been used in the commission of a crime. Matches could be made off the rifling pattern the gun barrel created on fired bullets. Each small nick or imperfection was as individualized as a fingerprint.

She likened this type of investigation to watching dominoes fall. Once the first one was set in motion, each finding could progressively trigger the next in a chain reaction. Hopefully, one of them would lead to the answers they were seeking. Penny had located the property owner for the house Paul Leonard had rented. She had a name and number to call for an individual who owned several other rental properties. There was another line Taylor wanted to pursue first.

Let's see who you are Paul Leonard. She turned her attention to making calls to Springfield, Missouri to inquire as to whether Mr. Leonard had been involved in any incidents beyond the ones on record. She dialed the number for the Green County Sheriff's Department and spoke with the receptionist. Within minutes, she was put through to Sergeant Arnold Keith in Investigations. Once Taylor had explained the basics, she waited for him to search their files.

"Let me see what I can find. This computer is so antiquated, I'll be retired before it spits out the answer. So beyond wrecking a vehicle, why are you looking for this guy?"

Taylor rubbed her forehead and looked over the notes she had. "Paul is the last owner of the vehicle involved. My sheriff found a pistol jammed up under the seat, serial numbers missing. The truck was broken into while it was in the impound lot. We're guessing they were coming back for the gun. The truck also has some sovereign citizen propaganda on it."

"We had a confrontation with that bunch of nut jobs, not too long ago. Fanatics. If you've got them in your backyard, take them seriously. They'll slap a lien on your home, and you'll never even know it. There have been some violent incidents with them not too far from here."

Taylor scribbled on her notes. "One of our natural resource officers had a run-in with one of them over a fishing license."

"You probably found Paul's record in the system. From what I can see, we've had a few run-ins with him that didn't necessarily result in charges. Tax liens on his parent's property. We ended up evicting him out of the house."

Taylor looked at the booking photo from 2002. "If there are more recent photos of him than his early booking photo for the narcotics sentence or the last driver's license he had, I'd appreciate you passing them on."

"I'd have to look through our local records. Right now, I'm not seeing any."

Taylor continued down her list of questions for the officer. "I know this is going to be odd, but the pistol I have is pretty unique. We haven't been able to run it down. I was hoping you might have something on it. I'd like to forward photos of the gun. There are some pretty intricate carvings on it."

"We've got a good database our gang task force has put together. Go ahead and send it. I'll check with them."

"I appreciate it, Sergeant." He gave Taylor his email and they discussed a few more details before disconnecting the call. She looked at the clock. She'd been working at her desk for six hours without moving much, other than to take Midas out and get those fingerprints on their way. Her officers had come in and out, and she'd fielded several phone calls with questions. She was grateful for the investigation as it made her feel useful even without being on the road. She picked up a picture of Jace and Penny in their backyard. There had never been a time in Taylor's life that she'd been so settled. All the pieces were in place, and for that, she was at peace with the things she couldn't fix, like her relationship with her brother. She looked at the burns on her hands and shuddered at the thought of what could have happened. Midas put his head on her knee as if feeling her unrest.

"It's all good, boy. I can't thank you enough for dragging my ass out of that fire. I couldn't have done it without you."

Midas nuzzled her hand and put a paw on her leg.

"I know. It's time to go home and see your buddy, Jace. Let's go get Mom and get out of here."

A noise from the door made Taylor look up.

Penny grabbed Taylor's Stetson off the hook. "I think that's an excellent idea. I'm all finished up for the day. Maggie said she'd meet us at our place."

Taylor stood and noticed the stiffness in her back. "I've sat for too long today. How about we get Jace and go for a walk?"

Penny stood in the doorway. "Perfect."

Taylor took the Stetson and seated it on her head as they headed out. "Yes, you are. Let's go home."

Chapter Ten

JAX SAT BESIDE CHANCE on the other side of Mrs. Macguire's desk. "So currently you have no qualified interpreter?"

Chance covered Jax's hand with hers. "There has to be a solution."

Mrs. Macguire took off her glasses and tossed them on the desk. "Our kindergarten was four hours last year and he had an interpreter as per his Individual Education Plan. the Individual with Disabilities Education Act requires that we accommodate students with needs. The kids were only doing four-hour days last year. This year, it will be a full school day. I've put in a request for a full-time tutor interpreter. I've yet to hear whether we've found a qualified applicant."

Jax sat up straighter. "School starts soon. What is he supposed to do if we can't find one? Sit in a corner and color while he falls farther and farther behind? The deck is already so stacked against him as it is."

"Mrs. Fitzsimmons, I share your outrage. Without question, I'm looking for specialized teachers to provide assistance to my students with need.

Chance stood and began to pace. "What if we found an interpreter that could help him strengthen his ability to communicate and tutor him? Would that be allowed?"

Mrs. Macguire turned to her computer and began typing. "If the individual is qualified, she'd be a candidate for a full-time position here."

Chance's gun belt creaked as she shifted from foot to foot. "When I first met Hunter, we started taking some basic sign-language classes from a woman who may be able to do it or know someone who can. We also have feeler emails out to recent graduates that my wife is waiting to hear back about." She leaned forward. "In a few days, Hunter has an appointment to have his hearing loss evaluated. We're working on hearing aids. We have little information as to why he doesn't already have some."

Jax's stomach was turning. She stared blankly at the cinderblock walls of the office. The cream-colored background was as washed out as she felt. How could there be so few resources available to someone who would never have a chance without them? Not on my watch, and not to my son. "Mrs. Macguire, we're going to do everything we can to help Hunter be happy and successful in life. I have little doubt that you're going to be part of that plan. We can work together to make that happen."

The principal clasped her hands on her desk. "Mrs. Fitzsimmons, my job is to make sure that every student succeeds, every single one. I'll be Hunter's advocate in every way. I put no student above another. I have an entire school full of children who have been born to addicts, some addicted themselves. I have an entire school full of children with any number of challenges." She ticked them off. "Poverty, addiction, sexual molestation, physical abuse, mental abuse, and that's just one hand. I have little doubt you've dealt with many of the parents, Sheriff. Hunter was among them, and it's my understanding that only through a tragedy did he escape. Most of the others never know anything else. Some are lucky enough to have a grandparent who can take them in. Hunter has you, the other two hundred students in this county would be lucky if they had advocates who cared even a sliver of what you do. Let's work together to give him the absolute best chance possible."

Jax held her hand out toward Mrs. Macguire. "Let's do it."

***

Jax laughed as she hugged her dad goodbye. "You can't tell that he's excited to spend the evening with you. We'll be back around eight. Will you be all right until then?"

Hunter was tugging on his hand. "We'll be fine. We've got the picture board. Go, I've got this." Mike stepped into the house as Hunter pulled him back through the door. "Go. We've got guy stuff to do."

Jax waved and smiled. "Okay, you two. Have a good time." She turned and got into the 4Runner, where Chance was waiting.

"He loves your dad."

Jax put her seatbelt on. "Dad loves him, so it's very mutual."

They drove to Elkins, arriving fifteen minutes before their class was to start. Chance pulled in next to the only other car at the DHHR office.

"Are you ready for this?" Chance looked at her and folded her hand around Jax's.

"As ready as I'll ever be."

Once inside, they signed in on the clipboard beside the door. A woman stood off to the side, stapling papers together. She looked up at them and narrowed her eyes. "Just have a seat over there." Her words were slightly clipped.

An uneasiness came over Chance as she sat down in one of the folding chairs that had been arranged in a semicircle. Jax sat beside her. Two more people walked through the door and signed in. Chance listened as the woman greeted the other couple with a markedly different tone and attitude. The man and woman sat a few chairs away from them. The door banged open, and a harried-looking woman rushed through, weighed down with two boxes of some kind of food and several file folders.

"Sorry, sorry."

Chance jumped up and grabbed one of the boxes of doughnuts. The pile nearly blocked the woman's vision. "I've got it."

"Thank you. That would have been a disaster."

"Happy to help. I'm Chance."

The woman looked at her full hands. "Sorry, I'd shake your hand, but mine are a bit occupied. I'm Sherry Trask, it's nice to meet you. We'll do a bit more of a formal introduction in a minute. If you could just set those down on that table with the coffee carafe, I'd be grateful."

Chance took the other box of doughnuts off the top of the stack. "I'll be more than happy to."

Sherry rushed up front and set down the rest of her items before stepping over to the woman stapling papers. The woman scowled and looked at her watch. It was still a few minutes before six. *This should be interesting.* Chance took her seat beside Jax and leaned in. "Something tells me the woman with the stapler has a bit of an attitude."

Over the next few minutes, everyone in the group introduced themselves. Wells and Tera Eckle were from Elkins. The scowling woman was Beverly Moss, one of the CPS caseworkers. Sherry passed out the paperwork Beverly held out to her. As she went, Sherry talked about the purpose of the classes and why they were a necessary part of preparing families for the possibility of taking a child into their homes full time.

Beverly spoke up. "Most of the kids in the system have some ADHD diagnosis or some other trendy psychological babble that excuses their bad behavior. Don't expect that you'll be fostering some little angel. Many of them will end up in juvenile detention or adult prison, given their biological parentage."

Sherry abruptly interrupted Beverly before she could continue. "What Beverly is trying to say is you have an opportunity as a foster parent to break the chain of emotional upheaval these kids have been living in. With love, time, and a lot of patience, we can keep these kids from becoming the next generation of adults to end up in correctional institutions."

Beverly continued with another snide comment. "That and medication."

Chance watched Sherry's jaw clench. "Moving on. The papers I gave you contain a course outline for the next few classes on the pre-service orientation. Let's get—"

Beverly interrupted again. "Some of you skipped this and were magically moved through the system outside of agency norms."

Chance felt the hair on the back of her neck stand up as she looked up from the paper. "Mrs. Moss, I will assume you are talking about us. I assure you, there were special circumstances to how things went down. My mothers have a long history of foster service and were able to guide us through the process. We went through all of the background checks, home visits, and screenings. If you are implying that we skipped any of that, I'd be more than happy to show you my law enforcement background credentials along with my federal ones. Now, if we have that out of the way, I'm sure Mrs. Trask has important information that we'll need to continue with our fostering, as well as our plan for adoption." Chance stared Beverly down.

Beverly scowled again. "Yes, I'm well aware of how you ended up with a child in a home that, by certain opinions, is less than suitable."

Chance held up a hand to stop Beverly before she could continue. "Mrs. Moss, I'd like to schedule an appointment with your supervisor at the earliest convenience. I'll be more than happy to discuss things that are less than suitable. If you're quite through, I'd like to continue this training so we can go home and care for the child who has been placed with us. His bedtime is at eight, and I'd like to be home for that." Chance put the papers on the chair beside her and crossed her arms as she glared at Beverly Moss.

"Beverly, thank you for covering for me as I ran late from that home visit, but I'm here now and capable of handling this training on my own. I'll see you tomorrow."

Chance sat back in her chair. Her jaw clenched as Beverly steamed. Jax put a hand on her thigh and lightly squeezed.

Beverly turned to Sherry. "We'll discuss this tomorrow."

Sherry stood taller, and Chance watched as she looked directly at Beverly. "Yes, we will, with April and Mr. Franks."

Beverly glared for a few seconds more before storming off down the hall and slamming the door.

"Okay, now that we've removed a few of the distractions, let's continue." Sherry stepped to a whiteboard with a marker in her hand. "I'll be happy to share supervisory names and numbers at the end of class."

Despite her attempts to focus on the bullet points Sherry wrote on the board, a prickling sensation at the base of Chance's spine made her uneasy. She tried to banish Beverly's harsh words and thought about how she would deal with the situation. *And I will deal with it. You can count on that.*

***

Chance held the door for Jax. She climbed in and buckled her seatbelt, then stared out the window. Her mind wouldn't shut off. Her brain was on overload with the information on Hunter's school, a lawsuit involving her ex-wife, an endurance ride that she'd likely have to take the lead on, and now, a disgruntled CPS worker. Jax knew she was close to her breaking point. If not for the woman who'd just covered her cheek with her hand, she'd likely cry.

"I promise, we will get that taken care of tomorrow. The bad thing is, she won't likely be our only stumbling block." Chance fastened her own seatbelt and started the 4Runner.

"I know. I just wasn't expecting it. With so many kids looking for good homes, I can't understand the attitude. Does she have a beef with Maggie and Dee?"

"I don't know, but it certainly sounded like it. I promise, I will find out. Let's go home and see our boys. Your dad's probably exhausted." Chance started the vehicle and pulled out of the parking lot.

"Dad's having the time of his life, trust me. He has the opportunity to be a real grandpa with Hunter. With Jessie and Jackie, he had to accept the role of father within my mother's expectations. With Hunter, he's able to enjoy the simple pleasure of spoiling a grandchild." Jax interlaced her fingers with Chance's and watched the traffic out the windshield.

"I can see the gears grinding in your head. What else is on your mind?"

"I think it's everything. With Matt's injury, I need to step up my leadership role with the Saddlebacks, but that takes time from Hunter.

Then there's that stupid lawsuit. I should hear from my attorney this week."

Jax relaxed into the way Chance's thumb caressed the back of her hand. The simple touch of understanding and caring made all the difference.

"I think you are under far too much pressure. How about, tomorrow night, I invite the moms squared over and we grill out? Kendra and Brandi are coming home and will be here all week. We'll have a relaxing evening with the family. You call Uncle Marty and invite him as well."

"That sounds perfect. I'm glad the girls will be here. Brandi is going to help at the clinic. For now, let's go home. I want to snuggle in with Hunter before he goes to bed. His mind is probably going a mile a minute too."

"I like the sound of that plan."

Jax put her head back on the seat. It felt as if her past and her future were colliding. She only hoped the fallout would leave her intact. *One day at a time, Jax. One day at a time.*

***

Chance listened as Taylor filled her in on her investigation into the abandoned vehicle and the recovered weapon. Little movement had been made in the case. Her workday was nearly over, and she was frustrated they couldn't pin down the gun or find Paul Leonard.

"Keep on that. Our answers are there, just keep digging. I'm worn out after the meetings with the county commission and a concerned citizens group on the mountain. We fought tooth and nail to get that license plate reader installed."

"I know they hate it, but we've found one stolen vehicle and been able to give information on a missing child because of that reader. If you aren't doing anything wrong, then why be worried about it? It just doesn't make any sense."

"I'm right there with you. For now, I'm headed over to Tuesing's to get some fresh ground beef for tonight's cookout. The moms squared are bringing Hunter home when they come over. Brandi and Kendra are in, so I need to get moving. I'd hoped Uncle Marty and Jax's dad were going to be able to come, but those two have a card game at Marty's with some friends. I'll see you tomorrow." Chance waved as she and Zeus headed out.

There was just enough time to go home and get the grill started. Her mom had also promised she'd take care of the side dishes, which would take a load off Jax's shoulders. She was running slightly behind because of the extensive hip surgery on an English mastiff. That surgery was one of the reasons Kendra and Brandi were home.

Chance pulled up to see Hunter running through the yard dragging a kite. Zeus whined inside the vehicle. "Hang on. I'll let you out."

Chance put the vehicle in park and hit the automatic door to let Zeus out. Hunter immediately dropped to his knees and wrapped his arms around the dog.

Kendra stepped over and took an armload of groceries from the passenger seat. "He's such a trip to watch. You'd think he was one of Zeus' pups."

"Sometimes, I think he is. Good to see you. I miss you." Chance wrapped her sister in a one-armed hug as they made their way up the walk.

"Brandi's been wanting to work some with Jax. She's been so pumped about today's surgery, and tomorrow there's a round of barn calls on tap."

"Well, whatever brought you home, I'm glad to see you."

There was a comfortable silence between them for a few minutes as they watched Hunter put his kite on the porch and grab the tennis ball to throw for Zeus. They stepped into the kitchen and found their moms. Maggie was cutting up fruit into a bowl, while Dee opened a bag of tiny marshmallows. Chance stole a kiss on Maggie's cheek and set the bags down on the counter. She popped a marshmallow in her mouth on her way to the fridge for a beer. She eyed Kendra closely and watched her crack her knuckles. *Uh oh.* That spelled trouble. She saw that Dee noticed as well.

She caught Dee's eye and pointed to the hamburger and made a motion like she was making patties. Dee nodded.

"Grab a beer, Bullseye. Let's go watch my dog wear that boy out."

They made it outside and stood with their arms on the railing, watching Zeus and Hunter chase each other around the yard.

"Spill it."

Kendra turned her head quickly to Chance. "Spill what?"

"Whatever it is that you're too nervous to tell me."

"I'm not nervous."

Chance turned toward her sister. "You never were good at lying as a kid, so don't start now. You're cracking your knuckles, dead giveaway." She watched Kendra's shoulders drop and took a drink of her beer.

"You can't tell Mom yet."

"Which one?" Chance couldn't help the smirk that formed.

"Either." Kendra took a swig of her beer and set it on the railing, turning the bottle around. "I'm graduating early. I have to report to Glynco, Georgia in thirty days. I've been accepted into the US Marshals."

Chance felt her stomach drop. She'd known it was coming; she just didn't know how bad it would hurt to hear that Kendra's first law enforcement job wouldn't be working for her. She took a deep breath. "I'm proud of you. Taylor will be stoked."

Kendra put her head down and smiled. "Thanks. I had several offers: ATF, FBI, and a few other three-letter agencies. One of which I didn't even begin to consider, because I don't want to disappear into the dark and live a life of complete deception."

Chance knew she was talking about life as a CIA agent. There was a need for people who could become someone else and delve into international espionage. Kendra didn't have the personality for it. She was far too honest with her feelings and emotions. Chance knew the Marshals' academy would change her, give her an edginess that didn't exist right now. Kendra would be an outstanding officer, and Chance was grateful that her chief deputy had enough contacts within the organization that she'd always be aware of how Kendra was doing.

Chance could feel her heart soaring and breaking simultaneously. It was as if each beat was on an alternate plane of reality. "Take a walk with me."

As the two walked along the fence where the horses were grazing, they came upon Hunter standing on the bottom rail, looking through the slats. They stopped beside him and watched the three horses graze contentedly. "Any idea where you'll try and get stationed?"

Kendra put a foot on the wooden slat. "Part of it depends on where there is an opening. Brandi isn't finished with school, and I'd like to stay close to home. Pittsburgh isn't that far away, and neither is the Eastern Panhandle. I know Brandi wants to work with Jax, and I won't take that away from her. I'm hoping maybe a position will open up in Elkins or Clarksburg. This is home, and it's where I want to settle down."

Chance put a hand on Hunter's head. "Bullseye, this will always be your home. I only wish I had a position open for you."

Kendra dropped her head. "Me too. You never know, someday I might change my mind."

Glenny came over and nuzzled Hunter's hand. He reached through the fence and scratched between her eyes.

"I couldn't be prouder of you. Feels like you've grown up on me overnight." Chance looked down at Hunter. "I can remember when you were about his size. My God, you were a handful."

Kendra snorted. "I guess I was. All my life, I've wanted to be just like you. I thought you were a superhero."

"You're going to be a better officer than I've ever been. You're smarter than I am, and you'll avoid the pitfalls I've jumped into. I've watched you puzzle things out in your mind for years. You are exactly what any department head wants on their team."

Kendra faced her. "If that's so, it's because I've had one hell of an example to follow. It's all I've ever wanted to do. I know you did a few other things before you settled into law enforcement, but all I ever wanted to be was a cop."

Kendra reached down and knocked on the fence Hunter was leaning on. He turned to her and she signed. *"Want a piggyback ride?"*

Hunter's face lit up, as Kendra turned to let him jump on her back. "And Chance?"

"Yeah?"

"You're a great mom. Something else you were always meant to be. It just took you a bit longer to get there than most people."

"Thanks, Bullseye." She turned a bit to Hunter and signed. *"It's time to eat."*

* * *

The Fitzsimmons crew sat on the deck after dinner, watching Hunter chase lightning bugs with Zeus. Jax took in a deep breath of the late summer breeze and leaned against Chance as they sat in an oversized Adirondack chair. Warm air was blowing through the trees around them, stirring up the smell of grass clippings and hay from the barn area. It had been a long but fulfilling day working with Brandi at her side. She sat with Chance's arms enveloping her as the in-laws sipped coffee at the picnic table.

Maggie set her mug down. "So, tell us how the visit with the principal went."

Jax smiled at her mother-in-law. Maggie was a devoted grandmother, who she knew had been busting to know what went on yesterday. "We found out a few things that shocked us."

Chance joined in. "It seems that last year, Hunter only had an interpreter for a few hours a day."

Dee squinted at her. "Was it a funding issue, or did they not have anyone available?"

Jax leaned forward. "Both. We've got to address that and soon. We've got feelers out for a full-time tutor experienced in dealing with children with hearing loss."

Chance rubbed Jax's back. "We also have an appointment to have his hearing evaluated and get hearing aids if possible. If they can amplify what hearing he might have, there's no telling what his potential is."

Jax watched the young boy sit beside Zeus and stare up at the sky. "We'll make it happen," she whispered.

"What'd you say, love?" Chance looked puzzled.

Jax shook her head. "I said we'll make it happen. Whatever he needs to be as healthy and happy as he can be. When he starts school, we might occasionally need help picking him up. I'm not comfortable with him riding the bus yet. My dad has offered to bring him home. Since I have Bill on staff, I'll be able to take him to school in the mornings."

Maggie shifted on her seat and looked out at Hunter in the yard. "You know Dee and I will help however you need. One of us can watch Jace and the other can pick Hunter up."

Jax leaned back into Chance's embrace in sheer wonder of the family she'd married into. "Whatever it takes."

＊

Long shadows stretched across the ground as Maggie and Dee said their goodnights. Brandi and Kendra were sleeping over so Brandi could ride into work with Jax. Kendra volunteered to stay with Hunter the next day. She'd promised him a horse ride that made it nearly impossible to get him settled after his bath. While Chance and Jax took care of Hunter, Kendra fed the horses and Brandi straightened up the kitchen. Once everything had been secured for the evening, the adults settled in to watch an episode of *Wynonna Earp*.

With her legs stretched out on an ottoman and Jax's head in her lap, Chance leaned back on the couch. She wasn't much of a television fan, but she did enjoy a show with a kick-ass female lead. As the show ended, Chance turned to her sister. "That show is just weird."

"Yeah, but she's hot." Kendra yawned.

Brandi rolled her eyes as she shook her head. "What time are we leaving, Jax?"

"As long as we're on the road by eight, we'll have plenty of time to be over at the Hauser farm. They have a herd of fifty dairy cattle that need checkups. You brought your muck boots, right?" Jax stood as well and pulled Chance up behind her.

"They're in the back of the truck. I'll grab them in the morning. Let's go to bed, Ms. She's Hot."

Jax pulled Kendra into a hug. "You'd better do some ass-kissing. Word to the wise. If you keep saying things like that, you'll find yourself sleeping on the couch. Love you. Thanks for watching Hunter tomorrow. He's so excited to spend the day with you."

"I'm the excited one. My nephew is one cool little dude. We have secret plans, according to him. I'll keep your advice in mind."

Chance raised an eyebrow. "Secret plans?"

"I'm sworn to secrecy." Kendra pretended to zip her lips, lock them, and throw the key over her shoulder.

Chance made her hands into claws and wiggled her fingers. "You know I have ways to make you talk."

Kendra narrowed her eyes and pointed. "You wouldn't."

"Try me."

Jax smacked Chance. "Like you never had any secrets from your moms."

"Oh, I did, but this is too good to pass up. I haven't tickled her since she was seventeen."

"Not happening, Five Points. I'm so much faster than you." Kendra grabbed Brandi's hand and ran toward the steps.

Chance let her hands drop with a laugh. "She's probably right about that. Sarah and Kristi are a go for a cookout. We haven't seen much of them over the last few months at all. I know Kristi applied to be the school nurse at the high school this year."

"You have barely been on any calls with the rescue squad of late. The last one was to rescue Matt and me." Jax wrapped an arm around Chance's waist.

"I've got a wife, a job, and a child with special needs. Hunter deserves to have two parents who put his needs, all of them, first. Something had to give. I'll go out on the big calls, but I've asked the other officers to step up to run the day-to-day operations while we're in the process of adopting Hunter."

Jax turned to her. This was new information that Chance hadn't even spoken to her about. The rescue squad was a big part of Chance's life. Her skills had helped save the lives of countless tourists and that of their friend, Rhebekka. "Are you sure?"

Chance nodded. "The only thing I've ever been surer of is loving you. Hunter deserves to be the priority. If it's something they need me for, they'll call. For now, I've directed the 911 center to call my second in command. He knows how to reach me if he can't handle it. I've spent years training my people. It's time for them to shine."

Jax stood looking at the woman she loved. Hunter wasn't the only one who had lost a great deal in his life. Chance had been forced to grow up knowing her biological mother died at birth and then losing her father to violence. If you asked Chance, she'd tell you she was blessed in unimaginable ways. She'd landed with people who wanted her and had raised her in a loving home. Jax understood Chance's desire to give Hunter that same opportunity. She was glad to be the other half of that equation. "You're pretty amazing, you know?"

Chance wrapped strong arms around her. "How about we go upstairs, and I show you just how amazing I can be?"

"Let me take those stitches out of your arm, and I'll be more than happy to take you up on that offer, Sheriff."

***

The next morning, Chance, Kendra, and Zeus climbed back in the vehicle after their run. At five thirty the radio was already hopping. Khodi was out on a stolen motorcycle incident, and one of Harley's troopers had come across an alarm going off at one of the schools. Chance listened as Khodi went in service and responded to back up the trooper. She took a long drink of her water while Kendra held Zeus' bowl for him.

"Sounds like the day is ramping up to be busy."

"It's that time of year."

"All the *tourons* will pour in here in a few weeks for that last little taste of summer."

"Let's go home and get ready for it." Zeus barked his agreement, and Chance started her vehicle, reporting in that she was back in service from T2, one of the trails that wound down into the canyon and back up.

"SD-1, you're in service at 05:45. I have a few messages, if you can call me when you get the time. Nothing urgent."

"Received, Comm Center. Give me fifteen." Chance wanted to get home where she could call in from her landline. Cell service in the area was always hit or miss.

"I'm trying to figure out how I'm going to tell moms squared that I'm leaving school early." Kendra stared out the window.

"Bullseye, I don't think that's the part that's going to freak them out." Chance glanced over at her sister.

Kendra leaned back on the headrest and stared out the windshield. "Am I making a mistake? I could apply to an agency that would guarantee to keep me close. Something like the state police, or maybe one of the local police departments."

Chance chose her words carefully. "Kendra, you can be whatever you want to be, wherever you want to be it. There are people I trust in all those departments, but I have to be honest, I think you have greater potential than any of them can offer, even mine. You're one of the smartest women I've ever met. You have quick reflexes, and your mental thought process works like a computer."

Chance tightened her grip on the steering wheel and continued. "You can work through complicated puzzles and word problems with almost freakish ability. It reminds me of Sarah. Any of those departments would be gaining a valuable asset. My one concern is that your abilities would never be used to the fullest. I won't lie and say that if you were on my hiring list, I'd tell you to go work on the federal level. I'd hire you in a split second, but that would be for incredibly selfish reasons. Part of which would be to keep you safe. The truth is, knowing you won't be working with me is a hard pill to swallow."

A few tears made their way down Kendra's cheeks. Chance reached out and squeezed Kendra's hand as they drove. There was no doubt in her mind that her sister was processing all she'd said and would do it over and over. She was going to be a great US Marshal.

Right before they turned into the gravel drive, Kendra said something that nearly broke Chance.

"You know, the US Marshal's badge has five points too. No matter what anyone ever tells me, they will always stand for honor, duty, courage, integrity, and empathy, just like you taught me."

Taylor's words came back to Chance with the force of a sledgehammer. *Those standards aren't just words you've said to her, Chance. They're words you've embedded in her heart and on her spirit.*

She won't forget them, no matter who her training officer is. Chance felt her own tears threaten. "I couldn't be prouder of you, and the moms squared will be too. It's part of what it means to be a Fitzsimmons, no matter where you started your life."

They pulled up to the house and got out. Zeus started his morning perimeter check as they walked up the steps. Kendra stopped her with a hand on her bicep before they went inside. "Thanks, Chance. I mean it."

Chance pulled her sister into a hug. They stood there in an embrace for several minutes, until Chance pushed her away. "Go shower, you stink."

"You don't smell like a spring rain either."

Kendra's smile gave Chance what she was looking for, a break in the tension and emotional overload. Kendra would be okay; they all would.

As they entered the kitchen, they both raised their noses to the smell of coffee and bacon. Brandi and Jax were preparing breakfast and greeted them with smiles and steaming mugs.

Jax kissed Chance and pointed. "Off to the showers with both of you. Breakfast will be ready in twenty minutes. Wake Hunter on your way back down."

Chance saluted. "I've got to make a call first. Love you, thanks for the coffee."

"You're welcome." Jax watched Brandi cup Kendra's cheek. "Everything okay there?" Jax nodded her head in their direction.

"It will be. I'll be back down in a bit." Chance sipped her coffee and headed up the stairs, grateful in the knowledge that it truly would be.

***

Jax stirred the bacon and glanced at Brandi. "She'll be okay, you know."

"Chance told you?"

Jax nodded. "She did. You know you can always talk to me. If anyone will understand, it's me. It's not easy loving what they do but much easier to understand why they do it."

Brandi cracked eggs into a bowl before mixing in milk and cinnamon. As she dipped Texas toast into the mixture, she slowly began to talk. "I'm scared to death, and she's not even in the academy yet. She wants to be on the fugitive apprehension team. One of the marshals from West Virginia died a few years ago, over in Elkins. A lot of people think the Marshals only handle prisoner transfers and witness protection but that's only part of it." She laid the egg-soaked bread in the skillet.

"She's got big dreams, and those dreams include you. Kendra will do everything in her power to come home to you every night. Just like Chance does for us." Jax cut some strawberries and watched for Brandi's reaction.

"How did you do it?"

"Do what?"

"Survive her being shot at?"

Jax wiped her hands on a dishtowel and pulled Brandi into a hug before looking her square in the eye. "I've never been so scared in my life. We weren't even a couple then. What scared me more was not having the opportunity to tell her how much I still loved her." Jax nodded toward the skillet. "Better watch that before it burns."

"Shit!" Brandi turned quickly and grabbed the spatula, using it to flip the golden-brown toast. It sizzled in the skillet.

Jax walked to the refrigerator and pulled out the pure maple syrup. She partially filled a large bowl with hot water before sitting the cold jug in to warm the syrup. "I can tell you this. You live through it by building a firm foundation. You tell her every day how much she means to you so that if that ever happens, she has something to make her fight to stay alive. You lean on those who love her too, and as a family, you act as an anchor for her to hold onto during the storm."

Brandi wiped a tear as she dipped another piece of bread in the egg mixture. "I'm so grateful to have you and Chance to help me deal with my fear."

"Maggie and Dee love you too, and they will be right there. There's no one stronger than those two. They lived through Chance's burns and all the other close calls she's had. Lean on them. When's Kendra telling them?"

Kendra came down the stairs, running a towel over her head. "Tonight. We're having dinner with them. I can't put it off any longer."

Jax came around the counter and held Kendra's face in the palm of her hand. "Stop worrying. They'll be so proud of you. They've known this was coming. It's just a little earlier than they will be expecting. Chance and I both believe in you, and Hunter thinks you're awesome. What more do you need?"

Chance came down the stairs carrying a sleepy little boy rubbing his eyes. "He sure does. You were the first thing he mentioned when I woke him up. All about the secret plans you two have today." Jax came over and kissed Hunter as she pulled out his chair.

She signed to him as she spoke. *"Juice or chocolate milk?"*

Hunter let a grin escape then made the sign for milk.

"I hope you're hungry."

Hunter yawned as Chance went over to the door and let Zeus in. Hunter immediately got up from the table and went about getting Zeus fresh water and some food. Jax and Chance stood back as they watched the K9 patiently wait on the little boy to give him the sign to eat before he got up and licked Hunter's face. The joyous sound of a child's giggle filled the kitchen as the four adults watched. Zeus gave one more lick, then started eating his breakfast. Hunter came back to the table, wiping at his face. Jax pointed to the sink.

"I'll help you." Kendra signed, then helped Hunter wash his hands in the sink as Brandi took the platter of French toast to the table.

Jax grabbed the bacon and maple syrup. The family ate together before Chance went to the gear closet and began to get ready. She emerged a few minutes later and put Zeus' vest on him. When she placed her Stetson on her head, Jax pulled it back off and kissed her.

"Be careful today, Sheriff." She replaced the Stetson and knocked on the chest plate of Chance's vest. "Remember, there's two of us depending on you to come home."

"That's the plan." Chance went over to Hunter and bent down. *"I'll see you tonight. Love you."*

Hunter wrapped his arms around Chance and hugged her. When he pulled back, Jax watched him look into Chance's eyes. *"Love you."*

The sight nearly broke Jax, but it filled her with a love she'd longed for. "Brandi, we need to get moving too. I need to stop by the clinic and pick up some meds before we go to the farm. Kendra, we'll be back around two."

Kendra ruffled Hunter's hair. "You guys get out of here." She tapped Hunter's chest, then made a motion like pulling a bow. "Hunter and I will clean this up."

Jax smiled. "What was that?" She mimicked Kendra's motions.

Kendra smiled as she carried a plate to the sink. "I read that most people have a single motion with the first letter of their name as their name sign. I started making one like I was pulling back the bow for him using the letter h. It might not stick, but it doesn't hurt to give him something special."

Chance laughed. "I love it. I've got to go. See you later. Let's go to work, Zeus."

The Malinois nosed Hunter's foot on the way by, causing a fit of giggles.

"That goes for me too." Jax walked over and kissed Hunter's cheek. He returned it and signed the sweetest words. *"Love you, Momma J."*

If Jax thought her heart was full before, her cup had just overflowed its rim.

***

Chance had been in her office for four hours, pouring through the never-ending stacks of paperwork on her desk. She remembered that she wanted to firm up the weekend cookout plans. She keyed the speed dial for Sarah and put the phone on speaker as she continued through the stack.

"Hey, Chance."

Chance looked at the phone as if she could see her friend. "Sarah, you okay?" Chance noticed Sarah's voice was rough, as if she'd just woken up.

"It was just a long night."

Chance furrowed her brows. "You've been pulling a lot of midnight shifts lately. I thought, as a supervisor, you mostly worked day shift."

There was a long pause. "I've got a medic out of service. Hanna got stuck with a needle the other day."

"Shit. Is she going to be okay?"

"We're in that wait-and-see period. The patient has to agree to go through a series of tests, but it wasn't one of our fine, outstanding citizens. Let's leave it at that."

"I was calling to confirm the cookout."

"What time? I'm off on Saturday. We've brought on some part-time help to fill in for Hanna while she's on light duty off the truck".

"How about you guys come over anytime around noon? I'm grilling burgers and dogs."

Chance looked up to see Taylor at her door.

"Sounds good. We'll bring some sides and a dessert. Anything Hunter particularly likes?"

Chance smiled. "If you bring something chocolate, he'll be your friend for life. Looking forward to seeing you guys. Get some sleep."

"Can't wait. I was watching some TV and dropped off. I think I'll try to go to bed and get some real rest. Thanks, Chance. I've missed you."

"Same here. See you this weekend."

Taylor came in and sat down in front of her desk. "That didn't sound like a call with Child Protective Services."

"It wasn't. I'm still waiting on that call."

"How about I fill you in with some information on that weapon? Sergeant Arnold Keith from the Green County Sheriff's Department got back to me."

Chance sat forward in her chair. "Really. Did we get a name?"

Taylor wagged her head back and forth. "Sort of. There were two of these particular .38 specials that were sold in Springfield, Missouri, where Paul Leonard was from."

"Please tell me one of them was registered to him?"

"We couldn't get quite that lucky. They were able to contact one owner and confirmed the gun was in his possession. The second was found to be missing or stolen. The owner apparently went to a range for shooting practice with several weapons and accidentally left that particular one at the range. He hadn't reported it stolen, but it can't be accounted for." Taylor flipped through a notebook. "The interesting part was that Paul Leonard was once employed there for about six months. The logo on the hoodie was from the business. He did maintenance work for them, three days a week. The owner let him go after ammo started disappearing."

Chance looked over at her. "They could attribute it to him directly?"

"They started keeping an inventory every night before the guy worked and again after his shift was over. He was the only one on and they were always short. They couldn't prove it was him because the camera in that area was on the fritz. They didn't want trouble, so they told him they had to cut back on staffing. Magically, no more ammo went missing. The last day Paul worked was also when the gun went missing. The owner had no idea the guy had a felony. I also checked with his former landlord. He said he hadn't seen or heard anything from him after he left."

Taylor passed Chance a piece of paper with Paul Leonard's last driver's license picture and the booking photos from earlier years. The two photos were definitely of the same person. The more recent picture showed that he'd beefed up considerably and had more tattoos, including the ones peeking up out of his shirt collar. "Do some social media searches on this guy. See if you can find any pictures of him, even if they are on someone else's page. See that mark on his neck? That looks like a tattoo of those sovereign citizen symbols we saw in class. See if you come up with any hits on known associates."

"Good idea. Sergeant Keith was able to connect with the individual who accidentally left the gun at the range. The guy was able to describe the intricate engraving in great detail along with telling him about the custom grip. I have little doubt this is his gun. It doesn't definitively prove who we're looking for, though it certainly warrants more investigation. I've got Penny printing up some flyers for each of our officers. I plan to have them discretely ask around to see if anyone's seen him. If we get a more current mug shot, we'll add that."

"I'll send it out to Harley as well. Even if he didn't wreck the truck, he's a good candidate for breaking into Granger's Towing. Keep me posted."

"Will do. You want to tell me what else is bothering you?"

Chance sat back and rubbed a hand through her hair. "Shut the door for a minute."

Taylor stood and shut it. "What's up?"

"Kendra leaves for the US Marshal Academy in thirty days."

Taylor sat back down and leaned forward in her chair. "You're kidding me?"

Chance shook her head. "No. She's working on graduating even earlier to finish her degree before she leaves for Georgia."

"I'll be damned."

Chance pointed to Taylor. "You're one of the reasons she applied. She looks up to you and has heard you talk about your time with the agency."

"You're the one she looks up to, but I appreciate being included in that same category. I still have some contacts down there. It's a tough academy, though I have no doubt she'll ace it. I expect she'll be a natural."

Chance blew out a deep breath. Her elbows rested on the arms of her chair, as she steepled her fingers near her lips. "She hasn't told our moms yet. She's watching Hunter today and swears she's telling them tonight."

"You think they'll be unhappy with her choice?"

Chance shook her head. "No, but they aren't ready for her to be an adult. They're just now getting used to her being away at school. They'll also be thinking about what happened over in Elkins when that Marshal was shot."

"That could happen with any law enforcement job. Hell, it's happened to you. We all go after wanted criminals. No matter what agency she ends up with, there will be risks involved."

"I know. I promise not to ask you to call about her every day, but if you'd let me know how she's doing, it will relieve my stress level some."

Chance's desk phone rang, and she picked up the handset. She relaxed, hearing Penny's voice.

"Sheriff, there is a call for you on line two, and can you have Taylor step out here for a minute when you're done with her?" Penny asked.

"Will do. Thanks." She hovered her finger over the line. "Your best half needs you for a minute."

Taylor stood and pointed at the phone. "If that's CPS, try to hold your cool. They're the ones in the hot seat, not you. Don't put yourself there."

Chance grinned. "Thanks for the advice. Now go." Chance pushed the line and watched Taylor leave. "Sheriff Chance Fitzsimmons, how can I help you?" She used her title deliberately to set a tone of authority. Something she rarely did but Beverly Moss' behavior was uncalled for, and Chance planned to let them know that.

"Sheriff Fitzsimmons, this is Arnold Franks, supervisor for the foster and adoptive services division. I have a note to call you about a complaint."

"Mr. Franks, my wife and I attended the mandatory parenting class the other night as part of the process to foster and eventually adopt the young boy currently in our care."

Chance went on to describe what had happened and the hostile inferences that had been made. She could hear a pen scratching across paper.

"Sheriff, you have my sincere apologies. First, my agency can't thank Maggie and Dee enough for what they've done as foster parents over the years. I know that not everyone considers them a conventional couple, but the children who have been put in their care have benefited more than I can say. They are a trusted source that has helped us out no matter what time or under what circumstances we've called them."

Chance rubbed her brow. "Then what's Beverly Moss' issue? She made it pretty clear that having them foster a child was less than desirable. In my mind, she can't feel any different about another same-sex couple. I understand that some people might have a prejudice against families like mine, but what's best for the child has to come first. Hunter is flourishing with us the same way my sister Kendra did with my mothers. The same way I did when they were forced into parenthood after my dad's murder."

"You're absolutely right. I won't even try to make an excuse for her actions. I can assure you, I'll do all I can to prevent a repeat."

"Mr. Franks, I've spent my life in public service, and most of that has been as a supervisor in one capacity or another. More than once, I've been placed in an uncomfortable position by a subordinate and have had to apologize for the actions of others. The blatant homophobia I felt from Mrs. Moss has no place when it comes to the welfare of children."

Chance heard him audibly sigh over the phone.

"Sheriff, again, I apologize. It's not our policy to discuss personnel complaint outcomes. I have no doubt, in your position as Sheriff, you've had days like this. I can assure you it will be dealt with."

"That's all I can ask Mr. Franks. If it happens again, I'll be forced to escalate my complaint within the next level of the administration."

"I would expect no less."

The two ended the call as her cellphone rang. She looked at the display to see Harley's name. "Harley, what can I do for you?"

"I think we have an issue brewing up in Dry Fork. Our office was contacted by a resident from the area. Do you remember the name Ted Eichland, from that sovereign citizen flyer?"

"I do. He was one of the violent offenders in comparison to the paper terrorist, right?"

"That's him. My complainant caught him tearing down an electric fence line set up as a temporary grazing pasture at the edge of his property. He ended up in a confrontation that nearly came to blows. Ted brandished a weapon and our complainant walked away. He called directly into the Parsons barracks when he got back to his house. A few hours ago, Milton went to check on his cattle. Several of them had been shot in the head."

Chance rubbed her eyes. "Damn. Sounds like our friend, Ted, was trying to make a statement."

"I'd say so. I've got one of my troopers up there recovering rounds from the cattle. Once we do an investigation, we'll see about matching it to anything in their possession. Someone put about ten thousand dollars' worth of Angus beef down in a field."

"That's a pretty devastating loss for any farmer." Chance jotted down a note on the pad at her desk.

"Especially when the cattle were on his property to start with and someone else decided they weren't satisfied with property lines. Anyway, I just wanted you to know we've got a mess brewing up there."

"I have a strong suspicion our break-in at Granger's is tied in as well. Taylor's working an angle on an unreported stolen gun. Once we get the information gathering done, I say we get together and see if we can connect the dots."

"I'm with you on that. Talk with you soon."

Chance hung up and looked at her watch. She was getting anxious about Jax's phone call with her attorney. Every time it seemed like they cut a tie with their past baggage, another tendril was discovered. With a sigh, she continued to dig her way out of the mound of paperwork on her desk. When her phone buzzed, she checked her text messages and found one from Kendra.

Check this out.

Kendra had sent a short video of Hunter with a small, compound bow drawn back. He was aiming at a target downrange. When he let the arrow fly, the point hit the colored circles just to the left of the center. Kendra's mug appeared on the video, wide-eyed, as she mouthed, "wow."

Chance typed a message. *That's pretty awesome. Seems like he's going to be a natural, like someone else I know.* She watched her phone as the three bubbles rose and fell, indicating Kendra was typing again.

He's really good for his age and never doing this before. He loves it.

So did you.

Still do. I learned at the hand of the master. Gotta go, secret stuff in progress.

Chance smiled and put her phone down. She was so grateful to have been around when Kendra was young. She'd been working for the US Fish and Wildlife Agency when Kendra was in her teens. Now, she was grown and about to go off to training academy and follow in

Chance's footsteps, albeit a path leading to a different agency engraved on her badge. The photos on the office wall showed some of Chance's accomplishments and people she'd helped over the years. Some were of her family. Among the award plaques and mementos of her past as a smokejumper was a framed photo of her and her father.

Chance rose and walked to the picture. It had been taken a few months before the domestic call that had cost him his life. She was sitting with him in his cruiser, and the smiles on their faces were miles wide. "I hope I'm half the parent you were, Dad. I hope you can see him from where you are. Watch over him if you can. I miss you." She touched the glass that covered the photo. Zeus nudged her other hand with his nose. "Us too, if you've got the time." With one more glance at the picture, she grabbed her hat. "Come on, Zeus. I say we take the rest of the day off and go spend some time with Kendra and your buddy Hunter." At the mention of Hunter's name, Zeus barked and went to the door. "I couldn't have said it better myself."

***

Jax clenched her teeth together. "Alex, I have a family, I have a business, and I have a life on this side of the country. I don't have the time or the desire to come back to California for a trial that has nothing to do with me."

"Jax, trust me, I understand that. If you remember right, I helped you make the things you just mentioned happen, minus the family part. I've done everything I can to keep the judge from requiring you to come back to California. The only way I see that happening is to offer a settlement, and before you cuss me a blue streak, I don't think that's what you should do."

Jax sat back in her chair and angrily pulled out the ponytail holder that kept her dark hair away from her face. "Alex, I haven't forgotten. Please don't act like you did all that out of the goodness of your heart. You do remember the check I wrote you?"

He chuckled. "Ah yes, my wife was more than happy to spend it on my son's college education. Seriously, Jax, I'm doing all I can to keep you out of court. The judge ruling on this case can be an ass. I don't want to piss him off before he has a chance to see you had nothing to do with this."

Jax could feel the skin around her eyes tightening from the impending migraine. Why was it when everything in her life seemed to be going so right, Lacey had to drag her into the muck. "Alex, I understand. If I were still in California, this wouldn't be such a big issue, but it is now that I'm back in West Virginia. We're in the process of trying to adopt a foster child in our care. I've also been thrust into the leadership role for an endurance race. I don't want to settle because it's not my fight. Just because someone wants to have more than one deep pocket on the hook. I'm divorced and one of the million reasons is that I caught Lacey with this woman. I can tell you she certainly didn't seem like she was unhappy as she screamed how good it felt. This is bullshit. I know it and you know it." Jax took a deep breath. "If there is no other way for me to do this then yes, I'll get on a plane."

"I don't think there is any way around this, but I'll keep trying."

"I still don't understand how she's tying me in as being complicit or sanctioning this." She listened to keys clicking in the background as she picked up a pen and doodled on her calendar.

"I'm sure she's trying to fall back on the times you discovered Lacey's infidelity and didn't divorce her. In her filing, she lists Lacey as a predatory employer who demanded sexual favors as a condition for employment, raises, and advancement."

Jax threw her pen across the room. "Again, how does that tie into me? I didn't have her on my service, and none of the bonuses or raises were tied to individual performance. We gave across the board raises when we met certain financial or scheduling goals. There were no advancement opportunities. You came in as a member of the office staff, janitorial, or veterinary technician. None of which had anything tied to it other than seniority for years of service."

"Jax, you're preaching to the choir here. I don't make the rulings. I'm trying to get you released from liability. I promise I am. We have a court date in February of next year. Unless you're willing to settle out of court, I suggest you book a ticket."

Jax rose from her chair and paced her office space. She was fuming, and her head felt like someone was busting up concrete with a jackhammer. "Okay."

"Okay you want to settle, or okay you'll be getting on a plane?"

"If it comes to it, I'll get on a plane and stand before a judge to say exactly what I've said to you."

"We've got a plan, Jax. I promise you. I'll keep you up to date. Try not to worry so much. You trusted me once before to lead you through this. Trust me to do it again."

"I'm counting on you."

She hung up and checked her email. Every day, she waited to hear from one of the people she'd contacted about being an interpreter and tutor for Hunter. School was just around the corner, and she was frustrated he might not receive the time and attention he needed to take in the material. *Junk mail, junk mail, junk mail. I need to check my settings.* She came across an email from a Julia Gerard, with several attachments. She opened each, reading through the impressive credentials. Jax began a response, talking aloud as she typed.

Dear Ms. Gerard,

Thank you for responding. I am impressed with your resume and would be interested in meeting with you. I see from your response that you are a native of Grant County. If you could send me information about when you would be available, my wife and I would like to sit down and discuss what we are looking for in order to help our son. As you know, school starts soon, and we'd like to find a way to have an interpreter-tutor in place as soon as possible. I hope to hear from you soon, Jax Fitzsimmons.

Jax sent the email, and for the first time all day she felt hopeful.

***

Uncle Marty walked into Jax's office. Jax remembered when she'd been so young and excited about her chosen profession. All of it was due to the man who stood in front of her.

"Kitten, how are you?"

Jax came around the desk and melted into her uncle's outstretched arms. "Better now. I've missed you. I didn't get to see you when you were at the house with Dad and Hunter the other day." She felt his arms tighten around her.

"I know, I'm sorry about that. I had a Lions Club meeting I had to preside over. The district president was coming. Our annual elimination dinner is a few weeks away, and we were discussing what programs we'd be able to sponsor this year." He drew back and looked at her. "You look tired."

They moved to the small couch in the office.

Jax smiled at him. "Keeping up with a six-year-old at my age will do that to you."

"Keeping up with that boy at any age would tucker out a border collie pup. He's full of piss and vinegar. Makes this old man smile. I'm happy for you and Chance."

"We're so blessed to have him in our lives." Jax wiped at a tear. "I never thought I'd have a child."

He pulled her to him. "You know your Aunt Mary and I couldn't have children." He sighed. "She wanted them so badly, but it just wasn't meant to be. That's why we loved having you come and stay with us so much."

"Those were the best days of my childhood. If I'd have had my way, I'd have never left."

He patted her hand. "Truth be told, we'd have loved for you to stay with us like you asked. My sister wouldn't hear of it. We got you and your brother as much as we could. We wanted to show you a loving home. Something I know was severely lacking."

"She loved the thought of us. The one where we were perfect children, seen and not heard. Jennings was much better at it than I was. I couldn't wait for the day I left for college. Now, all these years later, I'm back where I wanted to be all along."

"I only wish your Aunt Mary would have lived long enough to have enjoyed you taking over the practice for me. We had so many plans of what we'd do when I retired. She wanted to travel."

"I'm sorry I didn't come back sooner."

"Oh, honey, I wouldn't have been ready to retire when she left us. No use dwelling on the things we can't change. Now, there's something I want to discuss with you. I'm getting up there in age. Don't get me wrong, I'm still pretty spry, but I'd like a little less to take care of. I'm planning to put together a rent to own agreement with your dad for my place and move into Pineridge."

Jax sat up a bit to look at him. "The assisted living facility? Uncle Marty are you sick?"

He laughed. "Only of cutting grass and cleaning a house that I only use three rooms of. The place is just too big for me. Your dad's been renting that condo. Instead, he'll rent my place. He won't let me just give the damn place to him, so we worked out a deal that he'll purchase it on a land contract. It will make it so he has an affordable payment with no interest and will give me an income to help with my expenses at Pineridge."

"Uncle Marty, you do whatever you want. It's your house."

"Yes, I know that, but it's one I willed to you after I'm gone. This will change that."

Jax hugged him. "I want you to do whatever makes sense for you. Chance and I have our home. I don't know what I'd do with your place other than rent it. This way, the house stays in the family. I like the plan."

Uncle Marty held out a hand. "Help an old man up, would ya?"

Jax stood and held out both her hands for him to grab onto and pull himself up to a standing position. He cupped her cheek with his weathered hands that had gently held many newborn kittens.

"I've always told you that you were the daughter I never had. I couldn't be prouder of the woman you've become or the family you've made for yourself. Now, I know you're busy. Thanks for taking a few minutes to humor an old man."

"Uncle Marty, I've always got time for you. Always. You stop in anytime you want. I love you."

"Love you too, kitten. Now, there's a brook trout with my name on it. I best get to the river."

"Be careful. You have your cellphone?"

He tweaked her nose. "Yes, mother hen, and I wear that fancy vest you got me with the flotation device in it, in case I fall in. As a matter of fact, your dad is going with me, so I've even got my own lifeguard."

"Forgive me for being overprotective. I couldn't imagine anything else happening to you. It nearly broke me when—"

He put his finger to her lips. "It's all in the past. I love you. Now, back to work." He hugged her one more time, then left her office just as Brandi stepped in. He waved on his way by. "Keep her on track, Brandi. It makes me look good."

Brandi put her hand on Marty's arm as he passed by. "You've got it." She looked at Jax. "Booney is here for a checkup. Bill wants to know if you'd like to do it, or do you want him to?"

Jax took a deep breath and cleared all of the emotional turmoil she felt. "If we don't have anyone else, let's give him the gold star treatment. All three of us will see him. We don't have any more farm calls today."

"That means three times the treats, you know?"

"He's earned them. Let's go."

***

Jax was already running late when she dropped Brandi off. An emergency had walked through the door near the end of their shift. The two of them handled the case as Bill headed home to help take care of an issue on the farm with one of their cows. Jax had called home and told Chance to go ahead and eat. She'd arrived just in time to put Hunter into the bath. Once they'd accomplished the nightly routine, she'd wandered downstairs for a few slices of cold pizza.

Chance handed her a beer.

"You have no idea how bad I need this."

"Let me guess, you talked to your attorney."

Jax nodded. "Alex says I'm going to have to go to California unless we settle." She went on to explain all he'd said. When she was through, she rubbed her eyes. "This is so screwed up."

Chance wrapped her in her arms. "It is."

She melted into Chance's embrace. "I just don't get it. I finally have the life I was afraid to dream about. I have the woman I couldn't love more and a little boy sleeping upstairs with our dog. Everything I've ever wanted is right here, and yet my nightmare of a past is chained to my ankle."

"So, you go and get the shackle cut off. When do you have to be there?"

"Not until February, so we still have time to hope it will get thrown out. How did your call with CPS go today?"

Chance took a drink of her beer before she spoke. "I did talk with Mr. Franks. After I explained everything that happened, he assured me it wouldn't happen again. I still don't know what Beverly's issue is, but it seems she's not the only one in the organization that disagrees with same-sex couples fostering or adopting." She went on to share Mr. Franks' gratitude toward Dee and Maggie for their services as foster parents.

Jax swallowed another bite of pizza. "It just doesn't make sense. So many of these kids age out of the system never having known a family. We offer a home to a child in need, and someone sits in judgment of our family because we don't fit their narrow-minded concept of what one should be."

"I'm right there with you on that. I can't imagine having grown up with anyone other than the moms squared."

"You certainly hit the jackpot there."

"I agree."

Jax stretched. "In other news, I had an email from a potential candidate for our tutoring position. She's from Grant County and sounds promising. I asked her to look at her schedule and see when we could meet for an informal interview. I forwarded you the information."

"That sounds very promising. You let me know when and where, and I'll have Penny schedule it. Now, how about we go to bed? You look as exhausted as I feel."

"Yes, please."

"Grab your beer. Let's go."

On her way out of the kitchen, Jax looked around and saw Hunter's drawings on the fridge. All the little signs that he lived with them warmed her heart. With a sigh of contentment, she turned off the light and followed Chance up the stairs. *The dragons will still be there to slay tomorrow.*

Chapter Eleven

CHANCE SAT BEHIND HER desk talking to her sister who seemed to have drifted off in thought. Chance cleared her throat to bring her back to the present. "How'd they react?"

Kendra startled a bit, then shifted in her chair. "About like you'd have expected. They wanted to know about finishing my degree and where I'd end up after the academy. They're worried, but it's no different than how they worry about you every day. I think they knew it was coming."

Penny spoke up from the doorway. "How about I order everyone some lunch and we talk while we eat?"

"I'd like that. Thanks, Penny." Kendra grinned that crooked smile.

It didn't take long for the food to be delivered, and they moved to the break room, where a small, closed-circuit TV allowed Penny to monitor the front desk.

Taylor smiled as Kendra took a huge bite. "One of these days, you're going to choke." She took a bite of her own sandwich while Penny picked at a salad. "I hear you leave for Georgia soon."

This conversation had been coming for a while, and Chance knew Kendra would need to lean on Taylor this time more than her.

Kendra nodded slowly and straightened the bread on her sandwich. "Thirty days. I hate to alter my graduation, but that was one of their conditions for application. I had to be able to drop everything and be at Glynco within thirty days of my acceptance. I've been working to graduate early anyway. I have enough credits."

Penny jumped into the conversation. "What's Brandi think?"

Like a seesaw, Kendra's head waggled back and forth. "She wants me to be happy, but she's not crazy about being without me for that long."

Chance knew leaving Brandi was a huge concern.

"Her classes will take up a lot of her time," Kendra continued. "She's got clinical hours over her next few semesters. I expect she'll come back here and spend time with Jax at the hospital. That way, she won't get too lonely, and I'll know she's okay. Her family is so far away."

Chance sat forward and covered her sister's hand. "We'll take care of her, she's family to us. Take that worry off your plate."

Penny patted her arm. "Kendra, I'll be able to help Brandi when she has questions. Taylor and I hadn't been together too long before she went to the academy. I knew I'd wait for her. She'll tell you she wasn't worried about me, but the letters she sent told otherwise. She even had one of her best friends keep an eye on me." She winked at Taylor.

Taylor tried to deny it, but one look from Penny ended that protest. She sighed. "She's right. I did worry, but I'll never admit to having someone watch you. Mum's the word on that." She mimicked zipping her lips shut. "I did have a reason though. The first time I met Penny was in the commons area. She was a business major, tutoring this guy at one of the tables. He was becoming rather loud and persistent in his attempts to get Penny to go on a date. After I watched her remove his hand from her leg a third time, I intervened. We started talking, and before you know it, we were dating. Within a month, I got my letter of acceptance to the US Marshals Academy."

Taylor swirled the ice in her Coke. "It's a tough program, Kendra. Make sure you graduate as high as you can so you can write your ticket as to where you want to be assigned."

Kendra sat up straighter and looked her dead in the eye. "You can count on that. I'd like to end up assigned to Elkins or Clarksburg. Either of those posts will keep me close to home, so Brandi can join Jax's practice if she wants to."

Chance put a hand on Kendra's shoulder. "You're smart, Kendra, you always have been. You know this family has your back, and that means Brandi's as well. Your nephew thinks the sun rises and sets on you."

Kendra chewed another bite of her food before speaking. "Hunter's a cool little dude. I'm planning to keep up with my online sign language classes. We had the best time the other day."

The affection in Kendra's voice made Chance smile. "When we put him to bed, he showed me you'd put my old bow in his room. I have to admit, that choked me up a bit."

"He's part of the family." Kendra looked up at Chance. "You passed it to me, and now it's in the hands of the next generation of the Fitzsimmons clan. Exactly where it should be."

Chance prayed there wouldn't be any trouble with the adoption process. West Virginia had always leaned more toward conservative politics, though there were pockets of progressiveness. Many of the residents of the mountaintop area of Tucker County had started their lives somewhere else. That demographic tended to make the political, spiritual, and moral compass move in a wider arc than off the mountain. The woman at Child Protective Services concerned her.

The trash from lunch was discarded as the group made their way back into Chance's office. Taylor wrote down a series of contact numbers, emails, and a few places of interest Kendra could check out if she had time.

Kendra held up the paper. "Thanks for this and for the promise to help Brandi through it. I know it will mean a lot to her. As for those places of interest, the only thing that interests me is the pages of the books they'll give me and studying my ass off."

Taylor grinned. "I know, but once in a while, go have a burger. For a few hours, let your brain have time to reset. It will help you focus."

"You're probably right. I'll call and let you know how I'm doing."

"I'd like that." Taylor pointed at Chance. "Put your sister's mind at ease. You know it's killing her that you aren't coming to work here."

Kendra looked at Chance. "She knows it's killing me too. You never know where I'll end up. Until then, I'll be working for a kick-ass agency."

Chance waved as Kendra left. "That you will, Bullseye, that you will."

***

Chance left the office and stopped by the house. They'd received a complaint from a landowner in Dry Fork. He'd hired a local conservation agency to do some stream restoration on the far end of his property, back in the woods. The contractors found an area that appeared as if it was being used as an illegal firing range, where targets and brass casings littered the clearing. She patted Kelly on the side as she trailered the horse. "Good girl. Let's go for a ride."

The drive to the property would take close to thirty minutes. *I wonder how long this has been going on.* The family that owned the land was from out of state and planned to build a home there soon. She passed several people who waved at her. She dreaded the next year that would be consumed with campaigning for reelection. "Part of the job if you want to keep it, right, Zeus?" He barked in confirmation. "That's what I thought."

The trees were still green, and the leaves waved in the breeze. Rain had been spotty all summer long, which always led to the question about whether the fall colors would be dull or vibrant. Thoughts of last year's Leaf Peepers festival floated through her mind. Hunter, lying unconscious from an accidental overdose, led to Jax experiencing a contact overdose when she carried him to the ambulance in her arms. At that time, she had no idea that Hunter would become her son. Nor did she know her entire world could have been gone in one fatal blow. *Thank you for watching out for them, Lord. Did you see this coming? If you did, thank you for that too.* Maybe it was time to start attending church to show her gratitude to the being she prayed to frequently. *Something to think about later.*

She stopped at a locked gate and saw a man step out of a black Cadillac Escalade. He looked to be in his sixties and stood in jeans and a light-blue, button-down shirt. His hiking boots looked brand new. She drove through after he opened the barrier. She parked and released Zeus, who immediately came to her side in work mode as the stranger approached.

He held out his hand. "I assume you're Sheriff Fitzsimmons?"

She shook it and responded. "I am. I hear you have a problem with some trespassers."

He held out a stack of photos to her. "According to these pictures, I do. My name is Thomas Randler and I own the property."

Chance looked through the pictures, shocked at the volume of spent casings on the ground in large piles. "Any idea how long this has been going on?"

"Honestly, I don't. I can give you a vague timeline of what I do know. We purchased the property from one of your tax sales, about seven years back. Of course, you know the rules that are associated with the sale. The previous owners can buy it back if they pay the past-due taxes and fees within the allotted time, so we sat on it until it was clear. We'd originally planned to start building last year, but I changed jobs and we were unable to begin construction until now." He pointed to the photos. "This particular area is close to the property line. I'm not sure if the same people who failed to pay on these twenty acres are doing this. I hired Valley Institute to come in and restore a section of the stream that was plugged by some previous logging activity. The stream banks have been eroding, and the overflow gobbles up land when it floods."

"Do you have the phone number of the individual that took these pictures?"

He nodded. "I do, as well as GPS coordinates for the site."

Chance studied the pictures. "Are you staying somewhere locally?"

"I am. My wife and I have a room over at Canaan Valley Resort. We're meeting with a contractor to look over our plans to build. We'd like to get started on drilling a well for water, installing a septic system, and pouring a foundation. It's important to get that done before winter hits. That way they can get moving on the rest of it as soon as the weather breaks next spring."

"I understand. We have a short building season around here. I assume this will be more of a summer home for you? Access to this place would be difficult, at best, in the winter. You're beyond where the Department of Highway plows."

Thomas smiled. "Mostly. We have a plan for winter. I've got my eye on a snow groomer with tracks."

Chance shook her head and laughed. "You might need a road grader too. I'm going to take a ride out to this site and look around."

"By yourself?"

"I'm never by myself, Thomas. Zeus is the best backup I could ask for. I'm guessing you won't want to wait for me. If you're comfortable with it, can you give me the gate combination? That way, you can lock it when you leave. I'll secure it once I've got Kelly loaded up and we're on our way out."

"Not a problem, Sheriff."

Thomas wrote the combination on the back of a business card and left as she unloaded Kelly. She pulled the handheld GPS out of her BDU pocket and waited until the unit locked onto the satellites needed to guide her to the location in the photos. Before she left, she grabbed her mic. "SD-1 to Comm Center?"

"SD-1, go ahead."

"I'm out on that complaint in Dry Fork. I'm headed to the following coordinates on horseback."

Chance relayed the longitude and latitude of her destination to dispatch. With Zeus at her side, she wasn't concerned. The coordinates were merely a safety measure in case she was unable to use radio communication while out on the incident. The terrain would play into her travel to the site. There were parts of the journey that would be difficult for Kelly to traverse and a time estimation would be difficult. She did relay that if she didn't make contact in three hours to alert Taylor. With those things in place, she swung up into her saddle and looked down at her K9 partner.

"You ready, Zeus?"

He ran ahead of her and barked back at the mounted pair. She patted Kelly's side "I'd say that's a yes. Let's go, girl." The three of them set off at a leisurely pace toward their destination. *Let's see where this leads us.*

***

Jax watched Hunter and Jace play at her mother-in-law's real estate office. "The boys are having a good time."

"They certainly are." Maggie's smile was infectious. "I didn't expect you, but you're just in time to watch the afternoon wrestling match. Hunter is always sweet enough to let Jace win."

Hunter lay face down on the floor while Jace climbed all over him. Jax stood and watched how gentle her son was with her godson. No words were needed. When the wrestling match was over, Jax joined them and they pushed a few cars around on the floor. Playtime with the boys was exactly what she needed.

Maggie leaned on the doorframe. "You okay, honey?"

"Overall, yes. I needed a bit of a pick-me-up and knew these two would provide it."

"How about a cup of coffee, and we can sit and talk while they play?"

"I'd love one." Jace tried to put one of the cars in his mouth, and Jax pulled him into her arms to tickle him. Not to be left out, Hunter began to tickle Jax, until tears of laughter ran down her cheeks.

"That might be the best medicine there is for what ails you." Maggie took a sip of her coffee and set Jax's down on a side table.

Jax signed to Hunter to keep playing with Jace and she'd be back. He nodded and crashed his car into Jace's, making him laugh. She rose and pulled the warm cup into her hands before sitting down beside Maggie.

"It definitely is." She sat back and watched the boys, grateful for Maggie's silent companionship. She knew Maggie would wait for her to talk in her own time. It was a pleasure just to sit together and watch the two boys, who were different in age but seemed to have found a way to overcome the gap. Jace lay down on the playmat, his eyes growing heavy. It didn't seem to faze Hunter, who continued to play when his companion drifted off.

"Oh, to be that innocent again," Jax mumbled, more for her own benefit than Maggie's.

"Chance was like that as a baby. She'd play as hard as she could, then collapse wherever she was." Maggie sipped from her mug. "When Chance's mother died in childbirth, my brother had no idea what to do. Dee and I practically moved in with him to help him get comfortable with feeding and bathing her."

"I can't even imagine losing your wife like that. I'm sure he was grateful you were there."

"It was so hard on Ray. He was grieving his wife, and at the same time, had this tiny life that relied on him for everything. He threw himself into it, even though he didn't have a clue what he was doing. He'd been too little to help Mom with me when I was a baby. Plus, in those days, the men didn't do much with the children. That was women's work."

Hunter moved to a small table and began to draw.

"Such a different time," Jax said. "You and Dee certainly gave Chance great role models to be exactly who she is and, in turn, a great mom."

"Is that what you're worried about? That you won't know how to be a good mom because of how you grew up."

Jax looked away, feeling tears well up. "Partially. He deserves the best home he can have. I'll make sure we do everything we can to make that happen."

"When's your next parenting class?"

"Next week. The schedule says we have a total of five weeks of them."

Maggie nodded. "And your first one was filled with tension. When Chance came to live with us, there was no question. I was her only blood relative, and Ray had everything ready in his will. He'd prepared for the possibility because of his job. The children we took in later, as fosters, were a bit more of a challenge. We waited for years and jumped through every hoop they put in front of us. Kendra's story isn't much different from Hunter's. We tried for years to adopt her and met headlong with many of the bigots that run this system. Over time, there were some changes in leadership, and we were finally able to adopt her."

"Kendra and Hunter bonded the other day. He wouldn't stop talking about his time with her."

An incoming email buzzed Jax's phone. "Oh, this is from the tutoring candidate. She says she can meet us the same day Hunter has his hearing appointment. She's going to be in the Morgantown area that day."

"That's great news. Firm those plans up. Another opportunity might not come around as easily."

Jax sent back a reply with a tentative time and place, adding Chance to the email as well. *Please let this work out.* Once she put her phone away, she revealed the fear she was battling. "I assume Chance has told you I might be required to go back to California to deal with Lacey's bullshit."

"She mentioned it."

"Why is it that when my future looks so bright, my past comes back like a dark cloud over the sun?"

Maggie blew out an exasperated breath. "I wish I knew. Faith tried to drag Chance back as well if you remember. She couldn't accept what Chance was while they were together, until someone else who could was in the picture. Of course, you always had Chance's heart. She never got over you, ever."

"Thank the heavens for that miracle. So much time wasted."

Maggie put her arm around Jax. "That's up for debate. You both had paths to follow, and yours led you back here at a time in your life that you wanted the relationship more than anything else. She had wandering feet in her twenties. Hell, sometimes I wonder, if she hadn't been burned, would she ever have come back here for good? Despite all the pain, she's exactly where she's supposed to be and so are you. Hunter was waiting for you both."

Hunter came running over to Jax and handed her his drawing. He pointed to the figures and smiled.

Jax held the paper in her hand as if it were the most precious thing she'd ever been given. Chance's image had a star on her chest, while Jax's held a black bag like the one she carried at work. He'd drawn his own likeness with a big smile standing beside a dog she was sure was Zeus. There were hearts on the page. The bitterness in her heart disappeared with the sweetness of the drawing. She pulled him into her arms and looked at Maggie. "I think it was more like I was waiting for him."

***

Chance used her binoculars to look over the small area indicated by her GPS. She'd stopped short to assure herself as much as possible that no one was around. She'd waited nearly twenty minutes with no sign of anyone. "Okay, girl. Let's go. Zeus, *bewaken*." She'd been watching for any sign that her astute partner had noticed anyone. He hadn't. She was fairly confident no one was around.

At the edge of the clearing, she dismounted and tethered Kelly to a tree branch. Chance released the clasp on her weapon and adjusted her hat slightly to give her a wider field of vision. She slowly circled the outside of the area, taking note of the numerous shoe patterns in the dust. Most were from adult males, given the size, with a few smaller that could be a female or a young adult. Someone had built a railing that looked like it was used as a rifle rest for the makeshift range. Wooden posts were spaced at intervals that correlated to the targets downrange. She paced them off. *Twenty, thirty, and forty yards.* Some were set at even greater distances. The photos had accurately depicted the piles of discarded cartridges. Some had been gathered into five-gallon metal buckets that had once held asphalt sealant. The range of calibers was astonishing.

"Whoever they are, they've got guns of every size." Chance bent down and picked up brass for .38 and .45 shells. There were discarded cartridges from rifles as well. The casings that truly caught her eye were the buckets containing those from what looked like AK-47's and even some stray .50 caliber rounds. She and Zeus walked downrange to the metal cutouts, past trees with chunks missing from their trunks. When she got to the targets, she examined the bullet holes. *Armor-piercing rounds.* Her finger touched the metal where the copper jackets had been stripped by the quarter-inch steel. "These guys are into some heavy shit, Zeus."

With her cellphone, she took pictures of the damage and walked on down beyond the final targets. There were giant craters in the earth. "What the hell do they have?" She slowly made her way into the hole and found what looked like fragments of steel pipe. "Someone's been making pipe bombs, boy." Other than being on private property and littering, they hadn't crossed the line into anything of major concern until she discovered this. This crossed the line. She photographed everything and took a sample of the pipe, placing it in an evidence bag, before climbing back out of the blast hole.

Chance walked back up and collected some of the casings, including a cluster of .38's that had been dumped on the ground. She mused that they might be from the stolen gun she'd found in the truck. She put everything in evidence bags and took some video of the area, including the targets and the paths leading away from the site. She decided to put up a few blackout game cameras off the trail leading away from the range in places where they wouldn't easily be spotted.

Any more investigation without armed backup could be suicide given the obvious amount of firepower they had in their possession. She looked for any loose scraps of paper with a name or an address. Nothing jumped out at her. It was time to go before it started to get dark. "Let's go home, Zeus. We'll be back when we can find some of our friends to come with us." She mounted Kelly, and they headed back to the gate.

Chance thought about the scene she'd just left. What she'd found warranted more than a casual investigation. The pipe bombs, .50 caliber armor-piercing rounds, and the thousands of discarded brass casings told her she was dealing with someone who was an avid gun owner and had little regard for the law. She was aware of a few people disgruntled over tax sales since she had become the sheriff, but this sale would have happened under her predecessor. The previous owner of this parcel could be the same as the adjacent owner, and it was possible they still felt it belonged to them. *Without anyone on the property to monitor it, squatters can do as they please with someone else's land.* It was worth further investigation. She picked up the pace, eager to get out of the woods before dark. Tomorrow was another day.

***

Saturday morning, Jax sat on the porch watching her wife and son. Chance was beside Hunter on the concrete pad they'd poured at the end of the driveway to avoid stepping out in the mud during the rainy season. Chance fastened his helmet, then held the handlebars of the bike Grandpa Mike had bought for him. Chance had taken off the pedals to teach him to balance first. He threw his leg over the seat, then put his feet firmly on the concrete. Jax watched the instructions as Chance demonstrated what she wanted him to do.

Jax smiled. *She's a great mom and so patient with him.* The first few times Hunter pushed off, he wobbled. Chance brought him back to center. Jax remembered being little and the patience her brother had shown her. She'd been terrified, but Jennings had instilled in her the confidence she'd needed to try something new and scary. Hunter showed little fear and eventually pushed himself back and forth across the concrete from one end to the other without Chance's assistance.

The excited boy turned to the porch and signed enthusiastically in her direction. *"Watch me, Momma."* Hunter's smile beamed at his newfound confidence.

Jax's heart melted every time he called her mom. She stood and waved her hands to clap. She descended the steps that connected to the pad and came to stand by Chance. "You're a great teacher, you know."

Chance laughed. "I don't know about that."

"There's living proof right in front of us." Jax put an arm around her wife's waist. "He's having a great time."

"He still has to learn to pedal."

"Teaching him balance is important. He'll let you know when he's ready to move on. For a kid who never had anyone take the time to do something like this for him, he's taking to it like a duck to water."

Jax shifted to put her back against Chance's chest and covered the arms that wrapped around her with her own. "Teaching him to ride the horses helps with that too. His core strength has improved so much in the short time he's been with us."

Hunter stopped and looked over as if to see if they were still watching

Chance answered him by pointing to her eyes, then his. *"Keep going."* Chance waved her hand at him.

Jax pulled Chance's knuckles to her lips and kissed them. "I really hope Julia works out. We are so close to the start of school. I hate the thought of him being at any more of a disadvantage.

"Let's hope for the best. Until then, we just keep moving forward."

Jax nodded. "What time are Sarah and Kristi coming?"

"I told them they could come over anytime. We'd be here hanging out. I'm a little worried about Sarah. Something in her voice. I don't know, something just doesn't seem right."

Jax turned her face to look at Chance. "You think they're having trouble with Daniel moving in with Dezi?"

"I don't think so. They've practically been living together since he got out of the academy. I don't think that's what's bugging her. I can't put my finger on it exactly. She's had some tough ambulance calls over the last year. Maybe, if you get the opportunity, mention my concern to Kristi. See if she'll give you some insight. I'm going to see if Sarah will open up to me while we grill out today. I've never seen her this down."

"Well, if she's going to talk to anyone other than Kristi, I have no doubt it will be you, her best friend. You two are like sisters."

"We always have been. If we're able to adopt—"

Jax interrupted. "When we're able."

Chance laughed. "When we're able to adopt Hunter. I'd like to ask Sarah and Kristi to be his godparents, if that's okay with you. I want them to know I trust them in the way they trusted me all those years ago."

Jax turned in Chance's arms and placed her palms on Chance's cheeks. "Of course, it's all right. Other than your mothers, there is no one I could imagine raising our child if something happened to us."

"Nothing is going to happen to us."

Jax turned in her arms to watch Hunter. "I believe that, but I also know that we have to be prepared for anything. A look back at our last six months is all we need to confirm that. I want to talk with our attorney soon, as well. We need to get things established that will take care of him if something does happen to us. Even if, heaven forbid, they don't allow us to adopt him, I want his future secured. He deserves that. He's spent enough of his life wondering where his next meal would come from. No matter what happens, he will never go without, ever again."

Jax felt Chance's arms tighten around her as they watched their son triumphantly push himself across the pad for another lap.

***

Chance cleaned the grill as Sarah stepped up beside her. "How hungry are you? I've got burgers and dogs."

"I'll take a hot dog. Kristi made her famous chili."

Chance turned to look at her. "Just one?"

"For now. Lately, I haven't had much of an appetite." Sarah tipped her beer and took a deep swallow.

Chance finished the grill prep and lit it to let the lingering bits burn off. "You know, you and I never keep anything from each other. There's nothing I haven't told you since the first grade. I won't lie, I'm a bit worried about you." She turned to her best friend and studied her small frame. Sarah had always been lean. Lately, she looked nearly gaunt. If Chance's eyesight wasn't failing her, Sarah looked like she'd lost twenty pounds. Her shorts hung on her, and the T-shirt she wore nearly swallowed her. Dark shadows made her eyes look bruised. "What's going on?"

Sarah looked away and took another drink of her beer. Chance waited on her to speak, sipping from her own beer.

Sarah shook herself. "I wake up in the middle of the night, sometimes in a cold sweat. Other times I'm screaming, and Kristi has to wake me."

"About?"

"It varies. Sometimes I see you lying in a pool of blood when that guy shot you. Kenny bleeding out when they kidnapped Doc. I see Jax over that hill, or Rhebekka in that creek. Lately, it's Travis. You know he and Daniel played basketball together at the high school. He stayed at our house more than once. A great kid that got handed a shitty deal with his dad and mom dying. Now this."

Chance squeezed her shoulder. "That's quite a bit for one person, Sarah. I also know you worry about Daniel, and there's whatever is going on with Hanna. Your plate is so full it's got sideboards. When's the last time you and Kristi got away? I don't mean taking a weekend off. I mean turned the pager off, let someone else be in charge, and went somewhere. Just the two of you?"

Sarah stared off into the yard where Hunter threw the ball for Zeus. "Long before Daniel was born."

"Well, I think that's the first step. After that, maybe it's time to talk with someone. I know you don't want to hear this because none of us ever do. We always think we can handle all the shit we see. It doesn't bother us. The reality is it *does* affect us. I can't even imagine those in the emergency service areas that see that every day. We all have varying degrees of PTSD. After Kenny was shot, I broke down at home. I was the one that sent him on that welfare check at the clinic. It reminded me of the fire when I got burned. What could I have done to save more people?"

Sarah wiped at the condensation on the beer bottle. "I didn't think I was going to make it when Maggie called me about you being burned back then. When we landed and got to the hospital, I think a little part of me died seeing you like that. When I walked in to see you intubated and in an induced coma, I almost passed out."

"She always told me you were the pillar of strength. You helped them get through that."

"It's all I know how to do."

"Maybe that's the problem. You've never known how to let others help you process it and send it to the trash."

Sarah furrowed her brow. "What do you mean?"

Chance thought for a minute how to explain in a way that would make the most impact on her friend. "When we have a tough rescue call, what do we do after?"

"We bring everyone together for a debrief, then make sure everything is ready to go for the next call."

Chance threw the hamburgers, hot dogs, and Italian sausage on the grill. "Exactly. We go over the call and evaluate our performance as a group. We let everyone chime in with one negative and one positive. We critique any part of the operation that went wrong, celebrate the things that went right, and train to make sure we are ready for the next call. On big drills and exercises, we seek out the experts who can evaluate how we operate and what things we need to work on, right?"

"We do."

Chance turned to the one person she considered her equal when it came to their ability to handle tough challenges. She and Sarah had worked all their lives to turn something that could end up in tragedy into a triumph. "Then we go out, have a few beers, and thank our lucky stars we pulled another one out of our ass."

Sarah let out a laugh that nearly made her spit beer. "That too."

"My point is, we process it. We look it over, tear it down, fix the broken shit, and make it better. If we can't do it on our own, we find someone to help us. Do you get what I'm saying?"

"You're saying I'm not fixing the broken shit."

Chance rolled the sausage and hot dogs over before flipping the hamburgers. "I'm saying, if we don't fix the broken shit, we can't make the next call right. We just keep filling the forms in with the same information instead of clearing the fields and starting fresh."

Sarah sat down and leaned her elbows on her knees. "I don't even know where to start."

Chance joined her. "When I finally got out of the hospital, my parents and my department made me see someone twice a month. People died that day, Sarah. People I couldn't get to."

"You saved Richie and Topper."

"And I kept going back to that as a consolation for all those I didn't save. I had to process it in order to release it and truly move on from it, to clear the fields." Chance watched as Sarah sat back and seemed to contemplate her words. She hoped what she'd said had found its way into the part of Sarah's brain that analyzed data, diagnosed injured patients, and remembered complicated rigging setups. Last year, Sarah and Kristi had accompanied them on a double date at an adventure escape room. Sarah had solved the most difficult of the clues that allowed them to beat the timer. Jax and Kristi had teamed up and solved their parts, while she and Sarah had worked on others that involved complex movements. Sarah's mind could see processes without ever moving a single piece.

"You've always been a master chess player, Sarah. Your mind is the greatest puzzle you've ever faced. There are moves to be made and the board is wide open."

Sarah sighed. "Maybe you're right. Sometimes I feel so anxious, like I'm waiting for the next thing to go wrong. My sleep patterns are all fucked up, and I spend half the night out on the deck looking at the stars to let Kristi sleep."

Chance put a hand on her best friend's shoulder. "I know of an organization here in West Virginia that helps first responders find qualified therapists. What we do, the things we see, aren't like the average worker in a manufacturing plant would. It's a different mental trauma with physical symptoms. I know several police officers and firefighters that Armor Up has helped. I know of one guy they flew across the country for an inpatient treatment center. They do whatever they have to. Will you give them a call?"

Sarah wiped at tears that trickled down her face and nodded.

"Okay. That's all I can ask. The rest is up to you."

***

The group sat out on the deck with full stomachs, relaxing in the evening air. Hunter had fallen asleep on Chance's lap, and Jax idly ran her fingers through the exhausted boy's hair. Zeus had taken up protection detail at the edge of the deck. "I think you two wore him out playing kickball."

"I think it's the other way around. I'd forgotten what it was like to chase a little boy. Daniel's been well past that stage for a long time." Sarah looked at Kristi. "Remember how exhausted we were when he started walking?"

Kristi laughed. "I do. It's funny how, for that first year, we encourage them to walk and talk. As soon as they do, all we want them to do is sit down and be quiet for five minutes."

Jax moved closer and winked at Chance, then turned to their friends. "We'd like to ask you something. It's completely up to you, but we can't think of anyone we'd trust more. Once we've formally adopted Hunter, we'd like you to be his godparents."

Kristi sat forward, then looked at Sarah. Their smiles said it all.

"We'd be honored. I never thought I'd get to return the favor for Chance being Daniel's." Sarah wrapped an arm around Kristi's shoulders. "We only ask one thing. We'd really appreciate it if you could do your best to make sure this is only an honorary title. Hunter needs you two, and he couldn't have landed in a better place. When I remember what he looked like, even a month ago, it's unbelievable. The change is remarkable."

"I never imagined anyone would call me Momma, but I can tell you, it feels pretty awesome." Chance snuggled Hunter in a little closer.

Kristi patted her knee. "You've always been great with kids, Chance. With Jax by your side, you two are wonderful parents. I can't wait to watch him grow up."

"And just so you know, godparents have spoiling rights. I seem to remember that exact declaration cross your lips many years ago. He may not be able to hear right now, but I'm buying him every noisy toy I can find." Sarah grinned and pointed at Chance. "Paybacks are a bitch, my friend, and you've earned them."

Chance raised her hand. "I admit nothing."

Sarah rolled her eyes. "You don't have to, we have video evidence, and I have permanent ringing in my ears to prove it."

Chance scoffed. "Don't blame that on me, blame that on twenty years of sirens."

"When do you think everything be finalized?" Kristi took a drink of her coffee.

Jax took a deep breath and sighed. "If we had our way, tomorrow. As it stands, we have four more parenting classes. They've done all the evaluations, now it's just a process of crossing all the t's and making sure there is no blood family to be found. That will take a while, and they are always short staffed. We've been told to expect at least twelve months, possibly as many as eighteen. As long as they don't pull him from our care, we can keep putting one day at a time behind us."

A shudder ran down her back at the thought, and Jax wiped it from her mind. Hunter wasn't going anywhere as long as she had a dime left to her name. She knew Chance felt the same.

"So, Kristi, you're taking a job at the high school? That's great. Those kids could use someone like you." Chance rubbed Hunter's back when he whimpered in his sleep.

Jax watched Kristi's face light up at the subject.

"I'm looking forward to it. When Daniel was in school, our house was always brimming with at least two or three others, including your sister. Now that he's grown, the house is so quiet. I miss that interaction with the kids. We decided to stop with Daniel, but I think I have a lot to offer that position. Sometimes, as a nurse, you see things others don't. For a lot of these kids, the only healthcare they ever receive is through the school. I think it's where I need to be at this point in my life. The clinic work is wonderful, but I think I can make more of an impact at the school. At the clinic, I'm nothing more than a glorified assistant with a nursing degree."

"That's not true, honey." Sarah placed a tentative hand on Kristi's forearm. "Those patients think of you as family. I'll sure miss all the cookies and homemade treats from those octogenarians."

"You poor thing." Kristi covered Sarah's hand.

Jax watched the couple. She sensed an underlying tension between the two. Kristi's need to seek fulfillment wasn't a surprise. Her assessment of her current worth was. Sarah didn't look well. Something was going on, but Jax wanted to wait to get Kristi alone before asking if there was anything she could do to help.

Chance spoke up. "Rhebekka and I have been working with the staff on the drug problem. Xavier's death rocked everyone. It didn't necessarily stop anyone who was using, but I think some who were on the fence might have thought twice. You'll be in a position to spot kids in trouble. I'd like you on the task force, if you're willing."

"I'd be happy to help. You know our families were blessed that we never had any issues with Daniel or Kendra. It could have been so different. I attribute a lot of that to you and Sarah." Kristi leaned over and kissed her wife's cheek.

Jax watched as Sarah melted into the affection and caught the glint of tears in her eyes. *Definitely something going on there.* She made a mental note to call Kristi and invite her to lunch so they could talk. She hated to see her friends struggling.

Chapter Twelve

THEIR COMPANY LEFT, AND they put Hunter to bed. Jax wrapped the rest of the leftovers in aluminum foil and placed them in the refrigerator. "Did you think Sarah and Kristi were off tonight?"

Chance stopped and wiped her hands on a dishtowel. "I did. Something is eating Sarah up. I talked to her a bit tonight. I'm convinced she's suffering from PTSD. She half admitted it and half denied it. I tried to tell her there are resources out there. If I have to, I'll drag her ass to counseling myself."

"That's the thing about therapy though, you have to want the help. If not, every word the therapist says will sound like the teacher in the *Peanuts* cartoon, unintelligible noise."

Chance laughed and dried a set of tongs she'd been washing. "Sounds like you're speaking from experience."

"I am, in a way." Jax leaned against the counter. "When things started going downhill for my marriage, we tried counseling. It was wasted on Lacey, in one ear and out the other. Even the therapist described what she observed in those terms. It made complete sense to me. Lacey didn't want to hear what our therapist was saying because it would require her to change her behavior. Something she wasn't about to do."

"Do you regret that it didn't work? The therapy, I mean?"

Jax pushed off the counter and sauntered across the kitchen toward Chance. "Not for one minute." She traced her index finger over the curve of Chance's jaw, then softly across her upper lip. "If she'd have listened, I might have missed out on the love of my life." She moved closer and replaced her finger with her lips, kissing along Chance's jaw until she met the soft flesh of her wife's mouth. She slid her arms around Chance's waist and pulled her closer. Chance shifted, spreading her legs, and allowing Jax to move between them. Jax drew her tongue along Chance's lips, when they opened, she accepted the invitation to slide her tongue in, tasting the peppermint candy Chance had eaten.

She deepened the kiss and allowed her tongue to dance and tangle with Chance's. A groan slipped out when Chance worked a hand between them to cup her breast and squeeze. She pulled back and looked at Chance. "I think it's time we go to bed, Sheriff. I need a bit of one-on-one time with you."

"That feeling is mutual, Mrs. Fitzsimmons."

Jax grabbed Chance's hand and led her up the stairs to their bedroom. They peeked into Hunter's room before stepping across the threshold of their bedroom and closing the door. The baby monitor sat on the shelf, and Jax heard a slight squeak from Hunter's bed. She had no doubt Zeus was settling in as protector of their son. She pulled at the hem of Chance's T-shirt and slid it out of the waistband of her jeans. With feather-light touches, she scraped her short nails across the well-defined abdominal muscles of her lover, feeling her jump and buck her hips. Jax needed to feel Chance, needed to connect with her. She reached down to pop the button on the soft denim. "Off." Jax had plans, and no piece of fabric was going to stand in her way.

"With pleasure."

Jax watched as Chance moved back a few inches, pulled her shirt over her head, then dropped her jeans and boxer briefs to the floor. She slid off her socks to stand gloriously naked in front of Jax. "Pure perfection."

Chance stepped closer and deftly removed Jax's clothes until they stood with nothing but air between them. "You are so beautiful, Jax."

"I'd say the same about you, but beautiful doesn't quite fit. Handsome, strong, and perfect come to mind." Jax drew a single finger from the hollow of Chance's neck, down her collarbone, and over to the scars on Chance's shoulder. She traced the lines of raised tissue, then spread her fingers and covered them with the palm of her hand, swallowing back the tears. "Resilient, brave, honorable. All words I'd use to describe you that still fall short of my true feelings. When I think about how I might never have had the life I share with you now, it terrifies me."

Chance stopped her words with a hard kiss, and Jax felt strong hands cup her face. "All in the past. These scars are nothing more than silent reminders of my life before you. Broken and out of control."

"I love you so much, Chance."

"And I love you."

Jax felt those strong arms pull her in as she instinctively wrapped a leg around Chance's waist. The hand on her hips a silent request, she entwined her arms around Chance's neck and held on as she was lifted and encouraged to lock both legs around Chance's hips. She kissed her long and deep as Chance carried her to their bed and refused to let go, covering her body with warm skin pressed against her. "You feel so good." She shifted and moved her leg until her thigh was firmly pressed against Chance's wet center. "And so wet."

"It's what your kiss does to me."

Chance's body was hot to the touch, the evidence of her desire coating Jax's thigh. "Your body is on fire."

Chance groaned, pushed back, and looked into Jax's eyes. "You're killing me."

"Not yet, but I'm about to take you right to the edge." Jax slid her hand between them before finding Chance's soaked center. She glided through silk, brushing over Chance's clit, and finally burying two fingers inside the woman above her. "Ride me."

Chance panted in her ear before pushing back and doing as Jax asked. She watched in fascination as the strongest woman she knew melted into her touch. There was no doubt about Chance's dominance in their bedroom, but tonight, Jax needed to feel like she was in control of something. So many things were beyond even her influence, but this, bringing the love of her life to climax, was all in her hands.

She pushed deeper into warm flesh and heard Chance gasp as she continued to rock her hips with Chance's movement. She reached up and palmed one of Chance's nipples, delighting when her head drifted back, exposing her throat. *She's mine, all mine.*

"Jax!"

"I'm right here, Chance. Let go. I've got you." Jax reveled in the feeling of Chance rocking against her while her fingers were gripped so tightly. When the clenching became nearly painful, she watched the tendons in Chance's neck go bowstring tight as the rest of her body tensed with her powerful climax. Jax felt so privileged to feel her warrior shudder, then relax and collapse on top of her. Jax slowly withdrew and smiled when Chance's stomach muscles jumped. She watched heaving breaths finally settle into a relaxed rhythm just shy of normal, then kissed Chance's shoulder.

Chance moaned. "What was that?"

Jax pushed back a little so she could see Chance's face. "What?"

Chance raised her head. "You stole my thunder."

Jax let out a throaty laugh. "You mean that you normally make the move to please me first?"

Chance half nodded, half shrugged. "Something like that."

"Are you complaining?"

"Not in the slightest. I like this side of you."

Jax ran a finger across Chance's lower lip and smiled as Chance nipped at it. "Don't get me wrong, I like the commanding side of my indomitable sheriff, but sometimes, I want to give to you in a way that shows you I'm strong enough to love you, strong enough to walk through this life with you, and strong enough to survive any storm with you."

Chance swiped at the damp hair on her forehead. "There is no one else I'd want beside me. We started this family, and now, we've added Hunter. You are so much stronger than you give yourself credit for. You packed up your life and moved across the country after being devastated by someone who never deserved you. I've never had anyone love me like you do. Now, it's not just me you take care of, but a little boy who calls you Momma J. You are strong enough to shelter us even through the harshest winds, my love. I never look at you as weaker. My God, what you've been through would break most women, and yet, here you are. Don't ever doubt that you are just as strong as I am, stronger in some ways."

"Some days, I don't feel that way."

Chance waved a finger between the two of them. "That's why we're a team."

"Sometimes, I feel like we're down in the fourth period with time running out."

"That's when you put the ball in my hands. I'll hit the three, then go in for the layup. That's how I got my nickname."

Jax burst out laughing. "Oh, I'm aware of your legendary performance."

Chance slid down the bed. "Then let me give you a reenactment of the winning drive."

Jax lay there and felt Chance's hands move slowly over her body. She knew Chance would bring her just as much pleasure as she'd given, and Jax craved it. Strong arms slid under her and lifted her hips to bring her center ever closer to Chance's mouth. She relaxed and let the sensation of being completely loved wash over her. *Score.*

***

Monday morning, Chance stopped in to see her mothers on her way back home from her run. As Zeus lay on the porch, Chance sipped a cup of coffee at the table.

Maggie squeezed her shoulder. "You know I much prefer your visits after you shower, but I'll take what I can get. What brings you by, besides a free cup of coffee?"

Chance turned the cup on the table and met the gaze of each mother in turn. "I wanted to check in with you two about Kendra's news." She watched Maggie stop whisking the bowl of egg whites she was scrambling.

Dee took a sip of her coffee. "I'm not surprised. She's been putting out hints for a while, feeling us out."

"She didn't say a word to me before I questioned her the other night." Chance was shocked.

Maggie poured the egg mixture in the cast iron skillet and slid two multi-grain English muffins in the toaster. "I don't think she wanted you to feel bad. Her dream was always coming to work for you."

"If there was any way I could have added another deputy, I would have." Chance dropped her head. "I hate this."

Dee covered Chance's hand. "We know that, and so does Kendra. She's got a blade to forge, just like you did. She's going to be fine."

"This family never has been one to take the safe route." Maggie dropped the empty bowl into the sink and used a spatula to move the eggs around.

Chance noticed how hard the bowl had landed. "I'm sorry, Mom. I know I let you down on this. I always promised you I'd keep her safe."

Maggie continued to stir, then turned to look at Chance. "I want you to stop thinking like that. You've taught her how to stay safe. I have no doubt you would have put her on if you could. I do have concerns about something happening to her if she's stationed away from us. What if...." Her words trailed off as she went to the toaster and removed the muffins before returning to the skillet.

Chance stood and moved the eggs off the burner.

"Chance, the food will get cold. I'm—"

"You're not all right. I know exactly what you're worried about. I was far away when I got hurt."

Maggie's shoulders slumped. "You both grew up on me too fast. You're not little kids anymore, and I can't protect you like I used to. When you scraped your knee or got a splinter, I could fix you up with a Scooby-Doo Band-Aid and a Popsicle. Now, both my daughters will be facing people that want to kill them. You remember what happened in Elkins, hell for that matter what happened to you not long ago. We won't even discuss your dad."

Chance wrapped her mother in a hug. Fat tears ran down Maggie's face and soaked into Chance's T-shirt. She looked around the kitchen she'd grown up in, taking in all the familiar sights of her childhood. This room brought her great comfort and security. The same things she needed to extend to the women who'd raised her. "I know. We'll both do all we can to not get hurt. Sometimes, there isn't anything we can do, and we rely on our training and our abilities to make sure we come home to the people who wait on us. I know my careers have put you through hell, and I'm eternally grateful you've always been there."

Dee joined in the hug. "That's what you do for family, Chance. Kendra's going to be fine. You've been a great role model for her over the years. She'll take those lessons with her and make sure to use them to stay safe. I have complete faith in her, wherever she lands."

Chance stood there with the two women who'd stepped up to raise her as if they'd given birth to her. It was going to be all right, it had to be.

Maggie pushed Chance away. "You stink. Go home and let me fix our breakfast in peace."

Chance snickered then kissed her mother's forehead. "I'll do that. Jax is fixing blueberry pancakes and bacon." She watched as Momma Dee looked from the egg whites in the pan to the muffins Maggie plated.

A look of desperation came over Dee. She turned to Chance and mouthed "take me with you."

Maggie raised her spatula and pointed it at Dee. "Keep it up and you'll be back to oatmeal."

Chance kissed them both on the cheek and laughed uncontrollably on the way out the door. She stopped briefly to listen to the two women she loved with all her heart bicker back and forth. She loaded Zeus in the vehicle and scratched his ears. "There's no place like home, so how about we head there and see your buddy?" Zeus barked. "Glad we agree."

***

Chance drove to the office after she ate and cared for the horses. Hunter was always happy to help clean their stalls, even though he told Jax it was stinky. They'd bought him muck boots and stall tools in a smaller size. He never grumbled about the chores and took them on with purpose. *As soon as he gets a little bigger, we'll get him a pony.*

She stopped by Harley's office to check in with her about the incident with the cows and to share what she'd found on the property in Dry Fork. Harley was on a phone call as she walked in, so she and Zeus took a seat and waited.

Harley shook her head. "I swear to you, we're turning over every rock. I have no proof Ted Eichland shot your cattle. If I did, I'd be up there arresting him. We questioned him, and he denied everything."

Chance listened as someone, likely Milton Denver, chewed on Harley's ear. Harley made a fist then pointed her finger as if the person she was talking to was in the room.

"If you do that, I'll have to arrest you, and you still won't have restitution for your cattle. Give me and my officers time to do our job. I'll call you this week with an update." She paused. "You are more than welcome to call my captain, Milton. I'll have my secretary give you his number. Hang on please." Harley jammed her finger on the hold button and called an extension. "Lilly, can you give Milton Denver Captain Dawkins' number in Elkins, please." She rubbed a hand across her face and looked at Chance.

"I feel for the guy, but you didn't shoot his cattle."

Harley rubbed her temples. "And I can't arrest someone solely on suspicion based on their altercation. I went to talk to the guy. Of course, his version is vastly different, as you can imagine. I'm telling you, Ted Eichland is bad news, and he's got others living out there with him if the laundry on the clothesline is any indication. I didn't see any kid's clothes, but from the different sizes I saw, I'd say at least two adult males and a female. Nothing illegal was out in the open, but he never invited me in either."

"I'm amazed he let you that close to the house. I checked out the latest aerial photography. It showed a gate across that road."

Harley rocked back in her chair and put her hands behind her head. "Yeah, we went around and around about how I was trespassing on his land. He tried to charge me a fee for driving on his road. Apparently, someone went out the gate and must have planned to return fairly soon because it was open when we got there. The guy tried to shove his invoice in my uniform pocket."

"Let me guess, that didn't go over well?"

"He didn't care much for having his arm twisted. I put him down on his knees. He threatened to sue me every way to Sunday. I'll have to have the girls at the courthouse watch for him to come in and file a lien against me. Sovereign Citizens are extremely well versed in the judicial system they claim they can't be held to. Anyway, I doubt that's what you stopped by to talk about. What can I do for you?"

Chance swung her Stetson back and forth on her index finger. "It's likely related. I got a call from Thomas Randler. He owns property in Dry Fork, and someone has an illegal shooting range set up in a remote corner. I swear Harley, I haven't seen that much brass lying around other than at the training academy or Jibby's recycling. The variety was unreal. I even found .50 caliber shells. Check this out." She pulled up the pictures and videos on her phone and passed them over.

Harley swiped through the photos and stopped on one of the videos. She whistled. "Damn, are they planning for an invasion or what?"

"There's more. Keep swiping." Chance knew when Harley got to the most significant pictures.

"Pipe bombs?"

Chance went on to describe what she'd found and how much of it. "Thomas bought this property at a sheriff's tax sale before I took office. I haven't pulled up the property records, but I'm putting Penny on that as soon as I get in the office. The guy didn't even know that any of it was on his property until a crew he had working there ran across it."

"Crazy. I wonder if any of those casings match up to what we pulled out of Milton's cattle?"

Chance stood. "Hard to say. I put a few cameras on the trail into the place. I'll go back out, but I'm certainly taking a few more people for backup. It requires a good hike, or in my case, a pleasant horseback ride. I figured I'd take Taylor with me. She's itching to get back in the field, and I've got to cut her loose. I'm damned if I do and damned if I don't. Penny wants her behind a desk for a little while longer, and Taylor's climbing the walls. I need to get in touch with the ATF about the pipe bombs. Everything I saw could be purchased at the hardware store. The armor-piercing rounds have me a bit rattled too, but it's just one spoke on the wheel. Anyway, I'll keep you posted." Chance started through the door. "Oh, by the way, Jax checked with some of Lindsey's professors. They say she's doing great. We're proud of her."

"So are we. That girl works so hard and keeps her head above water, all while wrangling my daughter. She deserves a medal for that. I spent almost twenty years trying to figure her out."

"I hear you. Right now, I've got a little angel, but I'm sure we'll have our share of struggles."

Harley nodded. "No doubt, but it is so worth it. Be careful out there."

Chance threw her hand in the air. "Right back at you."

***

Jax had a busy day planned with a morning surgery and an afternoon visit from Rhebekka and Naomi. JJ, one of their cats, was due for her checkup and yearly shots. They were bringing Marley with them as well. Before she got started, she called Kristi.

"Do you have any plans today?"

"None, what's up?"

"Well, I think we should have lunch together. I know it's short notice, but I get the feeling you could use a little girl time." Jax turned a pencil over end on end.

"I certainly could. Would it be okay to come to your office? What would you like to eat?"

"That sounds great. You know me, I'm not picky."

"Jax?"

"Yes?"

"Thanks."

Jax inwardly sighed with relief. "You've been there for me more than once. I recognize the signs. See you at lunch."

Jax hung up the phone and pulled her ponytail clip out, gathered the long dark strands together, and reattached the clip. *Time to get to work.*

***

Chance pointed at the documents on Penny's computer screen. "That one. Can you get me any information on the previous owner, also the tax sale itself and any supporting documents?"

"I can." Penny made notes on a scratch pad by her keyboard. "Anything else?"

"Yeah, check out the property adjacent to it. Unless I miss my guess, they were the previous owners. Find me anything you can about them."

Penny turned back to her screen. "You got it. I think Taylor finally has some information back on that gun you found. She said to send you back her way when you got in."

"Okay. Is Jace with my mom today?"

Penny looked up and smiled. "Yes. According to Maggie, he and Hunter have a playdate scheduled. I don't know what we'd do without your moms."

"Isn't that the truth" Chance picked up the coffee Penny had ready for her and headed down the hall. "Good thing for both of us they love being grandparents."

She strolled into Taylor's office and sat down in the chair in front of her desk. Zeus and Midas were play-fighting in the corner. More than once, Chance had thought about getting a companion dog for Zeus. Now he had Hunter and that seemed to be all he needed. She tossed her phone on Taylor's desk. "Copy off that file labeled shooting range."

Taylor did as directed, then opened the file. She whistled. "Damn."

"That's what I said. It was unreal. From what I saw, they're loaded for bear and it's not even their property."

"Who the hell does that?"

Chance threw her hat in the chair beside her. "Assholes. I've got Penny running down some leads. I'm going to need to go back and retrieve the SD cards on the cameras I hid up there to catch whoever the hell it is. Hopefully, we'll catch clear facial images. When I go, I'd like you to ride up with me on the horses. It's a pretty good trek in by foot but an easy ride."

"Yeah, walking back in there alone wouldn't be advisable."

"I want to leave it a while to try and establish a pattern of their comings and goings. The last thing we want to do is ride in there while they're shooting their AK-47."

Taylor nodded. "Wonder if any of those are from a custom .38?"

Chance reached in a pocket on her uniform pants and pulled out the bags of casings. "I wondered about that too. There were too damn many up there, so I grabbed a few of each. Penny said you have something back on the gun?"

Taylor held up a report and handed it to Chance. "At least the prints on the gun. There were two sets. One of which belongs to Paul Leonard, as we expected. The other belongs to our one and only Mr. Ted Eichland."

"Well, well, well."

"At this point, we have a truck that was once owned by Paul, a gun that went missing where he worked, and a jacket with that range's logo. I can also say there is at least some contact or association with a known sovereign citizen. Add all that to the break-in where the wrecked vehicle was impounded, and it all keeps circling back that we need to find Mr. Paul Leonard."

Chance sighed. "This thing keeps twisting around itself more and more. Harley was at Ted's place not too long ago, investigating some dead cattle and a brandishing complaint. She ended up putting him in a wrist lock when he tried to give her some bullshit invoice for driving on his road. Anyway, once we go get that footage, let's hope we get a picture or two of Mr. Leonard with a firearm in his hand. According to his record, he can't legally own or possess a firearm in Missouri, where his last known residence was. He can't possess one here in West Virginia because he spent more than a year in jail on that distribution conviction. Prints on that gun show he's had it in his possession at one time or another. I'd say you don't have to be a genius to figure out he stole it from that gun range he worked at. Now, we just have to find him. If they're making those pipe bombs, might not be a bad idea to do a little surveillance if we can get a warrant for it."

Penny knocked on the door. "Here's the info you wanted. The property used to belong to Hansen Kilmer, but he died and left it to his daughter Patty. She couldn't pay the taxes on that parcel Thomas Randler bought at the tax sale. She filed several petitions about it but never came up with the money to pay."

Chance looked over the paperwork. "This says she's about my age. I don't remember her from school, but she could have gone to Harman High. Let's run a Triple I on her and see if we can make some connection between Paul Leonard and Patty Kilmer."

Taylor sat up and started typing on her computer. "That name sounds extremely familiar." She scrolled her mouse around and opened some files. "There it is." She pointed to her screen.

Chance and Penny came around the side of the desk, just as Daniel walked in.

"What am I missing out on?"

Chance smiled at him. "Detective work." She looked down at the screen. "Well, I'll be. I'm not even sure I remember that."

Daniel came around and crowded in beside them. "What am I looking at?"

Chance patted him on the shoulder. "The missing link. Damn good work, Taylor."

Daniel scrunched his brow. "Why would a letter with missing postage be important?"

Chance reached over and hit print on Taylor's computer, then retrieved the copy. "Remember that break-in at Granger's?" She watched him nod. "It's tied into a few things we were trying to connect." She laid out the evidence link that led to the printout she held in her hand. "Taylor remembered a call at the Davis post office. A woman was trying to demand the teller send a certified letter but wasn't willing to pay the proper postage. Patty Kilmer was that woman. Guess who she was trying to mail a letter to?" Chance pointed to Taylor.

"One Paul Leonard of Springfield, Missouri." Taylor grinned.

"Damn. Trying to follow that was like trying to drive up Cheat mountain in reverse." Daniel shook his head. "Let's hope a judge can follow the path easier than I did."

"I'll make sure the prosecutor does, even if I have to strap him in the passenger seat and take him for a drive." Chance looked closely at the paper. "I know it's Springfield, Missouri, but is it the address he was living at when he was evicted for taxes?"

The phone rang and Penny answered it. "Tucker County Sheriff's Office. How can I help you?"

There was a pause as Penny looked up to Taylor. "Yes, she's here. Hold one minute please." Penny placed the call on hold. "It's something about that gun you're investigating."

"This is Chief Deputy Taylor Lewis. How can I help you?" Taylor jotted down a few notes as the person spoke. Another call came in, and Penny went to her office to answer. Taylor hit the speaker button. "I have Sheriff Fitzsimmons with me. Can you repeat what you just told me?"

"Certainly, my name is Agent Mitchell Farmer with the ATF. You sent a weapon to the West Virginia State Forensics lab. They entered the particulars into the NIBIN. I assume the purpose was to see about possible matches to unsolved or known crimes."

Chance looked at Penny to see if she was following. "Correct, and I'm assuming this call means that it does."

"It does indeed, Sheriff. One that involves the shooting of an undercover officer who had infiltrated a group of sovereign citizens in Idaho. The groove patterns are a match for the bullet that was lodged in his spine."

Taylor leaned forward. "Son of a bitch, you have to be kidding me?"

"We've been trying to get a break in this case for months. Can you give me a little more detail on how this came to be in your possession?"

Chance relayed to Agent Farmer what they knew about the gun as well as several of the details with the cattle incident and the illegal gun range.

"Sheriff, I don't mean to alarm you, but I've got an agent who can't breathe without the assistance of a ventilator because of that gun. I'll be sending a local agent out of Clarksburg to dig a little deeper. I'd appreciate any cooperation you'd be able to give. Her name is Erin Southern. She's been with us for twelve years."

Chance leaned closer to the phone. "I know Erin. I've worked with her a few times when we were doing eradication operations."

"I expect she'll contact you before coming over then. Sheriff, I don't have to tell you how badly we want the guy who took our agent down. He has a wife and two kids. Right now, he's having a hard time. He thinks he's a burden to his family. I'd like to make sure we have an airtight case, if we can, for Myron's sake. He deserves it."

Chance glanced up to Taylor and Daniel and saw the steely determination she expected. "I know this is typically something your agency might want to come in and take over, Agent Farmer, but I want this to be a joint operation. I'm the primary law enforcement agency in this county, and we've worked very hard to build up a reputation of cooperation with federal authorities. Our community needs to know officers in this department are capable."

"I do understand that. I don't have enough agents in West Virginia at this time, and we'd welcome your cooperation as well."

"Then, Agent Farmer, you have a deal. Tell Erin to call me and we'll work something out."

"Will do, and thanks, Sheriff."

Chance hung up the phone and looked at Daniel who was petting Athena's ears. "Don't worry, I'm not leaving you out of this. I would expect Erin to call in the next few hours. She's good people." She looked to Taylor. "And family."

Taylor grinned. "Then it should be a fruitful operation."

Chance leaned back on a cabinet. Zeus watched her intently, as if he could sense her mood change. "Well crew, it seems things around here are about to get interesting."

Daniel laughed. "Is there a time around here that isn't interesting? For a small county in the mountains, we sure have our share of big operations. Between capturing those guys who kidnapped Doc Marty and busting the Kurst family, sure seems pretty damn interesting to me."

"It certainly feels like it, but I can remember years that went by where our only major issues were trying to figure out who was stealing Mr. Hampton's chickens and stopping the drag races out on Synergy Highway."

Taylor shook her head. "We could do with a few less interesting calls. I've visited you in the hospital one too many times in the last few years."

"I'd say Jax would agree with you." Chance looked at her two deputies, both family to her in one way or another. "You were at the training about these guys." She pointed to the phone. "Agent Farmer said there is an officer who requires a machine to keep him alive. He may never be able to hold his kids or wife again. Daniel, you're just starting, and I have no doubt you and Dezi will eventually have your own family. She pointed to Penny but looked at Taylor. "You have a saint standing at your shoulder. She went through hell to bring your son into this world." She pointed to herself. "I now have a family I never thought I'd have. Jax is back in my life, and I have a little boy who needs me around. No short cuts. No lapses in concentration. If we're lucky, we'll have many years to enjoy our families."

Daniel stood a little straighter. "I'm pretty sure my moms would like me to be around to give them grandchildren. If Dezi's willing, we plan to do just that."

Taylor reached out for Penny's hand to hold. "By the book."

Chance stood up straight. "By the book. One of the things I need to do, eventually, is retrieve my SD cards from my cameras and see if we caught anything. It's hard to tell who is out at Patty Kilmer's place. If this Paul Leonard is there with Ted Eichland, I won't be surprised if there are others. Daniel, do you still have that fancy drone of yours?"

Daniel's face lit up. "I do."

"Then let's do a little recon on that illegal gun range and see if it's safe to go in there and check on who's been traveling by."

Chapter Thirteen

JAX LOOKED UP WHEN the smell of baked bread wafted into her office. Her visitor stood in the doorway with a bag in her hand. "Tell me you made pepperoni rolls?"

"Fresh from the oven." Kristi walked in and began to pull out containers. "I've got pasta salad too. I know it's one of your favorites."

"What, no dessert?" Jax quirked a crooked grin.

Kristi put a hand on her chest. "What do you take me for, some amateur? I brought chocolate to commiserate with."

Jax put her hands in the air. "I will never doubt you again."

They ate for a few minutes before Jax spoke. "Kristi, don't take this the wrong way, but you look tired."

"No offense taken." Kristi moved the pasta salad around in her bowl. "I am tired. Sarah hasn't been sleeping, and without her tucked up against me, I can't sleep either. When she is in bed, she's tossing and turning."

"Do you want to talk about it? I've been told I'm a pretty good listener."

Kristi put the bowl down on Jax's desk and sighed. "I'm not sure what to do. I think it's a cumulative thing from all the serious calls she's dealt with lately. The overdoses, Chance going down, then your accident. I can't begin to tell you half the things she's seen. To be honest, I think Chance stepping back from the rescue team was pretty devastating to Sarah. She knows why, but they've been such a team for so long. She seems lost, and I can't seem to reach her."

"I was shocked when Chance told me she'd scaled back her involvement. She did say that they were aware she was available for serious calls. I didn't think she'd pulled completely away. Maybe I'm wrong."

"I think that's how I heard it." Kristi shook her head. "I'm trying to convince Sarah to get some help. I know she has the number Chance gave her in her pocket. I can't make her call. I just keep hoping she will."

Jax rocked in her office chair. "I'm not sure what I can do, but I'd be willing to talk to her. The other thing I can do is be here for you."

Kristi blew out a breath. "Sarah is talking to Chance, that's a start. I value our friendship. It's nice to know you're here when I need someone to vent to."

"Anytime. Have you heard anything about the new job at the high school?"

Eyes bright with excitement met Jax's. "I have. I'll be the new nurse at the high school with Mrs. Danner's retirement. I'm looking forward to it. Dealing with all those teenage hormones will be a challenge, and they have so much pressure on them. I'm hoping to be someone they turn to."

Jax leaned forward and took Kristi's hand. "You did a great job with Daniel. I have no doubt you will be someone very special in their lives." She took out a notepad and wrote on it. "This is the name and number of a spousal support group for first responders. Penny gave it to me not long after Chance and I got together. It's a place to find resources and sometimes just support. When she was hurt last year, I called that number more than once. I know that I have you and Penny, but sometimes you really need that anonymous person, just to blow off steam. Don't hesitate to call them. I started volunteering for the hotline several months ago. I can't do it as much as I used to, since that little ball of energy moved into our home, but I try to volunteer a day when I can. Call. I promise it will help."

Kristi took the paper and looked at it. She wiped at a tear. "Thank you for understanding. Sometimes, it takes one to know one."

Jax walked around her desk and bent down to hug Kristi. "I think you'll agree; loving them is the easiest and hardest thing we do."

"It definitely is. Now, how about that chocolate?"

Jax released her and grinned. "I thought you'd never ask."

***

Chance scrolled on her computer. She needed to strengthen the links between Patty, Ted, and Paul Leonard. The fact that Patty had been trying to send him mail years ago told her their connection didn't develop recently. Her phone rang.

"Yes, Penny?"

"It's Agent Erin Southern on line two for you."

"I'm on it." Chance punched the blinking button. "Sheriff Fitzsimmons."

A raspy voice came across the line. "Afternoon Sheriff, this is Erin. It's been a while."

Chance rocked back in her seat. "It has indeed. It seems we'll be working together again. How much do you know?"

"Just what Farmer told me. From the sounds of it, we've got trouble up in your beautiful neck of the woods."

Chance filled her in on the last few weeks, everything from the original wreck down to the illegal gun range with the pipe bombs.

Erin let out a low whistle. "Sounds like they've got some firepower from the variety of casings you found. I'm a gun enthusiast, and I can't imagine having a rifle that can hit something over a mile away. I don't have to tell you, we're pretty anxious to find whoever shot our agent."

"There's no doubt in my mind. I've got an idea. I've been talking with one of my deputies who owns a drone. When I was at the makeshift range, I put up some cameras with the permission of the property owner. We're going to put that eye in the sky to see if the area is safe to extract the camera card and check the images."

"These guys are bad news, Chance. I won't be surprised if they're running guns with the amount of firepower you found."

Chance thought about the agent on the other end of the phone line. She'd worked with Erin on different occasions and knew her to be a thorough investigator. The tall redhead knew her way around the backwoods, having run more than one operation with Scott Ross when he was with the DEA. "At this point, there is little that surprises me when it comes to how far people will go with their illegal activities. I had a deputy shot not long ago."

"I heard about Kenny. Isn't he going back to school?"

Chance looked up at a picture of Kenny and Tyson before he nearly lost his life. "He's still recovering, but yes, he's on track to become a lawyer."

"When are you planning to retrieve those cards?"

"Likely tomorrow morning, as early as possible. Most of these folks don't tend to be early risers."

"They do like the cover of darkness. Let me know when you've got the SD cards. I'll try and help with identification if I can."

"I'll hold you to that offer, thanks. I'll talk to you soon, Erin."

Daniel walked into her office with a stack of printouts. "You might be interested in flipping through this."

She took the stack and scanned page after page of hate speech and anti-government rhetoric. "Where did you find all this?"

Daniel quirked his mouth. "I'm the generation that grew up with the internet and social media as part of my daily life. It's not hard to find the stuff if you know where to look. You're pretty popular as the dyke sheriff on some of these sites." Anger crossed his normally cheerful face. "A lot of homophobic and bigoted bullshit, big talk about governmental overreach, vitriol about gun control, and a ton of other things." He sorted through the papers. "This one made me pause." He pointed to a few posts from someone called Sov88Eich. "This guy appears to be offering weapons training, and it sounds like it's with some of the weapons you saw casings for."

Chance read through the exchanges. "Is there any way to be sure if this guy is our Eichland?"

Daniel shook his head. "Not with our local resources, but I'm sure Agent Southern has access to a wider database. We could try running it through the WV Fusion Center as well."

"Let me check with Erin first. She may already have intel on it. If not, give it to Taylor, she's our Fusion Center liaison."

Daniel stood. "This is some pretty heavy shit, Chance."

She sat back in her chair and watched Zeus and Athena sniffing each other near the door. "And about to get heavier." She tapped the papers. "This is good work, Daniel. Really good work. I'm proud to have you working for this department."

He leaned against the jam. "I wish Kendra was coming to work here. She told me about the Marshal's position. She's pretty psyched, but I'd always hoped we'd get the chance to work together."

Chance drew in a deep breath and released it slowly. She steepled her fingers and let her chin rest on them. "Me too. I'm so proud of her, but I'll admit it's killing me. I've had a lot of people tell me she's got to make her mark. Subconsciously I know that. I can't help but worry."

"She's going to be okay. Look at Taylor. She started at the Marshals, and now she's your right hand."

"That's the only thing that's keeping me sane. Kendra has to do what's best for her. I support whatever she does."

"You taught both of us how to be good officers from the time we started dreaming about wearing the badge. Don't forget that. I never will."

"Thanks, Daniel. I needed to hear that more than you know." She picked up her phone. "I'll call Erin."

She watched him walk away with Athena, and Zeus came to put his head on her thigh. "Let's get to work, Zeus. We've got bad guys to find."

***

"Easy, Marley. I need to make sure this is all healed up. You guys did a great job keeping it clean. Did you have any trouble with the stitches?" Jax scratched under the tuxedo cat's chin.

Rhebekka held up her hand. "I confess, we had Amy do it."

Jax shook her head. "Well, she is a doctor."

Rhebekka looked contrite. "I was afraid I'd hurt her, and Naomi is the only one who can hold her so that she doesn't squirm."

Naomi snickered and looked at Jax. "When they took Rhebekka's stitches out, I had to hold her too."

Rhebekka rubbed her hand down Marley's back. "How's Taylor doing? I've been trying to catch her for the last few days, but since she's back to work, it's like trying to nail Jell-O to the wall."

Jax laughed. "That sounds about right. She's doing okay. The burns have almost healed completely. I think notifying Travis' grandparents hurt more, but it was hard on all of you to do that. Chance said she checked on them last week. They're still having a rough time."

Rhebekka nodded. "They are. I call them once a day. Travis was such a good kid. He took care of a great deal of the work at their place. They're pretty lost, so I have our after-school kids organized to visit and help out however they can. In other news, I talked to Penny not long ago. We're trying to schedule Jace's christening. I understand you and Chance are to be his godparents."

The thought of little Jace warmed Jax's heart and she let a true smile break forth. "We are. That little guy is so adorable. He and Hunter are best buddies. Maggie and Dee watch them on most days. Hunter is so gentle with him."

Naomi put Marley back in the crate and pulled JJ out. "How is Hunter adapting to living with you?"

Warm affection filled Jax from head to toe. "Better than anyone could have expected. Recently, he started calling us Momma J and Momma C. As a matter of fact, we have another parenting class tonight. All part of the hoops to adopting him and making him a permanent part of the Fitzsimmons clan, though not everyone seems happy about that."

Rhebekka looked concerned. "What do you mean? Who wouldn't be happy about a little boy getting a family?"

"One of the social workers, or whatever she is, made some snippy remarks about our family being less than ideal. She also made some comments about Maggie and Dee. Chance called the supervisor and complained. She was assured we wouldn't have to deal with her again."

Naomi crossed her arms and shook her head. Rhebekka rubbed her forehead. "West Virginia's come a long way, but it still isn't where it needs to be. So many kids are looking for homes, and yet there are agencies out there blatantly discriminating against LGBTQ families who could offer them wonderful homes. That's not even mentioning the poor kids that are LGBTQ themselves. One of our congregation members works over at the WV Children's Home in Elkins. She's told me about these incredible kids who will likely never live anywhere else until they age out of the system. Many will never have the opportunity because they are gay, lesbian, or bisexual. She knows of one transgender male being forced to live as a female."

Rhebekka cracked her knuckles. "Who is going to give those kids a home? Why are they throwaway kids who are kicked out because their parents can't deal? Some of those parents disown their children with no support, then spout off about their God being one of compassion and love. That certainly doesn't sound like it to me and definitely not the God I know in my heart."

Naomi put her hand on Rhebekka's back and kissed her shoulder. "That's why she told you, honey. She knows you will help her figure this out. We've always said there is a solution to every problem, if you are willing to be that solution."

Rhebekka covered Naomi's hand. Jax watched the couple with awe. Rhebekka spoke with such passion. Jax had no doubt Rhebekka would take the problem on. It was too important not to.

"Those kids need parents who will love them for exactly who they are." Rhebekka wiped away a tear. "No child should fear God because of something they have no control over or who they love. I spent my whole childhood fearing God, and that's such bullshit. It's like telling a toddler to be good or the police will arrest them."

Jax gave JJ her checkup and required shots. "Miss JJ, you have some pretty awesome parents." She handed the calico to Naomi. "Keep her on that special diet, and she'll keep getting stronger."

Naomi opened the crate to allow JJ to curl up with Marley. "They have the best vet in the world."

"You're too kind. I hope you two can come to dinner sometime. We so rarely get to see you other than at work. It would be nice to have a few burgers with some of that amazing Savior's Red from Redemption's

Road. What would be fantastic is if the visit didn't involve a heartworm pill or a death notification."

Rhebekka visibly relaxed. "That can be arranged. We have Salvations and Libations this Wednesday but we're pretty much free after that. Siobhan and her group are playing at The Confluence over the weekend, freeing us up. I could use a little time out at that beautiful farmhouse."

"Then we'll plan on Friday night, if that works for the both of you. You bring the beer. We'll provide the food and a six-year-old for entertainment."

Rhebekka grabbed the crate. "It's a deal."

"I'll walk you both out. It's about time for me to go home and feed that growing boy. Say a little prayer for us that our evening session goes well. We can use all we can get."

***

Chance sipped her coffee while reading over a file Taylor had sent her. Penny called her on the office phone.

"It's Agent Southern for you on line one."

"Thanks, Penny." She punched the line. "Erin, what can I do for you?"

I've got some information related to those chats your deputy found. Legally, I can't get too deep without a warrant. I've had our people do some searches related to that internet profile. In some of the pointed searches, we've found references to places, locations, and names of known subjects in your area. We're still digging, but what Daniel found is pointing to Sov88Eich being Ted Eichland. I need to warn you that Sov88Eich and others have shared the home addresses of local law enforcement including you, Taylor, and Sergeant Kincaid of the state police."

"Does it seem like they're targeting us?"

"Nothing specific points to that, just that they know where you live. As Daniel said, a lot of homophobic rants and plenty of anti-government rhetoric. Part of why I called was the coded wording used within the chats."

Chance put Erin on speakerphone. "What kind of coded wording?"

"I know that JD Hamilton from the FBI came in and did a class for your officers. I'm sure he told you about some of the unique phrasings many of them use."

"Yes, he said much of it is an attempt to try and separate themselves from government regulation."

"Much of it, yes. There are also pockets of substantially more violent sovereign citizens, which Sov88Eich seems to belong to. We've traced that chat name in several of the groups."

"I'm not going to like what you haven't told me yet, am I?"

"No. It seems like there is a meetup that will be going down. Some pretty heavy movers and shakers in the sovereign citizen movement are coming from out west and planning a visit to Tucker County. I'm bringing in another agent from the ATF, and I'm trying to get some surveillance warrants. We need to get some eyes on that Kilmer property as well as that illegal range you found. Something is getting ready to go down."

"Is it imminent, as in the next twenty-four hours?"

"More like this weekend or next week, which makes our surveillance even more critical. If we already have permission from the landowner for cameras, I'd like to add some of our more sophisticated equipment."

"We're planning to put Daniel's drone up in the morning to check our equipment. If no one is around, it might be the best time to put those items in place, if you have the equipment and manpower."

"I'll make it happen. What time?"

"Daniel doesn't have night vision on his drone so it would have to be daylight, which comes in around seven. We could get into position before that. It's a two-and-a-half-hour foot trek or a thirty to forty minute horseback trip. We've got the horses if your people can ride. If not, they're hoofing it. No pun intended."

Erin laughed. "I'm a farm girl, so horseback is no issue for me. Let me check with my people. I'm thinking I'll only need one other agent with you, Taylor, and Daniel there. Going in on horseback will help transport the equipment. We'll put in some night-vision cameras with the ability to transmit intermittently to avoid detection. If they're sophisticated enough to have jammers or detection equipment, we can defeat it. With the bigger names coming in, I won't be surprised if they do. I'm going to send you info on the names and backgrounds of the individuals we know that have shown interest."

"I appreciate it. I've got a parenting class in a few hours. I'll have Taylor start working on the particulars." She looked at the time on the bottom of the screen. "It's a little after three now. She'll have a more detailed plan worked out in a few hours."

"Sounds good."

They ended their call, and Chance immediately punched in Daniel's number and waited for him to pick up. An email came in from Erin which required the encryption software she'd installed to gain access.

"Afternoon Sheriff, what can I do for you?" Daniel asked.

"Get those batteries and whatever else you need for that drone charged up. We'll need to be close enough to that range by daylight. We'll be going in on horseback, so you'll be taking Jill."

"I've got a backpack for the drone, so that will work out fine. It folds down for transport. I took it out after my shift for a little practice too."

"Don't be nervous, Daniel. I have every confidence in you. If I didn't, we wouldn't be doing this."

"I know. It's my first big operation. I'm trying not to get the jitters, but you have to admit, this is pretty intense for my first year."

"It is. I'm not worried a bit. Get some rest. We'll meet at the barn around 04:30."

"I'll be ready."

"We all will."

Chance hung up and called Taylor, relaying the information from Erin and filling her in on what she'd told Daniel.

"I've got that parenting class this evening. I'll leave it to you to put the particulars together."

"It has to be easier than transitioning Jace to solid food. I'll see you in the morning, Chance."

"I think I've got the easy part, mine is potty trained and can feed himself. See you tomorrow, Taylor."

***

Chance flipped on her turn signal and merged onto the highway headed for home. The parenting class had gone much smoother than their first one. "Glad to see we didn't have to deal with our disapproving caseworker tonight."

Jax yawned. "Even Wells and Tera seemed more relaxed with Sherry leading by herself."

"If you don't mind, I need to call Taylor and see what she has worked out."

Jax put her hand on Chance's arm. "By now you should know you never need to worry about doing your job."

"It never hurts to include you in my decisions."

"And that's what makes me love you more and more every day. Call Taylor."

Chance used the Bluetooth system in the 4Runner to place the call. After their typical greetings, Taylor passed on the plan she'd worked out. Chance concurred. "Daniel knows to rest up and meet us at the stable in the morning. He'll be there in plenty of time to help load the horses and get to the property."

"Strange how the tip of the iceberg doesn't give you any clue as to how big the damn thing is below the surface. A simple leaving the scene turns into this."

Chance let out a sardonic laugh. "As long as we don't underestimate it like Captain Edward Smith, we won't find ourselves at the bottom of the ocean. Get some rest. I'll load Kelly up and meet you at the barn in the morning." She hung up and looked over to Jax, who'd let her head rest against the seat. "I'd tell you not to worry, but I know that won't help."

"I'll always worry, no matter how mundane the operation seems to be." Jax rolled her head to look at Chance. "From what I can gather, these are some sketchy people with a lot of firepower."

"Correct on all points. If they weren't doing anything illegal, we wouldn't have a problem. An officer on a ventilator knows how bad they can be. I don't want that in my county or for any of my officers to have a confrontation with them. This group doesn't believe in government oversite. They don't believe in rules and regulations or for paying their fair share of the taxes that help keep up the services and programs that put us above most countries. Many of them are involved in criminal activities that they see nothing wrong with. Not all of them are violent, but some are."

"I'm thankful there are people like you and Taylor who are willing to take them on. All I ask is that you remember the families that wait for you to come home."

"I feel very confident that Taylor feels exactly as I do about that."

"Then let's go home and put a little boy to bed. Luckily, he's already on a good schedule for school because that starts next week. Friday evening, Rhebekka and Naomi are coming to dinner. I'm telling you all this because I want you to remember that I have a lifetime planned with you. There's also a little boy who worships the ground you walk on. Don't ever forget that."

Chance drove them home thinking about all the things Jax said. Sometimes she wondered if it was time to get out of the business and concentrate on building her growing family. *I made a commitment the day I took office and the people of this county trust me to follow through. My commitments to Jax and Hunter are even more important. Balance, it's time to find balance.* She didn't know what that would look like in the coming years, but she was determined to do everything she could to achieve it.

***

Three thirty in the morning came long before Chance wanted it to. She held Jax for a few seconds longer, then kissed her forehead before trying to quietly disentangle herself from the warm body. Jax opened her eyes.

"Time to go?"

"It is. I was trying not to wake you." Chance relaxed for a minute longer.

"The second you pull away, I miss your heat."

"That's what hot flashes have turned me into, a living, breathing furnace."

"You're pretty handy in the winter. I went through a few years of them before they finally stopped."

Chance chuckled. "I feel like I'm in one constant flash. I swear there are days under that vest I'm ready to self-combust. One time, I stopped by the barn on the way to work. I rarely wear a coat in the cruiser, but it was two degrees when I stopped to check on the horses, and I didn't bother to take it off when I got back in the cruiser. Anyway, a hot flash hit. When I went to unzip, the damn thing got stuck. I ended up rolling down the window and turning on the air conditioner all the way to the office. It took Taylor with a pair of vice grips to get me out of it. I swear if it hadn't been a three-hundred-dollar coat, I'd have had her cut the damn thing off."

Jax laughed and burrowed into her neck. "Be careful. I want more three in the morning conversations. Maybe not until six, but I want more of them. Okay?"

Chance rolled on top of Jax and kissed her thoroughly. "Yes indeed. I love you, Jax, with all my heart. I'll be home as soon as I can."

"We'll be waiting."

Chance dressed and stopped by Hunter's room to retrieve her partner who was once again guarding his best friend. Chance leaned over and brushed the hair off Hunter's forehead and kissed him. She motioned for Zeus to follow.

"We'll come home to them, boy. They need us and we certainly need them."

***

Chance could see Taylor and Daniel loading Sabrina, Jill, and Kris, three of the department's horses, as she pulled into the barn area. She knew that Erin was bringing another agent, so she'd brought Glenny with her. Zeus whined behind her. "I know, your buddies are busy having fun without you." She let him out and watched as he bounded over to them.

Daniel walked Jill up into the trailer. "I don't know if I should say good morning or good night."

She shook her head. "Neither, because there's nothing good about leaving a warm bed at three in the morning."

He smiled at her. "Or the warm body still left in it."

Chance pointed at him indicating how correct he was. She looked at Taylor. "Is everything ready to go?"

"Almost. There's a tote just inside the door. We wanted the horses to get settled."

"I'll grab it while you get them secured." Headlights illuminated the gravel driveway. "That's probably Erin and the other agent. Let's hope they can ride."

The plain, charcoal-gray sedan came to a stop. Erin got out with another agent Chance hadn't met. She turned to Taylor before walking to greet them. "I'll get that after I make introductions. Erin, it's been a while."

Erin accepted her outstretched hand. "It certainly has. I get the feeling we're about to be spending a good bit of time here. I went ahead and rented a house in the valley to give us a base of operations in the county. If not, we'd spend half our day driving back and forth. Sheriff Chance Fitzsimmons, this is Agent Railey Timms. You'll be happy to know he grew up in Tennessee on a horse farm. No instruction needed."

The tall, wiry man held out his hand. "Sheriff, it's a pleasure to meet you. Every agent I talked to said they'd work with you in a heartbeat. I'm glad I'm the one getting the opportunity."

"Since you know your way around a horse, I'll have you ride Glenny, my wife's Arabian. She's built for endurance rides. My wife is a member of the local group."

"I promise to treat her like I paid for her."

"She's also my wife's baby, and I'd like to stay out of the doghouse. Let me introduce you to my team. Chief Deputy Taylor Lewis, this is Agent Erin Southern and Agent Railey Timms. The other individual here is Deputy Daniel Ryker. He has the drone experience. There's an office in the barn, let's have a meeting before we head out into the dark." As the group got acquainted, Chance took a few seconds to compose an email, letting Jax know they were about to head out and that Glenny would be ridden by someone with a great deal of experience. *Hug my boy for me, and when he hugs you back, remember that's from me too.*

* * *

Chance had Erin with her as they led the way in Taylor's vehicle out to the property where they'd unload the horses. "Let's hope the folks in question have had a long night and plan on sleeping in."

Erin looked out the window. "How are we going to ride up there in the dark?"

Chance chuckled. "Not exactly in the dark. The riding helmets we have are equipped with some powerful LEDs, and recently, we've also found ways to incorporate them into the halter while still protecting the horse's eyes. The light will follow wherever they look. We're planning to stop far enough away from the range that, even if someone is there, they won't see us. All Daniel needs is a small clearing to launch that drone as soon as it gets light enough for us to see. I'm planning on adding one of these to our arsenal and putting some thermal imaging cameras on it as well. The one we're using today is Daniel's personal property. He's the expert on its operation. If we'd have had this technology, even a year ago, I'd have found many lost people even faster."

Erin nodded. "Technology is always changing. Even with all the fancy equipment in the world, it still takes someone to put the clues all together to arrest the bad guys."

"Good thing for us or we'd be out of a job."

"Very true. I'd like to ask one thing of you, if I could?"

"If it's within my power, I will do whatever you need."

"Railey was partnered with our injured agent for years. He'd like to cuff Paul Leonard with Myron's handcuffs. It's possible Paul didn't shoot him, but he likely stole the gun that changed Myron's life forever. It would mean a lot to him."

"That's an easy request to grant. Is Railey okay on this operation? I can speak from experience that sometimes you can be too close, and it can cause you to lose focus."

Erin held up a hand. "Don't worry about that. Railey is rock steady. He wants to see justice done, nothing more. He and Myron were close. He was Myron's outside contact along with a few others that took shifts during the undercover ops. Railey wasn't even on duty when the meetup went down. He was at the hospital for the birth of his son. He knows it's not his fault, but that doesn't make it any easier to stomach."

"Completely understandable. There's the gate." Chance stopped and gave Erin the code for the lock and watched her swing the pipe gate out of their way. They drove through and parked to the side. "Here we go," she muttered to herself.

Taylor turned on a work light at the back of the trailer and illuminated the area. Chance turned hers on as well while Daniel shut the gate before helping Taylor get the horses out. It didn't take long to have everything ready to go. Chance had called the communication center at the barn and advised them of the operation before they left. Communications would be sketchy out here. Their radios worked on a relay system. If you couldn't hit the tower, you couldn't talk. This area was notorious for dead spots because of the dense rock formations that jutted up into the sky. She'd turned on the vehicle repeater in hopes they'd have communications if needed.

Chance lifted herself onto Kelly's back, settled into the saddle, and walked the horse close to the others.

Daniel put on the harness that held the drone and turned so that Railey could slide it in and secure the brackets. "Thanks."

Railey turned his ball cap backward and slid the riding helmet on. "Anytime. Ready to fly that thing?" Railey circled his finger like a helicopter blade.

"As soon as we see light, we'll get it up." Daniel put his foot in the stirrup and glided into the saddle.

Chance was enjoying the ease with which Daniel was fitting in. He was the youngest by far. She turned to see Taylor and Erin mount their horses and join them. "Okay, everyone. I've got my Suburban set up as a repeater. I've tested it with success. I'm not sure how it will be closer to that range. If that happens, the talk-around channel should work to communicate between us if we get separated. Everyone have their earpieces in? I'd rather not have radio traffic announcing our presence."

With nods of confirmation, Chance pulled on Kelly's reins, allowing her to slowly start to the edge of the property with everyone following in behind them. She knew with the LEDs, they glowed like a nuclear reactor, but it couldn't be avoided if they were to get to the small clearing where they planned to launch the drone from. "Steady as she goes, girl." She patted Kelly's neck and nudged her forward.

***

They traveled for just under ninety minutes, their progress slow and methodical through the dark woods. Chance heard sounds of the forest as it woke from its slumber. They'd already spooked a few deer and something else that never showed itself in the brush. The forest was misty, and the smell of damp earth and decaying wood hung heavy in the air. The three K9's loped along ears pricked. She pushed her watch to illuminate the dial, estimating they should reach the small clearing in a few more minutes. The sky was just beginning to lighten as they broke from the woods into an area of tall grass. "Whoa, girl." She pulled Kelly up short and turned to see the others entering the space. "We're as close to the range as I want to get without checking things out to see if it's clear. Once we know, we can go in and do what we planned. Daniel, let's get you ready to go."

The group dismounted, and Railey helped remove the drone from the backpack mount. Daniel pulled the battery packs out of the saddlebags and began installing them with Athena sitting at his side. He attached a tablet to the controller and synced the system so he could view the onboard camera. Once everything had been checked and rechecked, he fired up the drone and brought it into a hover, testing each of the flight movements with the small joysticks attached to the controller.

Daniel gave Chance the thumbs up. "We're good to go as soon as I have a bit more light."

Chance nodded. The night before, she'd given Daniel the GPS coordinates, which allowed him to program them in before they started their operation. She barely heard the drone as it lifted into the sky and headed out of their view. She stepped behind Daniel and looked at the screen as the machine flew above the trees.

"I'm going to adjust the contrast until the sun comes up a bit more. Sometimes, it's so hard to see even with the adjustments."

Chance patted his shoulder. "It'll be okay. Do your best, that's all I ask." She watched the treetops pass beneath the drone, the camera focusing on a small stream and finally on a barely visible path through the trees. Chance pointed to the screen. "That's it. To the right is the makeshift range. Further down is where I found the pipe bomb fragments in the pit. Right there."

Daniel hovered the drone as Railey squinted. "Are those buckets of casings?"

"Yes, and there are dozens of them. They must have more cash than brains with the amount of money they've left lying around. Daniel, make sure you do a wide sweep from a bit of a distance to see if there's any campfire smoke."

"Will do."

Erin stood at Chance's shoulder. "I know some of our offices have these at their disposal. It's absolutely amazing how much detail we can see."

Chance pointed to Daniel. "That's all him. It's proven its usefulness, and we'll be upgrading his personal one to something with a few more options."

For the next fifteen minutes, Daniel moved the drone around checking every available spot. There were no signs of anyone currently being there.

Chance stretched her back and rubbed her eyes. "Getting old sucks. Staring at a screen makes my eyes go buggy."

Erin chuckled a bit and rubbed her own eyes. "I'm with you."

Daniel turned to look at them both. "Neither one of you is old. I don't see anyone, Sheriff. I'll need to bring it back and change the batteries. Once we get up to the range, I can put it back up to do surveillance while we check your cameras and put the others up."

"Bring it home. Once we get it secured, let's get up there. We can move faster now that we aren't traveling in the dark. Railey, I'll leave it to you and Erin to get your equipment in place while Daniel and I take care of mine."

The drone returned, and Railey helped Daniel secure it again. They mounted up and rode through the forest. Chance followed her GPS until they reached the edge of the makeshift range. She tied Kelly to a tree branch and made her way into the hidden spot where she'd placed the game cameras.

"Check this out, Daniel." Chance pointed to the chew marks on the casing. "It doesn't appear the humans found it, but something with sharp teeth surely did."

Daniel looked around until he found a patch of bare earth with a paw print. He put his hand down near it for comparison. "I'd say a bear and a big one at that. I can't wait to see the pictures. I'm going to put the drone up again to check for any company that might decide to visit."

"Good idea."

She watched Daniel walk away, her heart full of pride for the young man she'd watched grow up into an intuitive police officer.

"We're fortunate, Chance. Every day, I see him emulate your core values," Taylor said.

"I can't take all the credit. His parents had a big hand in that as well." Chance watched Zeus and Midas for any sign that they could sense something she couldn't. The dogs were alert but not displaying tension. She traveled to the second camera, quickly pulling the card and replacing it. She heard a soft whir above her and realized the drone was up and hovering near her. *Thanks for watching my back, Daniel.*

The group, once again, gathered near the horses. Railey had a tablet out and was checking the connection and position of the new cameras.

He pointed to the screen. "They're operational and set to switch signals every forty-five seconds to avoid detection. They'll start filming on motion or heat signatures. Anyone or anything with a temperature in normal human range will initiate the recording feature. We might get a few animals, but only large ones."

Taylor whistled. "Those are some fancy toys you guys play with. How's the quality as far as facial recognition?"

Erin waved Daniel over to where one of the cameras would activate. "Excellent in daylight." She pointed to the screen. "At night, it takes a little digital magic by the techno whizzes, but we can still pick them out of a lineup."

Chance looked at Daniel's face on the tablet. "That's really clear." She looked at her watch. They'd been on the scene for a little under an hour. "Did you see everything you wanted to? I can tell you've got the cameras in place. I wasn't sure what else you wanted to do."

Erin nodded. "We can go. I took a video of the current state of things. Even if they try to haul it out, we've got video evidence."

"Let's hope these SD cards give us an idea of who we're up against." Chance patted her pocket and hefted herself into the saddle. "Let's get the hell out of here before we get visitors."

The group joined her, and they quickly made their way back to the horse trailers. Chance knew the operation was a long way from being over. For now, she wanted to put distance between their team and the people they were seeking. *Not done by a long shot.*

Chapter Fourteen

THE GROUP CONVENED BACK at Chance's office. They checked the video feed on the SD cards and found several faces that needed identification. One they could make out clearly, Paul Leonard. The other three individuals would require some facial recognition beyond the capability of the sheriff's office.

"If you can make me a copy of that file, I'll send it to our whiz kids in DC." Erin typed something into her phone, then held it to her ear. "I'm going to alert my supervisor that we've completed the camera installation."

Chance nodded. "Taylor, do we have any social media platforms with a current picture of Patty Kilmer?"

Taylor looked up from her laptop. "I'll check."

"Daniel, can you run that drone footage off and put it into a zip file?"

He moved to the door. "I can. I just need to pull out the microSD card. I think I have an adapter in my locker."

Carl leaned on the door frame and moved out of Daniel's way. "Oh, to be so young and eager again. I'm headed to the courthouse for bailiff duty. If there's anything you need, let me know."

Chance waved. "Thanks, Carl."

She continued to transfer the files from her hidden cameras to a secure thumb drive and waited for Daniel to reappear. Once they'd loaded his footage, Erin and her team could work on the identification of the others. She was fairly sure that one of them was Ted Eichland. They were in possession of a very old driver's license photo and a few surveillance shots JD had given her during his class. The man in the pictures taken without his knowledge had a thick beard and was wearing a hat and sunglasses, hiding many of his features. His build fit the tall and muscular profile of the flyer photos. The other two were definitely persons of interest, given what they'd witnessed in playback. Footage showed them operating Class 3 automatic weapons. She seriously doubted that any of these individuals had the proper background checks, ATF purchase approval, or the $200 tax stamp that benefited a system the sovereign citizens decried. Chance watched as one of them lobbed something into one of the blast holes she'd crawled into. The bright explosions happened seconds later. *Horseshoes and hand grenades. Things are about to get damn interesting.*

***

Jax looked at the clock. They had about three hours before Hunter's clinical diagnostic testing appointment. She rubbed the soft strands of his hair as she watched him shovel a huge bite of pancake into his mouth. She tapped him on his shoulder to draw his attention. She signed and tried to remember to allow him to read her lips.

"*Slow down or you're going to choke.*"

Hunter looked sheepish as he chewed. "*Sorry.*"

She leaned forward smiled. "*Try and taste your food.*"

He looked at her quizzically. "*It tastes like a pancake.*"

Jax realized sarcasm didn't necessarily translate into sign language. She nodded. "*Okay. Please finish eating and go get dressed.*"

He pushed another bite in his mouth. Jax wondered if wolfing down his food was an unconscious action from his years of being underfed and neglected. *He never talks about his birth mom. Time to schedule an appointment for him with that child psychologist.* Jax felt a pang of guilt that she and Chance would be the one to see Hunter grow into adulthood, under their roof, instead of with the mother who'd given birth to him. She hoped Crissy was watching down on him and relieved to see him thriving. Her phone chimed with a text. *On our way home. See you soon.*

She watched Hunter shove the last bite in his mouth. He jumped down and took his plate to the dishwasher. Jax teared up at how thoughtful he was. She knew it wouldn't always be like this, but for now, she'd enjoy it.

***

Twenty minutes after she'd sent her text, Chance returned home. She positioned the Suburban so the gate would open toward the barn. Hunter came barreling out of the house with Jax behind him. The second Zeus saw him, he came to attention and whined. "You love him as much as we do." Zeus barked, never taking eyes off his charge.

She put the vehicle in park and released Zeus to join the boy. Hunter giggled as Zeus licked something off his face.

Jax wrapped an arm around her waist. "Tired?"

"Not really. That will hit later tonight." She nodded in Hunter's direction with her head. "You'd think it's been days, not hours."

"When Hunter woke up, the first thing he asked was why Zeus wasn't on his bed."

Chance smiled and kissed her. "He'll make a fine K9 officer someday."

Jax laughed. "Let's let him graduate grade school before we start figuring out his occupation after college."

Chance led Jax to the back of the trailer. Hunter already had the barn door open and was standing with a brush in his hand. "I think someone is a little anxious to get to work."

"Everything at a run except sleeping."

They took care of the horses, grooming them all and giving them their morning feed, before turning them out into the pasture. After a shower, Chance dropped Zeus off to stay with her mother at the real estate office while they were at Hunter's appointment.

As she drove, Chance held Jax's hand and frequently checked on Hunter with quick glances to her rearview mirror. He was playing a game on his tablet. *This is what family is all about.*

"So, how did the mission go?"

Chance relayed everything they had found and suspected. "Now it's a waiting game on some facial recognition from the ATF and hours of watching footage from their cameras. 'Hurry up and wait' as they say."

"And you're sure there is something illegal about them?"

"Right now, we have evidence of explosives, trespassing, and at the very least, littering. There's more there to learn, but it will take hours of surveillance unless something breaks."

"I'm glad you all got out of there before someone showed up. From what you've said, I don't like your odds against an armor-piercing bullet. Why do they even allow that to be sold outside of the military?"

"Demand. Like with many other things, the regulations and laws rarely affect criminals."

"We've never discussed how you feel about gun control?"

"That's such a muddy issue. I believe that people should be able to own legally obtained firearms." She turned to Jax. "Within reason. No one, other than the military or trained law enforcement officers, should have access to fully automated weapons. No one with a violent felony background or distribution of narcotics should be able to have access to any firearms, period. They forfeit that right when they make poor choices in their lives."

"I think about the possibility of someone walking into Hunter's school and taking away that precious boy's life. It frightens me to death."

"A big part of gun control should have absolutely nothing to do with the firearm itself. We have to improve our impoverished communities, so they don't turn to a life of armed crime as a means to support themselves. Education has never been a priority in this country the way it is in others. Access to quality education, healthcare, and an actual living wage would go a long way to fixing why many of our young people turn to crime. We need to provide psychological care for those with mental issues. Far too often, they reach for a gun to solve a perceived problem. Law enforcement has to be a partner in all of it. It can't be us versus them. That sets us up as adversaries from the beginning."

"I love when you are impassioned about your role as a police officer."

Chance pulled Jax's hand up and kissed the knuckles. "Law enforcement has to be an integral part of the community, and violence should never be the first resort to conflict resolution. As officers, we also have to be willing to weed out those among us whose character and integrity more closely resembles the criminals we lock up than those who stand as that thin line between order and anarchy."

"Like Brad?"

"Maybe. I don't know if there was a time when he was a good officer or not. Did he become disenchanted with the job due to lack of support, changes in society, or was he always a bad fit? Somewhere along the line, we need to build bridges in our communities instead of surrounding them with razor wire. I'm a firm believer in de-escalation whenever possible. We have to emphasize to our police officers that deadly force is a last resort." Chance paused and collected her thoughts before swallowing the bile in her throat. "As a society, the life of a police officer has to mean something as well. We've sworn an oath to protect and serve, lay down our lives if we have to, for the public or a fellow officer. There isn't a day that goes by I don't think about the lives I've been forced to take. I pray that Kendra, and for that matter Daniel, never has to experience it. It profoundly changes you."

Jax rubbed the back of Chance's hand with her thumb. "That's why you and Rhebekka are pretty close, isn't it?"

Chance took a deep breath. She knew Rhebekka would never reveal their conversations where she'd poured out her guilt. Those talks closely resembled an odd form of confession. "One of the reasons. If anyone knows about forgiveness and grace, it's Rhebekka. Naomi as well. I lean on you for so much, and I'm eternally grateful for your love and support. No one can offer me absolution for the actions I've been forced to take, not even her. Talking to Rhebekka gives me a different perspective that is unique to her and her profession."

Jax rubbed her arm. "I'm not complaining, honey. I'm glad you have her to talk to. Please don't ever think I feel slighted about that. That's the farthest thing from my mind. Your mental and physical well-being are always my priority. Rhebekka's uniquely qualified to counsel you. I know she cares a great deal about you. I'm rather fond of her since she made my dream of becoming your wife come true."

"That was my dream from the time I met you." Chance smiled as she pulled into the doctor's office and put the vehicle in park. She looked in her rearview mirror to see Hunter smiling back at her. She released her seatbelt and turned to him to sign. *"Ready, buddy?"*

Hunter put both thumbs in the air.

"I'd say that's a resounding yes," Jax said.

Chance clapped her hands together. "Let's do this."

***

Chance sat watching Hunter put together a puzzle at a small table in the doctor's office. The minute he put the last piece in, he looked to her for praise. She delivered with a waggle of her hands that Hunter understood was a clap.

Dr. Clarissa Milan clicked through several screens on her computer. She stopped at one and turned it around. "We've run the MRI and auditory stimulus tests. There are a number of factors when we consider what a patient has available without assistance and what can be done to maximize it. That's where we'll start."

She proceeded to share with them the criteria and where Hunter was on the scale.

"Are you concerned this won't work?" Jax asked.

"No, it's a reality that his challenges will be greater because he's never learned to speak the way babies learn by listening to adults. It will require intensive speech and language therapy, and I'll be honest, psychological monitoring. Children are incredibly adaptive. Their inquisitive nature is beneficial, but children of his age are also prone to outbursts when they are uncomfortable, frustrated, or scared." Dr.

Milan stopped and picked up Hunter's history file. "From everything I'm reading, his short life has already been full of challenges that have nothing to do with his ability to hear."

Chance stiffened and stared Dr. Milan in the eye. "You don't know the half of it. Regardless of the cost and how long it takes for therapy, if this gives him a shot at being able to benefit from education, then we want to try. It doesn't matter to me if he ever speaks a word. He goes back to school next week."

"If these hearing aids even have a small chance to assist him, we're willing to provide them." Jax put her hand on Chance's arm. "Our plan is to hire an interpreter-tutor to make sure he's getting the most out of his education. We're actually interviewing someone after this appointment."

Chance nodded. "We're on track to adopt him. In our hearts, he's already our son, regardless of his biology. All we want is to give him the best possible opportunity."

Dr. Milan sat back in her chair. "Then let's get molds of his ears. Hopefully, in a few weeks, we can see if the advanced technology in these state-of-the-art hearing aids can help Hunter maximize whatever he already has."

Chance looked over at Hunter. *Life won't be easy, but it won't be because we didn't try.*

***

Chance and Jax waited on Julia at the Burger King close to the doctor's office. It had taken all they had to get Hunter to eat even a few bites of his meal. He was far too interested in the playroom. The restaurant had a ball pit and giant climbing tubes. He expressed his sense of accomplishment reaching the highest point of one by grinning and waving at them through one of the portholes. Chance and Jax both clapped in appreciation, wagging their hands back and forth.

Chance leaned back in her chair and continued to watch him. Very few things in her life had ever brought her such pride as witnessing Hunter become more and more self-assured.

"He gets that from you." Jax rubbed her back.

She turned and looked at Jax whose crooked grin was irresistible. "I had nothing to do with it."

"Keep telling yourself that, Sheriff."

"Do you think we're doing the right thing with the hearing aids and the school?"

"I think he deserves the opportunity to try. As you said, we won't love him any less if it isn't successful. We'll do our best not to build his hopes, or ours, up too much. We'll work with that child psychologist they suggested and follow any recommendations the school gives us. If we see he isn't thriving there, we'll back up and take another approach. My fingers are crossed that Julia will work out as an interpreter-tutor. That's all we can do. We're pretty lucky."

Chance smiled at her. "I agree. I hit the jackpot."

"Oh no you don't. I meant that about Hunter and me. No one loves like you do. You face every challenge with compassion and empathy. It's also what makes you a good police officer."

Chance felt her heart leap as she swallowed back unshed tears. Never in her life had she felt so understood and loved beyond what a parent could offer. She reached up and slid an arm around Jax's shoulders. "I'd argue with you, but it would only be circular. I'm the one who feels incredibly lucky to have both of you in my life. Before you came back, I went through my days focused on my job, on the things that the community needed from me. I never committed my heart to anyone on this level. I couldn't. I think the stars knew you were coming back to me, and when you did, my entire world changed for the better overnight."

***

Julia Gerard was in Morgantown for her own appointment at West Virginia University's speech and hearing clinic and had agreed to meet them. Their hope was that she could interact a bit with Hunter somewhere that he wouldn't feel intimidated and see if she was the right person to work with him. Jax had spoken with someone else earlier in the week but had discovered they were only interested in part-time and certainly not the type of extensive time it would take to work with Hunter.

Jax dipped a French fry in ketchup. "If those hearing aids work, we'll need to find a speech therapist that can help him develop a new set of communication skills."

Chance agreed. "A lot of decisions to make."

A young woman approached their booth. She looked about twenty-five, with dark blond hair and wore a Gallaudet University sweatshirt.

Petite and bright-eyed, she spoke and signed. "Are you the Fitzsimmons?"

Chance and Jax both rose. Jax spoke and signed back. "Are you Julia?"

She held out her hand and looked at both of them. "I am."

"Our signing ability is limited." Chance shook her hand as Jax signed.

Julia pointed to her ears and the hearing aids that curved around the back of them. "I didn't lose my hearing until age fifteen, so as a child, my speech and language were acquired more like a hearing child's. I can hear some, but I'll be reading your lips to supplement what I am able to hear with my aids. Speak normally, and I'll ask for clarification if I miss something."

They sat, and Jax pointed to Hunter as he climbed out of the ball pit. "That's our son, Hunter."

Julia turned to look at him. "He's adorable. I'm looking forward to meeting him."

They proceeded to talk about Hunter and his abilities, including what they'd found out during the earlier doctor's visit. There was some information on Hunter's preschool intervention and the basic signs his mother had used with him. Once all the background on Hunter had been addressed, they turned to the discussion about Julia's background.

Chance asked about her home in Grant County. "Do you still live there?"

Julia nodded. "It's home for now. My dad is a supervisor at one of the poultry plants, and my mom is an elementary school teacher. I graduated this summer from Gallaudet University with a Bachelor of Science degree in American Sign Language to English interpreting. My internship was with the Kendall Demonstration Elementary School, on the Gallaudet campus. I could have a job in another state, but that's not really what I want. West Virginia needs more qualified teachers with special skill sets like mine."

Jax pulled out a folder from her purse and placed it in front of Julia. "This is Hunter's evaluation and the direction we plan to head." She went on to explain the basics of how Hunter came to be in their custody and that they were in the adoption process.

"Wow, for only being in this world six years, much of it has been spent in turmoil. He's lucky there was any intervention at all." Julia's eyes shined with unshed tears. "Thank you for being willing to step up. I'm adopted as well. My birth mother gave me up when I was six months old. My parents couldn't have children. When I turned fifteen, I started getting dizzy spells and noticed I couldn't hear very well in school if I was too far from the teacher. At first, the doctors thought it was allergies and treated me with little success. Finally, my mom demanded an MRI. They found I had an acoustic neuroma interfering with the balance and auditory nerves in my inner ear. The tumor was benign, but it had grown large enough that I was left with severe hearing loss when it was removed. I wear hearing aids but rely primarily on lip reading and signing when possible."

Jax was looking at the printed form of Julia's resume, credentials, and recommendations. "Why this kind of teaching? I would think your skills and personality would offer you many opportunities."

Julia smiled. "I'll take that as a compliment. I could go teach in Romney, but I want to work with students who are involved in the hearing world as well. Many people are curious about how to interact and talk to a student that can't communicate the way they do. It's important to build bridges between the deaf and hearing communities. Working with Hunter is a great way to do that."

Chance smiled. "I like your philosophy, Julia. How about we see how Hunter reacts? Let me introduce you and see if you two hit it off. He has to feel comfortable with the person he's going to spend a great deal of his day with."

Julia lit up. "I'd like that."

They rose and headed into the play area. Hunter was building something with interlocking foam blocks. Jax stepped into his line of sight. *"Hunter, this is my friend, Julia."*

Hunter waved slowly, then looked down. Julia sat down in front of him and began to play with the blocks as well. Occasionally, she'd sign something to him, and Hunter would shake his head or nod. The two carried on small conversations where Julia used facial expressions and gestures that related to what they were doing.

Jax nudged Chance. "Will you look at that?" Hunter had moved so he was sitting much closer to Julia and smiling. "I think we just found his tutor."

There was much to be worked out, but Jax had a good feeling in her heart that this was going to be a milestone in Hunter's life, and maybe just maybe, a turning point as well.

***

Friday morning, Chance was looking over the schedule when the phone rang. "Tucker County Sheriff's Office, this is Sheriff Fitzsimmons. How can I help you?"

"Just who I wanted to talk to. Chance, this is Erin. How long will you be in the office?"

Chance glanced at her watch. "For at least the next three hours. What's up?"

"Railey and I are on our way to see you. We've got some news."

"I'm trying to determine if that's a good or bad thing."

"Both. I'll explain when we get there."

Jax had talked about bringing her lunch. She hit the speed dial and waited for Angie, the newest member of the clinic's staff to pick up. She was surprised to hear Jax's voice.

"Hey, you. What are you doing answering the phones?"

"Angie is up to her elbows bathing a group of kittens someone found in a box on the side of the road. Honestly, I just don't understand people. Enough of that, what can I do for you, my love?"

Chance looked at a photo on her desk of Jax and Hunter riding Glenny together. Little reminders of her family always made her smile. "I just wanted to let you know I'll have to take a raincheck on lunch. I've got an unscheduled meeting headed to my office."

"Not a problem. I'll miss you though."

"Right back at you. What time are Rhebekka and Naomi coming?"

"I told them seven. Are you picking up the burgers?"

"It's on my list. I'll see you at home."

For the next thirty minutes, Chance concentrated on paperwork. Daniel stood in the doorway.

"Got a few minutes, Sheriff?"

"For you, always."

He and Athena moved into the room, and the dogs greeted each other before settling near their partners.

"Heard anything from our friends at the ATF?"

Chance leaned back in her chair. "Funny you should mention that. They're on their way here with news. Unless you get called out, I invite you to sit in since you've been part of this from the beginning. I want you to look into a department version of that drone. I don't want you to have to use your personal one all the time. If something were to happen to it, I'd have to get creative on how to replace it for you. There are some grants available from the DOJ. I've sent you an email with some links to the information. I also know some training and FAA licensing our department would have to obtain. I'd like you to run point on all of that."

Daniel adjusted his gun belt and moved in the chair. "I'll get on it. I know some versions are a bit more durable. They were just out of my price range. Dezi about smacked me when I broke it last time. It cost me almost three Benjamins to get it fixed. She wants a house, and my toys don't fit into her budget."

Chance couldn't help but chuckle. "Are you planning on popping the question anytime soon?"

Daniel blushed and looked down. "Well, about that. Where do you suggest I go ring shopping? Her birthday is next month. She's working as a part-time teaching assistant at the elementary school until she gets her engineering degree. With school starting, we really can't go away for anything longer than a weekend. I checked the schedule, and I'm off for her birthday on the twenty-second."

"Sounds like you've got a plan. I promise not to mess with it. Now, about a jeweler, I'd recommend this little place in Shepherdstown. It's where I got Jax's ring. Small and handcrafted. You can go chain retailer, but as far as quality, they won't hold a candle to Kerry." She brought her laptop to life and clicked on a link which she copied and sent to him. Details are there in the email."

Daniel pulled out his phone and looked at the screen. "Thanks. I'll look at it later. When are they supposed to show up?"

Chance looked at her watch just as Erin and Railey walked up to the front door. "As a matter of fact, right now." She got up to greet them and ushered everyone into the conference room. "Good to see you two. I'm taking a wild guess here, but you hit on something?"

Railey nodded. "Understatement." He began attaching his laptop to the overhead projector as Daniel pulled down the screen and dimmed the overhead lights.

Erin passed Chance a set of stapled papers. "We've identified two individuals that visited the site with Ted Eichland and Paul Leonard in the last twenty-four hours. Two of them are wanted suspects and may still be on the property. One was involved in a bombing of a city hall in Blaine County, Idaho, ten years ago. The other is wanted for terroristic threats of violence against the Governor of Missouri. Both individuals have links to violent sovereign citizen groups."

Railey keyed up the photographs and information on the individuals in question along with additional information on Ted Eichland. "Ted once worked and associated with David Minor at ATK, a munitions manufacturer in Lewiston, Idaho. In 2009, David was accused of making threats to the Governor of Missouri after a report was issued on the militia movement. David was heavily involved in The Posse Comitatus. He's not anyone in the hierarchy but isn't above pushing the envelope. He repeatedly expressed his anger at what he perceived as the governor using his illegitimate authority to harass members of his group for their beliefs. He's suspected of putting an explosive package addressed to the governor on the front porch of the governor's in-laws. The incident was investigated by Missouri state troopers, the local FBI, and ATF offices." He pointed to a specific area of the report. "His fingerprints were found on several of the components of the bomb and appeared on the glue side of the packaging tape. He disappeared off the map until reappearing on those cameras we placed."

Erin walked up and tapped the screen in the next photo. "This guy, Helton Kyle, is bad news. He's a former ordinance officer in the US Army during the Gulf War. When he came back, he was all over the anarchist and anti-government movements. He moved around and finally settled in Idaho. Can you guess where he worked?"

Chance scowled and crossed her arms. "Would I lose money if I said ATK?"

Erin shook her head. "Winner, winner, chicken dinner. We found DNA evidence inside the bomb's box that matched system records from Kyle's army service."

Daniel scrubbed his hand through his hair. "What the hell are they doing here? I get it they worked together and might be friends, but it seems odd for them to come out of whatever hole they were in out west and show up here in Tucker County."

Railey clicked to another screen on his computer. "That's the next piece of the info I'm about to share with you. From what we can find, Patty Kilmer, Paul Leonard, and David Minor are related. We haven't worked out all the genetics yet, but there is a definite family tie from what we've seen."

Erin sat down beside Chance. "Here's where it gets extremely interesting. Part of the footage we've seen shows them opening a box of what appears to be some kind of plastic explosives. We lost a camera that was a little too close to those demolition craters. I don't know what the hell they're planning, but with the firepower we've seen and their demolition ability, it can't be good. We need to get some heavy-duty surveillance in there and track them back, see if they end up at that farm. The drone idea led us to a few other things we have access to."

Chance wondered if she was talking about some kind of military equipment or satellite imagery.

"There's chatter we've been monitoring about a meetup of some big players at a place they've been referring to as the kill zone," Erin continued. "We suspect that's the Kilmer Farm but need to confirm. I'm getting some warrants to allow for greater surveillance based on what we've captured on film. I've been in contact with J.D. Hamilton of the FBI as well."

Daniel stood and went to the screen, hands on his hips. "I thought most of these guys were paper terrorists. This seems so far over the top."

"Most are," Erin explained. "There are different factions in any of these movements, Daniel. Some, like these people, are extremists who often infiltrate even the peaceful groups. This is proving to be anything but. We almost lost an undercover agent, and everything in our investigation is leading me to the conclusion that Paul Leonard did the shooting."

Chance's cellphone rang. She looked at the screen. "Harley, haven't heard from you in a while. What's up?"

"It's always a busy time of year. Remember those shells we took out of the cattle? The ballistic analysis came back as a match to an unsolved road rage incident in Missouri."

Chance filled Harley in and invited her over to the office to hear what they were up against.

"She'll be here in fifteen minutes. This circle of suspects seems to be getting tighter and tighter around this group and where they've lived before. We need to come up with a plan, and from the sounds of it, yesterday."

Erin nodded. "I can't tell you how bad we want to get these guys."

Railey spoke up, the venom in his voice apparent. "They changed Myron's life forever. It's time we change theirs."

***

Jax looked at the clock that told her she had a few more hours until their company would arrive. Chance had called her at three, advising she would be home later than expected but would still arrive before Rhebekka and Naomi. Jax thought about the employment contract they'd signed with Julia. She would become Hunter's daily companion at school. She would work with him to develop his communication skills and be there every step of the way through his hearing aid fittings and speech therapy. Grandpa Mike had dropped Hunter off thirty minutes ago after a day of fishing with Uncle Marty. Jax had been feeling guilty that she wasn't able to spend more one-on-one time with him. She smiled at what he'd told her in response.

Hunter is your priority. He has to be, and more than that, he deserves to be. Your Uncle Marty and I are enjoying our fishing time and card games. I plan on being around a long time to take my grandson fishing. There will be plenty of time for us to be together. I love you, Jibber Jax, and my tiny fisherman as well."

She loved seeing the playful side of her father. He'd also informed her that everything with her mother was completely finalized. He'd refused to say anything more, even when she'd asked. More than once, her cellphone identified a caller as one Jaqueline St. Claire. She'd refused the calls repeatedly, sending them straight to voicemail, then deleting the messages before listening to them. Jax had enough going on. Her lawyer had called, advising her he had done all he could to dissuade a judge from ordering her appearance. Fortunately, there was still time for Lacey to settle. If that happened, Alex hoped he could get the part that claimed Jax was complicit thrown out. *If that doesn't happen, Lacey will be getting a call and not one telling her how much I miss her.* The screen door banged. Zeus ran by and straight up the stairs.

"We don't rank at all anymore, honey." Chance walked to Jax, wrapped her in her arms, and kissed her.

Jax melted into the kiss, her worries completely drained away the minute Chance's lips touched hers. The tension left her shoulders and traveled right down through the soles of her feet into the floor. "You have no idea how much I needed that."

Chance held her close. "Rough day?"

Jax leaned back and pulled Chance's Stetson off before running her fingers through the hair that was trending toward the salt and pepper she was growing to love. She tugged on the silver shock that had been there as long as she'd known Chance. "We'll talk about it later. Right now, I want some friends and family time. Are you going to shower?"

Chance walked to her closet where she removed her gun, put it in the lockbox, and pulled off her vest. "Yes, summertime in uniform is brutal. I can barely stand myself. I'll be back down in a bit. Need anything before I go up?"

"Just the burgers."

Chance snapped her fingers. "They're still on the seat. Be right back."

Jax watched her lover's long strides out the door, shivering at the thoughts running through her mind as she put Chance's hat on the hook. *Completely delectable.*

Chance brought the cooler back in and went to clean up. Jax worked to prepare the patties and side dishes. Hunter and Zeus had moved to the back yard. She stood at the kitchen window, watching them walk over to the pasture fence. Glenny and Kelly came over to nuzzle his hand as Zeus stood watch over them all. Strong arms wrapped around her from behind.

"He's adjusted so well. It's like he's always been here."

Jax leaned back and covered Chance's arms with her own. "I hope he'll always feel like this is his home. It's hard to imagine him not being here."

Chance kissed her head. "Not going to happen. We'll make sure of it. We won't give up, no matter what. We give them no reason to say no. He's thriving. I'll bet he's put on six or seven pounds in the time he's been with us. No one can argue he's not in better health or that he's unhappy. Stop worrying about something that isn't going to happen."

Jax tightened her grip on Chance's arms. "I'll try. In other news, Alex called. Looks like I'll be required to go to California early next year."

"I'm sorry, honey."

"I still have hope that Lacey will end up settling and take responsibility for this. If that happens, my attorney will move to dismiss my involvement. Either way, I'm not thinking about it anymore." She turned and kissed Chance.

"I like that idea. What can I do to help?"

"Let's get things ready outside. Go fire up the grill. They should be here in another thirty minutes or so."

Jax looked out the window again. Hunter lay in the grass with Zeus at his side. *Life is good Jax, just enjoy it.*

***

Chance wiped tears from her eyes. The stories her friends told always lightened her mood.

"The kids had just put in the last two pieces of a 5000-piece puzzle when Marley and JJ decided to play chase. They jumped on the table and things went flying everywhere." Naomi bent over laughing.

Rhebekka put a hand over her eyes. "The kids squealed, and the cats acted like we were crazy for trying to get them off the table."

Chance laughed until her sides hurt. "Cats. That's why ours stay in the barn."

Naomi watched Hunter put Zeus through some hand signals. "Is Zeus following Hunter's commands?"

Chance nodded. "He is. I taught Hunter four simple commands. Sit, stay, come, and jump. We blended Hunter's sign and the ones I use for Zeus to make the commands. Zeus picked it up pretty quickly. Some they developed on their own, like eat."

Rhebekka shook her head. "Amazing. We used to deliver food baskets to the apartment he lived in. I tried more than once to get Crissy some help. It's sad what's happened to him, but it looks like he's in a much better situation. I believe God watches over children. It doesn't mean bad things don't happen, but I think he puts people in positions to help. Like you two. He's a lucky little boy."

"We're the lucky ones. He's taught us so much in a short amount of time." Jax caught Hunter as he jumped in her lap and handed her a yellow dandelion.

Chance watched a myriad of emotions cross over her wife's face. *She was born to be a mother.* Jax fawned over Hunter's gift, offering to put it in water. The two of them headed inside, Zeus on their heels.

"It's so obvious how he feels about you both. I've always said blood isn't what makes people a family. It's love." Rhebekka lifted and kissed Naomi's hand, then looked back at Chance. "I talked to Travis' grandparents today. They want to set up a college scholarship to honor him."

Chance smiled. "I think that's a fitting tribute. Travis never went, but it would help someone else get there." Her phone rang, and the name Erin Southern was displayed on her screen. Jax and Hunter came back outside. "Excuse me for a minute, I need to take this."

Jax kissed her. "You're the sheriff, it comes with the territory. Go, Hunter and I've got this."

Chance waved as she walked away and answered her phone. "Erin, what's up?" As she listened, she knew her night would be short, and the coming day would be very long.

Chapter Fifteen

CHANCE, DANIEL, AND RAILEY crept to the western edge of the Kilmer property at midnight. Taylor was with Erin, a half-mile away in a makeshift command post with an ATF supervisor and several FBI agents. Harley, one of her troopers, an ATF agent, and one of JD's men approached from the south. Another team with FBI and ATF agents, along with Khodi, Randy, and their K9's, were coming from the east. Chance spoke to Railey in a whispered tone. "The intelligence on this had to be pretty good to warrant a large operation this quickly."

"Too solid not to act immediately," Railey admitted.

At the briefing held before they moved to the Dry Fork area, they were told there was a weapons exchange to take place at one in the morning. The exchange was also supposed to include some counterfeit currency. Erin and her team had obtained federal warrants and the go-ahead to move in. The kill zone had been mentioned several times in the correspondence leading the investigators to believe it had to be the Kilmer property. The directions given to the illegal range area confirmed their suspicions. Chance hadn't been read in on everything, but she had faith in the authorities she was working with.

She pointed in the dark. "We're not that far from the barn we plan to stage in. It should be another two hundred yards. Railey, you've got those super-agent, night-vision goggles, and I've only got a thermal imager, so you lead the way."

"With pleasure, Sheriff."

"Daniel, keep close. If I can't see you, I still want to make sure your mommas know I was watching out for you."

"I'm with you, Sheriff. I've got your back."

They continued through the tall grass, a coyote yipping off in the distance. It took them another fifteen minutes to hustle to the barn. Railey and Chance went to the loft, the ladder creaking as they climbed. Daniel and Athena stayed downstairs near the door. Railey scratched his head, watching Zeus as he came up the ladder and went straight to Chance's side.

"I'll be damned," he whispered.

Chance chuckled silently at his amazement. The loft smelled of dust and dry hay. She stifled the urge to sneeze as she looked through high-power binoculars. A dusk-to-dawn light illuminated the house. She detected movement as shadows passed by the windows. She checked the time. There was still almost an hour and a half before they were supposed to have visitors. Railey had his night-vision goggles on and crossed his arms into an x in front of his face.

He leaned close to her. "The other teams are in position."

They stayed hidden for an interminable forty-five minutes before Zeus turned his head. Chance and Railey looked down the driveway.

"We've got company," he whispered.

Chance was sure Athena had alerted Daniel as well. Three men exited the vehicles and looked around before approaching the door. Railey touched his ear as if listening to his communication device.

"Copy," he said, his voice barely audible. He leaned over to her. "They opened the gate with a code. Positive visual identification of our suspects."

Chance nodded. At the briefing, Erin's superior had identified who they were looking for on this mission. Two high-ranking individuals in Posse Comitatus and a gun runner from Texas walked to the side door. It opened, and Ted Eichland stepped into the light emanating from inside. The group exchanged a few words, then entered the house. Ted looked into the darkness before closing the door.

The plan involved watching the group make the exchange and letting the visitors leave, only to be taken down once they left the property, reducing the chance of them all joining forces. Chance's team, along with Harley's, would be handling the apprehension of Ted, Patty, and Paul. Khodi and Randy's group was to look for, and apprehend, David Minor and Helton Kyle. Chance hoped all of this could be done without bloodshed. *I can't imagine they'll come willingly.*

They didn't have to wait long before the three men who entered the house exited with Eichland, Leonard, Miner, and Keller. Chance's heart pounded as she watched Ted point to the barn they were hiding in and prayed that Daniel was seeing it as well. The sounds of Daniel and Athena scrambling up the ladder of the huge barn told her he had. The two settled behind some large bales near the hay loft's entrance. An engine roared to life and headlights turned toward the barn. Railey flipped up his night-vision goggles. In the light shining through the slatted barn wood, Chance watched him thumb off the safety on his Colt M4 carbine rifle. She did the same with hers, and Railey quietly alerted the other teams to the turn of events. She gave Zeus the hand signal to be alert and silent.

Within a few minutes, the barn doors were slid back, and the large SUV pulled in, the headlights shining inside. Heavy boots thudded across the rough wood as Ted Eichland walked to the center. He swept aside some discarded hay with his foot to uncover a set of handles. He opened one and waited for Paul to do the same. Cracks in the floor offered a view of steps that led down into a hidden area beneath the barn itself. They watched as several weapons were carried up and loaded into the back of the vehicle.

She glanced beside her to see Railey keeping his eye on the men. Zeus lay quiet but still on alert beside her. Helton Kyle went down and came up with a box he held by rope handles. An old tarp was thrown on the hood before Helton set the box down. David Minor pried the wooden top off to reveal what appeared to be small rectangular blocks packaged in dark plastic. He took one out, tossed it in his palm, then presented it to the largest of the three men who had shown up less than thirty minutes ago.

There's our plastic explosives. A nudge made Chance look at Railey, who pointed down and then to his eyes. Chance nodded. She knew what the plan was. Let them make the exchange, drive away, and be stopped away from the house. They wanted to avoid another Waco or Ruby Ridge disaster at all costs. Horrific images filled her mind. *Not here, not here on my watch.* The voices below them grew loud.

"How the fuck did you get this?"

Helton smiled. "I've got my sources. This isn't an easy thing to obtain, and you know it."

The man ran a hand over his beard. "Be careful how you talk to me. This is a very small transaction in the grand scheme. I'll walk out of here. You see my friends back there? They don't take too kindly to smartasses. I don't need this shit for anything more than the currency it will generate."

"And I don't have to sell it to you. I've got other buyers." Helton pulled the brick from the man's hand and put it back in the box. He slid the lid back on.

The man shook his head. "You're a cocky bastard, aren't you? You want to measure your dick against mine? Have at it, but I'll shut down your operation faster than you can take your next breath. I've driven a long way to buy guns. If you're interested in doing that, then let's get to it. All of you need to understand your place in the hierarchy. You barely move the needle. We want you to help the organization by moving some script. If you can do that, you'll be doing your part. If you aren't, keep showing your ass. I'll let the higher-ups know how cooperative you were."

Ted put a hand on his hip, close to the gun at the small of his back. "I think you're full of shit. My only loyalty is to my family, Posse Comitatus can kiss my dick for all I care. I might hold to their beliefs, but I owe them nothing. West Virginia ain't Idaho, but I've been able to do what the hell I want for years. Now, you interested in buying what I'm offering or not? This was something we thought you might have the market for. If not, we'll move on."

Chance listened to the tense negotiations. The last thing she wanted was to have the pissing battle turn into bullets flying around. The only things protecting her team were the vests they wore and the fact no one knew they were in the loft witnessing the transaction. There were agitated discussions over the price before the visitor pointed to the truck.

"Load it up. I want to get the hell out of here as soon as possible."

Money exchanged hands, and Chance watched Ted count every bill. He tapped the stack together.

"It's been a pleasure doing business with you. I'll start working that script into circulation. We've got a few gun shows coming up where we'll be able to turn it over. It'll take a few months, but we'll get it done. This is small potatoes. I was expecting something difficult."

Ted visibly stiffened as the visitor stepped close.

"Be careful your dick doesn't write checks your ass can't cash, Eichland. You won't know it's coming, but if you fuck with us, we'll bury you. You can count on that. You might be a big fish in this backwoods pond, but I swim with great white sharks. Remember that."

Ted looked down. Chance could see a large blade held in the visitor's hand and touching Eichland's side. To his credit, Ted held his ground and turned to Paul who stood with his pistol drawn and aimed at the nameless man.

Shit. Chance silently thumbed the safety of her rifle, ensuring once again that it was off. *This is getting way too tense.*

The visitor laughed and slid his knife back up his sleeve. "Let's get out of this shit hole."

One of the men jumped into the truck and backed it out of the barn as the visitor in black walked out into the yard. The third man walked backward watching the others inside the barn.

After the men got in their vehicles and left, Paul finally dropped his gun. Only the moonlight that poured in the open barn doors illuminated them. "That was fucking intense. It felt a lot like when I put a bullet in that rat out west, leaving him in a pool of his own blood. That influx of cash will keep us going while we build up the training site. Fuck them. We don't need them."

Ted cracked his knuckles. "You know they're gonna be all over us about that cash. We can't be done with them yet. Once we make good on it, then we'll be done. We need to start figuring out how to get rid of that jackass that bought the range. We can't lose that, and I'm not about to blow shit up here on this property. Those dykes will be all over us. The last thing we need is a sheriff and a trooper nosing around. Fucking queers. They've got that gun, and if they figure out who had it last, you're toast. They'll tie that back to you, and you'll find your ass sitting in Hazelton or worse. We let you come here because of the family ties, Paul. I won't let you fuck this up. We've been able to stay under the radar here for years. I'm not giving that up, even for you."

Minor and Keller stood with their arms crossed. "You two deal with your Brady bunch moment later. We just want to get paid and get the fuck out of here. We've got more shit to get out on the market."

Chance watched Railey tense. *Myron's cuffs are burning a hole in his pocket.* She wanted more than anything to take them into custody.

Ted counted out the money to them before he and Paul returned to the house. When they were all far enough away, Railey climbed down and offered cover for Chance and Daniel, as they made their way back to the ground floor. She signaled to Zeus to jump into her arms, and Daniel did the same for Athena. When everyone was ready, they trained their weapons out into the darkness. The radio clicked on with the agent in charge of Harley's team reporting their actions.

"We're going to take them in the yard. Minor and Keller are headed to their truck."

Railey spoke softly into the bone mic. "Paul's carrying a handgun. Ted's unknown but likely is, as are the other two."

When the two men were less than twenty feet from the door, Minor and Keller opened the doors to climb in the truck. Out of the darkness, an ATF agent, Randy, and Vader charged out, bright LED lights from their headlamps blinding Ted and Paul. Khodi and Echo followed the team that initiated a takedown of Keller and Minor at the truck. Shots rang out with return fire given.

Chance tried to keep her focus in the chaos. Railey and Daniel both trained their weapons on Paul and Ted. They each raised an arm to shield their eyes while reaching for guns at their backs. She held her rifle and heard Randy address the two men, giving them clear commands.

"Drop your weapons or I send the dog!"

Her team moved in from behind. Her eyes keyed in on Ted as he slid his hand to the waistband at his back.

"Zeus, *stellen*!" Zeus jumped at Ted and clamped down on his arm. Athena went for Paul, while Vader's teeth sank into Ted's leg at Randy's command.

Within seconds, the two men were writhing on the ground, screaming in agony.

"Get these fucking dogs off me!" Ted tried to strike at Zeus but was ineffective. Zeus continued to increase the pressure. Vader shook his head violently with Ted's leg in his mouth until Ted finally dropped the gun screaming in pain.

Chance looked over at Athena who had Paul's arm. She was smaller but made up for it in tenacity. Paul was doing everything he could to throw her off, trying to swing her off her feet.

Daniel ran forward with his weapon drawn. "Put your hands up! Stand still, or she'll tear your arm off! Stand still!"

Railey moved up beside Paul and hooked his leg with his own, tumbling both man and dog to the ground. Still, Athena held on.

Chance focused on Ted who was rolling on the ground, still screaming in pain. "Lay still or they'll keep biting!"

Randy put his gun directly in Ted's line of sight. "Lay fucking still!"

The fight went out of Ted. Chance knew Randy had the suspect covered, and she looked to see Railey and Daniel flipping Paul on his stomach. She turned back to Randy and pointed. "You got him?"

Khodi handcuffed one man as Echo held his arm in his teeth. Chance moved to Daniel's side. Her gun trained on Paul Leonard.

Railey straddled Paul's back and dragged the arm Athena didn't have behind him. He pulled Myron's cuffs from his pocket. "This is for the officer you left, as you said, lying in a pool of blood. I want you to know these are his cuffs taking away the one thing you value above everything, the right to do what you want, your freedom. Paul Leonard, you're under arrest for the attempted murder of ATF Agent Myron Ziker. That's right, you fuck, he lived, and he'll be around to see you go to prison for the rest of your life." He looked at Daniel.

"Athena, *los!*" The Dutch command to release flowed easily from Daniel's lips as he moved in front of Paul, pointing his rifle at him.

Chance's chest swelled with pride at her officer's abilities and determination. She turned back to see Ted also being taken into custody. She called Zeus off and he returned to her side, still on alert. Floodlights illuminated the yard, and Chance raised her weapon as the screen door from the house squeaked open. Harley escorted Patty Kilmer out of the house with her hands cuffed behind her back. Her hair looked as if it had been styled by the Serta sheep, giving every indication that she'd been asleep in bed as all this went down. Railey touched his ear. "All suspects at the kill zone are in custody."

Over the radio, someone called for an ambulance for one of the suspects at the truck.

"I need a fucking ambulance too, you fuckers. I'm bleeding. That damn dog better not have given me anything. I'll sue your ass off. I'll own you!"

Chance shook her head. "Always ready to take advantage of a system you claim not to believe in." She heard Erin's voice in her ear. "Excellent. Command copies. The other suspects are in custody. No injuries to our people. Good job everyone. We'll debrief after all the suspects are processed and resting uncomfortably with their new jewelry on."

Railey pulled Paul to his feet. "You have the right to remain silent. Anything you say can and will..." He rattled off the rest of the required Miranda Rights. The other ATF agent was dragging Ted Eichland to his feet. Chance held her fist out to Daniel who bumped it with his own. "Well done." His grin said everything she needed to know.

Large, black SUVs began pulling into the driveway. Chance shook her head. *By the time this is over, there will be an alphabet soup of agencies lining up for assignments.* Erin stepped out of the lead vehicle and walked to Chance as Ted and Paul were led away.

"Well done, Sheriff. This was big and it went off flawlessly. None of my agents have any new holes in them, and we have suspects still able to stand trial. I'd say that's a good operation."

"That barn was more than just a place to store hay. There's a trap door. No clue how big it is, but that's where they pulled out the guns and that nice box of Play-Doh that makes really big holes in buildings."

Erin's eyebrows went up. "At least it's now in our possession and not being sold to some radical anarchist group with an agenda bigger than these guys had. I've got our bomb tech team coming. From what you showed us, there's probably some unstable pipe bombs down there as well. We couldn't have done this without your intel, Chance. You've got a good team working for you. I hope you're planning to be around for a long time. Ted Eichland and this bunch are only one of the groups on our radar. This will put them on notice."

Harley came walking up. "I'm hoping we can get some compensation for Milton Denver. He's still out those cattle someone put bullets in. If we can figure out if one of these asshole's guns is responsible, we'll add that to the list of charges. Seems like it was a pretty good night."

Chance looked over at her team and her friend. "An excellent night for the good guys, and no one has to call Jax and have her meet us at the hospital. I'll take that as a win. Let's get this put to bed. We have much better places to be."

***

Hours later, Chance crept into the room and sat on the bed to take her boots off. She glanced at the clock to see it was closing in on eight in the morning.

"How'd it go?"

Chance turned, a wide smile on her face. "We got 'em."

Jax reached up and touched the greasy face paint. "What's all this?" She held up her fingers smeared with black, green, and brown.

"My interpretation of makeup. Nothing says love like camo, baby."

Jax chuckled. "Nothing says love like you coming home in one piece."

Chance stood and stripped out of her clothes. "Believe it or not, I actually made mention that the best part was no one had to call you and have you meet us at the ER." The sweat-stained T-shirt came off over her head, followed by the pair of tactical pants. Bits of straw and hay fell to the floor. She stood in nothing but the camo, jog bra and boxer briefs. "I'll clean that up, I promise."

Jax lay back with an appreciative grin on her face. "I kind of like that look. I think you're right. Nothing says love like camo."

"Told you. I need a shower. That boy of ours will want breakfast soon."

"We stayed up a little later than I'd planned last night. I think he was bothered that you went out. He settled down fine when I told him you'd be home when he got up. Don't you need to sleep?"

Chance shook her head. "I'll take a nap later. Right now, I just want to be home with you both. Zeus is chilling out on the end of his bed. I'm fairly sure he's still my partner, but he's definitely Hunter's dog when we step through that door."

Chance headed to the shower, grateful for the instant hot water feature they'd installed. She stood under the steaming spray, allowing the tension to wash away, along with the bits of chaff from her face and hair. She scrubbed at her face with a washcloth to remove the camouflage grease paint. It took more than one pass to remove it. Arms encircled her back.

"You were too far away."

Chance turned around with a clean face. "Then, by all means, join me."

Jax threaded her hands through Chance's wet hair and pulled their lips together. They met Chance's in a frenzy of want and need. Chance slipped her arm around Jax's waist while the other caressed a soft breast, drawing a pleasurable groan from Jax. In this moment, this place and time, there were no bad guys, no guns, and no decisions to make. There was just love and desire.

"I need you, Chance. I need to feel you."

"I'm here, baby. Right here, look at me." There were times when Chance sensed a fear in Jax that never seemed to abate until they were this close. In turn, she felt an urgent need to connect with the woman she loved, to complete her in every way, and drive away that fear. Chance dipped her head and took a velvet nipple in her mouth, rolling her tongue over it.

The sounds of Jax's need rushed out on a gasp, followed by a swift intake of breath as Chance's teeth bit and nipped at the sensitive flesh. She held tighter to Jax and moved to caress her lover's hip by drifting her fingertips over soft flesh. The course curls at the juncture of Jax's legs were inviting as she smoothly used deft fingers to part her and stroke through Jax's heat. Chance's palm bumped Jax's clit, causing her to jerk in her arms.

"Oh God, Chance. I need you inside me, please."

Chance didn't waver at the request and slid her fingers into Jax's depths. Nothing in the world felt like touching Jax.

"Yes, so good."

"I love you so much, Jax. Whatever you need, let me give it to you. I'm right here."

Chance began to slowly pump her fingers in and out of Jax's center with increasingly deeper thrusts. Jax panted into her shoulder and wrapped a leg around Chance's hip, allowing her more access. Chance spun her to the wall, pinning her with her body, all while never missing a stroke. She could feel the flutters begin around her fingers and wanted nothing more than to take her wife over the edge.

"I'm so close, Chance, so close."

Chance moved her hand just enough to increase the pressure of her palm against her clit. She moved until her lips were against Jax's ear. "I love you, Jax, so much."

"Oh, fuck!"

Jax bucked against Chance, riding the wave of climax. Chance felt red-hot pleasure wash over her. *She's so beautiful.* When her lungs screamed for her to breathe, Chance took in a tremendous gulp of air as she clung to her wife. "I've got you. When I touch you, I'm anchored in time and place at your side, in your heart."

As Jax slowly descended the crest, she held on. Chance felt delicate fingers digging deeply into her neck and bicep.

"You destroy me, then put all the pieces back together, stronger than I was before." Jax panted into Chance's neck.

"Two cords wrapped around each other are always stronger than a single strand. Bound together, they become one, an unbreakable cord that binds our hearts and anchors us in any storm. That's what love does."

They stayed like that for a few minutes before they sensually bathed each other. Chance loved when Jax washed her hair and reveled as the short nails scratched her skull. When the soap was rinsed out, she turned and kissed Jax.

Jax touched her face. "It's good to have you home."

Chance pulled her in close. "As the saying goes, there's no place like it. How about we get dressed and make some coffee."

"Deal."

They stepped from the shower and dried off. Chance stretched the scar tissue as she rubbed in the cocoa butter. She looked at her wedding ring and thought about all they'd been through to get to this point. She silently recited the words to her mantra. *Steel is tempered by fire, and gold is refined by it. No matter what flames are ahead, this family is my shelter.*

***

Chance enjoyed the morning as she sipped her coffee in a lounger with Jax leaning against her. Her mind was drifting to things she couldn't change.

Jax snuggled in closer. "If I guess what's on your mind can I get a kiss?"

"You never need to bargain for that." Chance kissed her.

"I'll take that deal any day. I'm guessing you're dwelling on Kendra heading to the academy."

Chance sighed and stared out into the yard.

"Want to talk about it?"

"I can't believe she's not going to be working for me. From the day I took office, there was always the thought we'd be working side by side."

Jax patted her leg. "We don't know what the future will bring. Didn't you tell me you worked with Taylor when she was at the Marshals? Nothing says that won't happen with you and Kendra."

"It's not that. I won't be able to watch over her. I think that's probably what's stuck in my craw."

"I think that's it exactly. You're the protector in this family. For once, you won't be able to take care of the things she'll face. It reminds me of when you talked about how helpless you felt when Dee had her heart attack, or when I was in surgery to fix my leg."

"Feeling like that isn't one of my strong suits. It's not in my nature to sit back and let things happen." Chance dropped her head to the lounger back and let the morning sun warm her face. All around her were the sounds of early morning and the life they'd built.

Jax patted her leg. "Now there's a true statement. Life isn't meant to be wrapped in a perfect package. Some things are meant to be unexpected and life changing."

The screen door opened, and Hunter padded out in his Paw Patrol pajamas. He climbed into Jax's lap and settled with his head against her chest, his arms tucked up near his chin. Chance set down her coffee and pulled them both in tight. She kissed Jax's head. "Unexpected and life changing indeed, Mrs. Fitzsimmons. As Pastor Rhebekka would say, 'thank the good Lord for that.'"

Hunter sat up and looked at them. *"I'm hungry."*

Jax eased Hunter off her lap and stood, holding out a hand to Chance.

Chance groaned as she stood, her knees popping and cracking along the way. She looked at Hunter and signed. *"Let's go eat."*

They wandered into the kitchen and started making breakfast. On a whim, Chance called her father-in-law. "Mike, if you've got anything on your agenda today, can you clear it? I think Hunter could use a little time at the river. Go pick up Uncle Marty and join us for breakfast."

"Breakfast? That sounds like a great idea. You're on."

"We'll see you in about a half hour."

Jax signed to Hunter that Grandpa Mike was coming and they'd go fishing after breakfast. She yelled to her dad, who was still on the phone.

"Come hungry, we're making waffles." Jax looked at Hunter and pointed upstairs. *"Please, get dressed."*

Hunter ran to his room with Zeus excitedly barking at his heels.

Chance walked over to the cabinet and pulled down the ingredients for the waffles her mother had taught her to make. "I'd say he agrees with our plan. That settles it, waffles all around."

Hunter came back wearing his boots with his life vest on over his PJs. Chance cracked up as she lifted him to her shoulders. "You work on breakfast, Momma J, while the mighty angler and I find something a little more appropriate to wear." She carried him up the stairs, content with her duties as the one thing she never thought she would be, a mom.

***

The weather was perfect for a day on the Cheat River. Warm sunshine had made Chance sleepy while the three fishermen caught their limit. Jax read a book and took pictures of the trio as Chance napped in her lap after her long night.

As the afternoon drew to a close, they'd left the river and taken Marty home before returning to their house where Mike's vehicle was parked. Chance and Jax hauled in the gear and cooler as Mike carried a sleeping Hunter into the house. He laid him down on the couch and tousled his hair.

Jax walked up beside him and slid an arm around her father. "That boy can pass out anywhere."

Mike pulled her in. "You used to fall asleep in the car as soon as the first wheel turned."

"He's had a big day. I've never seen him as excited as when he pulled in that bass."

"My grandson is a natural fisherman. He picked it up so quickly. He took to it like—"

"A fish to water?" Chance came in and stood beside them.

Jax patted her arm. "Don't give up your day job, honey. You've got to be exhausted. We have a big day Monday. It's his first day of school."

Mike turned to them. "Would it be okay if I rode there with you? You know, to learn the routine?"

Jax put her arms around his neck. "Admit it, you old softy. You want to watch him go to school."

Mike blushed and kissed her temple. "Do you blame a guy for trying? I can't completely act like a mush. I was a big tough cop, just like my daughter-in-law."

"Your secret is safe with me, Daddy."

Chance laughed. "We'll make it a caravan because the moms squared plan on driving over behind us. They swear they have an appointment in Thomas right after that. I'm just going to say, you grandparents are terrible liars."

Mike patted her shoulder. "We don't lie, we are just a bit creative with our reasoning. What time are we leaving?"

Jax walked him to the door. "Be here by six and you can have breakfast with us."

"Six it is. Goodnight you two. Tell him I'll see him Monday morning."

"Night, Daddy. I love you."

"Love you too, Jibber Jax."

Jax closed the door and watched him walk to his truck through the window in the front door. "I never thought I'd see the day."

Chance walked up and wrapped her in her arms. "That you'd have a relationship with your father?"

"It's more than that though. It's having him in my life, being married to you, and having my child call him grandpa. It's all of it."

"All things you deserve and more. He's a great guy. I'm thankful I've gotten to know him so well."

Jax grew quiet and wiped away a tear. "She's missing out on so much."

Chance looked at her quizzically. "Your mom?"

Jax nodded. "In her efforts to have the perfect family, it all splintered into a million pieces."

They walked to the kitchen and emptied the cooler.

"Have you heard from her lately?"

Jax put the soda back in the fridge. "A few calls. I let them go to voicemail but never listen. It's the same thing over and over. She'll never change and will continue to try and manipulate things to her advantage. I hear from Jackie that she's a shell of herself without Daddy to boss around. She wanders around that big house all by herself."

"The saying goes, 'you reap what you sow.' I harbor no ill will toward the woman, but she's put the people I care about, you and my mothers, through hell. I have no intention of inviting trouble."

"I wish I cared more. She's spent her life trying to control everything and, in the end, she has so little to show for it. Look what she's missing out on." Jax waved in Hunter's direction.

"By her own choice. Remember that. Pastor Rhebekka would be a good one for you to talk about your relationship with your mother. She chose religion over her children. Did you know they left home as soon as her sister turned eighteen? Rhebekka was determined to set her own course in life."

"Sounds like there's a story there."

"Oh, there is. One worthy of a book. She's walked a tough road paved with regret. She and Naomi almost didn't end up together."

Jax looked at Chance with pure astonishment. "I can't even imagine that. Watch them for five minutes and you'll see how perfect they are for each other."

"They have a story with a happy ending, just like us."

"Well, our story hasn't completely been written yet. Look at the chapter we just added."

"Truth is stranger than fiction. What isn't fiction, is how tired I am. How about we clean him up and we'll all go watch a few episodes of *Tom and Jerry* in our bed."

Jax cupped Chance's face in her hands and caressed her cheeks with her thumbs. "You've been full of excellent suggestions today, Sheriff Fitzsimmons, but this one will cost you."

"What price must I pay?"

"The best kiss I've ever had."

"With pleasure."

Chance leaned in and Jax melted into a kiss so powerful, her center clenched. Their tongues danced as their souls melted into one. When they pulled apart, Jax weaved slightly.

"Wow."

Chance chuckled. "Just wow?"

"Yeah, that."

"Then I've done well."

Jax stared into her wife's eyes. "Very well, my love. Very well indeed. Your wish is granted."

***

Sunday there were things Chance needed to do as a result of the takedown. She'd let Taylor do much of the paperwork the day before. Statements needed to be issued since the ATF and FBI had put out their official reports. She also had a dozen voicemails she needed to sort through. All of these things had required a trip to the office when what she wanted was to spend the day with Hunter and Jax hiking down to Blackwater Falls. She also wanted time with Hunter to practice riding his bike. She and Jax had purchased some so they could ride as a family. As she got ready to go in, she listened to Jax on speakerphone with the principal.

"I appreciate that Mrs. Maguire. Julia will be grateful to hear she has a full-time job with the school board's blessing."

"I won't lie, Mrs. Fitzsimmons. It was difficult, but I also know you were going to have a hard time finding someone on short notice. We just found out, Friday, that Mrs. Anderson, the woman who worked with Hunter last year, had to go on medical leave to care for her husband. Julia had all the credentials they were looking for, so we hired her on the spot. Hunter is our only student with hearing loss this year. This will allow Julia to stay with him for the entire school day. I know your financial assistance also helped convince the board to call the emergency meeting."

Chance watched Jax relax ever so slightly. *This is sounding better and better.*

"Even if it had to be completely on our dime, Julia would be tutoring Hunter. It will be a few weeks before we find out if hearing aids will help him at all. I'm working with Julia to get his speech therapy set up as well." Jax rubbed a hand down Chance's arm.

"He's a lucky little boy to have such advocates. I wish the rest of our students had parents like you."

Jax smiled triumphantly. "We're looking forward to many years of being just that, Mrs. Macguire. Thank you for your assistance. I hope, as we work toward adopting him, we can count on you as an advocate for us. Have a good day, and we'll see you tomorrow morning."

"I'll see you there."

They hung up and Chance took Jax in her arms. "Well done, Mrs. Fitzsimmons, and you didn't even have to go all badass on her."

"I'm glad it worked out, because I would have. This is the right fit for Hunter, I know it."

Chance held Jax close and swayed with her. "We'll always have his back, the same way we always have each other's."

***

Chance was awake most of the night, thinking about Hunter and the changes that were coming to his life. When the alarm clock went off, everyone got up and prepared for his first day of school. As had been suggested, Mike came for breakfast and was riding with them. He and Hunter sat in the backseat thumb wrestling. The squeals of laughter lifted Chance's spirits. Jax reached across the center console and wove her fingers with Chance's.

"He's going to be okay, you know."

"I do, but it doesn't make it any easier. What if he gets nervous?"

"Julia is going to be right there with him. He's going to do great."

Chance huffed. "Like there's any doubt, he's our son you know. Fitzsimmonses meet things head on."

"You kill me. He's going to be fine, momma bear."

"Momma bear is in the car behind us. I'm just a yearling compared to her."

Jax rubbed her arm. "You know, I'm betting your dad felt the same way on your first day of school."

Chance tried to remember but couldn't. "I don't know."

They pulled up to the school to see a myriad of vehicles in the drop-off area. Chance pulled into a parking space and looked in the rearview mirror to see Hunter wide-eyed. There was a timid smile on his face. She released her seatbelt and turned around to sign to him. *"We're here."*

He bit his lip and looked out the window.

Jax reassured him. *"Let's go find Julia."*

She was to meet them on the sidewalk. The mention of Julia's name made Hunter blush and grin. He released his seatbelt and turn to Zeus. The K9 licked him, and Hunter wrapped his arms around his neck.

Chance's heart nearly broke. When they got out, she left the vehicle running with the air conditioner on. No one was going to steal a vehicle with a seventy-pound Belgian Malinois sitting in the front seat. Hunter took her hand in one of his and grabbed Jax's with the other. Chance and Jax both knelt to his level and hugged him before they signed, *"We love you. We'll be back to get you later."*

Hunter smiled and turned to hug Mike, Maggie, and Dee. He grabbed Chance's and Jax's hands again as he started walking away from the 4Runner. Julia was waiting and greeted Hunter with a wave.

"Don't worry, I'll take very good care of him." She smiled at Hunter and held out her hand.

Hunter looked up to Jax, then to Chance, before releasing their hands and taking Julia's.

She reassured them. "It's tough, I know. He's going to be fine."

Chance held on to her gun belt. "You have our number if he needs anything, right? Don't hesitate to call. We want him to be secure that we are coming back for him." Chance shifted from foot to foot.

"I promise you, Sheriff, we will reach out if we need to."

Jax rubbed Chance's arm. "He knows that we will be right here waiting for him after school."

Chance turned to see the moms squared standing just behind them on the sidewalk with Jax's dad. "If he needs us, we'll drop everything and be here. He can count on us. We know this is where he needs to be, it's just hard to watch him go."

Julia turned to Hunter and swung his hand. *"Come. Time to go to school."*

Hunter nodded and walked with her halfway to the door before turning and running back to engulf the legs of both Chance and Jax. They dropped to their knees and hugged him tightly. He pulled back and held up the I love you sign before running back to Julia and taking her hand. He turned once more and waved at them, then stepped inside the school. Chance took a deep breath and fought back the tears. Maggie and Dee stepped to her side.

"Your dad felt exactly as you do now." Maggie wiped away a tear and wrapped her arm around Chance's.

"And how I felt watching you walk into the school in those Mary Janes your mother made you wear." Mike wrapped Jax up in a hug. "I thought the day would never end so I could pick you up. I took the day off because my nerves were so wrecked. I'd been through it once with Jennings, but watching you go ripped my heart out."

Dee patted both of them on the back. "He will be fine. He's a Fitzsimmons now and knows we'll always be there for him."

Chance turned to them and reached for Jax. "Whatever it takes."

Jax wrapped arms around her. "Whatever it takes."

They walked back to the vehicles and made dinner plans so that everyone could enjoy the tales Hunter would come home with. Zeus barely acknowledged Chance as his eyes stared intently at the school.

Chance rubbed his ears and leaned in. "I promise, we'll come back and get him. He's family and the Fitzsimmons clan sticks together. That's a promise."

Five Points Book Five

House of Refuge

Chapter One

1.   RHEBEKKA WATCHED THE SCREEN with rapt attention. Her heart felt like it was being ripped away from the arteries and veins that connected it to her body. She was lightheaded, and her cheeks stung from the tears that poured from her eyes and dripped steadily from her trembling chin. *Wolves in sheep's clothing.* The phrase repeated over and over in her thoughts. A sardonic chuckle bubbled up from her chest. "Christians my ass."

"Understatement. Come here." Naomi snuggled closer and pulled Rhebekka into her arms. "That's why you're different, why we teach of a God of love, not one of fear. They manipulated both of you for twenty years."

The program continued with one story after another about paperwork being kept in special blue envelopes and out of the hands of the authorities. Young girls being forced to be in a room with their male abusers and recount their molestation in front of a group of elders more concerned about protecting the organization than the child. The stories were horrific. It was wrong and immoral by any definition. Those children were now adults and fighting back to bring the abuse into the light. Those same women, and some men, were being labeled apostates by their former religion for daring to reveal the truth.

Rhebekka looked over at her sister who sat ramrod straight, mouthing the words to a song they hadn't listened to in over two decades. The music was a powerful trigger, and it was obvious that Ellie was just as affected as she was. She needed to be close to her sister. "Come over here." Ellie didn't move, and Rhebekka watched as Naomi gently touched Ellie's leg.

Ellie startled and looked over at Rhebekka. "That's what we are now, isn't it? Apostates? How many times did we see those groups on the sidewalks as we were ushered into the conventions?" Ellie was on her feet now and pacing. "I can hear Mom telling us not to look at them, not to even acknowledge them. All along, those protesters were telling the truth."

Rhebekka couldn't take it any longer. She paused the television and came to her sister's side. "Do you remember one of their tried-and-true catchphrases, the truth will set you free? We know the real truth. The only people who are perverting the message of God are those who hide behind the rhetoric to justify their actions and allow child molesters to be a part of their congregations. I thank my God every day for letting us get away."

Naomi joined them. "I knew it was bad from all the things you both have told me about your childhoods, but I could never have imagined people so bent on mind control that they would ignore claims of child abuse to protect an organization. I can't understand."

The three of them had been watching an investigative report on the Jehovah's Witnesses organization and the systematic concealment of thousands of pedophiles within their congregations worldwide. They returned to the couch where the three of them curled around each other, seeking shelter and comfort like tiny kittens huddled in a corner. Rhebekka stared at the still shot on the television of the familiar logo she'd seen on every piece of literature from the organization. A fortress to keep out worldly influences, the watchtower provided the seclusion to brainwash the victims within. From the stories being told, it also kept the abused inside to be prey for those who sexually violated children without fear of repercussions.

Naomi stroked her back. "I think we've watched enough of this today. Both of you are reeling from these revelations. How about we go for a walk and clear our heads? On the way back, we can stop by Karmen's and pick up something sinfully chocolate."

It was February and spring was still a good way off before it would start to poke its head out of the snow. There were no tender shoots of grass to be found poking through the muddy brown of the winter ground. Rhebekka was thankful that each day brought them closer to spring breezes and pops of color. She took a deep breath and turned off the television before looking at her sister. "Feel like a walk?"

Ellie sat there still staring at the blank screen. "A walk isn't going to clear my head. What I want is a strong drink and a piano."

Rhebekka reached out and grasped hands that felt like ice cubes. "Ellie, you're freezing. I'm not even sure your fingers will bend without breaking off." She cupped one in her hands and rubbed vigorously.

"Then a glass of Crown Royal is just what the doctor ordered to warm me up from the inside." Ellie pulled her hand from Rhebekka's and headed for the bar in the corner. "Can I get you one?"

Rhebekka shook her head. "A drink won't clear your head either, little songbird."

"Probably not, but it will help me forget what's in there."

Naomi got up and slipped on her coat. "I'm going to run to Karmen's and pick something up." She walked back over to Rhebekka and kissed her before whispering in her ear. "Tread lightly here. I get the feeling there's more to this than meets the eye. You two need a few minutes to talk. I'll pick something up and wait for you to text me to come back." She walked over and squeezed Ellie's arm. "Anything in particular you want?"

"Chocolate, anything and everything chocolate."

"You got it. I'll be right back."

Rhebekka watched Naomi go, beyond grateful for her wife's intuitiveness. She walked over to her studio and grabbed her Gibson. She strummed the chorus of a song she and Ellie had been working on for the last few days. Ellie downed one shot and was pouring another two fingers of the peach liquor blend, Crown Royal's latest release. It wasn't so much that Rhebekka was worried about Ellie's drinking. Her concern lay in the frame of mind that convinced her sister a drink was what she needed. When Rhebekka could stand the silence no more, she began to sing. "Ice-cold wind whips through my soul..."

Ellie joined her singing, "...and the long cold nights exact their toll."

The two sisters sang in perfect harmony about finding shelter and security away from the things that hurt them. As they continued through the unfinished verses, Ellie grabbed a pad and began to try out lyrics, using one phrase, then a different one, scratching out a word and replacing it until they had three verses to the song tentatively titled *Storm Shelter*.

Rhebekka let the last notes of the final chord fade away and smiled at her sister. The storms they'd survived were small in the grand scheme of the world but monumental in their own lives. "We've still got it, you know."

Ellie smiled. "Thank God for that or we'd all be going hungry. I'm starting to really like this as a single for Moxy Belles. "Martina and

Myranda ended up in the foster system when they were twelve and thirteen because their mother and father were drug addicts. Their extended family was incapable of taking them in. They were fortunate to land in the home of two exceptional men who raised them as their own in Vermont. Both Vince and Benny were music teachers and encouraged the girls' ambitions." Ellie walked to the keyboard and began pecking out the bridge of the song.

Rhebekka strummed along. "Wouldn't it be nice if all foster kids ended up in loving homes? Look at how far little Hunter has come living with Chance and Jax."

Ellie's eyes danced. "He is adorable."

"He's flourishing. They've been able to dial in his hearing aids so that he can hear some speech, and he has a fantastic interpreter. I can only pray they will be able to formally adopt him."

Ellie sipped her drink. "Is there a problem?"

Rhebekka put her guitar down and stepped over to the windows that overlooked the main drag in Thomas. There were signs of life up and down the street as people dressed in colorful ski jackets roamed the small shops. "There are some that are opposed to having a lesbian couple gain permanent custody."

"Are you telling me that they're good enough to foster him but not good enough to be permanent parents to someone whose only blood family overdosed and left him on his own?"

With a calloused finger, Rhebekka drew a heart in the window condensation. "Unfortunately, yes." She turned to Ellie. "Once again, the priorities of society are screwed up. Children aren't protected but instead used as political pawns. We have children in cages, children being thrown out of their homes for being gay, agencies preventing children from being placed in healthy homes, and religious leaders protecting pedophiles in the name of God."

Ellie looked away. "Let it go, Bek. I just can't right now."

Rhebekka swallowed hard. There was something Ellie wasn't telling her. Whatever it was, she would let her sister tell her in her own time. It didn't mean she wouldn't continue with gentle prodding, but for now, she'd let it drop. She picked up her phone and texted Naomi. She spoke softly to her sister. "Okay, El, but we're going to talk at some point. Count on it."

Ellie sighed and looked at her. "I know, just not today."

Before Rhebekka could slip her phone back in her pocket, it lit up with a call from one of her parishioners. "Hey Laura, how are you?"

A deep sigh came over the phone. "I'd be better if I knew what to do."

Rhebekka made her way to the office, looking up to see Naomi come back in the loft with a box from Karmen's. Pointing to the phone she waved Naomi over and put the call on speakerphone. "Maybe Naomi and I can help. What's going on?" Ellie joined them.

"Do you remember Lucian, here at the children's home?"

Rhebekka thought back. "Is he the transgender boy?"

"Yes, and he's run away. They say they have people out looking, but I've got to be honest, I'm really not sure how hard the institution is looking. Lucian will be eighteen in six months, and he'll age out. He's had such a struggle. They refuse to call him Lucian and continue to call him Lucy Ann. I believe they've contacted the Tucker County Sheriff's Office and Sheriff Fitzsimmons."

"That's ridiculous."

"It's like they're trying to force him into compliance, and I think he just had enough. Even the girls at the home aren't very supportive. They've made unfounded accusations against him. I've watched him withdraw further into himself. I've been trying to talk to him, but lately, he's completely closed off. The only time I ever saw any joy from him was when you and Naomi would visit to play music. Pastor, I'm terrified for him."

Rhebekka held her phone in her hand so hard, her hand started to hurt. She forced herself to relax. "Do you have any idea when he left or where he might go? How about what he was last seen wearing?" She knew she was peppering Laura with too many questions. She closed her eyes and took a deep breath. Her ears were ringing slightly, a sign that her blood pressure was rising.

"I wish I did. They took the kids on a field trip to skate at Canaan Valley State Park. When it was time to get back in the van, Lucian wasn't there."

Rhebekka patted her pockets. She'd had several conversations with Lucian, trying to comfort him and assure him that there was absolutely nothing wrong with him. Now he was out there somewhere, likely still in Tucker County. She looked at the clock and noticed it was two in the afternoon. Temperatures would be dropping, and night would be on them before they knew it. She needed to contact Chance. "Laura, I'm going to make some calls. If there is a search underway, I'll gather my folks and the kids from the after-school program if they're willing. If you hear anything let me know. We'll find him, I have to believe that."

Rhebekka hung up and started to call Chance when Naomi grabbed her hand.

"Let's ask for a little extra help first."

She didn't have the words. Her heart knew what she needed to say, but it was as if her mouth was frozen. Yielding to her wife's skills and powers of perception, she bowed her head and listened to the voice that had brought her back from the depths of her despair more times than she could count. She let her mind quiet and listened to the comforting pleas Naomi asked of God. Their God was one of love and compassion. When Naomi finished, her mind immediately went to the scripture in Matthew about a sparrow. *Not a single sparrow can fall to the ground outside your care. Please be with Lucian, for I know to you he is even more precious.*

Available in 2021

About CJ Murphy

I began to create lesbian fiction after my wife suggested I write her a story as a personalized gift. I was privileged to be mentored by another published author who helped turn a raw manuscript, into an actual novel. Upon completion, she encouraged me to submit to Desert Palm Press. DPP offered me a contract for my first novel, 'frame by frame' in 2017. My second novel, 'The Bucket List', was published in late 2018. I credit my storytelling ability to being an avid reader and having an adventure filled occupation for twenty-five years as a career firefighter.

Connect with CJ:
Email: cptcjldypyro@gmail.com
Facebook: CJ Murphy (Murphy's Law)
Blog: Murphy's Law Ink

Note to Readers:

Thank you for reading a book from Desert Palm Press. We appreciate you as a reader and want to ensure you enjoy the reading process. We would like you to consider posting a review on your preferred media sites and/or your blog or website.

For more information on upcoming releases, author interviews, contest, giveaways and more, please sign up for our newsletter and visit us as at Desert Palm Press: www.desertpalmpress.com and "Like" us on Facebook: Desert Palm Press.

Bright Blessings